# "BUT ONE OF THE DUELISTS IS A WOMAN!"

Griffith rubbed his eyes. "That woman is using a sword."

Like a flame above a slim white candle, her vivid hair struggled from under her coif and slithered down her back. Her eyes snapped with blue sparks. Her teeth sparkled white in a challenging smile. Her light step distracted Griffith from the sword she had balanced in the other hand.

Sweet Saint Dewi, but she was tall. She looked the handsome hulk of a man right in the eyes, and she did so boldly.

Griffith didn't like bold women.

**CRITICAL ACCLAIM FOR
CHRISTINA DODD'S *CANDLE IN THE WINDOW***

"A very special romance—heartbreaking and heartwarming, original, beautiful, compassionate, and well written. It is a story you'll never forget. *Candle in the Window* ensures Christina Dodd a place in readers' hearts."
—*Romantic Times*

*PRICELESS*

"Memorable characters, witty dialogue, steaming sensuality—the perfect combination for sheer enjoyment."
—Jill Marie Landis, author of *Come Spring*

AND *CASTLES IN THE AIR*

"Christina Dodd is a joy to read."

—Laura Kinsale

# Outrageous

## A STORY OF THE WAR
## OF THE ROSES

### ⚔ CHRISTINA DODD ⚔

**HarperTorch**
*An Imprint of HarperCollins Publishers*

This is a work of fiction. Names, characters, places, and incidents are products of the author's imagination or are used fictitiously and are not to be construed as real. Any resemblance to actual events, locales, organizations, or persons, living or dead, is entirely coincidental.

HARPERTORCH
*An Imprint of* HarperCollins*Publishers*
10 East 53rd Street
New York, New York 10022-5299

Copyright © 1994 by Christina Dodd
ISBN: 0-06-108151-5

First HarperTorch paperback printing: July 2000
First HarperPaperbacks special printing: February 1999
First HarperPaperbacks printing: April 1994

HarperCollins®, HarperTorch™, and ❦™ are trademarks of HarperCollins Publishers Inc.

Printed in the United States of America

Visit HarperTorch on the World Wide Web at
www.harpercollins.com

OPM   10  9  8  7  6  5  4  3  2

This book is dedicated to my critique group
with thanks and good wishes.

# AUTHOR'S NOTE

To this author's distress, the English have always had the regrettable tendency to name their monarchs the same thing, over and over again. For instance, there were six King Georges, seven Edwards, four Williams, and, most important for our purposes, eight King Henrys and five Elizabeths—two queens in their own right and three consorts to the king.

This story concerns Henry VII and his consort Elizabeth of York—the parents of the infamous Henry VIII, the grandparents of the awe-inspiring Elizabeth I. Together they founded the Tudor dynasty which provided stability to England, but they came from turbulent upbringings, filled with war, murder, adultery, and treachery of the blackest sort. The adultery and treachery shape the background for this tale of Henry VII and Elizabeth of York.

# Prologue

**August 22, 1485**
**Bosworth Field**

*Death whistled past* Griffith ap Powel as he dodged the knight's bloody sword. Shrieking his war cry, Griffith wheeled his stallion and swung his battle-ax.

The knight fell, but Griffith had no time to watch. Another knight took that one's place, and another, and another. None of these feeble Englishmen could match a Welshman's skill, but the warriors of Richard's royal army still tried, and tried mightily. Griffith spurred his horse. The marshland sank beneath the exhausted animal's feet, and the fetid smell of death and decay rose all around. Then the stallion gained firm ground, and with a clash of steel, Griffith met the main body of Richard's army.

Using mace and ax, Griffith cut a swath through the endless succession of knights. Moans and screams assaulted his ears. Sweat trickled in his mouth, tasting of salt and steel. He took a blow to his hip but dispatched his assailant impatiently. Blood seeped from a thousand tiny cuts, saturating the quilting beneath his armor, but he didn't care.

He had to get to Henry.

The morning mists drifted around Griffith. The slots of his helmet cut his vision, but on the hill above him he caught sight of the banner bearing the blood-red rose of the Lancasters. There he would find Henry Tudor, last hope of the Lancaster family.

There he would find the man who would be king of England.

He fought on the fringes of the battle, inflicting damage where he could but never losing sight of his goal. Closer and closer he moved, until, scattering Henry's bodyguards with the force of his charge, he roared in Welsh, "Henry! My lord, they must come *now!*"

In the tongue of his youth, Henry shouted back, "Do you think I don't know that?" He pointed first to one side of the battlefield, where an army waited, then to the other, where another waited. "I've sent word to each of the commanders, demanding they attack as promised. They haven't moved."

"Whoresons!" Griffith pulled off his helmet and greedily drank the water offered him by Henry's squire. "They swore they'd help us."

"They swore the same thing to Richard, I trow." Henry looked out over the battlefield. "They'll wait until they see which way the tide turns."

Griffith grinned in savage pleasure. "Richard's army outnumbered us and outmaneuvered us, but we've done them damage. We've killed his best commander, and his troops are disheartened. But look, my lord, and see what I see." He pointed across Bosworth Field. "Richard of York is coming for you."

Henry sucked in his breath in dismay as he stared at the charge headed his way. It was a large party, almost twice as large as the guard around him.

Richard himself led it, knowing full well that if Henry were killed, the Lancaster cause would lose its heart. An accomplished tactician, a hardened warrior, Richard might have been a good king, too, but he'd taken the throne from his own nephews. He'd had the two lads murdered, God knew how, and their bodies dumped in an unmarked grave. Even in England, home of royal treachery, that was the one sin neither commoner nor nobleman could accept.

Richard III had worn the crown for two dark years, and the rumors of his perfidy had grown. It was said that he'd had his good queen poisoned, that he'd wooed Elizabeth, his own niece. The sister of the dead princes, she would have given Richard the legitimacy he sought if she had wed him.

When, in fact, she was promised to Henry.

It was the perfect union—the red rose of Lancaster and the white rose of York. Griffith was determined it should come about.

Henry wasn't a warrior. Griffith hadn't chosen to follow him for his battle skills, but because Henry Tudor had the right to the throne. Son of the Lancasters through his mother's line, Henry was the Welshman promised by the ancient legends, the descendant of Arthur, who would unite England and Wales—and give Wales the autonomy it deserved. Griffith fought for Wales, for his home, for the promise of a better time.

As calmly as if he were the lord and Henry the minion, Griffith instructed, "Take your helmet from your squire and put it on. Loosen your sword in its scabbard. Sit relaxed in the saddle, and take good care to keep your shield ever before you. Keep a clear head, and remember"—he touched Henry's armor-clad shoulder with his mace—"I haven't followed you all the way from Wales to lose."

"It gives me comfort to hear you say so," Henry answered.

Giving orders in precise, accented English, Griffith ordered Henry's bodyguard into a line, told them to charge on his command, placed the standard bearer toward the back, then replaced his helmet. Returning to Henry, he said, "Don't worry, my liege. I will protect you with my life."

In wry appreciation of his danger, Henry replied, "You may have to."

Taking his place at the lip of the hill, slightly in front of the other knights, Griffith waited. Richard's party fought through the thick of battle. Griffith waited. The stallion beneath him trembled, anxious for strife. Griffith waited. Richard's party reached the hill. Griffith waited. The knights around him begged for release. Richard's party slowed as they started up the grade. Griffith lifted his hand. His companions clutched their weapons. Dropping his hand, he shouted, *"À Henry Roi!"*

The bodyguards leaped off the hill like avenging angels, taking advantage of the speed of the downward slope, the wind, and their opponents' battle weariness.

But Richard had picked his knights well, and these knights were as dedicated to Richard as Griffith was to Henry. They fought for Richard III, fought that he might retain the throne. Griffith whirled like a madman, thrusting, parrying, dealing death with each blow, and risking it with each defense. Each combat brought the end to another enemy; each combat brought another. Grinding Henry's men down with countless strikes, Richard's men moved them back up the hill, back toward Henry. Griffith tried to stop it, slow it, but Richard's men kept pressing in, more and more, overwhelming them with sheer strength of numbers.

Griffith had stared death in the face before, so he recognized it now. But he didn't give up. He couldn't. The dream was too strong, his need too dire. *"À*

*Henry Roi!"* he roared again, but the scream sounding close by his ear drowned the defiant cry.

Henry's standard bearer was down. Richard's men had circled behind Griffith, and nothing stood between Richard and Henry. For a fleeting moment, Griffith hoped Henry remembered his instructions. Then he heard the sound of thunder. The ground shook, and he turned, prepared to fight another charge, to lose the last battle of his life.

It looked as though an army had crashed into them. New knights, knights with unbloodied swords and pristine armor, charged into the midst of the crucial conflict. The waiting armies waited no more. They'd seen who struggled and who vanquished, and they rode to rally the strong and destroy the weak. Griffith sagged in the saddle, and his tired gaze sought Henry. He couldn't reach him in time; couldn't help him now. Only God could help him, and God seemed very far away.

Wearily he lifted his battle-ax and shield, not because he thought he could come out alive, but because it wasn't in his nature to surrender. But the attacking knights ignored him, and within a heartbeat he understood.

These troops fought for Henry. For whatever reason—the good of the country, the right of Henry's cause—they attacked Richard and his warriors. And they slaughtered them.

The fresh knights took pleasure in their work. They laughed as they killed Richard's men. They laughed as they killed the horses, too.

Sickened, Griffith thought, *Not the good of the country. Not the right of Henry's cause. But vengeance most horrible on Richard.*

Taking care to stay out of their way, he led his stallion back to Henry.

"They've got him," Henry shouted, but the triumph

was absent from his voice. "Look, they're killing Richard."

Of all his men, Richard alone remained upright. Knights surrounded the Yorkist king in a circle, and they hacked at him. He landed great and furious blows, and Griffith found himself cheering when he decapitated an enemy. But Richard's achievement only made the others more savage, and they drove him from one to the other, sticking him with their swords, chopping him with their battle-axes, smashing him with their maces.

In a final attempt to free himself—or perhaps just to die honorably—Richard brought his horse up. It whinnied as it reared, hooves thrashing, and knocked two knights from the saddle. One of them brought his sword up and the noble animal crumpled, a crimson slash in its milky-white breast.

Richard went down in a crash of armor, and the knights moved in. His breastplate and his helmet were flung out of the crowd, then blood flew in the air like rain.

The good English ground sucked up the rivulets of blood. The blood of foot soldiers. The blood of knights. And the royal blood of Richard III.

Henry Tudor watched the carnage, horror etched on his thin face. Turning to Griffith, he swore the oath by which he would govern England. "If that is how Englishmen treat their deposed kings, then I swear on the nails of the Holy Cross, nothing—no one will ever take my throne from me."

# 1

**Wenthaven Castle**
**Shropshire, England, 1487**

*The clash of swords echoed* through the long gallery of the fashionable castle keep, and Griffith ap Powel grimaced in disgust. "Dueling?" he inquired of his host. "You've brought me here to watch dueling?"

With a receding silver hairline, aristocratic features, and a pack of auburn-coated spaniels yipping at his heels, the earl of Wenthaven was the model of urbane hospitality. "I am but trying to fulfill your request."

Shrieks of laughter and sham alarm assaulted Griffith as they shouldered their way through the outer ring of spectators. "There is no respect for a warrior in this country," Griffith said. "In Wales, we fight in battle, to the death, with a good two-handed sword in our grip and an enemy before us. There is none of the so-called sport of dueling."

With one elegant gesture, Wenthaven dismissed Wales and its customs. "'Tis a French practice, actually, but many youths abide here with me, and they fight on any pretext. They fight for the pure joy of fighting, so I encourage dueling. The swords are light and have dulled edges, and their vigorous spirits are dampened with judicious training. Moreover, if you wish to speak to Lady Marian, the former lady-in-waiting for our uncrowned queen, then you must come here."

Already aflame with a sense of misuse and a total contempt for his mission, Griffith snapped, "Does this Lady Marian enjoy watching young fools slice at each other?"

Wenthaven mocked Griffith with a dimpled smile. "If you would but look closely, you would see the part which Lady Marian plays."

Griffith had the height to give him a clear view over the circle of cheering spectators. Two figures danced on the polished stone floor, dulled dueling swords in hand. The skill of both was extraordinary, a testament to healthy bodies and youthful spirits.

Then he rubbed his eyes. "One of the duelists is a woman. That woman is using a sword."

Like a flame above a slim white candle, her red hair fell out of its coif above her pale face. Her green eyes snapped; her teeth sparkled in a challenging smile. The hem of her creamy silk skirt hung over her arm, giving Griffith a glimpse of muscular, silk-clad ankles and calves. Her light step distracted Griffith from the sword she held in the other hand.

Sweet Saint Dewi, but she was tall. She looked the handsome hulk of a man right in the eye, and she did so boldly.

Griffith didn't like bold women.

Singing a tune off key, she ridiculed her opponent with the flash of her blade, with her amusement, with her height.

Both his hands were free to fight, and he displayed a skill and an agility that would tempt most men to back away. But he panted in great, billowing gasps, sweat dripped into his eyes, and he slashed with an aggression out of place for a friendly bout.

He was losing.

At Griffith's side, Wenthaven said, "She's good, isn't she?"

Griffith grunted his unwilling assent.

"I taught her all she knows."

Unable to tear his gaze from the too tall, too bold, too tall beauty, Griffith said, "You're mad. Why would a man teach a woman to duel with swords?"

Wenthaven chuckled. "A woman like her must have a way to defend herself from . . . shall we say . . . unwanted attentions."

The curved swords clashed, screeching as the blades scraped together in a shower of blue sparks. "A woman like her?"

"Aye." Satisfied with Griffith's avid concentration, Wenthaven announced, "That is Lady Marian Wenthaven."

Griffith turned to Wenthaven, missing Marian's coup de grace, but the clamor of the crowd brought his attention back to her. She gave a shout of triumph as her opponent's sword went flying. Glowing with victory, she raised her fists in celebration, and Griffith narrowed his eyes. "Flamboyance is most unattractive in a woman. Most unattractive."

He only wished his body understood what his mind believed.

Wenthaven clicked his tongue. "I don't suppose Adrian Harbottle ever stood a chance. He's just one of those landless knights, scarcely more than a churl."

Griffith glanced at the man Wenthaven disparaged so quickly. Blessed with golden hair, even white teeth, and sound limbs, Harbottle didn't look like a churl. He was so handsome, he made Griffith's teeth ache, and he reminded Griffith of something. Something familiar. Something reassuring.

Aye, Harbottle resembled the gilt painting of an angel in Griffith's mother's *Book of Hours*.

But Griffith would wager Harbottle was no angel. His breath still billowed his barrel chest, and he stared at Marian with fury. Griffith watched him, not caring for the malevolence his clenched fists betrayed.

Wenthaven rambled on. "He was a dolt to imagine he could challenge her—"

Harbottle sprang for Marian's sword, caught it up, aimed it at Marian. Griffith's protective reflexes whipped him into the fray before he considered the consequences. With a flying tackle, he landed atop Harbottle. Women screamed, men roared, as Griffith took Harbottle's wildly flailing body to the floor. Bones and tendons crunched on impact. Griffith rolled away from Harbottle and came to his feet as the sword skittered across stone.

Before he could reach it, another hand snatched it up. Another hand, a slender, feminine hand, pointed it at Harbottle's throat, and Marian's contralto voice snarled, "Coward and knave, stand and face the penalty for treachery."

Harbottle rose to his knees, his angelic face contorted and his breath a palpable heat. "Bitch, you betray not a shred of womanly compassion."

"Because I don't allow you to defeat me? To kill me? Must I die at the hands of some misbegotten knight to prove myself a lady?" She pricked at the open throat of his shirt with the shiny tip of the sword. "Get up, I say, and face this lady whom you have wronged."

She had been magnificent in her triumph, and now she wore her wrath like the robes of a queen. Griffith stepped close. If flamboyance in a woman was unattractive, why did her fire draw him to her?

Harbottle staggered to his feet and glanced at Griffith. "You hide behind your newest lover."

Without a flicker of interest, Marian dismissed Griffith. "I can kill you without the help of any man, Harbottle." And she drew back her arm.

Harbottle's blue eyes grew large. The whites turned red with strain, and fear shattered his facade. "You wouldn't . . . you can't . . ."

"Who would blame me?"

Her cheeks acquired a pallor, but Harbottle failed to notice. He concentrated solely on that unswerving tip. "I have money, if you want it—"

Her color blossomed again. "If I kill you, the world would be well rid of such vermin."

She took a deep breath, and Griffith now thought she would plunge the steel into Harbottle's heart.

"Have pity," Harbottle whimpered.

Her severity broke, and she gestured with the sword toward the door. "Go grovel before the priest. Perhaps he'll offer forgiveness. That's the best you can expect, for these gentlefolk will not forget."

Harbottle scurried backward, and when he was safe out of range, he cried, "Whore! You shame your family by bearing their name. Your little bastard bears the punishment for your sins." Griffith stiffened in shock, but Harbottle wasn't through. "That whelp you bore is an idiot!"

She lifted the sword to fling it, and the gaping courtiers dove for cover. Griffith caught her hand before she could, swung her around, and buried her face in his chest.

A bastard, he reflected grimly. She'd borne a child out of wedlock. No wonder she'd been banished from the court.

A bastard. A child unacknowledged by its father. Marian had brought herself disgrace and exile with her unseemly passion, and that lack of control she now exposed in her useless struggles.

Resembling a half-crushed insect, Harbottle took to flight, limping all the way.

Marian fought the restraint, furious that anyone dared come between her and that foul beast who maligned her son. In her ear a deep voice rumbled, "Anger is the wind that blows out the lamp of the mind, and you are the proof. Never threaten a man with death unless you mean to complete the deed. You've made a lifelong enemy, one who'll be satisfied with nothing less than your humiliation and defeat."

Wrenching her head free, she looked up, and up, and up.

The man was immense—and ill favored. His black hair, cut chin length, was combed straight back, leaving his face unsoftened and unadorned. His tanned skin had seen too much sun, too many battles, and the lines of experience that marked his brow found mates in the scars that furrowed his cheeks. His thin nose had been broken too many times, and his stubborn chin prickled with a day's growth of beard. Only his golden eyes betrayed a kind of beauty, and they glowered at her with such disgust that she stiffened even further.

"My thanks to you, but I am none of your concern."

He exhaled impatiently, and it ruffled the stray wisps of hair that fell over her forehead. She stepped away and heard him mutter, "If only that were true."

From behind her Wenthaven said, "This great Welsh beast is your newest emissary from the queen."

Marian swung on Wenthaven. "By my troth, Wenthaven. Why didn't you tell me at once?"

Spreading his hands in doubtful innocence, Wenthaven said, "I thought I did."

Dismissing him with a sniff, Marian tilted her head and examined Griffith, paying particular attention to his dull brown, unfashionable clothes. "He does resemble a beast. Does the beast have a name?"

Griffith bowed where he stood, and it brought his face close to hers. "Griffith ap Powel, if it please you."

He spoke softly, and his name brought a rush of blood to her face. "Griffith ap Powel? Griffith ap

Powel is no emissary from my lady the queen. Griffith ap Powel is the king's man."

Griffith straightened, a satisfied line to his hard mouth. "I am the king's man, and therefore the queen's, too, for they are wed and made as one by the holy ceremony of the Church."

Glancing around, Marian saw the crowd that had gathered to cheer her swordplay now hung on every word. Gesturing a page boy close, she handed him her sword and bade him clean it and place it with care. The time she earned gave her a chance to rein in her temper. "How is Elizabeth of York? Is my lady well?"

Griffith, too, noted the press of interested observers and offered his arm. "The king's consort is well, as is her son and heir, Arthur."

"The heir to the throne of England." Marian smiled at the irony of it. "And Henry Tudor is the father."

"*King* Henry Tudor is the father."

Marian almost laughed at Griffith's pomposity, but her years at court had taught her a respect for a king's power, if not a respect for the men who sought the position. So she took the proffered arm and agreed, "Of course. King Henry, seventh of that name, is the father of this child. Has King Henry let his wife be crowned yet?"

"Not yet."

"When the archbishop anoints Elizabeth's head and places the crown on her noble brow in Westminster Abbey, she'll be lifted above mere mortals." Marian clung close, content to use Griffith as a wedge to part the crowd. As they left the milling gentlefolk behind, she said, "The king is afraid. Afraid all will say he owes his throne to his queen."

Griffith corrected her without a blink. "He's cautious, and rightly so."

"The throne still totters beneath his royal behind."

"Totters? No. It does not totter, and only a fool

would say so. But those same fools who claim the throne totters might also claim he couldn't keep the throne without the support of Elizabeth's Yorkist kin."

"You aren't a courtier, are you?" Marian asked, smiling, more amused than embarrassed by the charge of foolishness.

"I am whatever Henry needs me to be."

"A lackey, then," she said, wondering if he would respond to the insult.

"At present, that is true. I am a messenger boy, delivering notes from one silly girl to another." Without asking her preference, he steered her out a door into the lavish garden, redolent with the scent of new roses basking in the warmth of the spring sun. "My reward for completing this mission is a visit to my parents in Wales."

The afternoon sunshine did Griffith no favors, Marian noted. It revealed his hair was not black, as she'd thought, but dark brown and shiny. It grew back from a point in the middle of his forehead, giving his narrow face a devilish quality, and it flared out like a lion's mane, lending him a beast's menace. The sunlight highlighted his harshness, accentuated the length and breadth of him, and she wondered what madness had encouraged Henry to send him.

Was Henry trying to intimidate her? What did he suspect? What did he know? And had he shared his knowledge with his messenger?

A strand of her bright red hair hung in her eyes, and she tried to tuck it back under her close-fitting cap, with little success.

He watched with a cynical lift to his mouth. "Do you dye your hair?"

Dropping her hands, she glared. In all her twenty-two years, she'd never met such a rude man. "If I did, would I dye it this color?"

He didn't smile, didn't twitch, didn't make false protestations about his admiration. Instead he took the strand between his fingers and efficiently inserted it beneath the coif. "Can we be overheard here?"

She could read nothing from Griffith's countenance except a vast distaste for her and for his duty. So much the better, she thought. Wenthaven's castle was the epitome of lavish country living, but she'd grown used to the excitement of court. Now she relished the chance to match wits with a haughty Welsh lord. "No one can hear us, but that's of no consequence. Everyone knows I was once the lady Elizabeth's chief lady-in-waiting. Everyone knows we communicate when possible, although the messenger is usually a little"—she ran her gaze up and down his form—"livelier." She held out her hand, palm up. "Do you have a letter for me?"

He withdrew a parchment from his belt, closed with the queen's seal, and picked at the wax. "Shall I read it to you?"

Snatching it, she tucked it inside her sleeve. "I'll read it to myself. Is there a purse?"

More slowly, he produced the heavy pouch.

She weighed it in her hand and sighed with relief. "Sweet Mary has blessed me."

"The queen sends you much of her meager allowance."

"Aye," she agreed, her thoughts on the two-year-old napping in her cottage. "She is ever tender of my well-being." Then she saw his outrage, which he didn't bother to hide. Sitting down on a stone bench, she cocked her head and smiled scornfully. "Why, Griffith ap Powel, whatever were you thinking?"

"I was wondering if you have some knowledge the queen wishes withheld, and so dip your hand into her pocket."

His bluntness proved his blatant disrespect for her, and anger, so recently subdued, again flashed through her. The light breeze off the lake accentuated the burn of her cheeks, and she glared at him. Then she remembered the secret that was not her own, and she dropped her gaze. In a careful monotone she said, "The Lady Elizabeth is no mark for a blackmailer. She's lived an exemplary life. How could she not? Her father, King Edward, cherished her first. Then her uncle, King Richard the Third, did his duty by her."

"*King* Richard?" He sneered. "The usurper, you mean. Richard was Edward's brother. Edward's sons should have inherited the throne, but where are they now? Where are they now?"

Clutching the leather, feeling the roll of the coins inside, she again repressed her animosity. "I do not know, but Elizabeth was their sister. She had naught to do with their disappearance."

"'Twas Richard who imprisoned them in the Tower, from whence they never returned." He put his foot on the bench beside her, leaned his arm on his knee, and bent his face close against hers. "They disappeared, never to be seen again. I fought for Henry and prayed he would be given the chance to unite the Yorks and the Lancasters in marriage, but when we came to London, we discovered the truth. We discovered the lady Elizabeth had danced with their murderer. She lived in Richard's court, wore the clothes with which he gifted her, and gave his court a legitimacy it wouldn't have had without her. Elizabeth shows the streak of decay that has riddled the House of York, and now that decay has passed into the Tudor line."

Without conscious thought, she swung the gold-filled purse against his face. His nose cracked. Staggering back, he covered his face, and while blood seeped through his fingers, she grasped his shirt in her hands and jerked him toward her.

The linen tore in small, high bursts, but her voice was low and intense. "My lady Elizabeth sacrificed everything to save her brothers. Everything. By my troth, do not ever malign her in my hearing again, lest I take my sword and run you through."

She shoved him away and rushed up the path, abandoning the purse in her haste and her fury. When she was sure she was out of sight, she picked up her skirts for more speed and lengthened her stride. She wanted to get away from that boor, that ass, that sycophant of Henry's.

It probably hadn't been politic to strike him. Especially not with that heavy purse. She'd heard a crack—had she broken his nose?

Yet how dare he accuse Elizabeth of collaborating with Richard in the death of her brothers? Marian knew the truth of it. She had been placed in Elizabeth's service at five, for they were the same age and related by blood. From the very beginning it had been made clear to Marian that she was to serve Elizabeth in every way.

At the same time, it had been made clear to Elizabeth that she was a sacrifice to the dynasty. Every motion, every word, every smile, was weighed and judged as worthy or not worthy of a princess of the House of York. A kind, amiable child, Elizabeth strove always to be judged worthy, and if her intelligence was not the highest—well, a princess had no need of intelligence.

No need, until her father, King Edward IV, died. Then came the days of treachery, and Elizabeth was ill prepared to play the political games that drove the country to war. Her beloved uncle took custody of her brothers, declaring he wished only to protect them—then in one sweeping, maddening statement, he had declared them illegitimate. He declared all of Edward's children illegitimate.

As Richard wished, Parliament named him king.

Marian had held her lady as she wept for her brothers, for her freedom, for her honor, now trampled into the dirt. She'd helped Elizabeth make plans. When Richard and his wife invited her to court, Marian and Elizabeth had first cried out in fury, then put their heads together and schemed. If Elizabeth were at court, if she played the role of dutiful niece, then perhaps she could discover her brothers' fates. Perhaps she could influence her uncle, perhaps she could help her brothers escape.

Marian and Elizabeth formed wild plans, trying to cover every eventuality—but they never could have imagined their own final role in Richard's doomed reign. If only . . .

Marian sighed. She could drive herself crazy with the if-onlys.

Her cottage stood close against the towering curtain wall that surrounded the castle and protected it from assault, and far from Wenthaven's keep. She liked it that way. Here she was remote from Lord Wenthaven, the politics he dabbled in, and the schemes he hatched. Here she and her son were safe.

Lionel. Would he be awake now?

Pushing open the gate into the front garden, she called for him, then grinned as the pudgy, dark-haired boy came toddling around the dwelling. She swung him up in her arms and exclaimed, "You're gritty. Have you been playing in your sand?"

He nodded, beaming, and patted her cheeks with his grubby hands.

"Building a castle?"

He nodded.

"With a moat?"

"Oh, don't ask him about a moat," his nursemaid said, coming around the edge of the cottage. "He'll want to go to the well for water, and then we'll have a royal mess."

A handsome girl, Cecily resembled Marian's mother to an astonishing degree. But where Marian's mother had been a long-ago, loving memory, Cecily had proved to be silly and easily swayed by fashion, by opinion, and especially by the appreciation of a man. Any man.

Still, she'd followed Marian, with scarcely a whimper, into the backwater of Castle Wenthaven. "Did he sleep?" Marian asked.

Cecily blew the hair out of her eyes. "He slept a bit, but he's been active for most of the afternoon."

Marian squeezed him, kissed him, and agreed, "Aye, he's a healthy lad."

"You'd never know he cried his whole first year."

"'Twas just colic," Marian said, her attention on Lionel as he wiggled to the ground.

"'Twas just awful," Cecily answered roundly.

Marian didn't answer. There were many things she didn't reveal, but foremost among them was her own initial antipathy to Lionel.

She hadn't wanted to be a mother. Had had no interest in children. When the midwife had first placed that bloody, waxy bundle in her arms, she'd reacted with quite unmaternal disgust.

"Early babies are always puny and fussy and ugly, they tell me." Cecily seemed to take Marian's agreement for granted. "Sometimes I thought he wouldn't survive his first months."

Sometimes, late at night when he'd been screaming for hours, Marian hadn't known if she'd *wanted* him to survive his first months. She hunched her shoulders against the remembered guilt and followed Lionel to the pile of river sand they'd dredged for him.

Cecily tagged along. "But for you, my lady, I'd have gone mad."

Marian's remorse had driven her to take on more and more of Lionel's personal care, and then . . . oh, then one day he'd smiled at her.

She'd never had a reason to believe in love. She'd never believed in one moment of illumination. But that first toothless grin from the baby in her arms had changed her. With each smile afterward, with each

childhood illness and each youthful triumph, he'd
bound her to him. Now his dark head bobbed as he
scraped the sand together, and she exulted in the
strength of her own devotion. She would lay down
her life for him—not because of duty or loyalty, but
because of love.

Cecily sighed as loudly as Lionel did when he was
seeking attention. "I wish I'd been there to help you
through his birth."

Marian glanced at her incredulously. "You? You
come over giddy when a man spits."

Hanging her head, Cecily admitted, "I know I do,
but I'm sure my womanly instincts would have taken
over."

Marian doubted it, but said nothing.

"Of course, you had to accompany the lady
Elizabeth into exile. She could hardly remain at court
with the rumors that were rife." Cecily peered around
the edge of her gable hood, her big eyes guileless.
"About her marrying the king, her uncle, I mean."

Fingering the letter hidden in her sleeve, Marian
said, "I know well what you mean."

"I'm still surprised you didn't take me into your
confidence. To face such a dishonor, by yourself,
without the support of your own dear cousin." Cecily
sniffled a little. "After all, I was your lady's maid."

"Cecily." Marian faced her full on. "Who's been
talking to you?"

Guilt flooded Cecily's face, and she faltered, "Why
do you think someone's been talking to me?"

"Because you know you never wanted to be at
Lionel's birth. Is one of your friends breeding?"

Confusion, dismay, embarrassment—Cecily displayed all those as she stammered, "N-nay."

Forthright as always, Marian continued, "If you
told someone you helped me with the birth, and you'd
help her, too, you'd best admit the falsehood at once."

Cecily's mouth puckered as if she'd bitten a lemon.

"I haven't told anyone a falsehood. But it's been hard, trying to explain why you left me at court and went off to have Lionel without me. The . . . other maids hint you didn't trust me."

"Not trust you?" Understanding now, Marian pulled the diminutive Cecily into her arms. "Of course I trust you." Marian compensated for the half lie with a hearty hug. "If the other maids are teasing, you tell them the truth. 'Twas my concern for you that made me leave you at court. I wanted you to find a husband, to settle down in your own home, before anyone discovered my secret. I didn't want you to be ruined with me—as you have been."

"Nay," Cecily mumbled.

"Aye, you have, and scarcely a word of blame have you uttered. I'm an ungrateful wretch if you don't know how much I appreciate your sacrifice."

Cecily pulled away. "Nay, you're not an ungrateful wretch. You've been good to me. You call me cousin—"

"You *are* my cousin."

"From the wrong side of the blanket." Realizing, perhaps, her faux pas, Cecily glanced at Lionel and mumbled, "Not that there's anything wrong with that. But I'm not like you. I'm not clever with letters, and I can't use a sword at all."

Marian grinned and knelt beside the ecstatic two-year-old. Scraping together a pile of sand, she said, "There are some who claim that's to your advantage."

"The men talk, and I hear them. Some of them think you're dashing."

"And some of them don't," Marian said, remembering the scowl that had blackened the Welshman's face and the blood that spurted when she'd taught him respect for his betters. Sir Griffith had a rough appeal, like that of an untamed mountain, all craggy and fraught with mystery, and she wished she hadn't hit him.

But he'd deserved it, and besides, God rot him, he'd made her drop the purse.

She'd have to go and beg him for it. And he would make her beg, no doubt. Marian squirmed. She had to have that money, but she didn't want to see the dark, tall man again. She didn't want to listen to that voice of velvet express his disapproval of her. She really didn't want to apologize, and she would have to, if she sought him out. Perhaps there was another way. Perhaps . . . Her eyes narrowed. Aye, she'd think of another way.

"That man today thought you were dashing."

Her mind still on Griffith, Marian frowned. "Oh, no, he didn't."

"He did, too. Why else would he have fought with you for the privilege of your bed?"

"What?" At first confused, Marian realized Cecily referred to that boor Harbottle, and she dismissed him with a wave. "Him. He's nothing but one of a legion of asses who think me easy prey. I taught him better."

"I've spoken to him. He'd marry you."

Her cousin's surrogate offer, made in a tone intended to induce gratitude, infuriated Marian, and she controlled herself only with an effort. "No doubt he would, to raise his station and lower mine. No, I thank you."

"If you don't marry, you'll not be able to have a legitimate child."

Marian stood in a flurry. "So I'm destined to have another bastard, do you mean?"

"No!" Cecily's full lips pouted in dismay. "No, I—"

"There may be bastards galore in England, and some of them may live rich lives. But their fathers acknowledge them. It proves how virile those noblemen are. How manly." Marian glared at her cousin, and Cecily shrank away. "Lionel doesn't have a father to acknowledge him. Lionel has only me, and I'll protect him, and nobody had better ever—" A tug on her skirt stopped her. Lionel stood, his hands clenched in the folds of her dress, looking up at her with distressed brown eyes, and the invective died on her tongue. She sank to her knees, put her arms around him, and lifted her face to the breeze. When she could speak civilly, she asked, "Would you like me to help you build a road?"

He nodded, his gaze sliding to Cecily.

Still angry at the serving maid, but angrier still at her own loss of control, Marian said, "Cecily can cut the bread for our supper, lovey. Would you like honey, too?"

He nodded again, but Cecily clasped her hands in supplication. "Oh, Lady Marian, I had hoped . . ."

Marian knew what she hoped. "Aye?" she asked, although she'd already decided to grant Cecily's wish, to let her go to be away from her.

"I hoped I could go into the manor and join with the others in their festivities."

"Join the others?" Marian knew she shouldn't tease, but her pride still stung from Cecily's tactlessness. "I thought you joined only one."

"I'll be out all night, my lady, if you don't need me."

"Oh, Cecily." Marian's heart twisted at the doom her maid courted, and she couldn't keep from asking, "Whom do you meet?"

Cecily's teeth gleamed as she smiled and sniffed. "He's a man of whom you would approve. He's clever and great."

"Then go, of course." As Cecily hurried away, already primping, Marian added solemnly, "But be careful, Cecily, lest you find yourself cradling a fatherless babe in your own arms."

# 2

"*Smacked ye a good one,* she did." Art pressed a cold wet rag on Griffith's nose. "I'd like to meet the lady."

"I'm sure you would." Griffith shoved Art away, then with careful fingers he felt the place where bone and cartilage connected. "Broken again. Saint Dewi preserve me, 'tis broken again!"

Art agreed. "Aye, she broke it for ye. Keep it up and ye'll have a face as pretty as mine."

The swelling caused pressure around his eyes, but Griffith observed his liver-spotted, snaggle-toothed, one-eyed servant. With a groan, he rearranged the rag on his face and wished he'd wrung Marian's pretty neck. Even more, he wished he hadn't maligned her lady.

Marian had proved herself loyal to Elizabeth. If Griffith had been a man less in control of himself, he might have given in to the impulse to reply physically to her challenge. But she was loyal, regardless of the danger to herself, and Griffith grudgingly respected that.

"'Tis not as if ye have a face to make a woman swoon, anyway. At least not with joy." Art chortled until he wheezed. "Yer nose was too big before it was ever broken. Yer hair's all wild, like some forest animal. Ye have the Powel chin—too square—and yer blessed mother's eyes—too yellow. 'Course, I don't understand it, but the women are always lining up for a peek in yer codpiece. Ye haven't said what happened with the lady . . . what's her name?"

"Lady Marian Wenthaven." Griffith rubbed his forehead and wished his headache would subside. "She's some relative of the earl's."

"Ye haven't said what happened with Lady Marian," Art repeated, "but I bet I know. I bet I know."

A sense of foreboding stopped Griffith as he prepared to lie down, but it couldn't stop him from asking, "Know what?"

"Fat ol' Lady Marian made a grab for ye." Art grabbed the air. "Ye fought the ol' hag." He fought with shadows. "And the ugly bitch slammed her ham fist into yer face."

Interrupting Art's imitation of womanly dismay, Griffith said, "She's not fat, old, or ugly."

Art straightened and his gaze sharpened. "Oh?"

Griffith flopped onto the feather mattress and arranged the pillows behind his back. The activity gave him time to make his plans.

He knew what Art was doing. His beloved body servant had for some reason decided Griffith should marry again, and he scouted every prospect most carefully. Now he fished for information, and if Griffith told him Marian was attractive, Art would be on him like stink on a pig farm. Worse, if Griffith told him she wasn't attractive, and Art caught sight of her, he'd know Griffith had lied. He'd construe the worst explanation for Griffith's evasion, so Griffith dared show no appreciation for Marian's appearance.

Not that he liked lithe women who smiled too much. Or was it too expressively? He told Art, "She's young."

Art pounced on the scrap of information. "How young?"

Lesser folk had to utilize words for the emotions Marian's smiles expressed. Griffith best remembered her scornful smile. Head tilted down, eyes amused, full lips curled just at the corners, a charming dimple in each cheek. "Twenty? Twenty-five years, perhaps?"

"The right age for ye," Art enthused. "Since ye're all of twenty-eight. What color is her hair?"

Nay, Griffith best remembered her dare-you smile. Shoulders thrown back, chest extended, all her white teeth flashing, a charming dimple in each cheek. "Red."

"Red hair?" Art frowned. "Englishwomen don't have red hair. Must be bright, ugly red from that dye women use."

Griffith squinted, pretending to think about it, but he remembered. He remembered too well. "It's not dyed."

"Copper, then?"

"Red," Griffith said firmly. "But some men might call it pretty."

"Like flame, then," Art said with satisfaction.

"Mm." Ah, but Griffith remembered her amused smile. Amused eyes slanted up, rosy cheeks lifted, full lips, white teeth, a charming dimple in each cheek . . . She'd been amused at him. How would she look when they laughed together? "Heated flame," Griffith mumbled.

Art lifted Marian's weapon—the purse—from the floor. "What color are her eyes?"

"Green."

"That's it," Art crowed, leaping in the air like a toad on a hot rock. "When a lad knows the color of a lass's eyes, he's in love."

"What?" Griffith roared, throwing aside the rag.

"When a lad—"

Griffith rolled out of bed and took a step toward Art. "I heard you! You gander-head, I don't even like the woman. She's immodest, rude, violent, flighty—"

"Sounds like the woman for ye," Art sang as he prudently backed away.

"She's not my type." Griffith drew a deep breath and contained his outrage. Keeping careful eye contact with his sniggering servant, he explained, "You know I like a domestic woman, adept with a needle, content to stay home. I don't like a woman who casts her gaze about freely, who fights like a man, whose red hair proves her freakish nature. I don't like a woman so handsome men fight for her and with her for the privilege of her bed."

Art limped to the bedside table and dropped the purse with a resounding *clunk*. "Ye just told me she was *not* old, fat, and ugly."

"So?"

"Ye didn't tell me she was handsome."

"So?"

Art hummed a little tune. "Are we going to stay here, then?"

"The sun's gone down, you silly old dickweed," Griffith answered. "Of course we're staying—tonight, and until I deliver that damn purse. But only until I deliver the purse. *So?*"

"So nothing. Ye're young and strong. Ye know yer mind best."

"And you'll not interfere?"

"Nay, master."

"Ha. When a cat can lick her ear!"

Pleased, Art limped back to the pile of saddlebags and leather pouches they'd brought from London. "Never seen a castle like this in Wales. Why don't ye lie down again? Ye're looking choleric."

Griffith grunted as he lay down. "Will I never win with you?"

Art ignored him, showing his Welsh contempt for the English and their fighting skills. "Instead of catapults and weapons, the grounds inside the walls are full of flowers. 'Twould be conquered in a fortnight in Wales."

Distracted, Griffith said, "Perhaps putting his castle on an island in a lake gives Wenthaven a feeling of security."

"Bah! They keep the chickens penned and his men-at-arms hidden in their own barracks."

"Not his men-at-arms," Griffith corrected. "These are mercenaries."

"Ah." Art comprehended immediately. "No wonder the earl keeps them separate from himself, then. They're likely to see a chance to conquer from within. Especially since he's hired a wad of them. Doesn't he know having yer own men is best?"

Griffith stroked his chin. "He *has* hired an army, hasn't he?"

"Heard a lot of Welsh out there."

"'Tis common knowledge the Welsh are the best fighters in the Isles."

"And why shouldn't our lads fight for English coin and English plunder? Want me to go chat with them, casual-like, and find out what's up?" While Griffith hesitated, Art opened the bags and dumped them onto the floor. "What do ye want me to save out?"

"Traveling clothes. We're leaving for home tomorrow."

"'Tis a shame not to stay and get acquainted with Lady Marian."

"Traveling clothes," Griffith repeated with emphasis. He didn't want to discuss Marian with Art anymore. He didn't even want to think about Marian.

An Englishwoman, he thought contemptuously. He'd learned the depths of an Englishwoman's love when he rode to London after the victory of Bosworth Field and heard the tales of Elizabeth of York.

He'd told Marian the truth. Elizabeth's callous dis-regard for her brothers' fate and the rumors of her willing liaison with Richard had sickened him. They had sickened Henry, too, and he dragged his feet about marrying the strumpet. Then Parliament made their sentiments known. Henry must keep to his pledge to wed Elizabeth. Henry had bowed to neces-sity, repeating his battlefield vow—that nothing and no one would take the throne from him.

Girding his loins, he'd met with Elizabeth—and come away with a changed attitude. Neither a blow to the skull nor a caress to the groin should have softened Henry so, but he married Elizabeth without another murmur and behaved in a seemly manner about it.

Elizabeth seemed a charming woman, Griffith admitted, but her betrayal with Richard could not be banished from his mind, and he wondered how Henry managed to subdue his revulsion. Perhaps he'd been seduced by her youth and charm, perhaps . . . Griffith remembered the tiny span of Marian's waist and speculated about the breasts he'd glimpsed beneath the fur-trimmed neckline.

Perhaps, Griffith admitted, Henry had lost his heart to an Englishwoman's arts. But sorrow, war, and anguish had hardened Griffith's character. He'd never chosen to bless any woman with more affection than he gave his falcons.

And he never would. He never would.

"I said"—Art rubbed his eye in exaggerated pain— "I *said,* this old wound's a-painin' me."

"I heard you," Griffith said, irritated. "You don't have to shout."

Crossing his arms across his chest, Art repeated, "This old wound's a-painin' me, and ye're daydreaming."

"I'm not, and your eye doesn't hurt. You know it. You always say that when you want your way."

"'Tis a shame not to check out Wenthaven's plans," Art coaxed.

Griffith hesitated. As the king's representative, he should try to discover what Wenthaven plotted, if anything. But Wenthaven was deep in the royal confidence and surely knew his future lay with Henry. "I'll send a message," Griffith said. "If Henry wants me to come back, he'll command me."

Sanguine, Art flung wide the doors of the carved wood cabinet. "Guess I'll put the bags in this fancy cupboard."

"Wenthaven can afford a fancy cupboard and a choice castle. He's one of the dowager queen's upstart relatives." Griffith stretched out on the bed with a sigh. "He married well and held some prime positions during Edward's reign."

Art nodded. "Got his money the hard way, then. By scheming." Holding up one of Griffith's shirts, he flapped the sleeves. "Look at this. This proves what I was saying. Yer arms are so long ye can scratch yer knees without bending down. Not that that doesn't give ye a good reach with a blade, and not that I haven't had reason to be thankful for yer reach. Yer big old chest makes ye look like a barrel, and yer legs are so long I have trouble keeping ye in hose."

"Are you trying to make me feel better?" Griffith asked irritably.

"Of course. How else can I prove this lass hasn't ruined yer looks? I say, if ye want her, better take her quick, else some other man will steal her from under yer"—Art snatched away the now-warm rag and replaced it with a cold one—"nose."

"I don't want her."

"Then why is the bone in yer drawers as puffy as that bone on yer face?"

Griffith came up with a roar. "Damn it, Art, shut your muzzle before I knock the rest of your teeth down your throat."

"Ooh, frightened, I am."

Removing the rag and throwing it aside, Griffith

insisted, "I'm not interested in a woman who has no control over her impulses."

As little awed by Griffith's severity as by his threats, Art cocked his head, his eyes as inquisitive as a sparrow's. "And why is she lacking in control?"

"She was the favorite lady-in-waiting of Elizabeth of York. Marian could have made a great marriage, been a great influence. Instead she destroyed her chance for one moment in a great lord's bed."

"'Tis not an uncommon sin."

"She bore a bastard." Griffith heard the condemnation in his own voice and knew Art would make him repent for it.

"Ah." Head bobbing, Art pranced around the bed in a sprightly step. "So her sin is not fornication, but gestation. Not the sin itself, but being caught."

The trouble with old and trusted servants, Griffith reflected grimly, was not their insights, but the fact they felt compelled to share them. Intent on discouraging any more of Art's ungainly strutting and critical comments, Griffith said, "Anyone who cannot control himself is not worthy of having mastery or authority over others."

"'Tis a country proverb, and a good one." Art stopped dancing and eyed Griffith's dour expression. "Too bad ye've not always followed it."

On this subject, Griffith could not shout—at least not at Art, who had lost his eye to Griffith's youthful folly. "I learned my lesson early."

"Perhaps Marian lass learned the same lesson, but the proof of her mistake is not so easily hidden."

Deep in Griffith's heart the knife of memory twisted, and he bled anew. The blade was a shard of glass, a broken icicle, or perhaps plain rusting steel, for memory, he'd discovered, had the capacity to wound forever and ever.

"There, lad." Art pushed him back on the bed and changed his rag again. "'Twas a low blow, and I'm sorry for it. I was just trying to point out we all make our mistakes, and ye've judged this girl too harshly." Turning away, he muttered loudly enough for Griffith to hear, "And all because she's got ye playing solo on yer skin flute."

Dignity had somehow escaped him, but Griffith answered, "I'm here on Henry's business—for no other reason."

Art opened a pocket on his own saddlebag, pulled out a folded paper, and extended it.

Scarlet wax fastened the edge, and Griffith recognized the design of the seal. With foreboding, he accepted it and looked inquiringly at Art.

"Our sovereign sent this letter—hand delivered by that little secretary of his—with instructions it should be delivered after ye'd met Lady Marian." Although he couldn't read, Art leaned way over the bed as Griffith skimmed the contents and inspected the writing with a knowledgeable eye. "Anything interesting?"

After rolling the paper, Griffith handed it to Art. "Burn it, then unpack the bags. We're staying at Wenthaven Castle, God rot it!"

Art scratched behind his ear where his last few wisps of hair remained. "The king doesn't say why?"

"It's Henry's style. Orders, but no explanations. That's why he sent a letter to you—by Oliver King, no less. If Henry had commanded me himself, I'd have demanded the truth."

"Crafty, isn't he?" Art asked in admiration. "What are the orders?"

"We are to remain indefinitely and watch over Lady Marian and her son."

Art thrust the parchment deep into the fire with an iron poker. "Why is the king worried about Marian lass and her son?"

Clipping his words, Griffith replied, "I don't know. Henry confided no worries to me."

"But it's damned strange he has an interest." Art

went back to the jumbled pile of clothes and stirred it with his toe. "Might as well hang all this up. Good thing ye were going home to Wales and ye brought every last one of yer garments for yer mother to clean, else ye'd be hard-pressed to dress for this fancy company."

"I had wondered why Henry insisted I visit my parents. No doubt he was troubled in his mind." Griffith swung his legs off the bed. "I had heard rumors about a setback in Ireland."

"What kind of setback?"

"The rumors claim the earl of Warwick is at large in Ireland."

Art sighed with the marked exasperation of a Welshman who prides himself on his ignorance of English nobility. "Is that supposed to mean something to me?"

"The earl of Warwick," Griffith explained carefully, "is the son of the late duke of Clarence."

Art sighed again.

"Pay attention." From the bowl of fruit placed on the bedside table, Griffith withdrew three apples and placed them on the table. Lifting the plumpest and rosiest, he said, "This is King Edward, father of Elizabeth of York."

"He's a fat one," Art observed.

"So he was. This"—Griffith lifted another, quite shriveled piece of fruit—"is King Richard, the usurper, defeated, and killed at Bosworth." Griffith lifted the last apple, smaller than the rest. "This is the duke of Clarence. These three men were brothers, sons of the house of York."

"Aye, I see the family resemblance," Art interjected.

"Two of them were kings, and although Clarence was not, he had a son."

"Ah." Light broke over Art's wizened face. "The earl of Warwick."

"Exactly. Nephew to two Yorkist kings and, by some accounting, heir to the throne of England."

"And now he's in Ireland?"

"Nay, the earl of Warwick lives safely under Henry's protection in the Tower of London."

Pressing his hand over his eyes, Art mumbled, "I'll never understand all these kings and king's daughters and king's nephews."

"Think about it," Griffith urged. "Edward's heirs disappeared into the Tower, never to be seen again, murdered by their own uncle"—he picked up the wrinkled apple—"Richard. Now Henry has taken another heir into custody. If you were a lord who hadn't supported Henry in his bid for the throne, what would you think?"

"That Henry had murdered this earl of Warwick."

"Right. And if you were a lord who hadn't supported Henry in his bid for the throne, how best would you depose him?"

Art dropped both his hand and his guise of confusion. "I would claim to have the earl of Warwick, raise a force, and try to take England from Ireland, where Yorkist feeling still runs strong."

Tossing the apples back into the bowl, Griffith said, "Ah, Arthur, you are ever the wisest—"

A knock on the door interrupted him, and he and Art exchanged looks. Opening it, Art revealed a round and wrinkled maid, smiling and bobbing a curtsy. "I'm Jane. I've been sent t' help ye settle in." She clucked when she saw the mess of clothing on the floor and immediately knelt beside it. Sorting shirts, hose, and mantles into separate piles, she chatted, "Looks like ye could use help, too. Never know why ye men must try t' do yer own laundry. Right awful, ye are." Shaking out a richly trimmed mantle, she pulled a disapproving face. "Look at this! Fer all that it's black"—she glanced down at the pile—"like most o' yer clothes, it deserves more than being thrust into a bag an' ridden all over th' countryside. I'll take care o' this one right away, an' ye can wear it tomorrow, master."

She took his agreement for granted, but when Griffith would speak, Art laid a restraining hand on his arm. *Let me handle this,* his look said to Griffith, and Griffith subsided. Art had a way with women, all women, and he stepped forward and bowed with a flourish. "I'm Art, the man who is eternally grateful for yer services."

Obviously well versed in flirtation, Jane dimpled coyly. "Glad t' meet ye, Art."

"Will ye be taking the rest of the clothes, too?" he asked.

"The rest o' them we'll work on, an' th' master'll have one t' wear every day ye stay. As th' winter deepens, though, we might have t' loan ye a warm cloak. But don't worry, we get visitors all th' time we need t' dress, an'—"

That proved too much for Griffith's restraint, and he demanded, "Why do you think I'll remain through the winter? I told Wenthaven I'd be leaving tomorrow."

Straightening, Jane stared. "Have I got th' wrong room? Aren't ye Griffith ap Powel?"

Art elbowed Griffith back into silence. "He is, and a surly, ungrateful lord to so scorn yer services. Now I"—Art moved close and picked up Jane's hand—"I cherish the tenacity which keeps ye working so late. Yer husband must be a lucky man."

Jane tittered as he kissed her knuckles. "I'm a widow."

"A widow? How sad." Art cooed the last word, making his true emotions clear. Jane smiled in response, and Griffith cleared his throat in disgusted admonition.

Recalled to her duty, the laundry woman stiffened. "All I know is, orders from His Lordship came down just as we were retirin' t' our pallets, tellin' us ye were stayin' fer a long spell an' we were t' tend t' ye as one o' our most honored guests. He said we were t' wait until tomorrow afternoon t' do so, but I said t'

Mistress Fay, I said—Is that th' way we treat honored guests? Makin' 'em wait fer their clothes to be cleaned an' pressed? So here I am, an' good thing, too, I say."

Astonished, the two men stared at the woman as she stood, clothing hanging from her arms and shoulders. When they didn't reply, she shrugged. "I'll have these back fer ye as quick as a wink." Peering at Griffith, she clucked her tongue again. "Ooh, Lady Marian really landed ye a knock. She always was a hot-tempered one. Will ye shut the door behind me, Art?"

Art hastened to obey, then faced his master with hand outstretched in a gesture of innocence. "I told no one about Lady Marian and yer nose. Someone must have seen ye quarreling."

"I'm not concerned about Lady Marian or her hot temper," Griffith snapped. "I want to know how Wenthaven knew I would be staying almost before I knew."

"The king's been in contact with Wenthaven," Art guessed. "Must be why he knew we would stay."

"Or do the walls in this manor have ears?" Griffith indicated the carvings that etched the wood panels in elaborate designs. Art, too, glanced around, instant comprehension in his gaze. Before Art could express his rage, Griffith said quietly, "Sleep with your eye open, will you, Arthur? With the blow to my head, I'm likely to rest hard tonight, and there's more to this than I had realized."


The whine of the spaniel sprawled on his chest woke him, and the earl of Wenthaven lay with eyes closed and listened. Something rustled in the bushes outside his bedroom window. Something . . . no, someone. He soothed the dog with a hand on its head and whispered a command, and the bitch subsided. Moving with the subtlety of an ox, the intruder climbed through the open window. He crept toward the bed, and the spaniel quivered with anticipation. Wenthaven waited until the intruder stood right over the bed, then cried, "Attack!"

The spaniel rose with a spine-tingling growl, the woman beside Wenthaven screamed, and the intruder cursed in a colorful mix of street language and aristocratic expression. Wenthaven recognized the deep voice, but he let the bitch take a few bites as he armed himself with a sword. Then he called off the dog, rewarding her with pats and praise, and faced Sir Adrian Harbottle. "What are you doing in my room?"

"Filthy goddamn dog," Harbottle fumed. "Sank her teeth into my wrist and my ankle. I'm bleeding and it hurts!"

"Well, don't do it on my carpet. It's new and it's expensive," Wenthaven replied sharply.

"It would be." Harbottle wrapped his wrist in a handkerchief and stepped off the carpet onto the flagstone floor.

"Again I ask—what are you doing in my room?"

Harbottle said, "I came to set things straight. I came for a bit of revenge."

"Revenge? For what?" Wenthaven kept his sword at the ready as he lashed Harbottle with his words. "For offering you my hospitality? For feeding you more than any one person should consume? For putting up with your boorish ways?"

"You contrived against me," Harbottle accused him.

"*I* contrived against you? I . . . ?" Wenthaven's tone became a croon. "Darling, will you light that branch of candles? The moon has just risen, and we need to throw some light on this wretched bit of humanity."

With shaking fingers, the woman touched the wicks to the solitary night candle and they sputtered to life.

Harbottle snorted. "You've got your plump, pretty woman in your bedroom and your pretty people in your pretty castle in the middle of a lake, but they all hang about you because you've got money—"

"Yourself included?" Wenthaven interrupted.

"I came here in good faith, glad of the food and the roof over my head. I didn't know I'd be paying for all of it with my honor."

Wenthaven laughed freely. "Honor? What honor concerns a younger son such as yourself? Your brother's a baron, you have no prospects except the ones you make for yourself with your face. . . . Honor? Please."

"You want me to do things no decent man would do." Harbottle's earnest face glistened with moisture. "You want me to listen in corners, pry secrets out of their hiding places, look under rocks where the evil things dwell."

"You're so good at it."

"I am not!" Harbottle shouted.

This young man would have to be handled delicately, Wenthaven realized. Nature had endowed Harbottle with such masculine beauty, he'd become spoiled. Conquest had become second nature to him. Nature, also, had endowed him with coordination and strength.

Ah, aye, Marian had dealt a blow to both Harbottle's conceit and his confidence, and a man in such disarray would seek vindication. Hot-tempered, hot-blooded, with delusions of his own virtuous character, Harbottle reminded Wenthaven of an untrained cur. Frisky, without direction, but teachable with the right master.

True, Wenthaven trained purebreds, but the principles were the same. Gesturing with his sword, he said, "Pour yourself some wine. It's the best from my cellar."

"You can't bribe me like a child," Harbottle

protested, but he poured the wine and sipped it. His face lit up. "It is good."

"Of course. Now sit down."

Harbottle's face clouded again. "Nay!"

A sharp blow, then a stroke from the master. Wenthaven planted the sword into Harbottle's chest. "Please sit down."

Subsiding like a good hound, Harbottle watched with mournful blue eyes as Wenthaven filled a goblet for himself and took the chair opposite.

"The way I see it," Wenthaven said, "is that I misdirected your talents. I should have seen at once you were too refined for anything as distasteful as seeking out information."

"Nay." Harbottle drank, and Wenthaven gestured to the woman who hovered beside the bed. She brought the pitcher and filled Harbottle's cup again.

"Nay, indeed." Wenthaven made a production of drinking but let the wine only touch his tongue. "Today you proved your sword is your strength."

Rising in a surge of indignation, Harbottle shouted, "I'll not be laughed at."

Wenthaven raised his eyebrows. "Who's laughing? I meant it as a sincere compliment." He watched the young man waver, then pointed at the chair again with his sword. "Sit."

This time Harbottle responded with less reluctance. He sat.

A pleased master, Wenthaven said, "When I encouraged you to fight the lady Marian, I should have warned you of her slyness. It was obvious to all you were holding back because of her femininity, and when she realized it, she took advantage of you."

Harbottle's full lips parted. "Indeed?"

"Of that there was no doubt. Word has spread about the excellence of your sword fighting."

"I am good! Damned good. That's how I've supported myself, and I'll wager you knew it."

"How would I know that?"

"The same way you know everything. Why, I'd wager every one of those noble folk who eat at your table pay your price in secrets. I bet you're the most well-informed man in the kingdom."

"You flatter me." Wenthaven tapped his teeth with one long fingernail and deduced it was time to dangle the proper treat. "But we're not here to talk about me. We're here to talk about you. You and the nubile Lady Marian. Isn't that correct?"

At the mention of Marian's name, Harbottle's hand shook and his voice rose an octave. "What about me and Lady Marian?"

A stud with the scent of a bitch strong in his nostrils, Wenthaven diagnosed. "You wanted to get to know her better, isn't that correct? She wasn't noticing you, and I suggested you challenge her. I thought when you defeated her, she'd show you some respect." Sadly, Wenthaven sighed. "I failed to think about the advantage she'd have. . . . I imagine her excellent figure might have distracted you. Hmm?" He peered into Harbottle's moist eyes, and Harbottle looked away. "It's no shame. If I do say so myself, Lady Marian's breasts are the finest in the kingdom. She isn't as comely as you are, of course, but there aren't many men who can match her height as you can. I imagine the men lucky enough to share her bed find she can wrap her legs around them twice."

The air around Harbottle wavered with warmth.

Allowing himself a private smile, Wenthaven now opened the gate to the kennel. "Lady Marian learned her swordplay from me, but I'm not a fool. I didn't teach her *everything*." Harbottle exhaled in a gasp, and putting sincerity into his tone, Wenthaven asked, "What would you say to private lessons? I'd be glad to teach you what she doesn't know."

Harbottle jumped into Wenthaven's trap. "I want a second chance at her. I want a second chance at

Mistress High and Mighty. When I defeat her, she'll be at my mercy. Of course"—he looked down at his well-shaped hands with a crooked smile—"she'll put up the obligatory struggle, but no woman has refused me yet."

The man's complacency staggered Wenthaven, and he wondered how many women had refused Harbottle in all sincerity and found themselves flat on their backs, struggling with this smirking jackass.

That wasn't what he planned for Marian. Marian would yet prove her value.

Wenthaven cautioned, "It will be difficult to lure her into another bout. Your remarks about her son were ill timed and ill advised."

Harbottle's mouth turned down. "That whelp's just a bastard."

Wenthaven felt a stirring of impatience, but he subdued it. If Harbottle was an imperfect weapon, still he was a weapon. Wenthaven needed every weapon he could lay hands on, for Henry Tudor had sent that towering Welshman to guard Marian, and that meant the king was suspicious. Wenthaven said, "The whelp is *her* bastard, and she's fond of him."

With a rising excitement, Harbottle said, "She's always hanging on to him when she should be listening to me. I'd like to smash him."

"Don't hurt Lionel." Wenthaven was alarmed. "The lad is precious to me. Nay, listen to my plan. Stay out of sight until I've taught you a few sword tricks she doesn't know, then you can insult her son, and she'll challenge you."

"And for my reward?"

"Your reward will be more than you ever imagined," Wenthaven promised. "Now exit out the window, there's a good lad—"

"Nay." Harbottle leaned forward, fists clenched around the chair's arms. "I'll not accept such a feeble promise again. If I do what you want and defeat Lady Marian—"

"What you want, too," Wenthaven reminded him.

"Aye, that's what I want, too. But I want to hear my reward. I want you to tell me what my reward will be."

Wenthaven hesitated. It went against his cautious nature to reveal his plans to anyone at any time. But what could it hurt? He could always have this virile, smelly mongrel sacrificed and served on a platter to Henry, and none would be the wiser. "If you challenge and defeat Lady Marian, she'll have to let you in her bed. And when you've thoroughly ruffled the sheets, then she'll have no choice but to wed you. I'll make sure of it."

"She might refuse."

In a tone as steely as his sword blade, Wenthaven said, "She's a woman. She lives on my charity. She'll do as she's told."

"When you speak like that, I almost feel sorry for her."

Harbottle didn't sound as if he meant it, Wenthaven noted. "Tell no one of our discussion, or you'll ruin the surprise we have planned for Lady Marian."

With a hop of enthusiasm, Harbottle slid out into the bushes. Wenthaven extinguished the candles, conscious of a job well done, then felt a nudge.

His latest lover snuggled her head under his arm and rested it against his chest. "I don't hang about you because you're wealthy," she whispered, all fake innocence and sensual appeal. "And you don't keep me to use me. That awful man didn't know what he was talking about."

"No." Wenthaven stroked her blond head and matched her insincerity. "We're eternal lovers, and when the time is right, we'll marry and you'll be my countess, for I could never use a woman who offers her love so sweetly."

And he smiled a secret smile.

# 3

*Someone was in the room.* Someone besides Art, who slept at the foot of Griffith's bed and whose hand shook him awake. With a warrior's instincts, Griffith worked to maintain an even breathing while his eyes adjusted to the contrast of dark and white light the night and the moon created. Slowly he turned his head and saw someone crouched beside the saddlebags. Too far away from the window's square of moonlight to be recognizable, the intruder used his hands to search the far reaches of the leather sacks, and Griffith watched carefully.

Did the scurrilous fellow seek gold? Or did one of Wenthaven's minions seek information?

Rising empty-handed, the thief revealed himself to be a plump youth, clad in hose and jerkin. He opened the cupboard and soundlessly groped through the contents, and Griffith eyed the distance to the door. If the youth made a move to leave when his spying was complete, Griffith would urge him to remain. Physically urge him to remain. And although this young man's legs were long, Griffith's were longer.

He would get to the door first.

But that proved unnecessary. Apparently dissatisfied, the thief shut the doors and moved across the floor to Griffith's bedside.

The bag of gold rested there on the nightstand. Marian's bag of gold.

With a quiet murmur of satisfaction, the youth picked it up, and Griffith rose with a roar. The robber shrieked and whirled on him. Griffith grabbed him by the waist and flung him on the bed. Pouncing, Griffith evaded the fists that aimed so unerringly at his nose. He caught the flailing hands. With a wrestler's grip, he leaned his arm into the intruder's slender throat.

The scent and softness and his own sure instinct brought reality with a jolt.

"Got him?" Art asked, fierce as only an old warrior can be.

"Got her," Griffith corrected sourly, and felt the mutinous body beneath him collapse.

"What the hell?" Art lit one feeble candle with his flint and held it aloft, and the flame reflected in the wisps of red hair around a defiant face. At once, Art subdued his savagery and broke into a smile. "Lady Marian, I trow!"

"Aye, 'tis Lady Marian." Still straddling her hips, Griffith sat back on his heels and surveyed what he could see of her. "Lady Marian, in a most outrageous outfit."

The long-sleeved jerkin, he could now see, was quilted and stuffed—quite fashionable and quite convenient for a woman wishing to disguise an unmanly chest. The short skirt that flared beneath the belt served, as well, to cover the curve of her hips. But the skirt ended at the tops of her thighs, and lying beneath him, as she was now, it rode up and revealed the codpiece. Or, rather—the empty codpiece.

"God rot it." Embarrassed, horrified, and . . . God

help him, was he aroused? Griffith jerked his gaze back up to her face. "What are you doing in here? And in this harlequin's outfit most absurd?"

Her full lips pouted and trembled like those of a child thwarted, but she maintained a pretense of dignity when she protested, "I could scarcely come to rob your room in my skirts and petticoats."

"Rob my—"

"And I wish you'd keep your voice down and blow out that candle," she scolded, her voice low yet strengthening as she recovered from her alarm. "The earl has spies everywhere, and by my troth, I'd be ill pleased to have this adventure bandied about."

Griffith glanced at Art, and Art nodded. Extinguishing the light, he said, "Ye'd best get off the lass before I'm forced to scold like an old maid chaperone and call for the priest." Griffith jumped off the bed like a scalded cat, and Art continued, "Ye'd best ask her about Wenthaven before she gets away."

"I'm not going anywhere." Marian avoided looking at either of them by lifting the purse from the nightstand. "At least, I'm not leaving without this. 'Tis mine, is it not?"

An undiagnosed disappointment sharpened Griffith's voice. "Mercenary *and* thieving."

"Griffith," Art groaned.

"Quite," Marian agreed in even tones.

Too even. Griffith's ear caught the firmness of a soul unjustly accused and resigned to misjudgment. He found himself excusing her. "But you can't be thieving. As you said, the money is yours."

She tied the heavy purse to her belt. "I'm only mercenary, then."

Like a benevolent gnome, Art threw his arm around her shoulders. "Not at all. Ye have to feed yer babe, don't ye?" Marian shied away from Art, but he pulled her close to the window. "Nay, lass, look at me and tell me ye don't trust this face."

Of course, she did trust him. Once the moonlight had touched his vivid blue eye and his wrinkled, half-plucked chin and his kind smile, she trusted him as surely as did every other woman in the world.

"Griffith, here"—Art extended a crooked finger— "Griffith doesn't understand why ye need Her Majesty's money, but Griffith's never been a father. He's never had to keep a growing child in shoes and clothes, or try to fill a babe's endlessly hollow belly, or pay a witch to come with her herbs to cure a wee fever."

"Or pay a priest to bury the tiny bodies?"

Marian's gentle inquiry startled Griffith. He knew Art's story, knew the pain behind the tale of the "wee fever."

But Marian must have heard the quaver in the old voice, for she asked, "Have you children, Art?"

Art cleared his throat. "Not any more, lass. I saved them from a battle and lost them—all six of them, and their mother, too—in the famine and sickness that followed."

She nudged him with her shoulder, the kind of a nudge a tabby gives when she wants to be petted. He raised a hand and smoothed her hair back. Then, with artificial briskness, he said, "Now tell us, like a good lass, is it a fact that Wenthaven knows more than most folks about his guests and their business?"

Her saucy smile denied she'd ever been touched by Art's story, and Griffith might almost have believed that moment of compassion never happened—except that Art wiped a tear off his cheek.

Waving at the walls around them, she whispered, "Wenthaven could sell information to the devil, but he's too greedy and keeps it for himself. This room is the richest, rife with places to listen and to peek, and Wenthaven puts only his most important guests here." She smirked at Griffith. "What have you done to so interest Wenthaven?"

"A just inquiry," he answered. "I'd like to know myself."

Her hand crept to the purse at her belt, and she rolled the coins around, looking at the wistfully appealing Art. "I'll move you to a different room. A safe room."

Griffith observed her betraying movements. "Why do you imagine you may move Wenthaven's guests and he'll not protest?"

Her hand dropped to her hip, and she smiled with cocky assurance. "I can handle Wenthaven."

"And how do you know the room is safe?" Griffith probed.

"You'll see." She moved out of the betraying moonlight. "Get your master's things, Art, and I'll take you there."

"Got nothing to bring." Art pulled a wry face. "Jane o' the laundry took it all. Guess I'll have to go looking for her tomorrow and have the clothes sent to our new room. Wherever that might be."

Marian stepped into the candlelit hallway and bent to pull on a pair of fine leather boots, appropriate for a young man.

Hand on her arm, Griffith swung her around. "Why didn't you just ask me for your gold?"

He wanted to know the truth. He wanted to know what she thought, and she infuriated him with a prevaricating, "When?"

"Tomorrow."

"You might have left tomorrow," she answered.

"If I had left tomorrow without giving you your gold, I would be a thief."

"No, not a thief, but possibly"—she looked at him, at his swollen nose—"but possibly an angry man."

"Is that what you think of me? That I would rob you as revenge for this puny injury?"

"I do beg your pardon," she said.

Offended by this affront to his honor, he retorted, "I would hope so."

"I shouldn't have hit you, no matter how insulting you were. But when you insulted the lady Elizabeth's integrity—"

"Wait. Wait." He held up one hand. "Do you mean you apologize, not for the slur on my own integrity, but for hitting me?"

Looking him full in the eyes, she answered sharply, "Only a fool would depend on a man's integrity."

"What kind of men have you known?" But she tilted her head, honestly puzzled by his outrage. Disgusted—not with her, but with the men who'd taught her such values—he gestured to her. "Lead on."

As she led them to the end of the hall, Griffith heard Art chortle behind him, and the old man's whisper floated to his ears. "She'll be a tough nut to crack. Mayhap ye *should* give up before ye've started."

Brow puckered, Marian glanced back to verify their presence . . . or was it because she'd heard Art? Griffith hunched his shoulders, stepped between them, and glowered at her.

"Don't you ever smile?" she asked, as if goaded by his ill humor. She didn't wait for a reply but plucked a candle from its stand. Showing no respect for the earl's possession, she placed it on a gold-and-colored-glass wall plate and opened a tiny door hidden in the paneling. Griffith had to duck to enter, almost tumbled down four narrow steps, and found himself at the bottom of a winding stair.

"The tower," he said, paying Marian a grudging respect. "Aye, I can see even Wenthaven would have difficulty placing a spy here."

She smiled, but her mouth was lopsided and she seemed to be uncomfortable. "Wenthaven doesn't ever come here." Moonlight shone through thin arrow slits, providing feeble help for the candle. She lifted it high, but Griffith could see only a black tunnel above. Beneath the stairs, the floor tumbled in a rough pattern of paving stone and boards.

"This is the old part of the castle." She looked up and around. "Even the rock feels ancient to me."

"Aye." Art took a deep breath. "Smells like the old times."

She flashed him a smile, and her boots clapped against the stone as she leaped up the stairs two at a time.

"Impulsive," Griffith muttered, but he followed just as swiftly. To guard her steps, he told himself, for no rail protected her from a fall, but he took the chance to study the undulating bottom and legs before him. It was a new perspective, and while a woman in hose should disgust him, he found it only piqued an already reluctantly whetted appetite. The strength of her calves, the smooth movement of muscles working to get her up the stairs, entranced him, made him dizzy, and when she stopped abruptly on the top landing, he skidded back a step and banged his knee.

She caught at his arm as if he were an old man. "Are you ill?"

"No!" Rubbing his new bruise, glaring at the cackling Art, he demanded, "Where is this room?"

"Here." She flung open a door he'd not previously noticed and waved the candle. "Go on."

He stepped inside and smelled dust. She followed him, raised the light, and he saw elegance—and melancholy. At the very center of the round room rose a dais. Perched thereon stood a carved wood bed shrouded in brocade curtains. Tapestries alive with scenes of long-ago hunts, battles, and domesticity hung on the stone walls. An immense fireplace gaped, hungering for fuel, for light, for warmth. Chests and cupboards, placed by an artistic hand, waited to be filled. Chairs ached to embrace a human form.

"This is no room for a guest," he objected. "This is—"

Marian chuckled, and the sound drifted on a current of air. At once the room seemed brighter, happier. "Wenthaven's countess used this room."

"If that's meant to reassure me," he said sternly, "it does not."

"They tell me she liked to be above the hubbub of the castle guests." Placing the candle beside the bed, she whacked the curtains. Dust flew, and she coughed. "The servants haven't been caring for this place, and with you here, they'll be forced to." She wiped a finger across the glass of the window and glared at the streak it left. "Lazy sluts."

Griffith said, "Wenthaven wouldn't want me to destroy the sanctity of a shrine he has kept so carefully."

"As you wish," she answered. "But wherever you go in this keep, beware of drapes that seem to cut the breeze, and tiny alcoves and passages that lead nowhere. They often hide the unseen listener."

He winced.

"I thought you wanted to be able to freely speak to Art. To know no peering eyes watch you dress, or snigger at the holes in your hose. To piss without embarrassment—"

"M'lady," Art chimed in, "the watchers would but envy him."

"Shut up, Art," Griffith snapped. "That is scarcely the point."

Marian insisted, "That's all the point. There's no place in this castle where Wenthaven's spies cannot go—except here."

Griffith was a man used to solitude. To the open length of a Welsh seashore and the hushed call of a woodland owl. Living here at Wenthaven Castle for an indefinite time would be strain enough. But never knowing when someone eavesdropped on him . . .

From the doorway, Art asked, "So are we staying?"

"Wenthaven will toss us out when he discovers our impertinence," Griffith insisted.

But he was wavering, and Marian knew it. She smiled that lopsided smile again. "He won't mind."

Art stepped in and dropped the bags. The thick carpet swallowed the thud, and he wiped his palms on his jerkin. "What happened to her?"

"The countess?" Marian's gaze shifted away toward the window. "Eighteen years ago she fell down the stairs and broke her neck. That's why this room is safe for you. Wenthaven never comes here. I'm told she was the only thing he ever cared about."

"So we trade the nosiness of Wenthaven for the constant presence of his wife."

Art's whisper chilled Griffith.

Marian moved close to the old man, seeming unsurprised by his claim of a haunting. She laid a hand on his arm. "Is she really here? Some of the servants claim she is. They say the room's too cold and the air's unfriendly, but I've never felt that."

Art patted her hand. "Of course not. She didn't die unshriven, did she?"

"Nay. She still lived when they found her, and the priest gave her last rites. Then they tried to move her. . . ." Marian dropped her hands in a final gesture.

"So she's not a cruel ghost," Art said, "but a gentle shade whose work on this earth was left unfinished. She'll have no patience with idle maids or lusty knaves. But she likes ye, Lady Marian. Aye, she likes ye."

Delighted, Marian smiled at Art, and Griffith found himself even more annoyed by the friendship springing up between his manservant and his . . . and Lady Marian. "Arthur," he snapped, "you've never claimed to be a sensitive before."

"Do ye think ye know everything about me?" Art snapped back. "Ye young runt, ye."

Marian tossed back her head and laughed aloud. This time the change was tangible. The room brightened, and Griffith looked for an explanation. There, outside the east window, the sun flung its earliest glow. Dawn wouldn't be for another two hours, but Marian saw it, too, and said, "I have to go. I've been gone too long as it is." In a hurry now, she strode to the door. "I'll get the servants up here as soon as the cock crows. And I'll clear it with—"

"I'm going with you," Griffith said.

"What?" She paused. "Where?"

"To see you to your room. 'Tis not safe for a young woman, dressed as you are, to wander about." He tried hard to keep the censorious tone from his voice, but apparently he had ill succeeded.

"It's safe for me," she retorted.

"Nevertheless, I will go with you." And when she opened her mouth again, he added, "Or you'll stay here until sunup."

Her smile expressed a savage impatience. "Come if you wish, then, and be damned to you."

"Ladies do not curse so bitterly," he answered.

She pretended not to hear, but the set of her shoulders as she ran down the stairs told him she had. She led him past his former room, past the corridor to the main door, and into a smaller passage that wound down to the kitchens. Taking a tiny stairway, she led him up again to a door. She pushed it up a crack, said, "It's me," and it was opened by a hulking man-at-arms.

He stared fearfully when Griffith emerged into the apple orchard at the west side of the keep. "M'lady, this passage is supposed t' be secret."

"Sir Griffith'll never tell," she assured him, brushing her knees.

The giant rubbed his chin. "Then I suppose I'll not have t' kill him."

"I'm grateful," Griffith said, eyeing the assortment of weapons the fellow carried.

"So you should be," she answered. "Billy is our fiercest soldier."

Billy basked in her approval, then handed her a knee-length coat. "Put it on, m'lady," he urged. "Th' way ye dress is a scandal. Some men"—he glared at Griffith—"might get wrongful ideas about ye."

"That's impossible. Sir Griffith already knows all about me," she said. "And he's quite disgusted."

"Put on the coat," Griffith said.

Grinning, she did as she was told.

"Do ye want me t' walk ye t' yer cottage, m'lady?" Billy asked, giving Griffith the first clue to their destination.

"I'll make sure she runs into no trouble," Griffith assured him.

Billy pointed at Griffith's nose. "Are ye sure ye can handle it?"

"I'm sure." When Billy seemed about to say more, Griffith leaned close and looked him in the eye. Holding the contact, he repeated, "I'm sure."

Billy backed up. "Aye, Sir Griffith. As ye say, Sir Griffith." But as Marian and Griffith walked away, he called, "Ye watch yerself, Lady Marian. Not even yer Sir Griffith can be trusted over much."

Griffith hoped Marian would have the good sense to keep her mouth shut. Billy's suspicions didn't amuse him, and he wondered if all onlookers could see the bubbling broth of desire and disapproval Marian had brewed within him. He hoped she realized he could boil over; hoped she realized how hot a fire she'd built with her very self.

At the same time, he hoped she would be unwise, and the thought shocked him. Speaking to himself as much as to her, he said, "Women should never indulge in fornication without the protection of marriage."

Marian stuck her thumbs into her belt and swaggered along a row through the trees. "You're a virgin, then?"

"That's what whores are for."

"To cure an unfortunate case of virginity? Tell me"—just outside of the orchard, she turned and smirked at him—"how bad is your case of the pox? It certainly explains your vile disposition."

A cottage—her cottage?—stood in the shadow of the curtain wall, but he couldn't look away from her to examine it. Instead he caught her narrow jaw in his hand and lifted her smiling, scornful face to his. "I haven't a case of the pox."

"Then you're one of those men who believe in depriving girls of their virginity to retain your own purity."

"No, damn it! Stop baiting me. I was wed, and my wife fulfilled my needs, and I've had no woman since her death."

"And how long ago was that?"

"Two years."

"Two years." She still smiled, mockingly. "By my troth, I'm surprised you're not mad with desire by now. Billy certainly seemed unconvinced your motives are pure."

Her mockery broke his control, and he smiled back, both glad and alarmed at his lack of control—but mostly glad. "Billy is a smart man. I *am* mad with desire. Would you like me to demonstrate?"

Her flare of alarm delighted him, as did the strength of her shove against his chest. "Nay."

"Too late." He lowered his head to hers.

She didn't want to kiss him. It had been long since she'd kissed a man, and those experiences had been so unremarkable, she'd convinced herself men bored her. But Griffith . . . Griffith didn't bore her.

Infuriated her, aye. Amused her, challenged her . . . attracted her.

Not with a handsome face. Not even his mother could call him handsome. Nay, 'twas his rugged build, his slow deliberation, his honesty. He gave her a sense of security, as if she could trust him to care for her.

Her own stupidity embarrassed her.

But she still kissed him back, for—damn it!—he kissed remarkably well. In fact, for a man who claimed celibacy, he kissed wonderfully well. His lips were firm, his tongue restrained. He took care not to grind his face to hers and hurt her with his whiskers. He smoothed her lips with his tongue, not demanding entrance but savoring the flavor, the privilege, of her. And he let her go when she pulled back.

God rot him, he'd piqued her interest.

The spicy scent of cottage pinks, the cool autumn breeze, the stars overhead, the moon on his strong features . . . She traced the ridge of his brows with her finger and observed the spark of his eyes. Her hand wandered lower, and she touched his mouth as if she could discern his magic without being affected by it.

It didn't work. His breath warmed her palm with his long, slow exhalations. His lips felt lustrous as a glass heated by spiced wine. His very patience intrigued her, made her want to indulge her curiosity. Cautiously she whispered, "Again."

Carefully he pulled her close. "Again."

Their bodies kissed. Their lips embraced.

The resulting heat burst on them, a storm of spring mating.

Surprised, she leaned into him.

Amazed, he lifted her coat and cupped her bottom.

They fought to get closer. She grasped the hair at the back of his neck and pulled him, opening her lips wide. He tasted her, then sucked her tongue into his mouth. Moaning, they rubbed together like mating wildcats, frustrated by clothes yet as pleasured as if they were without.

She tried to wrap a leg around him. He tried to help her—and she smacked his nose with her head.

He yowled with pain. She moaned, sorry yet exasperated at herself—then she realized what she'd done. What she'd almost done. The vows she'd almost broken, the imbecility, the—

"I beg pardon," she said, jerking away.

"Think not of it." He reached for her.

She leaped back. "Sir Griffith, I do beg your pardon."

He froze. "Why do I think you're apologizing for more than my nose?"

"I never meant . . . I never should have . . ." With one glance at his face, she ran toward her cottage.

She didn't have to look to know he was right behind her. His long strides ate the distance between them, and when she stumbled on a clod of dirt just inside the fence, he caught her by the shoulder.

She whirled again to face him. "I beg your pardon. I truly beg your pardon. I never should have—"

"*We* never should have," he corrected.

"What?"

"There were two of us back there, and you're right. We never should have."

She might have believed him more if he hadn't retained a glow, a fierceness of manhood.

He continued, "But I said I would escort you home, and you're not home yet."

"I'm here." She pointed at her cottage.

"I will see you to the door," he said. "I will escort you home."

She opened her mouth to argue, and he placed one finger over her lips. "Home," he whispered.

"Home," she repeated. His touch reminded her of things best forgotten, so she walked away. After fumbling for the latch, she pushed the door open into the hut's single room and saw, in the light of the night candle, her son. Sitting up in bed, he rubbed his eyes sleepily. Chastising herself for leaving him alone, wishing she had never gone, she knelt beside him. "Did we wake you?"

He shook his head and pointed out the window.

"Something out there—" She paused, remembering the noises that had escaped as she and Griffith struggled for satisfaction.

Bright-eyed, Lionel nodded, and his mother blushed.

"He seems to have an affection for you," Griffith observed.

Promptly offended, she declared, "He's my son!"

"Women of less rank and wealth than you have pawned their jewels to hire a nursemaid."

Her mood shifted from offended to defensive. "He has a nursemaid."

"It would seem he has everything he needs," Griffith answered.

His amusement embarrassed her, made her aware she'd been jumping to extremes. Looking down at Lionel, she found him inspecting the stranger. When he had gleaned all he could from one searching glance, he buried his head in her chest.

Stroking the dark head, she explained, "He's shy. He's not given to liking strangers, and he doesn't speak yet."

Griffith examined her with the same care her son had given to him. "Can he hear?"

"Aye."

"Then he understands every word you say, and you shouldn't talk about him as though he weren't here."

Her mouth dropped at his cool pronouncement, and dropped even more when Lionel pulled his head away from her and inspected Griffith again. Then her shy child smiled and extended his arms to the big man. Griffith picked him up with the efficiency of one long accustomed to children. "Most adults talk that way in front of children, but this lad deserves better." He glanced at Lionel for confirmation, and

Lionel nodded without hesitation. Griffith continued, "I didn't speak much my first few years, either. But then my mother said I just opened my mouth and out came entire sentences. Entire speeches. Stories in Welsh and English. Songs and ballads. Why, when I started talking, they couldn't get me to shut up."

Marian crossed her arms over her chest and glared. "Obviously."

Griffith swung Lionel into the bed, then knelt beside him and patted the pillow. "Lie down now, my lad, and sleep 'til the cock crows."

Lionel shook his head.

Griffith laughed. "You don't look like your mother, but you act like her."

Marian and Lionel exchanged glances.

Griffith only laughed again—deep, low, and like the purr of a pleased cat. "Please yourself, but if you don't get a good night's sleep, you'll not be rested for our early morning walk."

For a moment Marian thought he spoke to her, but Lionel had no doubts. Flinging himself back on his pillow with a thump, the boy squeezed his eyes shut as if that would deepen his slumber. Griffith pulled up the blankets, gave the shiny black hair a brief caress, then rose.

He seemed unsurprised at his victory over one stubborn child, she noted, and she wondered if he always picked his weapons and fought his battles with such success. If he did . . . She squirmed. Was that the purpose of that kiss outside? The petting? Was that kiss only a method of controlling her? He'd tried insult, would he now try conquest?

Did he think, like all the rest, that she was wanton?

As if to confirm her suspicions, he smiled at her. His first smile to her, and she staggered from the effect. His somber expression gentled to strength, his golden eyes warmed to kindness, his lips . . .

His lips reminded her of his kisses, and his kisses reminded her of her loneliness.

No wonder he apportioned his smiles.

"Go to your bed now," he said, "and we'll take you for a walk tomorrow, too."

"Go to my bed," she repeated, captivated and enraptured.

Then the words penetrated her mind and jerked her back to reality.

To her bed? Did he plan to tuck her in, too? Did he plan to loose his hold on his celebrated celibacy tonight? Touching her lower lip, she wondered—what kind of lover would he make? If he'd truly been abstinent . . . But did it matter to her? How could it ever matter to her?

Would he leave without urging, or had he been pretending an interest in her son to cajole her? Casually she strolled toward the door, and he followed. Stepping outside, she saw the moon still rode high through clusters of clouds. The trees still rustled, and the breeze brought her the scent of cottage pinks. The chill of an early spring night had deepened, but she didn't shiver because of that. She shivered because of the warm memories waiting to pounce. Elaborately casual, she pretended she'd forgotten those heated kisses, forgotten the brief burst of wildcat passion. "The earl has arranged for a hunt tomorrow, and I'll act as hostess. I'll have no time for walking."

Griffith's heavy brows snapped together. "A hunt?"

She was startled at his surprise and even more at his displeasure. "Weren't you told?"

"Nay."

"You rode in yesterday, so I suppose Wenthaven thought you wouldn't wish to come." After she'd excused Wenthaven, she added, "You're welcome nevertheless. The earl's hospitality is never less than flawless."

She watched him, anxious to hear his reply. He studied her in return, looking first at her face, then at the overcoat and the length of calf below, but he seemed to find no pleasure in the sight of her. "You'll not go dressed like that."

"What?"

"You'll not go on a hunt riding astride a horse like some loose woman without morals or upbringing."

Her *"What?"* wasn't as astounded this time.

"Just because you've borne a child out of wedlock, it's no reason to live down to everyone's expectations."

His gall took her breath away. All her pat answers, all her practiced replies, flew out of her head in the surge of rage. "You dare tell me how to behave?"

"It appears someone must."

He sounded so insufferably stuffy and looked so sure of himself, she wanted to hit him. But she'd done so, and she'd regretted it. Instead she took a deep breath, calmed her fury, and annihilated him with a brilliant, cutting comment. "You aren't my father!"

She could have groaned. Where was her renowned wit?

But he answered, and his answer was stupid. Stupider even than hers. He said, "If your father were here, he'd be horrified at the way you're acting."

"If my father were here . . ." Head extended like a turtle, she stared at him. Didn't he know? Didn't he comprehend?

But no, he didn't. His expression set in self-righteous indignation, and just like that, she'd been given the power she sought. Using his own ignorance, she could have the last word. Triumphant yet bitter, she retorted, "My father *is* here. Didn't you realize? I am the heir to Wenthaven. The earl is my father."

# 4

*How odd, Griffith thought.* He lay in the countess of Wenthaven's bed. He lay in Marian's mother's bed and lusted after her daughter.

It made him vaguely uncomfortable, as if the spirit of the countess peeked into his thoughts and caught him with his hands in Marian's codpiece. Yet at the same time . . . well, surely the countess couldn't approve of the way her daughter had turned out. Fighting with swords, dressing like a man, giving birth to a babe without the benefit of marriage.

"Who do you suppose the father is?" Griffith murmured.

At the foot of the bed, Art popped up like a child's toy, comprehending Griffith's mind with the ease of old friendship. "I was wondering when ye'd think about that. Could the child's paternity have anything to do with Henry's peculiar interest in Marian and Lionel?"

"The woman hides her mysteries well." Griffith leaned on his elbow. The room, so dim and dusty last night, looked cheery this morning. Even Art looked good, thought Griffith, although it baffled him how a one-eyed man with skin like wet leather could look good.

"Ye're looking better this morning," Art said, unconsciously twisting Griffith's thoughts. "The swelling on yer proboscis has almost disappeared."

Griffith touched the broken place with tender fingers.

Art's head bobbed on his skinny neck. "Maybe the countess cured ye during the night. Maybe she approves of ye."

"Maybe she does." Cold emanated from the walls of cut stone, a cold that bit at his nose, and Griffith breathed deep, reveling in the free flow of air. "She'd be foolish not to."

Propping his elbows on his knees, Art examined Griffith through one critical eye. "I thought we settled the issue of yer beauty last night."

"I'm not talking about my appearance," Griffith said. "I'm talking about my character. I can say, without conceit, that I'm stable, respectable, and moral."

"God's blood!"

"I'm the kind of man a mother would wish her daughter to wed," Griffith added complacently.

Art's one eye blinked at him. "Damned dull, is what ye are. And what's this about ye wedding Lady Marian?"

"I didn't say I was going to wed her, I just said . . ." Staring at Art, Griffith decided he could not win this argument. Turning the subject, he asked, "Did you know Wenthaven is Marian's father?"

"Ah." Art scratched his ear. "I'd wondered. She seemed so sure she could do as she liked in his house. And there's the resemblance. 'Tis a little too pronounced for cousins."

"Resemblance? There's no resemblance between that strutting sack of dung and—"

"And the strumpet ye've been sent to guard?"

Griffith bent his most intense frown on Art, intent

on quenching the old man's sparkle. "She's not a strumpet. A little high-spirited, mayhap."

"Such a shift since last night!" Art marveled. "I wonder what could have changed yer mind. 'Tis the smile, ye know."

"What?"

"The resemblance is in the smile. Wenthaven and Lady Marian both smile readily, and use their smiles to express so much."

Collapsing back on the pillow, Griffith considered. "In Marian's case, it's mostly scorn."

"In Lady Marian's case?" Art cackled. "In Wenthaven's case, it's mostly scorn."

"No, that's malice," Griffith corrected absentmindedly. Art was right. Griffith had changed his mind about Marian during the night, and he didn't have to wonder why. She'd responded to his kisses sweetly, hotly, with a hunger long denied. Then she'd bolted like a startled hind. It proved what he desired, that she'd been chaste for many the long days. Since the birth of her son, likely, and before. "It's not that I think she's a strumpet. She's like a wild bird, needing a man's capable hand to control her."

"'Tis coincidence ye've trained falcons," Art interjected.

Griffith ignored him. "Like this morning. She's off on a hunt with the other guests."

Art looked curious. "Ye're not going?"

"Nay, I'm taking her son for a walk, but I told her quite sternly how she was to behave."

Art sounded faint when he asked, "How she was to behave?"

"Most especially, I told her to dress like a lady." Remembering how she looked in hose, Griffith felt appalled—and aroused—all over again. "Can you imagine the scandal if she rode astride?"

Art choked and flung himself back on the mattress.

"Aye, I feel the same way. With a little bit of

guidance—" Art choked again, and Griffith cocked his head. "Art?"

Art's shriek of laughter rose from among the bed-clothes like the cry of an Irish banshee, making Griffith's blood run cold.

Griffith sat up and stared at his writhing, kicking servant. "Art?"

With snorts and coughs, Art caught his breath. "Ye . . . told her . . . to dress like a lady?" At Griffith's nod, he vented more of his disbelieving merriment, holding his side against the ache. "Aren't . . . ye . . . the clever one? That will no doubt cure . . . her every mad impulse."

Before Art could finish, Griffith was off the bed and dressing in yesterday's garments.

When Art could contain himself, he sat up with a blanket around his still shaking shoulders. "Going to take Lady Marian's laddie for a walk?"

Griffith cast him a caustic glance as he swung his cape around his shoulders. He stormed from the room, then stormed back in again. A fine glass mirror hung on the wall, and on the table beneath it were a lady's accoutrements. Rummaging among the dusty things, he found a comb and drew it through his hair.

Art shrieked with laughter again, but as Griffith ran down the stairs he heard Art call, "Happy hunting."

Marian walked her horse into the trees and dis-mounted. As she tied the animal securely to a branch, she wondered morosely why she'd come on the hunt.

She'd forgotten how the men stared when she rode astride in a man's clothes. She'd forgotten how the ladies tittered as she strode about in her pointed black boots.

She'd done it often when first she came from court. Then her still twitching reputation lay in shreds around her feet. Her friends had deserted her, and all that mattered, it seemed, was the wailing babe she tended every night. Her own father had encouraged her to ride like a man, to swear like a trooper, to practice swordsmanship like a squire. Angry, defiant, she'd reveled in thumbing her nose at the gossips, lived to feed the flame of her own destruction.

The memory of those days made her squirm, and she tossed her felt hat to the ground and rumpled her braided hair. Forget it, she told herself, knowing she would not.

Wandering along the low ridge, she watched the ground carefully. If she remembered correctly, along here somewhere . . . With a crow of triumph, she dropped to her knees and pushed aside the brambles. Wild vines crawled along the ground, and on them tiny strawberries begged to be picked. Creeping along, she filled her hand while memories filled her mind.

'Twas a small thing that brought her to her senses. Nothing more than the letter from the lady Elizabeth, telling of her marriage to King Henry. Henry had spared no expense, but the elaborate ceremony had been marred by one thing and one thing only: Elizabeth's dearest friend, Marian, had not taken her place as Elizabeth's chief maid-in-waiting.

Marian had laughed. Then she'd cried. Then she'd rocked Lionel until dawn, clothed herself in a modest dress, and set out to be a respectable lady. It had proved difficult, for even in court she'd been the wild one, willing to run for miles, to dance all night, to walk the fence on a dare. But she flattered herself that she'd done well.

Of course, Sir Griffith didn't think so.

Marian frowned. Thanks to him and those kisses, she'd been awake all night. Her lips felt irritated, not because he'd been brutal, but because she'd bitten them repeatedly as she tried to understand why he'd been so passionate.

She'd finally decided he hadn't been passionate. He'd kissed her because he was angry and wanted to teach her a lesson. He couldn't possibly desire her.

Unfortunately, last night had proved she didn't despise Sir Griffith. If those kisses were anything to go by, she positively admired him.

Those kisses. She wouldn't think of them—or him.

Popping a strawberry into her mouth, she closed her eyes and savored the first sweet taste of summer.

How she always hated winter! How she then missed the days at court! The games, the laughter, the fires that chased away the chill.

At Castle Wenthaven, they played the same games, but the laughter sounded shrill and desperate. Wenthaven's fires were built not for warmth, but for show. The people huddled around them weren't friends, but watchful adversaries.

Yet every winter Marian had been forced to accept the feigned hospitality of the manor house. When the storms raged outside, the cottage shook in the blasts, the fire sputtered, and like any healthy, growing child, Lionel rampaged in ever-decreasing circles. Cecily whined, and to Marian's chagrin, Marian herself developed a cough. A cough easily cured in the dry environment of the manor.

The first winter had been the best. She'd moved into her mother's room, and she liked it there, away from the beggars who surrounded Wenthaven. Lionel's colic had eased. He'd learned to sit up and crawl—and he'd wanted to crawl down the unrailed, dangerous stone stairs.

The next winter found Marian, Cecily, and Lionel safe in one of Wenthaven's luxurious apartments, well ventilated with peek-holes and manned by spies.

An unpleasant sense of wet matter startled Marian, and she opened her fist. Smeared across her palm was a streak of red pulp and she chuckled at her own silliness.

After all, what did it matter if someone watched her? She had no secrets Wenthaven could discover, and soon she'd live at court once more. Soon she'd be among the great and near great. Soon all would know what she already knew—that Lionel, her son, contained within him the seeds of greatness.

Licking the mashed strawberry from her palm, she wondered: did Griffith have such secrets? She didn't know. She didn't even know—couldn't imagine— why she'd given him her mother's room. Except he seemed like a person free of pretense or artifice.

Seemed like?

She grinned. He was. Witness his tactless handling of her. Most men talked to her like a lady and treated her like a tart. Griffith had played no such games. He'd chided her in plain language, spoken like a pompous ass, then treated her like a lady.

Except when he kissed her. He hadn't kissed her as though she were a lady; he'd kissed her as if she were a woman.

Was that what made her prod him? The pleasure of seeing a genuine reaction? Today she'd dressed like a man in defiance of his order, and now she waited for him to find her just to see more of Sir Griffith's authentic indignation.

Would he come and find her? She thought so. And if he didn't—well, she'd have her ego crushed, and Lionel would have strawberries to eat. She opened the pouch at her belt, lined it with a clean cloth, and set to work, picking the hidden fruit until her bag bulged.

Then she heard it: the crackle of brush behind her. Turning, she smiled into the sun, squinting at the tall man blocking it and the golden glow around his head. "It took you long enough to get here." Then he moved into the shade, and she shrieked as she made out his features.

Hand on hip, Adrian Harbottle smirked at her open welcome. "I'm glad to see you, too, sweetheart."

Her breath came with difficulty, and she scrambled to her feet. "I didn't know it was you!"

His smirk changed, turned down into a sulky frown. "Who else would you welcome so generously?"

"Not you." She tried to jumped back when he lunged for her.

Catching her arm in a bruising grip, he repeated, "Who else would you welcome? Huh? Why not me?"

Glancing around, she asked, "Where's the rest of the hunt?"

"I left 'em to find you. Who else?" He shook her. "Why not me?"

She was alone with this pathetic imitation of a gentleman, and just yesterday she'd humiliated him in front of all Wenthaven's guests. When she was without the protection of her sword, he'd win any contest, and the truth of Griffith's reproof had been proved. She'd made an enemy with her temper, an enemy who lusted for revenge—and for her.

Cautiously she tried out the first, and best, of her weapons. "The earl of Wenthaven will be looking for me."

Harbottle honked with laughter.

"At the least, my father"—that title tasted odd on her tongue—"will be unhappy with you for being alone with me. Why don't we—"

She tried to walk away, but he pulled her in a circle back to him. "Aye, why don't we?"

She couldn't bear to watch him as he licked his generous lips.

"You looked fetching with your little arse wagging in the air, looking for berries." He smiled with practiced, whimsical appeal and reached for her mouth. She jerked her head back, but he brought away a tiny bit of fruit still clinging there. Sucking his long finger, he said, "Strawberries, were they? I like strawberries. Why don't you share some with me? Show me where they are?"

"They're right there."

She pointed, and he pouted as charmingly as if he'd practiced it in front of the mirror until he achieved perfection. "That's not what I meant. Come on." He tried to tug her down. "Show me."

Show me. He was trying to charm her, but if the charm didn't work, he'd use force, she knew. He'd use force and not even realize it, because he'd probably never had to in his life. He'd chosen his place and time well. No one could stop him or even notice if she didn't come back. After all, she'd left the hunt by herself. And in the end, who cared if Wenthaven's slut of a daughter tumbled a minor nobleman in the woods? Or if she'd been raped? She wouldn't dare complain, or she'd have a parade of men to her cottage, seeking favors.

Oh, God, she couldn't bear it again. It had taken a sharp sword and an aggressive chastity to keep them at bay after Lionel was born—nothing would do if Harbottle had his way.

So, think, Marian, she urged herself. Think. "I'd love to show you where the strawberries grow."

If her smile was less than genuine, he seemed oblivious. His gaze slipped to her bosom. "Aye."

"But I have so many clothes on."

His gaze slipped lower, and he began to pant like one of Wenthaven's dogs.

"Won't you at least help me out of my boots?"

"Oh, aye." He dropped to his knees and leaned toward her. "Oh, aye."

She couldn't believe he was so credulous; when he reached for her boot, she lifted the other foot and kicked him square in his bare throat. He tumbled backward, and she took to flight. Stumbling on the rough ground, she could hear him trying to scream, heard the squawking noise he made instead. In a kind of horror, she wondered if she'd injured him enough to kill him, but she stilled the impulse to help him.

For if he didn't die, he would kill her. Of that she had no doubt.

With fingers that fumbled, she untied her horse's reins, then spun in terror as she heard hooves thundering behind her. "Griffith." She clutched her fist at her chest, pleased to see him, close to tears. Then irrational fury swept her—where the hell had he been when she needed him?—and she shouted, "By my troth, you're too late to play the gallant rescuer, Sir Knight." Swinging her leg over the saddle, she sat defiantly astride, but he snatched her reins from her.

"What do you mean?" He leaned forward, looking twice as menacing as Harbottle had. "Rescue you from what?"

It was too late for second thoughts, Marian realized. Too late for wisdom.

Harbottle still knelt on the ground, fighting for breath, but his gaze on the two riders raised the hair on Marian's arms. He'd found the answer to his question "Who else were you expecting?" Regardless of the danger to himself, he expressed hostility with his red-rimmed eyes, with his feral snarl.

Marian grasped Griffith's arm urgently. "Don't bother with him. I already hurt him badly."

Shaking his head as he dismounted, Griffith murmured, "Nay, dear one. Nay, he's vermin and deserves to be crushed."

She tightened her grip. "'Tis not your concern."

She dropped her hand when he lifted his gaze. He, too, showed teeth in a snarl. The perception of being a bone between two rampant dogs swept her, and Griffith's guttural voice frightened her. "It's been my concern since last night. Now go home, Marian. Wait for me there."

He turned the head of her horse, and as it moved away he slapped it on the rump. It started, then broke into a gallop—a gallop that she couldn't control, she told herself. It wasn't that she was obeying Griffith, just that she couldn't *not* obey him.

Castle Wenthaven rose on an island in a tiny jewel of a lake, and she galloped across the drawbridge to find the stables almost deserted. Thank God, the hunt hadn't yet returned. The stable boys sprang forward when she rode in, and she slid out of the saddle and tossed them the reins in one graceful motion.

It wasn't a desire to avoid Griffith that made her hustle from the stable yard. It was a desire to get away from the curious lads.

But before she'd ducked into the orchard, she heard the hard noise of hooves on the drawbridge, and her prevarications dissolved in panic. Taking to her heels, she wove through the trees, knocking off blossoming tips and leaving deep footprints in the soft ground.

A trail, but she didn't care. The longer it took Griffith to find her, she reasoned, the more time he'd have to cool down. It would be nice if he had worked off some of that fury on Harbottle. It would be nice if he hadn't killed him, either. But that was of lesser importance when compared to—

Griffith caught her arm and swung her around. "To where, dear Lady Marian, do you escape so impatiently?"

He whispered as if he dared not speak aloud, as if he would shout if he loosened the restraint on his poise, and she babbled, "Home. You told me to go home, and I'm—"

Looking tall, dark, and beastly, he said, "I want to talk to you."

"I guessed."

"Don't be clever with me."

She opened her mouth and then shut it. He watched with a sort of satisfaction as she wondered if she shouldn't use the feminine skills she'd ignored lately. They might appease him. But she had to know one thing first. "Is Harbottle alive?"

"Aye, he is, no thanks to you."

Her feeling of conciliation faded, and she stepped back until she bumped into a trunk. The tree shook; a few apple blossoms fluttered to the ground.

"But he'll not lift a sword for a few months," Griffith added.

"I didn't ask him to follow me."

"Some men don't wait to be asked." Waving his hand up and down the length of her, he declared, "And some men would consider garb such as you're wearing an invitation."

With a smile of well-practiced scorn, she declared, "A man would have to be a dunder-whelp to be attracted to me in this outfit."

Clutching the front of her coat, he pulled her close and glared down at her. "Are you calling me a dunder-whelp?"

Her smile faded. This man, this broad and stalwart oak, looked sincere. Looked insulted! When she knew, she *knew* he must be jesting. "You aren't attracted to me!"

"Indeed?"

You despise me, she wanted to say, but she satisfied herself with, "I look like a boy."

"You do not look like a boy. You do not walk like a boy or act like a boy, and you could never fool a man with half his senses into thinking you are a boy." Warming to his subject, his voice rose as he insisted, "It's not your clothes that tempt a man, it's the body beneath it—no!"

Her head spun with his contradictions. "No?"

"It's not even your body. It's the challenge of your personality." Stroking his chin, he stared into space, looking for answers. "You can read. You've traveled with the court. What can a man offer you? You look right at a man, and you're not looking at the clothes he wears or the horses he rides, but at *him*. A man always knows you've judged him and found him wanting, and he wants to prove himself. Most men"—his eyes focused and narrowed on her—"think they can prove themselves in bed."

She couldn't help it; she laughed with contempt. "No man has ever proved himself to me in bed."

"Aye, no doubt you've told them so when they lie panting and smug beside you. 'Tis a miracle one of your lovers hasn't murdered you. I tell you truly, Marian, if you'd mocked that pretty boy after he finished with you today, he would have strangled you and buried you under a bush, and thought nothing more of it."

"I know."

"That's why I told you not to wear"—he plucked at her jerkin—"this."

Furious with his assumptions, she said, "I'm the victim here." She pointed to herself. "Me. Every time a man rapes a woman and feels a niggling guilt, he blames the woman. 'She tempted me.' 'She asked for it.' Well, I didn't ask for it, and I don't care what you say, I'm not tempting in this garb."

"You little fool."

"I'm not the fool. It shouldn't matter how I dress. It shouldn't even matter how I act. Harbottle's a grown man, he should be responsible for his actions. I didn't want him to touch me. Maybe I could be wiser, but it's discouraging when"—to her horror, her voice caught, but she steadied it—"when I behave with all the circumspection of a nun"—it caught again—"and because of one sin I'm considered easy prey. A sin I didn't commit alone, may I say." One tear trickled down her cheek, and she wiped it away on her shoulder. "I'm sorry I wore these clothes. It was a stupid impulse, but—"

"But I almost dared you."

She wanted to look into his face, but to do so would reveal her watery eyes, and she couldn't bear that. Instead she looked at his hands as they slowly closed around her arms and he pulled her closer. She didn't want to cooperate—after all, she had her pride—but after one moment of stiff dignity she relaxed. Just a little. Just her body. And she held her head erect.

His arms wrapped around her, he rocked her back and forth.

She kept her eyes open.

"You're right, lass. Of course, you're right."

She memorized the weave of the fabric in his coat and admired the fur trim on his cloak.

"'Twas just that I was frightened when I realized you would go out on the hunt dressed like a man and looking so much like a woman." He hugged her a little tighter, and his voice rumbled close to her ear. "Then I found Wenthaven and his guests, milling around while the dogs scared up game, and you weren't there. No one knew where you were, or cared, and I imagined you lying broken in a ditch."

He spoke faster and faster, and she found her head drooping closer and closer to that broad, comforting chest. His displeasure was understandable—how often had she wanted to smack Lionel when he frightened her with some childish escapade?

When had anyone cared enough about her even to be worried?

"Then I searched for you, and discovered that charlatan had found you first."

His mention of Harbottle made him as stiff as she had been when he first held her, and she snuggled her head into his chest. His heart thumped within the padded stomacher, and she tried to give back the comfort he'd given her. "He didn't hurt me," she said, low and earnest.

"No?" Rage brought a quiver to his massive frame. "Would you like me to kiss you now?"

"What?"

"An arseworm like Harbottle must give a woman a distaste for all of God's masculine creation."

Now she understood, and without hesitation she lifted her face. "I would very much like you to kiss me. You see, I could never compare the two of you."

His golden eyes glowed with flame.

"And you are very good at kissing."

He looked as passionate, as violent, as he had when he sought his vengeance on Harbottle. But when his lips touched hers, he transmitted only the passion.

The heat of the previous night rekindled as if it had never been extinguished. As if she'd spent the night and day contemplating it. As if he saw, as he claimed, beyond her boyish garb and her mocking smiles.

His mouth touched hers tenderly and with an intimacy that initiated her into a world she hadn't imagined.

"He didn't kiss you," he whispered, as sure as if he'd been there.

"No," she agreed.

"I still should have killed him."

This time the kiss was not as kind, nor his caress so comforting. He lapped at the corners of her eyes, taking possession of her salt tears as if he had a right to them. He put his hands under her coat, stroked her breasts, and unerringly found the places she liked, places she touched when she touched herself.

He pushed her against the tree and one of last year's apples broke loose to thump him in the back. He didn't seem to notice, but she rubbed the place and he purred like a kitten.

A big kitten. A beast kitten.

His mouth opened on hers, and willingly she gave up her pride and solitude. Whether she was assuring him of her admiration for him, or he was assuring himself of her safety, or they were both simply feeding a need, she didn't know or care.

Lifting his head only an inch, he muttered, "We've got to find someplace."

Her mind had fled, and she proved it when she offered, "My cottage."

"Lionel?"

She groaned. "Asleep."

"Alone?"

"Nay." Desperate, in heat, she said, "Behind the cottage. There's a place between the back wall and the castle wall. With trees. My private place. No one knows." He didn't even look doubtful, but she begged, "Please."

He kept his arm wrapped around her back. She kept her arm around his waist. They hurried along, unable to loosen their grip, clumsy with giddiness.

Almost mindless, Marian wondered briefly if he would notice the place where she'd buried her treasure and decided he wouldn't. She wished they could walk faster and prayed they could pass the cottage without Cecily noticing. She skidded to a stop before they left the orchard and nudged Griffith toward the shady side of the castle wall. She glanced at the cottage—then glanced again.

Something was wrong. Something was very wrong.

"Griffith?"

But he'd seen it, too. "Why are the windows broken? Why are there feathers floating in the yard?"

Panic smacked her, knocking sense in as it knocked passion out. "Lionel?" she said on a rising note. "Lionel?" Without a glance at Griffith, she raced toward her home and vaulted the fence. The door hung open on its hinges; inside she found utter destruction. The mattresses had been cut open, the shelves torn from the wall. Dust floated so freely that she could taste it on her tongue, and the small room smelled of kitchen spices, mustard, and honey. Every cupboard had been opened and the contents trampled.

And Lionel was gone.

# 5

*Marian stood poised* on tiptoe, ready to run, not knowing where. "Lionel?" she called calmly. But her hands were outstretched, braced for a fall. "Lionel?" she called again, stepping over the piles of rubble.

"Would Lionel have run?" Griffith asked, reeling with shock yet concerned about the child he'd been sent to protect. About the child, and about Marian.

She looked as if she didn't remember his name. "He might have. That's what we've practiced."

"Practiced?"

"We practiced running away. But he's not yet two, and I don't know—"

She left it dangling, but he heard the unspoken words. *If the men who had done this had let him.* Careful to sound confident, Griffith said, "I'll look in case he's hiding and afraid to come out." Diving into the ruin of Marian's home, he lifted furniture, piles of clothes, remains of beds, looking for a small body. When he stood, covered with feathers, holding only the bag of gold he'd brought from the lady Elizabeth,

Marian was nowhere in sight. Stepping outside, he could hear her calling, "Lionel!"

He sought her around the corner of the cottage and heard her exclaim, "Cecily!"

"Thank God, my lady," Cecily answered, and a long, slow sigh floated through the air.

"By my troth, you can't faint now."

A small stand of trees stood fast against the castle's curtain wall, and Griffith bounded there in time to see Marian slap Cecily with the flat of her hand. Cecily bounced off the ground, her eyes sparking, but Marian demanded, "Where's my son? Who did this? Where's Lionel?"

"I removed him from his bed and ran when I saw that man sneaking into the yard." Grass stains marred Cecily's skirt at the knees, and her steeple headdress hung askew. "I ran all the way to the manor with Lionel and saw him to his hiding place, then ran back to watch."

"He's safe?" Griffith asked, and Cecily's gaze found him. She looked away, then looked back speculatively.

Marian grasped Cecily by the arm and jerked her back to face her. "Lionel's safe?"

Cecily nodded rapidly. "Aye, I'm sure he's safe."

Marian set off at a run toward the manor. "Let's find him."

More a lady than the lady she served, Cecily tried to hang back, but Marian dragged her. Griffith heard her cry of dismay, saw Marian's disgust, and he glanced around him hastily.

Marian had spoken of this coppice as her own private place. A hammock swung between two trees, and sunlight dappled the trunks, the grass, the bare spots of dark ground. It seemed a place of solitude, quite out of character for the lively Marian. It roused his suspicions, and he resolved to come back and seek out Marian's secrets.

He caught up with the women as they raced through the flower beds. Cecily's pointed headdress had slid off the back of her head and she clutched at the useless veil, but Marian scarcely noticed. As they approached the gray stone walls of the keep, the smaller woman set her feet. "Lady Marian, I'm not going to run through the house like a hoyden."

"Then stay."

"Lady Marian." Cecily tugged at her. "Do you want everyone to know you've lost Lionel?"

Marian glared at her, but Cecily pushed her advantage. "Do you want everyone gawking when you find him, asking questions about the cottage and wondering what you have that someone wants?"

Marian's chest rose and fell. She shut her eyes, and when she opened them all trace of anxiety had disappeared. To pass the inspection of servants and guests, she became the Marian whom Griffith had first met. The carefree Marian, unbound by conventions.

Griffith watched as she leaped up the stairs and wondered, Was this a chimera to deceive the world, or did she have another, more hidden reason for her deception?

She nodded at the footman who held the door for them. Down the main hall she pranced in her masculine garb, leading Griffith and Cecily past a gaping priest. "Good morrow, Father," she said, but she didn't turn back when he called to her. Instead she turned down the corridor where Griffith's first room had been.

"Where *is* Lionel?" Griffith asked.

The door to the tower was in sight, and Marian's stride lengthened.

Cecily pointed to the door. "In there."

Comprehension burst on Griffith. "In the countess's tower?"

"I pray it is so," Marian said fervently.

Cecily scoffed at her concern. "Many months ago

you insisted we make a place for him under the stairs, with a blanket. He'll stay there."

But when they opened the door, no little boy ran out of the dark to meet them. "Lionel?" Marian's call echoed up the empty stairway, and her breath caught audibly.

Cecily's inelegant curse reminded Griffith of the duty she had forsaken, and it reminded Marian, also.

"How could you have left him? The stairs . . ." Marian dropped to her knees, searching the floor with her hands as if she expected to find his tiny body smashed on the stones. "Lionel?"

Griffith ran lightly up the stairs.

"I wanted to see what was happening," Cecily babbled. "I wanted to help. I wanted to see who destroyed our home."

"I've told you and told you your first duty is to Lionel." Marian was out of control, panicked. The light of one thin arrow slit shone on her face. "Where do we look for my son now? Up the stairs? Outside in one of his favorite places? Back at the cottage?"

Cecily whimpered.

"What if he ran into the brute who searched the cottage?" Having examined the floor, Marian leaned her back against the stone wall and pulled herself up. "What if someone took him? Cecily—"

Faint and far away, childish laughter sounded, and Griffith hissed down the stairway. "Shh."

Immediately Marian hushed and listened. It came again, a little more clearly, and Marian took the stairs two at a time. Griffith got to the countess's room first and opened the door for Marian.

Bent over a silver ball on the floor, Art and Lionel looked up with astonished faces as Marian rushed in. When she stopped and took in the domestic scene in a glance, Griffith again observed her transformation. Not Wenthaven's wild daughter, nor Lionel's frightened mother, but a pillar of strength only slightly chipped by life. "Well! Have you had a good time, Lionel?"

It was a good act, but Griffith saw the anguish and relief behind it.

Lionel grinned, showing baby teeth and a plethora of dimples.

"That we have," Art said, his gaze going from one to the other. "He's a bonny lad, Lady Marian. Ye should be proud."

"Aye. I am." Marian knelt on the rich carpet and extended her arms. They shook, and her voice shook, too, defying her attempts to steady it. "Lionel, have you a hug for your mama?"

With a childish lack of tact, Lionel shook his head and picked up the ball in one dirty hand. He hugged it close, and a bell hidden within jingled. Jiggling back and forth, he called forth the pleasant toll.

Clucking like a hen with a wandering chick, Art said, "Yer mama will not take the ball from ye, and we'll play again when ye've kissed her."

Lionel stuck out his lip, and tears closed Marian's throat. He didn't mean to be cruel, she knew. If he'd been frightened before, he'd forgotten it. She'd interrupted his play, and he had no time to spare for his mother. But she needed that hug, needed that reassurance of his chubby arms around her neck and his firm body pressed to hers.

"Lionel," Art crooned, "why don't ye roll the ball to yer mother?"

Lionel stared at her suspiciously.

"And your mother will roll it back," Griffith encouraged.

Unable to speak, Marian nodded.

Proud of his new possession, Lionel hefted the ball and threw it as hard as he could. Art cried out, Griffith moved to intercept, but Marian's hand flashed out and snatched it from the air. "You've a good arm, son." She tossed it up and caught it. "Come here and I'll teach you to aim."

Lionel trotted forward, giving Marian a chance to embrace him. She kept it brisk, then turned him in the circle of her arm and fulfilled her promise. As he pitched to Art, she asked, "Did he climb the stairs by himself?"

"Aye, that he did."

Marian's teeth nearly chattered at the thought of her baby climbing those steep, dark, stone stairs. "Only two," she murmured. "By the saints, he's only two." As she hugged him once more, he wiggled free impatiently and toddled to Art.

"Now, lass, 'tis not so bad," Art soothed. "Except for his fright, he came through all right. I found him hiding in the bed when I came back from visiting the laundry. A wee scrap of a boy, all eyes and hair. He liked me not at first, not until I told him I lived in this room and had this ball just for him."

For the first time since she'd entered the room, Marian noticed her surroundings. No dust lingered on the surfaces. The windows glistened in the late afternoon sunlight. A fire burned in the large fireplace, and the tapestries looked clean and alive. "Oh, Art," she said, "you've done a lovely job in here."

"'Tis a comely room, and yer servants needed only a bit of a nudge to clean it." Art grinned. "Only a bit of a nudge, and I provided it."

"Art's good at nudging." Griffith didn't mean it as a compliment.

"Ye don't have to make me sound like an alewife." Art rolled the silver orb across the carpet toward Lionel.

"If the boot fits . . ."

Her mind on days gone by, Marian said, "I think I remember playing up here when I was a child, as he is. Hearing the bell as it jingled. Smelling the scent of summer roses and seeing a smile."

"Yer mother," Art said. "She's a sweet woman."

At the door, Cecily shrieked. Everyone turned to stare at her, and Marian surveyed her cousin unfavorably. "What's wrong, Cecily?"

Cecily held on to the door frame and pointed at Art. "Have you seen the ghost of the countess of Wenthaven?"

Art cupped his hand and blew his nose into it—because he had no kerchief or as a commentary about Cecily, Marian did not know. She only knew Cecily annoyed her, and she ordered, "Come and sit down. Tell us what happened."

Disheveled and breathless from the climb, Cecily collapsed onto the nearest bench. "A blond man came and knocked on the door and said through the window he had to come inside. I told him no, but he frightened me, so I took Lionel from his bed and ran out the back."

Griffith put his foot on the bench beside her and leaned forward. "Why didn't you get help?"

Cecily's vague air vanished. "From who? Almost everyone was gone, and I didn't know but the stranger had instructions from—"

"You did well, Cecily," Marian said.

"Why?" Griffith demanded.

Lionel accidentally kicked the ball, then scrambled after it. Ignoring Griffith, Marian watched her son with a steadfast interest, but Griffith came to Marian, planted his boots where she could see them, and demanded again, "Why? What do you suspect, that your maid shouldn't seek help from your father's men?"

Marian looked up until her neck bent back, resenting his height and his unfair use of it. "Some questions are best left unasked in this castle. Some questions I don't want answered. But I do want to know"—she craned her head to see Cecily—"have you ever seen this blond man before?"

Griffith paced away until he stood before the fire.

Cecily plucked at the veil connected to her steeple headdress. "I couldn't see him exactly. I didn't wait for him to come through the door. But something about him looked familiar."

"Familiar?" Marian prompted.

"He was tall and handsome, with broad shoulders"—Cecily showed the span with her hands—"like a knight."

Griffith jumped to a conclusion he knew was false. "Harbottle."

"Aye!" At the name, Cecily sat up as alert as a land spaniel prepared to flush a woodcock. "It looked like Harbottle."

"Not unless he has a twin brother," Marian said. "Harbottle was with me."

Griffith asked, "All the time?"

"Nay, but he was with the hunt and saw me leave," Marian said.

"You didn't notice him in the hunt?"

Griffith sounded like the clerk in a church court, and his tone rankled Marian. "Why would I?"

He strode to the fire and stretched out his hands before he answered. "Because I doubt he would admit to you he'd been robbing your cottage."

She couldn't argue with Griffith, although she longed to dispute his right to interfere. Men never helped unless they wanted something; she could never depend on their strength, for her disappointment was all the greater when they demanded their reward.

"Lady Marian, you talked to him?" Cecily sighed. "Oh."

Marian almost grinned at Cecily's disappointment. "Aye, Harbottle's convenient, isn't he? He has a reason for wishing me ill."

"There are others who wish you ill." Cecily clasped her hands while tears trickled down her cheeks. "Oh, my lady, I am so frightened."

"As you are meant to be." Griffith sat on a chair before the flames. "Did the knave steal anything?"

"How would I know?" Bending over her skirt, Cecily picked at a thread. "I didn't go in afterward."

Lionel's ball jiggled as he walked to stand in front of Griffith, and Griffith held out his hands. "Do you want to sit here, lad?"

Lionel examined Griffith, then thumped his head into Griffith's lap.

"Lionel!" Marian cried, and half rose to her feet.

"Fret not." Griffith waved a restraining hand at her, but he sounded strained and his face paled. "He's just being affectionate."

"Affection like that could kill a man," Art said, and Marian covered her mouth with her hand.

Laughing would be bad form, even sympathetic laughter.

Art continued, "Still and all, ye might as well slam yer jingleberries around. Ye don't make use of 'em."

Cecily giggled. "Jingleberries?"

But all of Marian's amusement fled. Griffith had been planning to use his jingleberries not an hour ago, and with her.

If Griffith remembered, he gave no indication. Instead he took a restorative breath and hoisted Lionel onto one leg, making sure the boy's feet kicked away from him. Wiping the sweat from his brow, he said, "Cecily, you saw him leave, you said. Was he carrying anything?"

"I didn't say I saw him leave."

Lionel wiggled to make himself comfortable, and Griffith adjusted him carefully. "You said you left Lionel and went back and watched the cottage. That means—"

"He didn't take anything . . . that I noticed."

Cecily's color had risen, and Marian and Griffith exchanged looks around her. Marian knew they both wondered if the girl lied about her vigil outside the cottage. It would be like Cecily to want to help but lack the courage to do so. Watching her closely, Marian asked, "From where did you watch?"

Cecily's lip stuck out. "The orchard."

"You can't see much from there," Marian said. "It's too far away."

"Well, where do you suggest I stand next time?" Cecily retorted, too provoked for tact. "On the fence?"

Art stepped between Marian and Cecily and pointed at the wooden ladder that led to the trap door in the ceiling. "Best go up and prepare a bed for yer mistress and the little master afore ye say something ye'll regret."

Cecily paled. "We're not staying here. Are we, my lady?"

Griffith answered almost before she finished. "You're not staying anywhere else."

Marian spread her hands. "We'll go to one of the bedrooms below. After all—"

"You'll stay here," Griffith interrupted.

"—what can happen to us in my father's house?"

Looking more like a beast than ever, Griffith shook back his dark hair and frowned until his eyebrows met in the middle. "The same thing that would have happened to you if you'd been in that cottage today."

Marian shrugged. "Probably nothing."

"Woman, you don't understand." Griffith's voice became more emphatic. "Whoever tore your home apart was no kindly servant doing his duty to your father. Someone wanted something desperately. If you'd been in the way, he might have put you out of the way."

"My father—"

"I don't understand why you think it's your father. What would he want to steal? What would he be seeking?" Griffith asked.

She looked everywhere but at him. "I don't claim to know my father's mind."

"Even if he had ordered it done, how safe do you feel with some of his lackeys?" She flinched, and he saw it. "Aye, now we're getting somewhere. We have no answers to our questions, and until we do, we'll keep you close."

She glanced at him, then away. "I can't stay here with you."

"Because of your reputation, do you mean?"

Was he being sarcastic? She didn't know and didn't care. At least, not much. "I'll not have them saying I'm warming your bed."

"Cecily will sleep in the bed with you," he decided.

"I won't," Cecily said with spirit.

Before Griffith could respond, Art walked up to the girl and cuffed her ear. "Ye'll stay!"

The abused steeple headdress swayed, then toppled to the side, held only by Cecily's wimple. Her cry may have protested the rough treatment or the order to remain, but Art didn't care. He pointed up the spiral stair and said, "No lickspittle English serving woman's going to contradict my master. Now get ye hence afore I slap the other side."

Marian reproved him, but Cecily didn't wait for her mistress to vindicate her. Her tears spilled as she jumped up and stood wavering between the door and the stairs. She looked at Marian for one long moment, then sobbed, "I can't leave you," and climbed the stairs.

Marian wrung her hands. "Now look what you did. You made her cry."

Art sneered. "Stupid twit must cry all the time."

"Aye, and then she changes pillows to leave me the soggy one."

Griffith chuckled with satisfaction. "So you'll stay."

She drew another breath to argue, but Art announced, "The hunt has returned."

Standing, Marian dusted off her seat. "Then I shall go speak with Wenthaven."

Griffith tried to stand up, but Lionel clung to him and he sank back. "You can't go alone."

"You can't go with me." He tried to protest, but she cut him off. "You're not a complete fool. I have to know if Wenthaven sent that messenger of hell to my cottage. If he did, I have to know why. If he didn't . . ."

"If he didn't?" Art asked.

"If he didn't, he's slipping. He used to brag he knew everything that occurred on his property." Marian lifted an amused brow. "I would enjoy telling him that more than anything."

"Marian." Griffith's deep, resounding voice called her back.

"What?" Even to her own ears she sounded surly, but she didn't want another lecture. Didn't like the responsibility this man wanted to take for her.

He dangled a bag. "I have your gold."

"My gold! I'd forgotten."

"Forgotten? How could you have forgotten the gold? 'Twas what the thieves sought, was it not?"

Griffith sounded as if he suspected the truth, and she suspected it would be too easy to tell him. She'd never wanted to confide in anyone before, and she didn't understand what alchemy this servant of the king had used to tempt her.

She crossed the room without replying, but when she would have taken the bag, he snatched it away. "I'll let you go alone to see your father for a promise."

"And what's that?"

"That you return here to spend the night. Give me your word." His upraised hand cut off her protest. "Give me your word, or I'll not give you the money."

She eyed the leather mutinously.

"As long as you keep to your bed upstairs," Griffith went on, beguiling as the serpent in Paradise, "your reputation will be in no danger.

And you should have no difficulty with that, for you like me not. I'm an ugly beast whose complete loyalty lies with Henry Tudor. I think King Henry should beat your lady Elizabeth for her treacheries during Richard's reign, and I think you should be wed to a man who'll beat you twice a day so you'll not stray."

She repeated the phrase she'd lived by since her return to Castle Wenthaven. "I'll never wed." But the words meant nothing to her.

"I think you will."

It was a challenge. Everything he'd said had been a challenge, emphasized by the warmth of his gaze. His eyes glowed a golden color: like sunshine, like fire. He reminded her of her surrender in the orchard.

Griffith hadn't forgotten, as she hoped. He looked, instead, like a man biding his time.

"I'll come back," she finally said.

He handed her the bag of gold without a smile, but she felt waves of his satisfaction lapping over her.

Before she could repent her foolishness, Art plucked the bag from her fingers. "I'll put it here"—he made a production of placing it atop the tall cupboard—"and ye can get it later. And my lady, don't worry yerself about the other. Griffith *is* an ugly beast, and unworthy of ye. Why, I wager ye don't even know the color of his eyes."

Marian squinted at Art. "They're rather . . . yellow."

"Brown as mud," Art scoffed. "'Least, when he's not excited."

"I've never seen them look like that," she protested. "They're golden as England's crown."

Art smirked at her, then at Griffith. She looked from one to the other, confused by the unspoken communication between them. When it became clear they wouldn't enlighten her, she swirled her coat and left.

The solid oak door could not be slammed. It was too heavy and the hinges too unwieldy. But it gave a muffled thud as if she'd given it her best try, and Griffith pressed one finger lightly above the bruise that discolored his nose. "Do you think I convinced her of the danger?"

"Ye convinced her there is danger, but I believe she perceives a greater danger inside this room," Art said.

Lionel threw the ball, and Griffith let him down to toddle after it. "I've made damn poor work of protecting her."

"Henry will not be pleased."

"Henry be damned," Griffith snapped, aggravated beyond tact. "I would that I knew from whence danger approaches. We arrived only yesterday. Was the destruction of her home the result of our arrival?"

"Or did we arrive just in time?"

The doleful inquiry struck at the heart of Griffith's worry. "Has someone perceived the hazard we could be to their plans, or did someone know why we came?"

Art picked up the thought. "Someone like Wenthaven?"

"Aye, Wenthaven."

With a crooked smile, Art asked, "Want me to go down to the laundry and rub up against the widow Jane?"

"So I do." Standing, Griffith hoisted Lionel in his arms. "And I promised Lionel a walk this morning. 'Tis afternoon, but mayhap Lionel and I could visit the mercenaries. They could show Lionel their armor and weapons while I chat with their captain."

"And keep an eye on the lady Marian and Wenthaven?"

"And keep an eye on the lady Marian and Wenthaven."

# 6

The cacophonous sounds attacked Marian's ears as soon as she stepped out of the manor. Dogs snarled over the remains of the boar and some unfortunate squirrels they'd caught. Disheveled women shrieked to one another. Horses stomped and snorted, tired yet still high-spirited. Men slapped one another on the back and shouted in sham camaraderie. Servants ran through the crowd with mugs of ale and platters piled with meat, answering bellows of, "Here, boy. Me first!"

The whole yard smelled of blood, of virility, of hunger and thirst and tethered carnal passion. The titillation of the hunt was not yet over and wouldn't be until all of Wenthaven's guests had indulged themselves in food and drink and sex. Like hunting dogs on the trail, the men sniffed at the milling women, then one by one cut a female from the pack. The tables, the corners, the corridors, would be rife with indulgence tonight.

Marian skirted the crowd cautiously, watching for Harbottle while searching for her father. Grasping the sleeve of a maid, she demanded, "Is Wenthaven in the kennels?"

The maid rubbed her well-pinched rump. "Where else would he be?"

Marian looked distastefully over the heads of the frantic revelers. "Aye, where else?" Of all her father's traits, this was the one she least admired. He organized excitement, provided a plentiful supply of drink, then sat back and watched as women destroyed friendships over a strutting cock and men dueled to the death over whores.

Tomorrow morning, at a huge breakfast, a suave Wenthaven would question each participant of the hunt. He would point out any indiscretions that might have escaped general consideration and smile as he bound ever more captives to his bounty. For where else could they go? No respectable household would welcome one of Wenthaven's soiled cohorts.

Marian stepped inside the wooden fence of the kennels and knelt in the grass to greet the filthy, panting spaniels. "Did you have a good time?" she crooned as she petted their heads.

Sheldon, the kennel keeper, strolled up, wiping his hand on a cloth. "Aye, that they did, m'lady. They're th' best o' th' breed in all England."

Amused, she asked, "Only England?"

He grinned. "Even th' filthy Spaniards can't sire 'em any better than we do."

She scratched behind the ear of one of the smaller spaniels and asked the animal, "Did you flush some woodcocks?"

"Got a dozen or more!" Sheldon answered for the dog.

A panting in her ear alerted her, but not soon enough, and a long tongue licked her cheek and ear. "Ugh! Don't kiss me," she said, pushing at the large dog.

Mathe dropped to the ground and rolled onto his back in total submission, his eyes sad, his tail swishing.

Sheldon said, "Mathe thinks everyone should get a kiss today. He flushed a red deer, an' he's feelin' proud."

"A red deer?"

"Aye, an' they're none so plentiful as they once were."

Relenting, Marian rubbed the dog's stomach. "Clever lad. Clever boy. But must you grovel?"

Shaking his head at the pathetic demonstration, Sheldon said, "He only grovels fer ye, Lady Marian. 'Tis a proper response fer any male when confronted by a female strong as yerself."

Marian laughed out loud and stood. "I wish the other males understood. The tall males." She indicated a man's height with her hands.

"They're just fightin' their instincts," Sheldon said. He shooed the dogs away from her. "Yer father's back helpin' with th' dippin', if 'tis him ye seek."

Nodding her thanks, she sauntered through the yard, noting the pristine condition of the runs and kennels. The lavish enclosure would have made many a stable hand weep with joy, for Wenthaven spared no expense in his breeding program. His land spaniels, both large and small, had gained a reputation in this part of England as the best game flushers to be obtained, and his dogs alone kept Wenthaven on civil terms with his nobler neighbors.

That was the reason, he had told Marian, he took such care of the dogs. But seeing him now, his torso bare, his arms deep in dirty water, rinsing a struggling bitch, Marian didn't believe it. "Ah, Wenthaven, if your enemies could see you now."

Wenthaven couldn't have heard her soft step on the grass through the constant barking, yet he didn't seem startled. "If they could see me now, they'd want to buy this ill-mannered spaniel, and I'd let them have her. Damned dog." Releasing her, he watched as she scrambled out of the tub. One of the kennel keepers scooped her up. "Dry her well. I don't want to hear her coughing again," Wenthaven ordered.

"Aye, m'lord." The kennel keeper bowed, then called, "Here, boys! M'lord needs clean water fer th' next dog. Hurry!"

Two kennel boys struggled to empty the washtub and the rinse tub as two more ran to the well with buckets. In a well-rehearsed drill, they scoured the tubs clean, put them back up on the benches that raised them to waist level, then filled them with fresh water.

Wenthaven grumbled as he examined his wet and wrinkled fingers. "I have to watch them all the time, or they'll not care for the dogs properly."

"Sheldon's capable, isn't he?" Marian asked.

"He's the best kennel keeper in England. I'd have no less."

"Then trust him."

"I do trust him." Wenthaven stepped back up to the newly filled washtub and whistled. His favorite bitch leaped to her feet and jumped in. Water flew, drenching the apron Wenthaven had tied around his waist, and in the tone he reserved for his favorites, he crooned, "Ah, you're a sweet doggie. Aye, you are." The small blond spaniel splashed in the water, trying to lick his face, and Wenthaven put his cheek down. "Such a good dog. Such a good Honey." He plunged his hands into the soft soap he used to kill fleas and transferred a gob of it to the dog. With a jerk of the head, he indicated Marian should stand opposite the tub where he could see her, then asked, "What brings you here?"

She took her position boldly: fists on hips, legs astraddle. "The ransacking of my cottage."

The bitch in the tub growled at the angry tone of Marian's voice.

"Someone ransacked your cottage?" Wenthaven asked.

"On your decree, I vow."

Wenthaven sounded quite mild as he denied it.

"Come, Wenthaven," Marian said. "You have your finger in every pie for fifty miles about. Don't tell me you didn't know about this."

"I try to keep my finger in every pie," he corrected. "It would seem I failed, and most miserably. What was taken?"

"I don't know. I only know . . ." She faltered as the impact of the destruction struck her. Before, she'd been concerned with Lionel. Now, she realized how many of her personal items had been demolished. Mementos of the court, gifts from Lady Elizabeth, treasures of her childhood, all gone in a whirlwind.

"Your son escaped without injury?"

She dabbed at her eyes with her sleeve. "Aye."

"That's all that matters, is it not? You're like your mother in that. Your child is all you live for."

She drew a breath and let it out in a sigh. "That's correct."

Wenthaven leaned over Honey and scrubbed the soap into her neck. "So. You've come to me for money to replace your clothes? Were your clothes included in the ruin? No matter. 'Tis time you had new."

Frustrated, she cried, "I didn't come to you for new clothes! I came to you to ask you why you had someone—"

"Could someone, perhaps, have been searching for something?"

She averted her gaze. "What would they want?"

"That is indeed the question. If I had had someone search your cottage, you'd have never known, and why would I have someone rip it to shreds? Be logical, Marian. That's not my style."

She hesitated slightly before agreeing.

"And why would I steal from you? Everything you have is mine."

"Not everything."

"Aye, there's the gold the queen sends you. But you hoard as much of that as you can, don't you? I wonder why."

His faint smile kept her anxiety at bay, and she answered honestly. "Lionel must have every advantage, and that'll take money. Living off your charity is not so dreadful, I've discovered. The only fatality is my pride."

"You've developed a rather wry humor about your situation, haven't you? Most amusing." But he looked as if he'd found half a worm in his apple. "The new clothes, I confess, are nothing but a sop to my conscience. I obviously have failed to maintain a decent surveillance of my property."

Cheered by his perturbed expression, she said, "Perhaps your grip on your followers is slipping."

"You'd best hope not, my dear, or chaos would ensue."

"Speaking of chaos, did you set Adrian Harbottle on me?" she demanded.

Wenthaven stopped washing the dog to peer at her. "Well, well. You are discerning. I thought I had hidden that from you."

Instantly enraged, she shouted, "You told him to rape me?"

Honey growled again, and again Wenthaven calmed her as he stared at his daughter. "Rape you? When?"

"Today. At the hunt."

To her horror, her whole body shuddered, and his cool gaze noted the betrayal of her emotions.

"You defended yourself successfully, of course."

"There is no 'of course'—but, aye, I did."

He suggested, "Most women would be honored by the attentions of—"

"Of a stupid peacock with ambitions above his station?"

"Sometimes, my dear, you show signs of having my intelligence. It fosters a kind of paternal pride—an alien emotion, and a disconcerting one." He scrubbed at the dog. "So use that intelligence, and tell me—would I give my daughter to some man as a gift?"

"You might if you could use that man to control me."

He laughed, short and sharp, and he avoided a direct reply to that accusation. "You are an heiress yourself, and even besmirched as you are, you're worth much on the marriage mart. Men are willing to forget much for a large dower."

"I've not been overwhelmed with offers since my return from court."

Wenthaven chuckled, soft and low. "There have been some, and as the memory of your sin retreats, they increase. I've simply seen no reason to bother you with them."

"They weren't lucrative enough?"

"I'll not sell my daughter for money."

"Ah. The offers were not from powerful families."

"How well you know me."

"Aye, I know you. Know you well enough to wonder if you're telling me the truth."

"In all honesty, I assure you, I will never offer you to Adrian Harbottle. He has slipped his leash."

"Then what did you encourage him to do to me?"

"Ah. I'd hoped you'd forgotten that."

She waited, tapping her toe.

"I encouraged him to duel with you."

Confused, she demanded, "In the name of the Virgin, why?"

"For excitement."

"I don't like being prodded like a bear facing a bull."

"Most people don't—if they realize it. When you first came to Castle Wenthaven, you paraded every grievance. But as time has gone on, you've conformed more and more to society's demands, and—dare I say it—you've become dull." He waved his hand, and drops of water flew. "Witness the marriage offers I told you about."

"Why did you encourage me, when I came from court, to do mad things?"

"Give a dog a bad name and hang him, my dear. You'd ruined your reputation in the worst, most permanent way, and you might as well be hanged as try to recover your good name. You wanted to show you didn't care, and I helped you show it."

"Despite the further damage it did me?"

"Did it?" He leaned forward until his forehead almost touched hers. "Do you remember when you were a tiny lass of five, and I sent you to Lady Elizabeth to serve her? Do you remember the advice I gave you the night before you left?"

Looking into his eyes, she could almost imagine the years had melted away and she stood before her father once more—afraid to leave her home, more afraid to tell him so, and clinging to the hope that if she did as instructed, she would make him proud enough to bring her back. Did she remember? "Aye, I remember. You told me to cultivate the ability to please, to recognize my lady's misdeeds and advise her against them, and if she did not listen, to exhibit the most extreme loyalty and take responsibility for the results."

"Was it good advice?"

Without hesitation she said, "It was."

"Now I will give you more good advice. Never apologize for events past. Never explain, never ask forgiveness for who you are. You are Wenthaven's daughter, and you are a force to be reckoned with in England." He leaned back and returned his attention to his task. "Don't ever forget that."

Somehow she felt like that frightened child again, trying to comprehend something just beyond her grasp.

"That young man will have to be watched," he said.

"Who . . . oh, Harbottle. I don't think so."

Wenthaven lifted Honey from the slimy water. "Did you kill him?"

"Not I. I kicked him—"

"How unimaginative."

"—in the throat—"

"Better."

"—but Sir Griffith rode up in a fortuitous manner, and he assures me I should worry no more."

"Sir Griffith ap Powel?" Honey yelped as if Wenthaven had tightened his grip too much, and he placed her gently in the rinse water. "Powel is quite the chevalier."

She didn't like the way he said it. From Wenthaven, it sounded like an insult.

He continued, "As a matter of curiosity, why did you move him into the tower?"

His daughter, Wenthaven noted, wasn't as skillful at juggling the truth as he was. It made her uneasy, and it gave him, finally, the upper hand. The whole conversation had been a revelation to him, a worrisome indication of his own incompetence. He'd thought Harbottle too stupid to take the initiative, but he'd underestimated both the youth's conceit and the size of his cock-stand. He'd have to do something about Harbottle.

He'd underestimated his daughter, too.

In all his dealings with royals, with courtiers, with common folk, he'd not found a soul in this world with half his intelligence or capacity for intrigue. But his daughter—damn, she was good. What he'd originally taken for stupidity had proved to be naiveté. With a little guidance, she could easily be his equal.

That should have alarmed him. Instead it fostered pride in him—an unfamiliar notion. Now he would have to probe her mind to discover the depth of her interest in this Griffith ap Powel. It pleased him when she stammered, "He—he wanted a room where he could speak without having your spies listen."

"And how did he discover my spies were listening?"

"I don't know." She threw out her arms in an excess of innocence. "I don't know, Wenthaven. I only know his servant questioned me about your spies. Probably King Henry knows about it. Probably the king's spies are spying on your spies."

That was a thought. A depressing thought, and one worth investigating. But he wasn't done with Marian yet. "Why were you in Powel's room in the middle of the night?"

She made it clear she didn't like it, but she answered bluntly, "I was collecting my money."

"Of course." He didn't believe that, but it wasn't important. "Back to the original question—why did you put him in the tower?"

"I don't know what you're asking."

A fine parry, but he thrust under her guard. "Is Powel your newest lover?"

"Nay!"

Well accustomed to interrogation, he leveled an accusing stare at her. "You wanted to put him in the tower because there you could indulge yourself without my knowledge." He felt that stab of pride again when she visibly pulled herself together.

"Nay. Sir Griffith is ill tempered, ill mannered, and ill favored. He thinks me a whore and despises me for my wantonness. I've remained celibate since Lionel's birth. Why do you think he would tempt me?"

Wenthaven wondered how well she'd learned the fine art of acting during her latter days at court. Did she hide an ardor for this Griffith ap Powel? Better than most, Wenthaven understood the illogic of pas-

sion. With his hands cupped, he lifted water from the
tub and poured it around Honey's ears. "Your mother
wasn't the most beautiful woman I've ever met, nor
the most interesting, but I never stopped pursuing
her, even when she was mine. Even now, when I see a
woman who resembles her . . . but they're never the
same."

As he had intended, this glimpse of his soft underbelly fascinated Marian. "So you mourned my mother
when she died?"

For some reason, he told her the truth in a neutral
tone that he hoped disguised the old anguish that was
still alive after almost twenty years. "If I could, I
would level the tower that killed her."

"It would be difficult, but not impossible. Why
can't you?"

"She won't let me. I planned to do it once, and
went into the tower to explain to the workers what
must be done, and she . . ." He recalled a whisper of
silk, a scent of rose, a quick turn to see . . . nothing.
He pressed one wet wrist to his forehead, then
plunged it into the water again. "I haven't gone back
since. It's not a pleasant feeling, being dictated to
from beyond the grave. Especially not by a woman
who said so little when she was alive."

"Does she disapprove of you?"

"Your mother was an innocent." It made him
angry that he still remembered, still longed for her.
"She never approved of my activities, my little forays
to gather information. She didn't like the people I
keep around me."

He didn't look at her directly, but from the corner
of his eye he could see her gathering her courage. He
braced himself for another probe about her mother.

But she asked only, "Why *do* you have those people here?"

"What people?"

"Those pathetic imitations of courtiers. Those

poor souls who hang about, looking for a handout. These dogs have more dignity than they do."

"From your lips I heard the answer. *Poor souls.*" He relished the phrase. "If I didn't take them in, who would?"

"They'd have to do something useful with their lives."

"How? Most of them are noble. They have no skills. The younger sons can tilt at tournament, recite their own dreadful poetry, sit a horse—one of them can even recite a mass. He was a priest destined for high office in the Church until his bishop caught him with his hand up his daughter's skirt. The bishop's daughter's skirt, that is." Wenthaven rolled his eyes. "No political acumen."

"And the women?"

"Ah, the impoverished daughters!" He blew an annoying strand of silver hair out of his eyes. "Who'll pay for needlework and gossip? The unfortunate souls are dependent on me for everything."

"And that gives you power."

He slid her a sideways glance. "How clever of you, darling."

"Why do you want so much power?"

"Ah. Are you asking about my motivation?"

"I . . . aye, I suppose I am."

He clucked his tongue and kept his tone smooth. "'Tis the first time you've shown interest in me and my background. I'm flattered."

She wisely kept her mouth shut.

He rewarded her acumen with a glimpse of his past. "When I was a youth, I was one of the unfortunate souls." Lifting the dog out of the tub, he told the approaching kennel keeper, "I'll care for Honey." To Marian he said, "I was a poor relation of the Woodville family, and they were not, at that time, related to royalty. But when Elizabeth Woodville married King Edward and produced all those children—starting with your own Lady Elizabeth of York—that changed. Cousin Elizabeth Woodville—she's the dowager queen of England now—had King Edward give me a title. She found me an heiress whose lands were not entailed, and I wed."

"My mother?"

"Your mother." He pointed at the stack of drying clothes. "Hand me that towel, would you?"

Marian obliged. "What did she think of the marriage?"

His smile wavered. "Your mother was not an easy woman to read."

"Did she love you?"

"Aristocrats do not love."

"Then, did you love her?"

He looked at her, noting the coltish grace of her legs and the tilt of her chin. For the first time in his life, he'd slipped. He'd revealed too much, and she'd gotten above herself. She imagined she could insult him without consequence. In the cold tone he often employed with such success, he replied, "I am not so low a breed as you think, my lady Marian. Not so low a breed as a pathetic soul who comes running home with her bastard and begs me for sanctuary."

She jerked her head back as if he'd slapped her. "You never reproached me before."

"Reproached you? For the failure of my dreams? For destroying the chance I bought for you?"

She leaned across the dog to grab his arm. "I did what you told me to do."

With a snarl, Honey sprang toward her. Wenthaven grabbed the dog, and with a cry, Marian tumbled backward onto the grass. Barking frenziedly, Honey fought to escape him, to protect him. He wrestled with the dog, desperate to restrain her, furious with Marian for provoking the attack and more furious at himself.

He should have let Honey maul Marian. It would

have not only taught her a well-needed lesson, but put enough marks on that pretty face to stop Harbottle and Griffith and whoever else she'd been toying with.

But in instinctive reaction, he'd pulled the dog back.

He didn't want Marian to bleed. He didn't want her in pain.

"Damn the dog!" Marian cried, her gaze fixed on the sharp teeth Honey kept bared at her. "Why did she do that?"

He calmed Honey until she subsided into a fit of low growls. "She was protecting me."

"I wasn't going to bite *you.*" She sat up and flapped her coat, trying to dislodge some of the grass and mud. "Honey never liked me."

"Of course not. Honey is the dominant bitch in the kennel, and she's responding to the threat to her domain."

Still defiant, she said, "I don't threaten her!"

"I know that, but you'll never convince Honey." He tapped her untouched cheek. "She recognizes your scent, and after all"—he smiled with all his teeth—"you are top bitch in the kennel."

# 7

*Lionel wiggled* on Griffith's shoulders, and Griffith adjusted him without giving it a thought. How could he, when his discussion with the Welsh mercenaries, and particularly with the scarred and ruthless captain, proved so much more interesting than one small boy?

But Lionel wiggled again, then tugged Griffith's hair sharply.

"Hey, lad!" Griffith swung Lionel down to his feet. "What do you mean by it?"

Lionel laughed, a light, joyous sound, and pointed toward the kennel enclosure. Griffith's gaze fastened on the tall, graceful youth closing the gate.

Not a youth, but a woman with too much faith in a costume and too little in a man's perception.

Marian.

The mercenary proved Griffith right with a grin that revealed a few broken stubs of teeth. In Welsh Cledwyn said, "Th' earl's mad daughter. I have plans t' visit her some night."

Griffith gathered the front of Cledwyn's grimy,

knee-length garment—the only one he wore—in his fist and pulled him close. Looking deep into his eyes, Griffith replied in Welsh, "I'd reconsider, if I wanted to keep my family clappers intact."

"Is she"—the flesh of Cledwyn's face quivered—"under yer protection?"

"My protection, and King Henry's."

"King Henry? Ooh, 'tis frightened, I am." The mercenary shot two fingers out toward Griffith's eyes.

Griffith deflected them with a slash of his flattened palm.

Cledwyn considered Griffith. "Ye can fight, can ye?"

Calmly, making it clear he did it because he chose to, Griffith loosened his grip on the mercenary's filthy garment. "How did you lose your teeth?"

"Mace swing t' th' head." Deprived of the structure that teeth lent a face, Cledwyn looked like a clay molding mashed from jaw to forehead. "Only a Welshman tough as me could live through it."

Griffith nodded. "'Twould be a cruel irony if it happened again. I doubt you'd be lucky enough to live through it twice."

Not at all alarmed, Cledwyn again considered Griffith. "Some Welshman ye are, threatening yer fellow countryman."

"Some Welshman you are," Griffith countered, "dealing treacherously with King Henry of Wales."

Cledwyn seemed more surprised than sullen. "There's money t' be made."

Lionel pulled on Griffith's coat, but Griffith only patted his head and answered Cledwyn. "That doesn't absolve treason."

"Money absolves everythin'." Seeing a chance to challenge Griffith, Cledwyn sneered. "Especially when Henry remembers he's a Welshman only long enough t' secure his arse on th' throne, then do his dirtiest t' my own dearest country o' Cymru."

He ended on a sob that didn't impress Griffith at all. "Your affection for Wales isn't worth piss." Lionel tugged at Griffith again, and Griffith shook him off. "If enough Welshmen think as you do and hire themselves out to a petty lord with dreams too big for his codpiece, Henry'll have reason to betray Wales, won't he? All of Cymru will be squeezed out at the little end of the horn."

Cledwyn's voice rose. "Save yer breath t' cool yer porridge. Ye'll never convince me—damn little turd!"

Griffith jerked Lionel away from Cledwyn's hairy leg and swung him away just as the mercenary's hand descended.

"He bit me!" Cledwyn shrieked, lunging for Lionel. "Th' half-wit whelp bit me!"

Griffith's hands were full, so he aimed his kick to Cledwyn's groin and let Cledwyn's forward momentum drive the blow home. Cledwyn's arms flew out, and he paused like a man dangling from a sky noose. Then he crumpled while his fellow mercenaries cheered.

Griffith took no notice of their approval, knowing well they'd have cheered just as vigorously had he suffered the defeat. To the groaning Cledwyn, he said, "I did warn you about your clappers."

"Mama!" Lionel pointed in the direction of his old home. "Mama!"

Jolted, Griffith stared at the lad. "You can speak!"

"Damn clear, too," said one of the mercenaries.

"Been practicin' on his own," another commented.

As proud as if he were Lionel's father, Griffith grinned. "His first word, and he said it to me."

"Mama!" Lionel insisted.

Griffith glanced around, but Marian had disappeared. "Where did she go?"

Apparently deciding he'd said enough, Lionel again pointed. With the child in his arms, Griffith set off at a trot through the orchard, searching for

Marian. He found her just as she slipped through the gate of the cottage fence. He wanted to call her name, but she skulked along so furtively, he stopped himself. Lionel, too, seemed to have detected the need for secrecy, and withheld his astonishing cry.

Marian avoided the cottage and crept around toward the curtain wall. She was headed for the copse and, to Griffith's disgust, disappeared among the trees. He shifted his position but she still remained out of sight. No matter how he moved, he couldn't see her, and he knew now why she'd chosen that place to conceal her secrets.

When she emerged, he stepped back, hiding himself.

He didn't like doing it. It was not the act of an open and honorable knight, but when dealing with wild creatures, with kings, and with women, Griffith had sometimes found cunning to be essential.

With Lionel safe in his arms, Griffith slipped around to the walls of the castle that so closely overshadowed the copse. He used the rough stone as a protection against spies from above and depended on the unremarkable black of his mantle to hide him from any other gaze.

The copse looked the same as it had only a few hours ago, but the sun no longer touched it, and it seemed less a haven and more a place of enigma and shadows. Same trees, same hammock, but something niggled at Griffith. Something *was* different. . . .

Lionel pointed. "Mama."

Griffith stared at the deepest shadow beneath the trees but saw nothing.

Taking Griffith's chin between both his palms, Lionel turned it toward his own face, looked into Griffith eyes, and slowly enunciated, "Mama's."

Griffith grinned at the lad. "You're my ally in this, aren't you?" Walking into the trees, he saw what Lionel insisted he see. A fresh mound of dirt, hastily dug, hastily tamped over. Placing Lionel in the hammock, he dug, too, and found a black waxed box.

It was empty.


"Why do you wear such ugly clothes?"

Marian's question broke a silence as profound as a monk's meditation, but no one in the tower room seemed affected. Cecily didn't move, preferring to sit close against the fire, her arms wrapped around her belly. Lionel lay on a blanket by her, sucking his thumb and looking smug as only a secure two-year-old can. Art and Griffith straddled a bench, playing chess, drinking ale, and muttering in a language quite incomprehensible to Marian.

She wondered if she'd only dreamed she'd spoken and said more loudly, "Griffith ap Powel. Why do you wear such ugly clothes?"

Griffith lifted his head. "Are you talking to me?"

"Is your name not Griffith ap Powel?" Marian asked, exasperated. "And are you not the only person in this room wearing ugly clothes?"

Griffith looked at everybody in turn, his gaze lingering on Marian. She smoothed the tight bodice of one of the gowns her father had sent up to her, wished the skirt were long enough to cover her ankles, and wished she wore a wimple to shield her expression.

Instead she tucked the loose strands of hair back into the braid and stared boldly at the dismal brown surcoat Griffith wore over his linen tunic. "No one's worn a surcoat of that mode for fifty years, and it looks as if you've been rolling in the mud."

Only mildly interested, he looked down at himself. "'Tis an admirable color for stalking prey, and what does it matter if it's old-fashioned? I'm not a peacock spreading fine feathers for a mate."

Dismissing the subject—and her, it seemed—he returned to his play.

It had been a very odd evening.

When Marian had returned to the tower room—as instructed—there had been no one there except a wide-eyed, terrified Cecily, who jumped every time the ceiling creaked and babbled about Countess Wenthaven's malevolent spirit. But it seemed she was more afraid of Art, so she had stayed.

Marian had taken the garments sent by Wenthaven up the stairs to the tiny room, and there she had changed and hidden the treasure she'd retrieved from the grove behind her cottage. When Griffith returned with Lionel, she had been kneeling before the hearth to start the fire.

She had wanted to say something snappy about her own obedience to Griffith's commands, but the sight of Lionel held so tenderly by the giant knight stopped her words. Then she was glad she'd held her peace, for obviously Griffith was in no mood for repartee. In fact, he had been so grimly, thoughtfully silent, she'd jumped with pleasure when Art arrived.

But even the exuberant Art seemed tired and tight-lipped.

She'd imagined an evening rife with the gripping tension that existed between Griffith and her. Instead he'd ignored her, and she'd had a chance to let down the hem on the other two gowns Wenthaven had scrounged for her.

She couldn't even pick a fight with Griffith, and it embarrassed her that she wanted to. Was she a child seeking attention?

But Lionel rested quietly, content with his thoughts, and the comparison did not flatter her. "Come, Lionel," she said, rising off the bench. "You've had a big day. Let's put you to bed."

As always at bedtime, Lionel's lip stuck out, but this time he surprised her. He said, "Nay!"

Marian froze.

Cecily choked, then asked, "Did you speak?"

Amenably Lionel repeated, "Nay."

"You little darling!" Marian flew to his side and knelt on the blanket. "Say it again."

"Nay. Nay, nay, nay."

"Did you hear that?" In her pride, Marian included every occupant in the room. "He said his first word. Nay." Her tongue lingered on it as if it were the best syllable ever created. "Nay."

Cecily wet her lips. "He . . . is that really his first word? Probably 'nay' is all he'll say for a long time."

"Actually—" Griffith began.

Delighted with the attention, Lionel interrupted him. "Mama."

Marian's heart swelled. She could scarcely breathe with emotion. "Mama?" she whispered.

"Mama." He crawled into her arms, all grins and wet kisses. "Mama."

Dropping her head on his shoulder, Marian shed a few tears. Embarrassing tears, tender tears, tears too precious to contain. Her baby, her perfect baby, had just said his first words.

"Can he say anything else?" Cecily asked, and her voice trembled.

Philosophical as any experienced father, Art answered, "We'll find out soon enough."

"Sweet Jesú," Cecily whispered.

Blindly Marian put out a hand to Cecily, and Cecily grasped it tightly between her palms. Lifting her wet face, Marian smiled at Cecily through the blur of tears. "Dearest cousin, you've been my rod and staff these last years. How wonderful to share this moment."

"Aye," Cecily agreed. "I never expected to be so flustered by one tiny word."

Still hugging Lionel, Marian gathered his blanket and stood. The flames behind her cast themselves through the thin material of her makeshift skirt, outlining the length of her legs, and if Griffith could have moved, he would have covered Art's eyes. Instead he sat, frozen and stupid, while she wrapped up her son. Halting before the stairs, she said, "Lionel, wish Griffith and Art a fair night."

Still too overwhelmed by Lionel's miracle to believe in it, she didn't wait for a response.

But Lionel said, "Griffith."

Pride and horror took alternate possession of Marian's features, and she staggered as if Lionel suddenly weighed too much for her.

For the first time in years, Griffith found the blood rushing to his cheeks, and he cleared his throat before replying gruffly, "Sleep well, young Lionel."

"Guess this answers the question about him saying anything else," Art said, as close to crowing as Griffith had ever seen him.

Cecily held out her arms to Lionel. "Let me take him, my lady."

Reluctantly Marian gave him up, then turned her dewy face to Griffith and Art. "His first word was 'nay.' Does that mean he'll be a warrior?" She gurgled with laughter and followed Cecily upstairs.

Griffith stared after her. From the hole in the ceiling, he could hear sounds of bedtime preparation. Lionel squawked but settled easily, worn from his stimulating day. The murmur of women's voices floated down. In the silence that followed, Griffith unshrouded his own long neglected imagination.

Was Marian in bed? Did she still wear that wisp of a too small dress, or had she bared herself to the chill of the sheets? And if she had—

Art masked his meddlesome stare when Griffith turned to him urgently to say, "Lionel said 'Mama' first. He said it this afternoon. Should I tell her?"

"Not if he said it to ye," Art answered, scandalized.

"Better she should think his first word is 'nay,' and that he said it to *her*."

"That's what I thought." Griffith rubbed his aching head. "I'm glad I did one thing right this day."

"Did ye talk to the mercenaries?" Art asked.

"Aye."

"Then ye did two things right."

"There's treachery afoot." Griffith again glanced at the hole in the ceiling. "And I know not from where it comes."

"Not from Marian lass," Art protested, indignant at the unspoken suggestion.

"Not from her, but about her, I trow." Griffith touched Art's shoulder. "Let's build up the fire and sit beneath the canopy on the bed. 'Twould be warmer and less noisome to the occupants above."

Art squatted in front of the fireplace. "Ye carry the wood. I've tired myself in yer service today."

Surprised, Griffith complied with the unusual request, stacking the logs where Art could reach them and squatting beside him. "I've not heard that complaint before."

"I never thought I'd see the day where I'd make it." Art poked vigorously at the fire, and sparks flew. "Did ye know the widow Jane has buried five husbands?"

"Ah"—Griffith scratched his chin as he tried to understand—"nay, I did not know that. Five, eh?"

"Five." Art pointed at the bed of coals. "Put the log there. Five husbands, and I trow why they died."

"Poison? Witchcraft?"

"Exhaustion. She worked the poor squids to death, and she damn near wore me out, too."

Confused by Art's indignation, Griffith asked, "Doing laundry?"

"Doing her! That woman—"

Griffith started to laugh.

"—can dance the buttock jig more times than any woman I've ever had"—Art glared at the convulsed Griffith—"and I've had quite a few."

"That I should live to see the day," Griffith gasped when he could speak.

"She coulda killed me."

"At least you'd have died happy."

"But then ye'd not have had the information for which I sacrificed the Roaring Jack," Art snarled.

Griffith promptly sobered. "Which is?"

"The winter has brought a slow buildup of mercenaries here, mostly foreigners and mostly savages." Art blinked his one eye against the smoke as he set the bellows to the fire. "Wenthaven's cottagers kept an anxious eye on it, fearing a battle nearby what could wipe them out, but 'tis worse than that. Rough bunch, these mercenaries are, and impatient to start looting. Crooked the elbow too many times one night and visited the village down the road. Raped the women too many times, roasted a baby on a spike, set fire to half the huts."

Remembering Cledwyn's scarred face and his promise to visit Marian, Griffith leaned into the fire. "Sweet Saint Dewi."

"Four families burned out in the cold. Wenthaven paid for it all, and the mercenaries haven't been loose since, but—"

Griffith slipped out of his shoes and set them to the side of the hearth. "Does your widow know why they're here?"

"Nay, but I bet I do." Art stared into the flames as if God's truth were written there. "To join forces with those Irish rebels ye were telling me about."

"With the impostor earl of Warwick? Perhaps. But Lady Marian has secrets, and I suspect 'tis her secrets which Henry fears."

"Ye believe her secrets are the reason for Wenthaven's private army?"

"I know nothing. I only know what I saw." Rising, Griffith gestured to Art, and they met on the canopied bed. Pulling Art into a huddle, Griffith murmured, "What if Lionel has a royal father?"

Griffith could see he had jolted the sharp mind camouflaged by Art's aging facade. "Not one of the princes who disappeared in the tower, for they were too young. How about King Edward, their father? He was a right rotten lecher."

"Even if Edward had died while conceiving Lionel, Lionel would still have to be at least three years old."

Licking his lips, Art reluctantly offered the name they were both thinking. "Richard?"

Griffith didn't agree, he only watched as Art looked alternately contemplative and distressed.

At last he burst out, "But if Richard, why? Why would she do it?"

"Power? Wealth?" Griffith suggested. "The chance to be queen when Richard's wife died?"

Art reared up, fist clenched. "I'd like to smack ye sometimes. What kind of noddy-pate would think such a thing of Lady Marian? She's as sweet a lass as any I've met."

Griffith hooted. "Sweet?"

Art hushed him.

Griffith lowered his voice. "Sweet? That's the last word I'd use about Marian, but in sooth, I share your doubts. When she broke my nose, she said something. The pain may have previously driven it from my mind, or I may have been too noddy-pated to think it important."

"That's better." Art subsided.

"She claimed the lady Elizabeth had sacrificed everything to save her brothers from Richard's lethal embrace." Griffith pulled off his surcoat over his head and tossed it to the foot of the bed.

"She's right, ye know," Art said, his gaze on the brown material. "'Tis ugly."

"I'll dress like a peacock on the morrow," Griffith retorted. His tunic followed the surcoat, and then his hose. Naked and shivering, he drew a rug over his shoulders and thrust his feet beneath the covers.

"Mayhap we've discovered the explanation for Elizabeth's behavior at Richard's court."

This time Art hooted. "Ye were so convinced Elizabeth was a right horrible villainess."

"I admit it." Griffith valued the chill of the sheets, for it kept his mind alert, and he needed to be alert. He was a warrior, simple and rough. He often failed to find his way through the maze of intrigue in the court, and he feared this intrigue would end in death—his own, Art's, Marian's, Lionel's—if he trod unwarily. The responsibility weighed him down, yet at the same time it challenged him. "But Henry took Elizabeth to his bosom with affection and seems to value her above all others. Henry's no fool, so—"

"So ye believe Lady Marian sacrificed everything for the young princes, also?"

Griffith gave her her due ungrudgingly. "She's loyal."

"Aye, and valiant beyond all sense. Are ye suggesting King Richard Arsewedge the Third killed the princes, then used their sister to get respectability and encouraged her chief lady-in-waiting to think the princes could be helped by the forfeit of her virginity in his bed?"

Art had a way with description Griffith usually appreciated it, but not tonight. Not about Marian. The thought of Richard blackmailing her, raping her, infuriated him. "'Tis a possibility we must consider."

"While his own wife lay dying." Art rubbed his stomach. "Makes me want to puke."

"'Twould explain why Henry sent us to Lady Marian and her son."

Art slid from the bed and brought the pitcher and two mugs, and together they sipped the ale. "Do ye think Henry means to kill the lad?"

"Richard had other bastards, and Henry hasn't killed them." Art stared at Griffith, and Griffith admitted, "He hasn't treated them well, either."

"Damn, I don't like this, Griffith. It fits too well. Lady Marian has a child by Richard, Wenthaven discovers it and sees his chance to be regent to the king"—Art drained the rest of his mug—"if only he can get Lionel on the throne."

"So Wenthaven hires mercenaries and plots with the Irish to depose Henry." Griffith again sipped, then handed over his mug with a grimace. "Or maybe he just plans to use that insurrection to cover the stink of his own activities."

"Meanwhile, Henry discovers the boy's paternity, catches wind of Wenthaven's plans, and sends us to care for Lady Marian and Lionel, knowing full well he might have to order us to kill the lad."

"I couldn't kill a child, and Henry knows it. That's the inconsistency." Griffith pounded his fist in his hand. "Why didn't Henry tell me what he feared? What part of this scheme have we missed?"

Suddenly they heard a soft footfall. They spun around, knives drawn and ready.

Marian stood between them and the stairs. "Put the knives away. I'll not hurt you."

Her voice sounded firm, but her tall figure swayed like a willow in the breeze. She still wore her dress, but her fingers clutched a woolen wrap around her shoulders, and the ruffles on her cap fluttered as she trembled.

Griffith calmed his instinctive fight reaction, then exchanged a glance with Art. Together they sheathed their knives and offered identical, boyish, and, they hoped, innocent grins.

"Lady Marian, lass, ye surprised us," Art said.

"Old habits." Griffith patted the pillow that hid his knife.

"I heard your voices, and I thought . . ." She shuffled her bare feet on the cold board floor.

"Sure, and we're glad to have ye join us." Art winked his one eye and created such an odd effect that she smiled, if only briefly. "Er . . . did ye want to talk about what we were talking about, or did ye have another topic in mind?"

"I didn't understand what you were talking about. You were speaking in Welsh again."

"So we were," Griffith agreed heartily.

"'Twas only a dull discussion of how Welsh ale is superior to English ale." Art poured Griffith's discarded cup full and offered it to her. "Ye'll want a taste before ye agree."

She stepped forward, her gaze on the mug, and Art lured her with a low, pleasant chuckle. "'Twould be treason to agree without a taste, but ye'll see what makes the men grow strong and the women grow beautiful when ye try Welsh ale."

She took another step. "But that's English ale. How will I compare?"

Art struck his forehead with his palm, as if the quandary had just occurred to him. "Ye'll have to come to Wales with me, I trow, to make it fair. Ye'll like Wales. The mountains are rugged and beautiful, with Snowdon towering above them all. The people are kind and generous, poetic and full of song. Castle Powel is set on a hill above the rugged Atlantic coast, where the waves pound and the seabirds sing. Aye, my lady, ye must come to Wales with us."

Griffith watched as she wavered, wanting to make the last step but frightened of the consequences.

And he didn't want her to make it.

All well for Art to entice her with a silly challenge and a bit of laughter. Art didn't see the braid that draped over her shoulder and imagine the red hair loose. He didn't imagine her comb as it dug into the waves and tamed them. He didn't observe the flex of her slender fingers and imagine them wrapped around a sweet Welsh bundle of a babe. He didn't look at her long, bare feet and imagine them placed on his legs on a cold winter's night. Art wasn't imagining the pleasures a man imagines when he's wanting a wife.

But Art knew Griffith was, and he was intent on making it well-nigh impossible for Griffith to deny them.

Her gaze was still fixed on the mug. She seemed frozen in place, and Art could wait no more. He took the final step, clasped her hands around the mug, and urged, "Drink."

"I can't," she said. "I'm cold."

"Ye're shaking, lass," Art observed, then hurried to the fire.

She *was* shaking. Griffith could see it. She shook in ripples, in waves, like someone fighting to repress some emotion too great to contain. He grasped her wrist and found it trembling in his hand. Other signs of distress were visible, too. She bit her lip. She looked at him, then her glance slid away.

His bold, valiant Marian was afraid.

Without his realizing, he softened the grip of his fingers, softened his normal rough growl. "What bothers you, sweetheart?"

She flinched away as if burned. "I just wanted to . . . ah . . ."

Leaning off the mattress, he put his hands over hers and lifted the mug to her lips, helping her as he would Lionel.

"Drink," he whispered, and she obeyed.

When she finished, he placed the cup on the table and again asked, "What bothers you?"

Her gaze slid up his body beneath the covers, lingered on his bare chest, then reached his face. "I had a . . . oh . . . the baby was sleeping, and I didn't want to wake him, so I . . ."

Comprehension began to dawn on him, but he encouraged her. "Why did you want to wake the baby?"

"I didn't want to wake him. Only hold him for a wee bit."

She shivered, and he knew the heavy wrap she wore could not be keeping her warm.

Art elbowed his way forward. "I've wrapped a stone, warm from the fire, and I'll place it here, in the middle of the bed." To Marian he said, "I've an assignation with a sweet widow in the laundry, and I must be going, but Griffith will take care of ye." He shoved the foot warmer between the sheets and rapped Griffith sharply on the leg in the process. "Won't ye, Griffith?"

"Arthur, don't go," Griffith commanded, but Art slid out the door without a backward glance. "Damn the man! I hope she sucks him dry."

The wrist in his hand trembled more, and Marian whispered, "You're angry."

"Nay. Not at you," he assured her, but he couldn't tell her to sit on the bed and warm her feet on the stone. He could scarcely keep from kissing her palm, and the years of celibacy drove him like a spur in the flank of a spirited horse. Grimly he pulled himself under control, reminding himself he was the rider, not the ridden.

Tugging at her wrist, she said, "But you're right. I shouldn't have come down. I'm sorry. Let me leave you in peace."

He kissed her palm. "I'm concerned about you. You had a nightmare, you say?"

Never realizing his ruse, she covered her eyes with her hand. "It was awful. They were burning the cottage, and I couldn't find Lionel, and when I found you, you'd been stabbed through the heart. . . ."

With his free hand, he drew her fingers from her eyes and felt the dampness of her tears. Saw them glisten on her cheeks. Heard her sniffle. He put his hands to her waist and lifted her onto the high mattress. After tucking the blanket around her sock-covered feet, he tightened the tie of her robe, then said, "Sit beside me."

"Why do you do that?" she burst out.

"What, lass?"

"Toss me around, make me do what you wish, then tell me to do it?"

He chuckled, comfortable with the press of her hip against his, pleased with the formidable barrier of sheet between them. Urging her down on the pillows beside him, he said, "Lie down. I've found you get your way when you don't give people a choice."

"Especially not women?" she asked peevishly.

"Especially not weak-minded folk," he corrected. Before she could respond, he asked, "You couldn't hold the babe, so came to hold me instead?"

Her shivering diminished. Instead she squirmed, and his whole body clenched. She was frightened, emotional, vulnerable. Every maid had been warned of the dangers of frequenting a man's sleeping chamber. And Marian herself had discovered the truth of it—Lionel proved that. But she had overcome her reluctance at least enough to come to him.

Only in the throes of fear, but she'd come to him.

So he would contain his outrageous impulses and give her the human contact she craved.

After sliding his arm around her shoulders, he pressed her head down until it rested on his bare chest. She resisted, of course, but she never had a chance against his strength and her need.

"Rest on me," he murmured.

With a sigh, she relaxed. Her breath puffed along his skin, her hand smoothed his crinkled hair from beneath her nose. "I only wanted to look at you," she whispered.

He smiled at the top of her head, glad she couldn't see the countenance her confession engendered. "All the lasses like to look at me. 'Tis only a privileged few who get to touch."

His uncharacteristic teasing did bring her head up, but he gently pushed her back down and asked, "Can you hear my heart?"

"Aye."

"'Tis not stabbed through. 'Tis healthy enough to—"

She kissed him.

Oh, just a light and innocent touch of her lips. Just the skin in the middle of his chest. Just the skin *over* his heart.

But it broke another of the reins that restrained the cavorting horse that rode him . . . that he rode.

She laid her head back down, and he thought he couldn't draw a breath big enough to fill his lungs. She could hear the betraying race of his heart, he knew, but he didn't know if he cared. The glory of her fiery hair drew him, and he lifted his hand. Touching her forehead, he stroked his palm slowly along. On their own accord, his fingertips wandered around her ear and down to her neck. They stroked down her back to the very tip of her braid. Then he lifted his hand and began again.

"Lass, have I told you how beautiful your hair is?"

"Nay."

The word was scarcely audible, but her breath warmed his nipple, and he closed his eyes against the pleasure of it. "How long is it when it's unbound?"

"It reaches my . . . ah . . ."

His hand patted her posterior, then surreptitiously released the ribbon that bound the end of her braid. "That's what I thought."

"I can sit on it when it's loose. It would be longer, but . . ."

He pulled the wool wrap back from her shoulder and massaged her through the thin material of her dress, and she broke off as if she were confused.

"But?" he encouraged.

"When I was a child, I hated the color. Everyone teased me about it, so I took some scissors and—"

"You're too impulsive." He wondered how he had the gall to chide her when they lay entwined on his

bed at his own behest, and he was carefully unplait-
ing her hair.

"When I was young, perhaps. By the time I was
five, I well knew my duties and had control of my
mad impulses. My father saw to that."

He wanted to ask her what it was, then, that had
landed her flat on her back in some man's bed, but
that would anger and alarm her, and he found himself
unwilling to sacrifice the warmth, the small talk that
was teaching him so much. Maybe it was the near
darkness, their isolation, the strangeness, but they
were talking.

Not snarling, not snapping, but exchanging information—and he liked it.

"Your father?"

"Aye, before he placed me with Elizabeth, he personally drilled me in my duties to my patron."

"Personally?"

"Of course." She chuckled. "But for no honorable
reasons, I assure you. 'Twas only to advance the for-
tunes of the family. The House of York seemed
secure then. I was to make myself indispensable to
Elizabeth, to remain totally loyal to her. And I did."

"For your family?"

"For Elizabeth," she corrected. "She loved me
more dearly than a sister."

"And your father loves you not at all."

"My father loves me as well as he can love.
Mayhap not at all."

As he pulled his fingers through her hair like a
comb, he said, "You take his lack of affection well."

She shrugged. "One can't miss what one has never
had."

Remembering his own warm relationship with his
parents, he wondered . . . But she was right, of
course. She wasn't suffering.

"If my father had had one drop of affection for me,
he wouldn't have sent me away from my home, and I

wouldn't have been there to help Elizabeth." She shook her head. "Now *she* was impulsive. She would do anything for love."

His fingers tightened on her shoulder. "And what would you do for love?"

He meant—had she given herself to help Elizabeth?

But it sounded like a personal appeal.

She was warm now, he knew it. Her toes touched the stone, and her body absorbed heat from his. Yet a fine trembling began in her again, and she lifted herself on her elbow to look into his face. "What would I do for love?"

She seemed to absorb his needs like a disciple and in her gestures responded to his unspoken query.

He wanted her to love him, to give him everything she'd ever given to another man, and more.

"I can't," she whispered.

"I would never force you." But he seduced her with a smile and never gave a thought to his battered countenance. The Griffith he saw reflected in her eyes was painted in all the hues of adoration and beauty.

"'Twould be disaster."

"'Twould be"—he laughed, deep in his chest—"magnificent."

Triumph swelled in him when she responded. Her unbound hair sifted around them in a slow cascade of autumn color, and she leaned forward.

He'd tasted her before; now he savored her. Her open lips, the peach color of her cheeks, the spicy scent of cedar lingering in her long stored dress. The sound of her wrap hitting the floor, the rustle of her bows as he untied them, the firm, long, athletic legs that kicked the dress down, the fire of her pubic hair. "If this be the mouth of hell," he murmured, "I would die unshriven."

She laughed, huskily, pleased and amazed. "I like you, too. Your chest hair and your . . . all your body hair is black." Her fingers skimmed through his head hair. "This is dark brown. Do you dye it with walnut juice?"

Too indignant to remember, for a moment, their first meeting, he protested, "Nay!"

Then her gurgle of laughter reminded him, and he punished her with a kiss that started at her lips and slid in slow, careful increments all the way down to her toes.

He didn't perform any extraordinary feats of lovemaking. He scarcely touched the places she longed to have touched—it was a punishment, after all. But she didn't seem to realize how he'd cheated her. The soft cries she muffled in the pillow, the clutch of her fists in the covers, the arch of her body, tense as a drawn longbow—they proved an innocence her lover had left untouched, and Griffith set out to make this time the first time, the best time.

She faltered, "You shouldn't . . ."

"Forget your back? That's true." Pushing her onto her stomach, he worked his way up to the nape of her neck.

She liked it, and she showed him by the strength of her embrace when he turned her to face him again. He pressed her into the mattress, using his whole body to brand her whole body with his ownership. He pushed his hands into her hair on either side of her thrashing head, held it still, and looked deep into her eyes. "You are mine," he said.

As with everything else, she erred in her reply. "For now."

It wasn't the answer he sought. He wanted to teach her that what burned in him would burn forever, but in her face he saw the rebirth of sanity—and he couldn't stop now. He was out of control, crazed with desire and desperate for her. He knew, without conceit, he could create in her the same desire, the same desperation, for although he might not be the world's most accomplished lover, he was her mate.

Though he already held her, he directed her, "Hold still. Let me show you. . . ."

Everything.

With a kiss that wrung whimpers from her, he taught her the finer points of pleasure—taught her until she forgot her inhibitions and her sanity.

This was worship, direct and simple. Her hands slipped and fumbled, she blushed and looked astonished, she seemed shy and overwhelmed, and she made him feel like lord of the heights. He monitored her as if he were initiating a virgin, and she reacted like one, right up to the moment he began to enter her.

"You're so tight," he murmured. "You're so tight."

Something about that bothered him, but conscious thought had been blocked by pleasure. Shivers ran up his spine, and he could only fight to control himself. He kissed her deeply, touched the breasts that had proved so sensitive, and stroked the one place he'd not yet touched.

He'd been saving it, depending on that final, sensual pleasure to push her over the edge.

And it did.

She moaned deep in her chest. She panted, she writhed, she bucked at him, and the muscles inside her sucked him in.

At least that's what he imagined, but he'd obviously gone mad, for he would have sworn, have *sworn,* he broke through her maidenhead.

She moaned, but her moan spoke of pain, not passion, and he reared up to look at her.

The pinched mouth, the trickling tears, the tight-shut eyes, told the story.

She had been a virgin.

By the saints, she had been a virgin.

# 8

*She tried to stifle her shriek,* but it was too late.

What had she done? Sweet Mary, what had she done?

Did he realize?

Could she hide it?

Opening her eyes, she looked.

He looked back, and he was furious. His gaze wasn't friendly, but it was hot. Aye, so hot. Then he smiled with all his teeth, and said, "I hurt you, but sweetheart, 'twas unavoidable. Now . . . now I'll show you real pleasure."

When they finished, the bed was destroyed. The pillows had disappeared, the sheets were untucked, the blankets kicked off. If it was cold in the room, she didn't know it, for his revenge for her deception had been, as he promised, real pleasure.

More pleasure than she could tolerate.

Like a stained-glass window whose components had been scattered never to be gathered again, she couldn't seem to pull all the pieces of herself back together. She groped for deceptions with which to cover herself.

But he gave her no time to think, to plan. He leaned over her, stroked her throat until she opened her eyes, and mocked, "All those years of riding astride—for nothing."

He'd found satisfaction. She didn't know much, but she knew that. His roar of primitive rapture had been part and parcel of the greater picture he'd created with her. Yet now his gaze poured heat over her, and when she groped for a blanket to cover herself, he stopped her.

Her voice quavered. "What do you mean?"

He smiled again like the beast he'd proved himself to be. "Riding astride didn't break your maidenhead."

She jerked in nervous reaction.

"I *know*." His voice lingered over the words.

She tried again for the comforter. Again he denied her.

"I'm cold," she complained.

"I'll cover you."

But he didn't mean with the blanket. He pulled her half under him, and like his eyes, his body burned, too. She tamped down the panic, prepared to face the consequences of her stupidity, but not the consequences of her passion.

He commanded, "Tell me again how you came to have Lionel."

Putting her hand against her lips, she felt them move as she spoke. Spoke yet said nothing. "I've never told you anything of importance."

Her evasion angered him further, and he crowded her deeper into the mattress. "Yet you lie with me in the most primitive sense. So where's the truth in this?"

"The truth is not for me to reveal. I gave you myself. Don't ask for more."

"But you didn't give me yourself. You gave me

your body, and beautiful though it is, it's not enough." Pressing his fingers to her temples, he whispered close against her ear, "I want what's in here. I want to know the mind, the soul, of Lady Marian Wenthaven."

"You can't. You'll be leaving soon, and I will stay here. . . ." He was shaking his head, and she asked, "Why do you deny it?"

"I mean, I will stay close to you as commanded by my sovereign, good King Henry."

Her sweaty palms slipped when she pushed at him, but he sat up obligingly. He was openly, impressively naked: corded muscles and a light dusting of body hair sliced, here and there, by scars both old and new. He watched her as she, too, sat up, and this time he didn't stop her when she groped for the covers.

But her need to hide herself was second to her need to understand him. Whispering in incredulous dismay, she asked, "What do you mean, King Henry commanded you to stay close to me?"

"In a letter he sent with me, he ordered me to remain and watch over you."

It would have been kinder if he'd struck her. She could have borne it better than this betrayal, this proof of her own folly, this mockery of love. "You came to spy on me?"

"I came to deliver gold from Henry's wife to his wife's former lady-in-waiting, then remained to protect her and her son."

"Spy on me?" Ignited by the pain of betrayal, her cheeks burned until they hurt. "Like my father spies on me?"

"Protect you—"

"A different term for the same thing." Her vision blurred with a sudden influx of tears. "I spit on the protection men such as you offer. I spit—"

He covered her mouth when she would have followed words with action, and his fury was no less palpable than hers. "Don't push me, little girl. You've lied to me from the first moment I saw you, and this self-righteous indignation can scarcely compete with the existence of the bloody stain on the sheets. You are not who you say you are."

She knocked his hand away. "I am."

"You are not Lionel's mother."

More emphatically, she said, "I *am.*"

With his fingers, he pushed his thick, tangled hair out of his face. "The virgin birth occurred almost fifteen hundred years ago, and so I say to you, that child upstairs is not the child of your body."

The chill in the room pressed in, cooling her temper, making her realize the danger to Lionel. She'd allowed herself to be seduced by kindness, by warmth, by a tender touch and a rumbling voice. She'd given herself to a man she thought she could trust and he'd just proved his deceitfulness. "You know aught of what you speak."

"May I remind you, I am the only man who knows of what I speak when you are spoken about."

She caught his hands and squeezed them until his bones and tendons creaked. "If you say anything about me—"

Quickly he slipped his hands out and caught hers in his. "I said I would protect you, and to speak about this would be to do you—and, I fear, Lionel—a great disservice. But you must believe in me for my protection to be effective."

His obstinacy pulled a frustrated little scream from her. "Believe in you? In *you?* I don't want your protection. I don't need your protection. I wouldn't take help from one of Henry's flunkies—"

"Not even if Lionel's safety depended on it?"

She sat frozen, her mouth slightly open, and he leaned forward to plant a kiss on her lips. The first flush of his anger had faded, and sweet reason supplanted it. "You need help, sweeting, whether you admit it or not. Your father's making some kind of plans."

She looked alarmed. "What do you mean?"

"Have you not wondered about the number of mercenaries your father has hired?"

"Wenthaven has never indicated interest in . . . me."

"Nay, not in . . . you." He mocked her. "But is there anywhere that's safe for a *royal* child?" Her anguished gaze told him more than she intended. It told him the truth, if not the details, of his suppositions. He brought her close against him and lay down, taking her with him, squelching her ineffectual struggles. "Ah, lass. Stay and sleep with me. Things will look better in the morning. We'll talk in the morning, and you'll see I'm right."

Alarmed at her limp acceptance, he arranged the blankets to cover them and tucked her under his chin. "We'll talk in the morning," he said again.

The passion, then the anger, had washed through him, leaving him relaxed and refreshed. He hadn't felt this good in years.

He hadn't felt this good, ever, and he couldn't help marveling at the miracle of this woman. His woman. His love.

She curled up tight as a babe, and he smoothed his hands over her, massaging her, trying to convey confidence in him, in them, through his touch. From beneath the covers where she hid her head, he heard, "But I don't know you."

He chuckled. "You know me better than any woman has for over two years."

"Only a fool thinks a bed partner can be trusted."

He hugged her to him. "Then call me a fool."


"I'm a fool!" Griffith's Welsh roar echoed down the stone stairway and around the tower. "A stupid, gibbering fool!"

Art pulled him back inside the countess's room. "Saint Dewi save us, man, don't announce it to the world."

The door rocked on its hinges when Griffith slammed it. "Where could she have gone? And with a babe?"

"More to the question—why did she go?"

Art accused Griffith with his question, with his tone, and Griffith thrust his face close to Art's. "Because we did what you had urged us to do."

Art flushed with anger. "Did ye treat her so awful she had to escape?"

"Oh, Arthur." Griffith flexed his fists. "Oh, Arthur, you don't know how you tempt me to wring your neck. I treated her better than she deserved. She'll not forget me for a long time. In fact"—he paced across the room—"she'll not forget me ever."

"Conceit!" Art cried.

"Not at all," Griffith said smoothly. "You yourself said a woman never forgets her first lover."

"Aye, I know I said that, but I—" Art stopped, and his eyes bugged out. "What do ye mean?"

Griffith walked over to him, wrapped his hands around Art's surcoat, and lifted him to his toes. "I mean, 'tis not Lionel's father we must wonder about. 'Tis Lionel's mother."

Art's mouth worked silently, then he released a slow, long whistle. "So that's it, is it?"

"Aye, that's it."

With a jerk, Art pulled his clothing from Griffith's grasp. "Ye have to take extra care with a virgin. Did ye take extra care?"

Griffith laughed bitterly and leaned against the windowsill to look out. "I took extra care, aye. For all the wrong reasons, but I took extra care."

Art opened the cupboard and pulled Griffith's clothes out into a pile. "Where do we start looking for her?"

"I don't know. Look!" He picked up her dress. "She left everything behind. Look!" He gestured toward the fireplace. "Even her sword."

Art rescued the blade from its place in the wood chips. After wiping it with a rag, he leaned it against the fireplace stone. "She might come back for it," he said.

Griffith stomped to the ladder which led to the loft and shook, calling in English, "Cecily, get down here. Get down at once!"

Cecily's blond head appeared in the hole in the ceiling, proving she'd been listening, and Griffith knew with grim satisfaction that she hadn't understood a word of the complex Welsh language. He pointed to the place in front of him, and she climbed down hastily.

"My lord?"

"When did your lady leave?"

She blinked. "Is she gone?"

In Welsh Art said, "Aye, and ye know it, ye strumpet."

She glanced at him, but he was stuffing clothes into the saddlebags and didn't look up.

"I might have heard her in the middle of the night," she admitted.

Griffith's hand itched to slap her. He didn't like silly little half-wits, especially half-wits who told a lie when the truth would serve. "Why didn't you stop her?"

She widened her blue eyes. "I thought I dreamed. My lady has never left me before."

"Hasn't she?" Griffith snapped. "Not ever?"

Those wide eyes slid away from his gaze. "Only once. Only because Lady Elizabeth had to go into exile and Lady Marian wouldn't let me go with them."

"Why?"

"Because she wanted me to find a husband at court."

"Nay." Griffith reined in his temper. "I mean, why did Lady Elizabeth go into exile?"

"Because of the rumors she was going to marry King Richard."

Art stopped packing.

"When did she go into exile?" Griffith asked.

"Two years ago. Well . . ." She blushed. "When Lady Marian bore Lionel, in fact."

Art started packing again.

As Griffith realized the implications, he wiped the sudden sweat from his brow. "So you heard Lady Marian leave in the middle of the night last night."

"I didn't hear anything," she said. "I didn't hear *anything.*"

"Heard too much," Art commented, again in Welsh.

Cecily turned on Art in a fury. "I don't know what you're saying about me, but it isn't true. I don't know where Lady Marian went, and I don't know when, and I don't know why. But I'll wager"—she drew herself up and glared at Griffith—"that somebody here knows."

Art scratched the gray stubble on his chin, and said, in English this time, "That might be true."

Emboldened, she turned on Griffith. "And if you've ruined Lady Marian again, Wenthaven will kill you both. Another baby will destroy his plans for her."

Art's Welsh phrases sounded lyrical, but what he said did not. "Ye've one of yer own in the oven, missy. Ye'll be high-bellied afore long, yerself."

Griffith glanced at Cecily's waist, then back at Art.

Art nodded. "I recognize the look. In another fortnight, everyone'll know."

Cecily flushed under their scrutiny, and her hand went to her stomach in a betraying gesture.

"So you don't know when she left," Griffith said to her. "Do you know where she would have gone?"

Sullen now, Cecily said, "Oh, she's probably hiding somewhere on the estate. She wouldn't leave unless she thought Lionel was in danger."

"And if she thought Lionel was in danger?"

"Then she'd go as far away from the danger as she could. Back to Lady Elizabeth, I guess," Cecily muttered.

Griffith jerked his thumb toward the door. "Go break your fast, and remember—don't tell anyone about Marian's disappearance."

Cecily scuttled out, and the men fell into their native Welsh.

"How long until the whole castle knows?" Art asked.

"Not long."

"Do ye think Marian lass is on the grounds?"

"Not likely."

"Do ye think she returned to Lady Elizabeth?"

Griffith slowly shook his head.

Art dropped his voice, not trusting even the protection of a foreign language. "Elizabeth is the mother, isn't she?"

"I suspect." Griffith started up the stairs. "Let's see if Marian left us any clues."


Sir Adrian Harbottle sat in the mercenaries' quarters, clutched his shoulder, and smiled the first smile he'd indulged in since meeting Marian in the woods. It was the first smile since Griffith had twisted his sword arm and the bone slipped its socket, rendering him useless, in pain, and without income.

Cledwyn smiled, too, for much the same reason and with much the same affability.

The bitch and her whelp were loose.

She'd slipped out in the first light, dressed in her men's clothing and leaving a trail any fool could track. Their first impulse had been to follow her at once and take their very pleasurable vengeance, but common sense had reasserted itself. She was too close to Castle Wenthaven. Worse, Griffith would take exception to her rape, and he'd proved himself lethal in ways both men understood.

So they destroyed her track, provided several quite acceptable false ones, and waited for the hue and cry to begin.

"We're going to enjoy this," Cledwyn said.

Harbottle smiled again. "Aye, we're going to really enjoy this."

Marian glanced around the woodland meadow and back up the track from whence she had come. Then she slid out of the saddle with Lionel tied in a sling before her. Before she could loosen the tie, Lionel struggled out, falling on his face. Before she could examine him for injuries, he was up and running across the spring grass.

"Don't go too far, Lionel," she called.

"Nay!"

She squinted against the sun, then removed the heaviest of the saddle pouches from the horse and put him out to graze.

Two years of waiting to hear Lionel's first word, and after only a day she was sick of hearing it. But she was too tired and too worried to demand obedience. He didn't like the deep shade. She knew that from her previous stops. So he would stay within sight.

Within sight. A dreadful phrase. Someone had been keeping *her* within sight. She fingered the well-honed eating knife she kept at her waist and touched the sword that hung from the saddle. She wished she had her own sword, but taking it had been impossible. It had rested among the wood chips in the lower room, much too close to Griffith. Instead she'd removed a sword from Wenthaven's extensive store of weapons.

If only she could use a sling or a bow, she'd feel more secure, both about her son's safety and about the precious treasure she had placed in a leather pouch and strapped to her leg. But she didn't need an arsenal, she comforted herself. She'd finally shaken her trackers loose from her trail.

At first, she'd been afraid it was Griffith. It could have been Griffith. She wouldn't have been surprised if it had been Griffith. And she didn't want to face Griffith. Not after last night. Not after the shared ecstasy and pain.

Then she'd realized Griffith wouldn't skulk behind her like a thief. He'd come tramping up and demand to know what she was doing. He'd be loud, indignant, and offended and insist she do what he commanded, but he wouldn't hurt her. He surely wouldn't hurt her, or Lionel.

That wasn't necessarily true of anybody else. So who *was* following her? Her father's henchmen? Or someone who wished her ill?

Sinking onto the ground beneath a tree, she uncorked her water jug. "Lionel, come and have a drink."

"Nay."

Pressing her hand to the hollow pit of her stomach, Marian sipped the water in hopes it would ease the ache therein. She was horribly frightened, for there were many people who might wish her ill.

Stupid, bullying Sir Adrian Harbottle.

King Henry Tudor.

And her father, the earl of Wenthaven.

Griffith's accusations of the night before had alarmed her. Was Wenthaven hiring mercenaries on Lionel's account? If he was, he was doing it without consulting her, and while she might wish to use Wenthaven in her plans, she wanted to be the one making the decisions. She wanted to be important again. She wanted to be in control.

Suddenly it seemed she'd lost that control. The falsehoods of which she had been warden now escaped her. They flew randomly through the kingdom, and she knew not where they landed or who possessed them.

And Griffith was right. Lionel was a royal child, and a royal child was an easy pawn for those who sought power.

So today she had doubled back and doubled back again: listening, watching, muffling Lionel's cries with her hand.

She had lost them. She was sure of it. Except . . . sometimes, she imagined she heard the soft shuffle of a footfall and the wheeze of a man's panting.

Her horse was good: well trained, strong enough to travel the dreadful English roads, swift enough to leave pursuit behind.

But she couldn't utilize his speed effectively, for she had to stop too often. Traveling with a rambunctious two-year-old strained the resources of her patience—and his, too, she supposed.

"Lionel," she called. "Look at the squirrel in that tree."

He looked up, clapped his hands, and, when the squirrel disappeared into the forest, cried, "Nay!"

He'd been limply, deeply asleep when she'd lifted him from Cecily's side and taken him to the stable. He hadn't stirred when she'd cajoled Billy into lowering the drawbridge and letting her go. But that had been the last of her peace.

He woke with the sun, prepared for a new day of exploration, and balked when he didn't get it. He didn't want to ride, he wanted to run. He didn't want to look at the trees, he wanted to touch them. He didn't want to eat dried meat, he wanted to eat dried mud.

He wanted down, and she had put him down less often than he wanted and more often than she liked. Torn between the frantic need to flee and her son's demands, Marian's frazzled resolution faltered.

Catching sight of a tall, four-legged, red creature with antlers, she called, "Lionel, look quick. There's a deer!"

Lionel spun around, looking everywhere but in the shadows.

"There," she said again, but the deer turned tail and vanished. "Ah, he's gone."

"Nay," Lionel said firmly.

Why had Henry sent Griffith? What did Henry know?

When he'd married Elizabeth, Marian had cowered, waiting for the denouncement. But the wedding night passed, apparently without incident. Couldn't Henry see? Was he so stupid he didn't know the difference between a virgin and a woman who'd been in childbed? Was he so befuddled with passion that he had not realized he'd been cheated? Or was he so desperate to retain the throne that he'd kept quiet and reproached Elizabeth in private?

"Lionel, don't eat the bugs."

He looked up from his meal of cricket, antenna waving from between his lips. "Nay!"

She stood up and moved toward him. "Yech. Spit it out."

"Nayoo!"

The cricket took advantage of Lionel's opened mouth to hop out, distracting Lionel and saving Marian from a tantrum. She offered bread in lieu of bugs, and he accepted, though grudgingly.

She watched the play of light on his dark hair and thought how much he looked like his father, how little like his mother. She thought how much she wanted for him and how difficult it would be to get it for him. She thought how alive he was now, and how likely he wouldn't see his third birthday. And she knew she would defend his life with her own, for despite what Griffith said, he was her son. The son of her heart.

Griffith. He knew too much now. He thought he knew everything, but he didn't. No one knew everything except Elizabeth—and her. The others who had known were dead. All dead.

Why hadn't he told her sooner that Henry had sent him to watch over her and Lionel?

Maybe because he hadn't had the time or the place. Maybe because he'd been so annoyed with a mission he perceived as inconsequential. Maybe because she'd annoyed him so much.

But she hadn't only annoyed him. She'd challenged him, mocked him, laughed at him. It had been a dreadful, backward flirtation, born of . . . what? Springtime and flowers? Need and passion? Or the simple recognition of one lost soul by another?

His seduction had struck at that wretched conceit she'd harbored, the conviction she would do nothing to jeopardize Lionel's safety. That had made his betrayal strike all the deeper. He'd been sent to spy on her—or worse, he'd been awaiting the order from Henry. The order to assassinate her child.

What had he said?

That she must rely on his protection, for Lionel's safety depended on it. What did that mean? Did that mean he would protect Lionel if she cooperated with him? If she bribed him, if she slept with him? Was that what he meant? How long would he be satisfied with such a bargain? Until he tired of her? Until Lionel annoyed him? Until Henry sent word Lionel should be killed?

Damn him and his rugged face and his muscled body. He had masqueraded as a dread warrior, then he'd proved to have the heart of a poet and the mind of a scholar. He had lulled her into trusting him, then he'd proved to be deceit personified.

If she had understood how their minds meshed, she would have been prepared. She would have been resistant. She wouldn't have fallen in his bed like some round-heeled draggle-tail paid twice the normal fee.

Could something that wonderful be so disastrous? Could a man who punished with pleasure be all bad? Could she have misjudged him so badly?

Suddenly she lifted her head and glanced around. Could Lionel have gone so far in so short a time?

"Lionel?" He didn't answer. "Lionel?"

She listened, but she couldn't hear him. He was hiding from her. 'Twas a game they played in less stressful times, but now it brought her to her feet. In a singsong, laughing voice, she called, "Where's Lionel?"

A giggle answered her, and she relaxed. He wasn't lost. He wasn't kidnapped. Now she had to pick him up and put him on the horse once more for another bone-jarring, weary ride.

"Lionel?" She stalked her son. "Where's Lionel? Where's Lionel?" With each giggle, she got closer. At the last moment, he broke cover and ran—right into a stream. "Oh, Lionel," she exclaimed, chasing after him. The water topped her boots, soaking her hose. He stumbled and fell. She swooped him up, wetting her sleeves and the hem of her coat, and dragged him onto the bank. "You're all wet," she lamented, holding the dripping child out straight. "I hope you don't get sick. Oh, Lionel."

Too much. This was all too much. She held back tears as she changed him, emptied her boots, squeezed out her sleeves.

Bright, cheerful, and phony, she chirped, "Time to go, Lionel."

"Nay."

She wrestled with him. "Mama put you in the sling—"

"Nay!"

"—and climb on the horse—"

"Lionel no go," he said clearly.

She faltered. Yesterday he'd said his first word. Today he'd said his first sentence. She spared a thought for Griffith's mother, who had complained of Griffith's sudden eloquence, and for Griffith, who had promised her Lionel would speak. And she wished the man she had thought Griffith to be were there, for the birds had stopped singing and once more she heard the faint echo of a stranger's footstep.

# 9

"*My arse is tired* of sitting on this horse. We've searched half of Lancaster in the last two days, and for naught." Art waved at the threatening forest around them. "All we've found is tracks that lead nowhere. No one's seen Lady Marian, and if ye want my opinion, we've been duped. She probably *is* still at Castle Wenthaven, hiding in a comfortable room with a bed."

Griffith grunted. "Perhaps. But I would have sworn she would run like a flushed deer. Think you someone else is playing us false?"

"Someone has her, ye mean, and is laughing through his socks as we make fools of ourselves searching?" Art rubbed the aforementioned posterior. "'Tis possible. I'm starting to think 'tis probable."

Turning his horse toward Castle Wenthaven, Griffith said, "Let us go back, and try flushing our game another way."

Art followed willingly, tired and showing his age, and Griffith resolved to wring Marian's neck when he caught up with her. If he caught up with her. If she were well. Could it be normal to wish to embrace and punish all at the same time? Or was it simply another of the ways Marian had discovered to undermine his control?

He'd ask her when he found her. If he found her.

"Do you still have the letter from Elizabeth?" he asked.

"Ye're worried about that letter, aren't ye?" Art patted the pouch that hung at his side under his jacket. "Aye, I've still got it. It says nothing seditious?"

"'Tis a plain, loving letter from a lady to her friend in exile. It says nothing . . . unless one knows what to look for." Griffith ducked beneath a branch and surveyed the area. They weren't far from the road. Before the afternoon ended, they'd be among the discontents and misfits of Castle Wenthaven. They'd be searching for Marian with stealth, and their every word would be monitored. Art, with his devious turn of mind, might shed a new light on the contents of Elizabeth's letter—a light Griffith couldn't see for his involvement.

Slowing his horse, Griffith pulled alongside Art and, drawing from his formidable memory, recited:

*From the Lady Elizabeth to her dearest Sister of the Heart, Lady Marian. I greet you well and send you God's Blessing and mine, asking most tenderly about your child, Lionel. I pray this finds him in good health and sturdy, and pray also for a long and varied report of his boyish and learned behavior. I find much comfort in your tales of his bright wit and charm, knowing full well that my son, Arthur, must soon follow along the footpaths Lionel now treads. I would that they could be together and much mourn your absence and miss the comfort you would bring me. Arthur fills the hole in my heart I believed burned away when my brothers disap-*

*peared and all around me betrayed my trust. All
except you, dear Sister.*

*Therefore I must tell you of my dear Lord
Husband, the King. He often speaks of you kindly,
although he's never met you, and is most generous
and encourages me to send money to you, for he's
beholden for the support you gave me during my
most trying times. In memory of those days, please
take this purse and use it as needed for the support
of your dear son; my godson and the child of
whom I think and pray every day.*

"The poor lady," Art said, his sympathies easily
aroused. "She's torn in her loyalties, and trying to
warn Lady Marian not to upset the fishcart or it'll
cause a terrible stink."

"Do you really think that's what she's saying?" A
great weight lifted off Griffith's mind. "Because that's
what I thought she was saying, but at times I've been
known to misconstrue a woman's true meaning."

"Ye're the only man in the world to do that."

"And with Marian, I've made mistakes."

"If ye hadn't told me, I'd have never known."

"But if you think that's what the lady Elizabeth
was saying . . ." He observed Art's smirk. "Arthur,
are you making a jest of me?"

"Nay, my lord, why would I do that? I wouldn't
dream"—Art ducked when Griffith swung his riding
gloves—"of making a jest of a respected warrior such
as yerself. Why, when I think of the wisdom contained within yer smallest finger"—he ducked again,
cackling—"I couldn't imagine sitting in judgment . . .
in judgment . . ."

His voice faded as he lifted a hand and tilted his
head in a listening attitude. Griffith, too, halted in
midswing and heard the sound of a man running. He
urged his horse onto the main road to see Marian's
guard from Wenthaven round the curve toward him.

Billy lifted his gaze from the ground just before he reached them and skidded to a stop. "M'lord." He put his hands on his knees and panted, trying to get enough air to speak. "If it pleases ye . . . I have news o' th' lady Marian."

Griffith and Art exchanged glances, then Art handed Billy a water jug. Billy drank greedily and poured the rest over his head, and when Griffith judged Billy could speak, he commanded, "Tell us."

"She left two mornin's ago."

"How do ye know?" Art snapped.

"I let her an' th' sleepin' babe out o' th' gate meself." At Art's indignant outcry, Billy defended himself. "She's th' lady, an' she'll do what she wants, an' I thought 'twould be better if I did it than some other one who'd see th' chance t' do her ill. Good thing I did, too, 'cause I wasn't th' only one what saw her leave."

Griffith straightened in his saddle. "Has she been captured?"

"Nay, m'lord. Th' last I saw her, she was fine. I stood guard, ye see, after I let her go. That mercenary captain knows too much what goes on at Wenthaven, an' his men are always a-pokin' their noses where they don't belong, an' I don't trust any o' them. An' first thing I know, there's that Cledwyn, observin' her. Then that Harbottle joins, an' they go a-followin' m'lady, an' they don't realize I'm a-followin' them."

"Good man," Griffith said.

"'Tis me duty," Billy answered. "Besides, I don't much like all these foreigners comin' t' Shropshire wi' their strange languages an' such. Beggin' yer pardon, m'lord."

Griffith well remembered Billy's challenge the night he walked Marian home and inquired curiously, "You mistrust Cledwyn and Harbottle, but not me?"

"'Tis a hard choice fer a simple man like me, m'lord, but"—Billy straightened and stared at Griffith with accusing eyes—"there's no one else at Wenthaven what cares about her. Ye care . . . although I don't like why ye care. Sniffin' around her like one o' Lord Wenthaven's spaniel studs wi' a bitch."

"This stud'll do right by her," Art said.

The testimonial left Griffith unimpressed, but Billy eyed Griffith with much the same consideration as he would a prize spaniel. "Aye, I'm thinkin' his intentions are good even if he's thinkin' o' dippin' his wick."

Annoyed with the men who should behave as his servants, Griffith spoke through his teeth. "I'm going to wed the lady."

Like a lazy wind clearing a cloudy sky, relief eased Billy's furrowed brow. "'Tis good. She's not as worldly as she would have ye believe. Ye keep her busy wi' th' babes, one a year, an' she'll not have so much time t' gallop about seekin' trouble."

"That I will."

Griffith gave his pledge solemnly, as if Billy were her father, and Billy accepted it just as solemnly.

"So where is she?" Art demanded.

Billy shuffled the dirt with his feet, looking worried and uncomfortable. "I can't tell ye exactly where she is right now. I had t' come an' get ye, ye ken." He brightened. "But I can tell ye where t' start lookin' fer her. Cledwyn an' Harbottle followed her south fer most o' th' mornin'—an' me after them—an' she finally turns west, toward Wales, an' keeps a steady line straight into that pagan country—beggin' yer pardon—an' th' two eel-skinners satisfy themselves that's where she's a-goin' an' turn back."

"Into Wales?" Art was incredulous. "Why would she go into Wales? She doesn't speak the language, and Wales is our home. To go to Wales would place her in our power."

"If ye catch up wi' her," Billy reminded him.

Griffith stroked the two-day growth of beard that covered his upper lip and chin. "Madness, but a sensible madness. She thinks we would never look for her there—and we wouldn't, without Billy's information. It keeps her well out of Henry's grasp, and to disappear so completely within England, one must travel north to the Lake Country. That's a fair ride."

"Ye think she went to—" Art sighed and confessed to Griffith, "Ye're not the only one who doesn't understand women. The men in Wales are not these mealy-mouthed, contemptuous lizards who live to bask in the sun—like the men of England."

Griffith smothered a grin. Art was getting his own back.

Art continued, "They're warriors, and live to kill the English."

"That's not what you told her," Griffith reminded him. "Remember? The night she left, you wove her some lyrical tale of a beautiful Wales whose welcoming people would take her to their bosoms."

Art's horror was genuine. "Billy, are ye sure? We tracked her south."

"Cledwyn an' Harbottle camouflaged her trail several times, not wantin' anyone else t' know where she was a-goin'."

"And created the false trails, I trow," Art marveled. "Ye got to admire those sly dickweeds."

"I do?" Griffith was furious he'd not thought to check Cledwyn's whereabouts before he left Wenthaven, and even more furious he'd not killed Harbottle when he'd had the chance. "They're going to be worm food."

Billy approved. "That's th' spirit, m'lord. I followed Lady Marian fer two days, an' she's definitely in Wales, but movin' slow 'cause o' th' child. Let me take ye t' th' last place I saw them, an' we'll go from there."

"Take us to the last place you saw Lady Marian, and Art and I will go from there." Griffith leaned out of the saddle to get closer to Billy. "You will go back to Wenthaven. Perhaps there are some obstacles to be placed in the path of Cledwyn and Harbottle."

A grin inched across Billy's wide face. "Aye, perhaps there are. Perhaps there are."

"Ah. Billy." Wenthaven smiled at the guard who hovered in the doorway of his bedchamber, patting Honey's head when she growled and giving her the command to cease. "Billy, come in, and welcome."

Wenthaven ignored the uneasy servant as he shuffled, inch by inch, into the room. He ignored the dirt Billy shed on the fine rug and the way Billy breathed through his mouth in noisy, moist exhalations. Instead Wenthaven poured two hearty cups of ale, called the spaniel to heel, and strode to the cushioned chair he called his own. "Come and sit down, Billy, and let us drink together."

"M'lord." Only new serving maidens sounded so shy and embarrassed. "I can't drink wi' ye."

"But why?"

"'Twouldn't be proper."

Wenthaven chuckled indulgently and sank onto the chair, Honey at his feet. "I think I'm in the position to decide what's proper, don't you? After all, if I choose to have an ale with one of my oldest and most trusted men-at-arms, who's to say me nay?"

Billy mumbled an inarticulate reply.

"Now, come and sit here"—with his shoe, Wenthaven scooted his cushioned footstool close— "and we'll talk."

He ignored Billy's groan, smiling with fixed goodwill until Billy crept forward and lowered his bulk onto the low stool.

"Are you comfortable, Billy?"

Clearly Billy wasn't, but he nodded.

"Here's your ale, Billy."

Billy took it with a hand that shook visibly.

"Now, Billy, how long have you been one of my men?"

"Ah . . ." The cup clattered against Billy's teeth when he tried to drink. "Ah . . . in years?"

Wenthaven closed his eyes in pain.

He missed Marian. He missed having someone with whom he could match wits. He missed having one person out of all the fools around him who wasn't incredibly stupid. Opening his eyes, he watched as Honey rose and began sniffing as if she'd picked up a scent. To Billy he said, "That would be fine."

"Ah . . . I came into th' troop when I was about eleven, m'lord, an' now I'm . . ." Billy squinted as he tried to cipher. "Ah, I guess, I'm thirty-two . . . ah, nigh onto sixteen years, I think, m'lord."

The earl almost sagged on his chair. Stupid, stupid, stupid. "That's fine, Billy." Honey reached the drapes that hung in folds against the wall and snuffled more loudly. "And how often have you left Wenthaven in those sixteen years?"

"Never! That is"—Billy squirmed as he realized the direction of Wenthaven's interrogation—"just two days."

"Yesterday and the day before?" Honey stuck her head under the curtain and wagged her tail.

"Ah . . . aye, I suppose ye'd say that."

"Drink your ale, Billy. I hate to see you so uncomfortable, you make me feel an unworthy host." Curious and suspicious, Wenthaven walked to the drapes. "You're shivering. Does the breeze bother you? Would you like me to arrange the curtains to block it?"

The drapes swayed, the dog leaped back, and Wenthaven almost laughed aloud as he realized what was happening.

"Nay, m'lord, I'm quite warm," Billy said. "I'm not cold, truly."

Wenthaven tapped the drape with his fingers, then

nodded. "As you say. I'll not open the drape . . . yet. Come, Honey." He returned to his chair. "Is the pillow soft enough?"

Billy blurted, "Aye, m'lord, my arse has never been so at ease."

"That's wonderful, Billy. Wonderful. 'Tis almost like we're old friends, then."

"Aye . . . er . . . nay, that is . . . m'lord, I left fer good reason."

"Do you"—Wenthaven examined his nails—"want to tell me about it?"

"I went t' protect yer daughter," Billy said stoutly.

"She left quite early one morning, I understand?"

Billy's face was a study of confusion and distrust. "Aye, m'lord, but who told ye?"

The way Billy demanded to know, quite as if it were his right, made Wenthaven smile. Marian had learned the lessons he'd taught her—she'd bound this oaf to her with chains of kindness, and Billy had proved a good servant. In reply, Wenthaven said, "There have been several unexplained absences lately, and I could not restrain my curiosity. I called young Harbottle in—are you acquainted with Harbottle?"

"He ain't worth scrapin' off th' bottom o' me boot."

Unwillingly delighted, Wenthaven said, "I see you *are* acquainted with Harbottle. When I spoke to him, he seemed to have met with an accident. One which pulled his shoulder free from its socket. One called Sir Griffith ap Powel."

Billy had relaxed enough to admit, "Now he's a good man."

"Do you know him, also?" Wenthaven asked in feigned surprise. "For he disappeared at about the same time as my daughter."

Billy's forehead furrowed as he tried to think. Too obviously, he didn't trust Wenthaven. Just as obviously, he didn't wish to betray Marian or Griffith.

"Sir Griffith was sent to my humble abode by King Henry himself."

Billy brightened, clearly impressed.

"But I don't know why the king sent Sir Griffith, and it worries me." Wenthaven placed the back of his hand to his forehead. "Could Sir Griffith's mission be less than honorable?"

"Nay," Billy said, sure of himself. "Sir Griffith is as dedicated t' Lady Marian's safety as ye an' . . . as I am."

"Very interesting. And how do you know this?"

"Because he gave me his pledge."

A chill swept Wenthaven, and he leaned forward. "His pledge?"

"He pledged himself t' marry Lady Marian."

Billy faltered in the face of Wenthaven's wrath, but Wenthaven couldn't control himself. "To marry Lady Marian?" His voice rose. "He pledged he would marry my daughter?"

"Aye, an' give her a babe a year t' keep her busy an' safe."

Then he shrank back, raising his hand in reflexive defense, but Wenthaven never thought of striking him. It was not Billy with whom he was angry. It was Sir Griffith, for daring to imagine he could wed the earl of Wenthaven's daughter. And it was Marian, that round-heeled slut, for not accepting her place in his plans.

She was his daughter, damn it. He thought she'd failed him when she brought home a bastard, but she'd refused to apologize or explain, and when Wenthaven had mastered his anger, he saw why.

Her son—what was his name?—Lionel? Lionel looked just like the York family. Just like Richard, king of England.

Royal bastards weren't worth much, of course, especially the children of a deposed king, but Wenthaven had his suspicions about the circumstances of the birth. And after all, what if he were wrong? What could he lose? He was one of the dowager queen's

Woodville relatives, and as Henry became more secure on the throne, so had he become less interested in retaining Wenthaven's—and any other Woodville's—goodwill. Wenthaven could see his position eroding with each day of Henry's reign, and his oath to Henry couldn't compete with his youthful resolution to become a power in England.

So he was grateful to Marian. She'd brought him a royal child to manipulate. Maybe she hadn't meant to, and maybe she didn't want him to, but he was her father and he knew what was best.

He had comforted himself with an insight into her character. She hated being so far from the court. She wanted the best for her son. He knew she'd appreciate his efforts when they came to fruition, so he'd waited and planned for the proper moment. And now the proper moment was at hand, but Marian had escaped—into the arms of a minor Welsh knight who imagined himself good enough to be her husband.

Wenthaven clutched the clothing over his stomach. God rot her, Marian had brought a fire to his gut no amount of wine could quench. And look at her champion, Billy. He'd fled to the other end of the room and was eyeing the exit longingly.

There were those who had told Wenthaven he looked quite diabolical when he lost his temper, but too much was at stake to lose it now. His task, as he saw it, was to ease his way into Billy's confidence— not easily done, for Billy had been witness to too many years of fatherly neglect. But everyone could be molded under the correct pressure, and Wenthaven had to find the way to mold Billy.

How could he convince Billy he wanted only Marian's safety? He could intimidate Billy into telling the truth about Marian's whereabouts and Griffith's role in her disappearance, but he couldn't force Billy to do anything to harm Marian or her son. Calming himself, he called, "Honey. Here, girl."

The dog sat up and wagged her tail in delight. When Wenthaven patted his lap, she leaped into it as if she trusted him with her life.

Which she did. This dog, loving, loyal, anxious to please, had never failed him, nor had he failed her. She worshiped him, and he was well aware of the contrast her golden coat made against the rich cloth of his doublet. He was more aware of Billy's reaction, a reaction Wenthaven anticipated.

No man so beloved by a dog could be all bad. No man who cared for his pet could purposely hurt his daughter. Wenthaven knew, without looking, that with each stroke of his finger through the spaniel's hair, Billy relaxed more and more. When he thought the treatment successful, he glanced up casually. "Billy, bring us that loaf of bread and the cheese. We need to replenish ourselves while you tell me how Sir Griffith came to give you this pledge."

Weighing every word before he spoke, Billy told him, "He was trackin' Lady Marian, just like I was, an' I wouldn't let him go alone unless he gave it. Last I seen him, he was a-followin' her int' Wales."

"Into Wales?" True surprise colored Wenthaven's tone. "What made her go into Wales?"

"Sir Griffith claims she didn't think he'd follow her there. I think"—Billy tapped his forehead with one beefy finger—"she was just runnin' in a panic."

"Why would she be panicked?"

"Don't know."

"She spent the night in Sir Griffith's bedroom."

Billy shook his head.

"Didn't she tell you that? And I'll warrant Sir Griffith didn't." Billy was off balance, no longer so sure in his judgment of Griffith, Wenthaven noticed, and he congratulated himself on a successful attack. "So we discuss Lady Marian's safe return."

"Her safe return?"

"Of course." Wenthaven scratched behind Honey's ears. "Lady Marian has to come back."

Billy fumbled among the foodstuffs kept always on the table. "Not if she's goin' t' wed Sir Griffith."

"Billy, we're not discussing a peasant girl. We're discussing the earl of Wenthaven's daughter. If Sir Griffith wants to marry her—and I don't doubt he does—he'll do it, but rest assured, he's not doing it out of affection. Marriage to Lady Marian Wenthaven is a rich plum. His family will want to know the extent of her dowry, and I'll want to know what dower they will provide in case she's widowed. There will be contracts to discuss, lists of the linens and clothing she will bring. Lady Marian will come back, for there's lands and money to be transferred."

Shuffling back to him, Billy kept his gaze on the loaf and cheese in his hands. "Sir Griffith ain't marryin' her fer her money."

"Perhaps not. Would you cut the bread? I hate to dislodge my dog when she's so comfortable. But Powel won't reject the money, either. My money is going to Wales. I can scarcely credit it."

"That bothered me, too. Not yer money, but that Sir Griffith is Welsh." Using the knife from his belt, Billy cut a chunk of bread and handed it over. "Think ye he's a savage?"

"I wouldn't want to meet him on the battlefield, if that's what you mean, but I doubt he'll hurt Lady Marian." Wenthaven fed Honey a crust. "Not seriously." He glanced up and met Billy's horrified gaze. "But then there's Harbottle . . . I threw him out, incidentally."

"Good fer ye, m'lord," Billy said warmly.

"Aye, he was a bad piece, but Griffith showed true savagery—and a great deal of subtlety—when he pulled the bone of Harbottle's sword arm free of its socket." Wenthaven bit into the bread and chewed meditatively. "Did Lady Marian have any broken bones the morning you helped her leave?"

"N-nay," Billy stammered. "Nor any bruises, either, but 'twas dark an' I couldn't see."

"Mm. Well, she probably ran away from Griffith in silly, maidenly embarrassment. She's not a maiden, of course, but 'tis possible." The bread and rich cheese eased the knot in Wenthaven's stomach, and the result of his campaign to discredit Griffith seemed only too successful. Relaxing back into the cushions, he began once more to plan. "I wish I could believe she's a willing bride. I wish I could help her if she escapes the Powel fortress. But there's no way I could ask a good Englishman to patrol in foreign territory, just so I'd be at ease about my daughter."

Billy lifted his hand, but Wenthaven waved it aside.

"Nay, Billy, let me think." He broke off a chunk of cheese for Honey. "I have the Welsh mercenaries, and they'd blend into the countryside, but in sooth, I don't trust them. They'd take their pleasure of Lady Marian before they returned her, and demand their payment, too."

"I beg ye, m'lord—"

"If there were some way . . ."

Wenthaven took a large bite, filling his mouth so much he couldn't speak, and Billy burst out, "But m'lord, there is a way. Put me in command o' th' mercenaries!"

Wenthaven gulped down the cheese and cleared his throat. Looking into Billy's shining eyes, he said, "You can't command all those mercenaries. And who'll take care of Wenthaven's defense? You can't leave Wenthaven empty of its men-at-arms."

"Ye've English men-at-arms," Billy replied. "Ready an' willin' t' defend Wenthaven. But if ye've got t' keep th' Welshmen, then give me three men. Three men, an' I'll get Lady Marian out o' Wales."

"God save us, you might just have an idea," Wenthaven said. He nudged the dog to the floor and bent over to pet her, hiding his face for fear his triumph would show. "Why, I'd be willing to give you five men. Take five of the mercenaries. They'll get you through Wales, and you'll bring Lady Marian home to me."

Billy moaned, so slightly Wenthaven almost didn't hear it. "But what if she wants t' marry Sir Griffith? I woulda swore he was an honorable man."

"There are many honorable men who don't treat their women well," Wenthaven said, and Billy agreed. "But although I had greater plans for her, if she wishes to wed Sir Griffith, I'll give her my blessing and her dowry, and call the Welsh my dearest kin."

Billy looked rather ill at the suggestion of Welsh relatives, but he rose, satisfied. "I'll pick out me men—"

"Take Cledwyn," Wenthaven ordered.

"He's not trustworthy."

"He's the mercenary commander, and he speaks both Welsh and English. You must take him."

Billy wrestled with that, but in the end he couldn't think of an alternative. "As ye say, m'lord, but I'll keep an eye on him."

"I would." As Billy moved toward the door, Wenthaven murmured, "And he will keep an eye on you."

Billy halted. "M'lord?"

"Billy, my thanks. You've relieved my worry." Wenthaven waved him out the door with a smile and leaned down to Honey once more.

When he was sure the guard was out of hearing, he walked to the window and flung out the dregs of the ale. At the table, he poured two cups of wine, then lifted one and strolled to the drapes against the wall. With a mighty thrust of his arm, he flung back the curtains. "Come out and drink with me, dear one," he said. "And never think you can spy on your master."

# 10

"*Marian lass is in there?*" Art eyed the wretched hut as the wind and rain battered it. "Here?" He looked around the miserable hamlet in the Welsh mountains of Clwyd.

"It boggles the mind, does it not?" How Marian had come so far alone, and why she'd stopped, Griffith did not understand. The inhabitants of the village had denied her presence at first, but a shiny coin tossed to one of the children elicited a nod at the hovel at the edge of the village. Now, sullen at being deprived of their wealthy boarder, the villagers huddled in their doorways and watched through the gale that swept down the west side of the valley.

"Why didn't she stay with the reverend brothers?" Art demanded. "At least she'd have been safe and warm."

"And been easy to find," Griffith added. It was a cold comfort to discover he understood her so well and even half sympathized with her need for flight. Except that she fled from him.

Art unknowingly fanned the flames of his ire. "She'll snap at ye when ye try to remove her."

Drenched with a combination of rain and sleet, Griffith mocked, "Why, Art, do you mean you think she'd remain here rather than come with me to a place that's warm and"—he lifted the soggy corner of his cloak—"dry?"

"She's a spirited one." Art swept a glance over Griffith. "That's probably why ye look like a warrior about to break a siege. Are ye going to sweep in like a thunder cloud or trample in like a stone giant?"

Griffith glared and started forward.

"A stone giant, then," Art said with satisfaction.

Griffith thrust open the pitifully small door.

"And a thunder cloud," Art observed.

Bending down, Griffith stepped inside. A peat fire burned in the middle of the floor, emitting billows of smoke that swirled in the inescapable draft. The only furniture was a bench and a bed. Marian didn't need to worry about spies in this hovel. Chunks of wall had fallen to the dirt floor, leaving holes no man could hide behind.

But the wind and rain blew through, and Griffith blinked, his eyes irritated by the smoke. Marian huddled in a blanket on the tiny frame bed with her eyes closed. Beside her, Lionel piled sticks and bits of wood together. Glancing up, Lionel saw Griffith, gave a screech of joy, and scattered his blocks with a kick of excitement. "Griffith," he said.

"Nay, sweeting," Marian whispered hoarsely, not opening her eyes. "No Griffith."

Griffith had come in prepared to roar, to fight, to use his strength unfairly—and found himself uncertain. Why did she lie so still? Why hadn't she opened her eyes when the door blasted open? He walked to her bedside and squatted beside mother and child. Lionel extended his arms, and Griffith hugged him. "I'm here, Marian."

Her eyelids fluttered open. Recognition dawned, and with it a flash of joy—then a flash of fear. She struggled to sit up. Her mouth moved—"Griffith"—but no sound came out.

He would have laughed at the irony of it, but her hectic flush and desperate gaze told him the truth of it. She was sick, so sick she could scarcely speak, so sick he feared for her life.

She collapsed back on the bed, too weak to stay erect. She tried to reach for Lionel, but her arms were too heavy and fell to her sides. Her eyes filled with tears at her helplessness, and he ached with sympathy and distress. After removing his cloak and pushing up his sleeves, he pressed his hand on her forehead. The heat of it made him wince and summon Art with a jerk of his head.

Art dragged his feet, as Griffith knew he would. Art had the courage of a lion coupled with the compassion of a monk. He didn't fear death for himself, but he feared it for those he loved, and he already loved Marian. Looking down at her with tear-filled eyes, he whispered, "Is it the fever?"

"Arthur," Griffith rebuked. "Do not mourn the living."

Marian's hand snaked out from under the blanket and took Art's palsied fingers. She pressed it to her mouth and kissed it, croaking, "Art. My son . . . shield him . . . keep safe."

It was a plea, an effort made with the last of her strength. Looking every day of his sixty years, Art vowed, "We're going to help ye."

"Lionel," she insisted, her thin hand clinging to Art's.

"We'll take care of him, lass."

"You." Her fear-filled gaze flashed to Griffith, then back to Art. "*You* swear."

Stunned, Griffith tumbled backward, his rump hitting the ground with a jarring thud.

She didn't trust him. She feared for her son's life with him.

No matter that he, too, had wondered at Henry's intentions. No matter that it was logical to assume he was an assassin sent by Henry. Damn it, she should trust him. He'd told her to trust him. He trusted her; he'd given her his seed.

Art comprehended her terror more slowly, but when he did, he protested, "Lass, Griffith would not—"

"Swear to her, Arthur."

Horrified, Art spread his hands in appeal. "But she thinks—"

"I know what she thinks." Griffith could almost taste his bitterness, his hurt. "Swear to her. Put her mind at rest."

With an uncharacteristic stammer, Art swore to protect Lionel with his life, against all peril, forever.

Marian's hand slid to rest on the mattress, and she looked with weak defiance at Griffith.

Keeping his gaze fastened to hers, Griffith instructed, "Art, you take the lad."

"Griffith, she's sick. She doesn't know what she says." Art leaned down and hoisted Lionel onto his back.

"Aye, she does. Go buy a cart."

"Ye'll not shout at her?"

"Nay, I'll not shout at her," Griffith replied with formidable patience. "And buy all the blankets in this godforsaken hamlet."

Art jiggled up and down, rocking Lionel into tranquillity, watching Griffith. "Ye've got a fierce temper."

"Do you not credit me with the strength to control it?"

What he saw seemed to satisfy Art, for he only warned, "These villagers are going to squeeze me for every coin."

"Tell them"—Griffith bared his teeth—"that if they're not reasonable, they'll have a fierce knight to deal with."

"Better than that. I'll tell them the lass has brought the fever to the village, and we're taking her away."

Griffith almost smiled at Art's back, but he found his mouth too stiff to bend into that simple curve of pleasure. Because of her. Because of his disappointment.

Coming to his knees beside the bed, he leaned over Marian. "Look at me," he demanded. *"Look* at me. See *me."* He deliberately filled her vision with himself: with his shoulders, his chest, his arms, and the face Art disdained and she had found desirable.

Her lower lip quivered and a few more tears welled in her eyes. But she pushed her face into the rough blanket to clear them and did as he instructed. Her gaze roamed the length and breadth of him like a wayfarer seeking shelter, and he waited until her explorations were through before he said, "I'm a warrior. A man bred to fight. If I wished, I could break Art's neck with one blow and take Lionel from him."

She could only mouth the words. "Not Art."

"Nay, I wouldn't hurt Art, and so you chose Lionel's champion well. But who will protect you?"

He could see her thinking. The process seemed to be a painful one and certainly was a long one. Then, with a questioning look, she indicated him.

He tapped his chest with his fingers. "Aye, I will care for you."

Again she considered him.

Why did she even have to consider? What did she imagine? That he would leave her here? That he would kill her on the trail? Or that he would neglect her illness until God took her and his conscience could be clear?

Did she realize how she slashed him with the knife of her distrust? He thought she did, but she was too weak to hide her true emotions. Still, he didn't know if he could ever forgive her.

Then she nodded acceptance, and the rock of his frustration began to crumble. But he had one more question. "Do you trust me to take care of you?"

Without hesitation she nodded and gave him a slight smile.

He almost groaned. When she looked at him like that, he feared he could forgive her anything. Grudgingly, because he didn't want her to know the extent of his softness, he said, "Well, that's some progress, then." He put the lie to his tough voice when he lifted her carefully and wrapped her shivering body close. "I'll build up the fire, feed you some hot broth, and get some strength in you." He rubbed his head against the mat of her hair and smiled at last. "Then I'll take you to my mother."

She had no strength to object, and during the journey, misery rendered her mute.

Dark and damp, fevered and frozen, awake and asleep. Wooden wheels hitting every hole in the road. Bones aching, head swollen, teeth chattering.

The cart stopped rolling and Marian opened her eyes, but it made no difference. She couldn't see. It was still dark and stuffy, and in some distant corner of her mind she wondered, had she died? Was she trapped in a coffin? Who would care for Lionel?

She stirred in agitation, waking the pain in her joints, and remembered—Art would care for Lionel. Art had sworn to care for Lionel, despite Griffith's displeasure, and Art would keep his vow.

And she couldn't be dead. She was too miserable to be dead.

Around her, at a distance, then close, there were voices, shouting in that strange language. That strange Welsh. Then, beside the cart, she heard, "Mother, I've brought you something."

Griffith. Had they come to Griffith's home? They

must have, yet he was speaking English. She had no time to worry about it, for a lively, pert voice replied, "Your laundry can wait."

Bellows of laughter greeted that, but Griffith answered, "'Tis the gift you've been asking me for these last ten years. A grandchild."

A grandchild? Marian stirred restively. What plot was this? How dare he introduce Lionel as his own? No wonder he had spoken in English. He wanted her to hear and understand. The laughter around the cart died, and the silence that followed spoke volumes.

Good. Griffith's people were as indignant as she was. She could hear nothing until Lionel piped up, "Griffith."

Art agreed, "Aye, lad, and this is Griffith's mama."

If only she could speak. She braced herself for his mother's rejection—and almost fainted when Griffith's mother betrayed nothing but approbation. "He's a beautiful lad, and heavy, too. How old is he?"

Griffith answered, pride in his tone, "He's not yet two years, but bright and active."

A male voice spoke, sounding much like Griffith. "Do you have something you need to confess, Griffith Rhys Vaughn Ednyfed Powel?"

"I'll tell you all, Da, but first . . ."

Marian braced herself, but nothing could prepare her for the impact of light when Griffith pulled back the rug. She flung her arm over her eyes, trying to block out the blinding rays.

She scarcely heard his mother's cry. "Saint Winifred's head, is she alive? Take the babe, Rhys." The cart dipped, then a hand smoothed Marian's cheek. The sweet voice scolded, "Griffith, you have no sense. This girl is ill, have you not eyes to see? You can't drag her across half of Wales as if she *were* your laundry. Dear girl—"

"Lady Marian," Griffith supplied.

"Lady Marian," his mother repeated, "I am

Angharad, mother of Griffith, wife of Rhys, daughter
of the line of that most ancient physician, Rhiwallon.
We are noted healers, and I will help you."

As she spoke, Marian slowly lowered her arm. The
cart was inside a high, beamed stable rich with the
scents of hay and livestock and rich with the sounds
of falcons at their roosts. The light was dim, not
bright, as she thought before, but still she squinted. A
ring of servants and stable hands surrounded the cart,
and a clump of men—Griffith, Art, and another man
as tall as Griffith—stood close by her shoulder. The
tall stranger held Lionel, so he was Rhys. But it was
Angharad who captured Marian's attention.

An old-fashioned white wimple wrapped the
woman's head all around, showing only her pink-and-
white face. Her round cheeks dimpled when she
smiled, and her creased face gave evidence that she
smiled often. Her eyes were a most unusual color—
light, golden, like Griffith's, but without the stern
control that straitened his soul. "Poor little thing,"
Angharad cooed, pressing Marian to her ample
bosom.

Maybe it was the smell of fresh-baked bread that
clung to her, maybe it was this unexpected acceptance, but Marian began to weep. Silent tears racked
her body and tore at her throat.

"Poor little thing," Angharad said again. "Griffith,
pick her up and take her into the keep at once."

Griffith leaned into the cart and lifted Marian out.
"Come," he commanded, as if she had a choice. The
agony of movement brought a new gush of tears, and
her head fell back against his shoulder. He sounded,
for the first time since Marian had met him, unsure.
"Mama?"

"I'll take care of her," Angharad said. "Art, throw
that wrap over her so she won't get wet. Rhys, bring
the baby."

A light woven blanket settled over Marian's head,

but she clawed it away. She didn't want her sight blocked or her breathing muffled. She wanted to see, to inhale fresh air. She caught a glimpse of Art's distressed face as he said, "It's the fever that makes her act so."

"Don't distress yourself, Art. She'll be well soon." Angharad tucked the blanket around Marian's neck. "Is that better?"

Griffith said, "I'll put her in my bedchamber."

"Are you wed?" Rhys asked.

"Not yet."

"Then there will be no shared bed in our house."

"As you say, Da."

"She's a widow?"

Rhys asked as if he had every right to interrogate Griffith, an attitude that shocked Marian. She had known Griffith only as a dictatorial knight, yet here was a man who demanded Griffith's respect—and received it.

"Nay, Da, she's not a widow."

Rhys shifted Lionel in his arms as if he'd suddenly found him too hot to hold. "She's not still married?"

"Not at all, Da," Griffith said solemnly. "She's as yet unwed."

In a display of either tact or insensitivity, Rhys nodded approvingly. "Good. I was wondering if we could expect to be besieged by some outraged husband."

"You can question Griffith later," Angharad said, making Marian wonder if Rhys's authority was indeed absolute. "Now we need to care for Lady Marian. Griffith, take her to your sleeping chamber."

"Wife . . ."

Rhys's voice sounded ominous, but Angharad seemed unaffected by it. "Griffith can sleep in the great hall with the servants."

Rhys groaned. "Little tyrant."

Angharad dimpled and curtsied to him, then

clasped her hands in her apron. "Saint Winifred's
head, I must start the maids to work on the chamber,
and the cook to preparing a proper dinner!" She ran
off, as light-footed as a true angel with wings.

Griffith watched after her with a smile that
brought a lump to Marian's throat, then he looked
down at her. "You lost your mother," he pledged, "so
I give you mine." Clasping Marian more tightly, he
started out the door.

A gentle rain sprinkled Marian's face, mingling
with the tears that dappled her cheeks, but she
blinked it all away and looked about her at Castle
Powel. The massive outer walls dwarfed the guards
who stood on them, and the four towers dwarfed the
walls. The keep, sturdy and gray, stood on a knoll
within the bailey, and Griffith climbed toward it. It
seemed to grow taller as they approached—intimidating, strong, unyielding—reminding her of something.

Griffith.

She wanted to huddle into his arms, and at the
same time she wanted to run away. This place had
cradled and formed Griffith into its likeness. Like
Griffith, it dealt harshly with its enemies yet protected those who sheltered in its shadow. If she chose
to yield to Griffith, she would be sheltered, too. Yet if
she did not, she would be battering herself against the
stone of his determination—uselessly, she suspected.

They stood before the great oak door and as it
swung open to swallow her, she struggled in blind
panic.

"Marian."

Griffith called her name, and she glanced up at
him wildly.

He knew what she feared. "In Wales, some practice the tradition of carrying the bride over the
threshold. 'Tis a remembrance of those days when
the bride was stolen from her family. Is there a similar tradition in England?"

She wanted to shout. She could scarcely whisper, "Cur. Louse."

He stopped her mouth with a swift kiss and passed into the keep. Climbing the stairs to the great hall, he paused to let her absorb the sight. "Your English King Edward built castles to subdue the wild Welsh rebels, and we built Castle Powel to fight him. We lost, of course. Castle Powel stayed in English hands until my lick-dog ancestor groveled before his new master."

Right behind him, Angharad gave him a push. "Upstairs to your room, Griffith. Lady Marian can hear the glorious Powel history when she's well. 'Tis a musty old keep, and nothing to brag about."

Marian understood Angharad's complaint. The keep showed its age in the lack of built-in comfort, but this had been compensated for with cushions, tapestries, and continuously burning fires. The chimneys scarcely smoked, the windows captured all the outdoor light to be had, and the servants performed their duties with a smile.

Art stepped up and pulled the now damp blanket off her. "Ye'll be good for Lady Angharad, won't ye?"

Marian hesitated, and his hands began to tremble.

"No matter what foul-tasting medicines she gives ye, ye'll swallow them, won't ye?"

She set her chin, and his one eye filled with tears.

"I never told ye, but ye remind me of my own eldest daughter. I couldn't bear to lose another such dear girl."

"Blackmail," she whispered, but she knew she'd lost. "I promise."

Art grinned, his tears dried as if by magic. "Ye do as Lady Angharad says and get well, and I—" he glanced uneasily at Griffith, but went on anyway as he took Lionel from Rhys—"I will take care of yer lad, just as I promised. Don't fret yerself about him."

"Nay." But she faltered, for how could she not fret about Lionel? "I'll not worry."

The room to which Griffith took her bustled with
the activity of many maids. They warmed the sheets,
fanned the new-laid fire, sprinkled savory herbs
among the clean reeds on the floor. A kettle of water
bubbled on the hearth, and Angharad said, "Good.
You brought my medicines."

The maids bobbed and smiled as Griffith laid
Marian on the sheets. Leaning over, he placed a fist
on either side of her head. *Croeso i Cymru.*
Welcome to Wales."

Had she been relieved to see him in that hut in the
mountains? If so, she didn't remember why. He was a
pushy, obnoxious man who thought too highly of his
lovemaking and the rights it gave him.

Agitated, she tried to push him away. Angharad
did it for her. "Leave her to me," the older woman
said.

"Let me stay and help," Griffith said. "I've cared
for her all the way to Powel—surely I can be of help
here."

"No!" Marian croaked.

Angharad glanced toward the door. "Rhys?"

Rhys stepped forward. "We have matters to discuss. If you would excuse us, Lady Marian. Lady
Marian . . . ?"

Responding to the implicit question, Griffith said,
"Lady Marian Wenthaven."

"Wenthaven?" Rhys said sharply. "From
Shropshire?"

Alarmed, Marian lifted her head.

"Aye, from Shropshire," Griffith replied. "But
why . . . ?"

Rhys placed a hand on Griffith's arm. "We must
talk now."

With a glance at the bed, Griffith followed his
father, shutting the door behind him.

He was pleased with this day's work. He'd been
half-frantic every time he'd looked at Marian's

cheeks, which were ruddy yet drawn with a wasting fever, and at her dull, anxious eyes. But it seemed as if his home had already begun working its magic on her.

Yet trouble had followed them, he guessed, and he turned to his father to ask, "Why do you know the name of Wenthaven?"

"An elderly beggar came to the gate only two nights ago, wrapped to his chin in rugs and cloaks and hobbling quite convincingly. We practice Christian charity, of course, and we brought him to the hearth to feed him." With a sideways glance at Griffith, Rhys added, "I was quite interested in this Englishman beggar."

"He was an Englishman?" Griffith straightened his shoulders. "Here?"

"Quite a long stretch out of the way for your normal beggar, I thought."

"Aye. Did he have an explanation for his direction?"

"Not at first. Not until he'd imbibed a large portion of a cask of wine. Then he complained of warmth, and threw off his wraps." Rhys smiled grimly. "Then he complained of a need, and tried to entice the maids. If he'd been sober, he'd have been good at it, I suspect."

"Handsome face? One hand?" With sinking heart, Griffith identified him. "Harbottle."

"Ah, you do know him. Recently of the household of Wenthaven in Shropshire, and recently the lover of the daughter of the house."

Griffith roared, "That miserable lying son of a decayed maggot! Where is he?"

"Follow me." As they walked to a chamber not far from Marian's, Rhys told him, "He's locked in here. He's served three meals a day and as much ale as he can drink. Your mother popped his shoulder back into place, and bound it. She nursed his wine ache, and the last I heard, two of the maids were visiting him of a night and nursing his stone ache. 'Tis as I suspected the first evening—he *is* a handsome brute."

"I'll cure him of that," Griffith vowed.

"Your gentle mother wouldn't approve of such violence to a prisoner," his father said. "She can no more resist a child or an invalid than she can resist your own smile, and you know she'll make Lady Marian well. By the same token, she made Harbottle well." He fitted a massive key into the hefty iron lock and pushed the oak door. It creaked open to reveal a fire, a cot, a bench, a table, and a tray of morsels to tempt a capricious appetite. With a weary gesture, Rhys indicated Sir Adrian Harbottle, bound by his roped ankle to the bed. "Her compassion knows no politics."

Harbottle's glance absorbed his hosts' menace, and he snarled like a wolf at bay. "Griffith ap Powel."

With a bow that mimicked the sweeping gesture of a courtier, Griffith said, "As soon as I heard we had a guest, I came to greet you. 'Tis such an honor to welcome the best swordsman in England." He stepped across the threshold of the tiny chamber. "Or is it the second best?"

Clutching his bound arm with his other hand, Harbottle proved his defense was less teeth and muscle than soft underbelly. "If you touch me, your mother will be angry."

"My mother is taking care of Lady Marian Wenthaven and is far beyond reach of your screams."

Marian's name brought a subtle change to Harbottle. "Lady Marian?" He seemed to savor the name. "She has arrived?"

Griffith's hands rose and clenched as if they were wrapped around Harbottle's corded neck.

Harbottle straightened. "Or are your words as false as your hospitality? Was she here all along?"

Rhys caught Griffith's arm and murmured,

"Steady, lad." Shutting the door behind him, he told Harbottle, "We came to share a civilized conversation with you, nothing more."

"You wanted to put me in the dungeon!" Harbottle accused. "You would have, too, but your lady wife wouldn't let you so treat an injured guest."

"And I'm known for the best hospitality in Cymru," Rhys marveled. "Consider the welcome you would receive elsewhere."

Paling, Harbottle muttered, "I wish I'd never come."

"Did Wenthaven send you?" Griffith demanded.

"Nay."

Harbottle clearly wanted to say more, but he restrained himself. For fear of Wenthaven? Griffith wondered. Most likely. The long arm of Wenthaven reached all the way into Castle Powel.

"Then why did you come to Wales?" Rhys urged. "'Tis a lengthy, chilly walk in the spring rain."

"I came to get what was promised me."

It was a sullen boast, but a boast nonetheless, and Griffith asked, "And what was that, pray tell?"

"He promised me Lady Marian for my bed."

Scornful of his claims, Griffith asked, "Why would the earl of Wenthaven promise you his only daughter? His heir?"

"For services rendered." Griffith and his father exchanged assessing glances, and to cover his slip, Harbottle added hastily, "Besides, 'twould not have been such an unseemly match."

"He's an earl, a rich and influential man. He could do better than you for Marian. If you're telling the truth"—Griffith suspected the opposite—"I wager you proved anxious to collect your reward before you performed the services, and he threw you out."

Harbottle's breath sounded harsh in the room, but he said nothing.

"What services," Griffith asked in fake conviviality, "did he ask you to perform?"

"Wouldn't you like to know?" Harbottle said with sulky defiance. At the look on Griffith's face, he cried, "Only to defeat her with the sword!"

"You tried that once."

"He was going to teach me the strikes she didn't know. We were to fight again."

"To kill her?"

"Nay, I . . ." Harbottle's voice trailed off. "Nay, he wouldn't . . . well, she's his daughter, after all. What use in goading me to kill her?"

"Is it her son, perhaps?" Rhys suggested, and Griffith hushed him with a gesture.

"Her son? Who's he?" Harbottle scoffed. "Nobody even knows who the father is." His blue eyes sharpened, and he stroked his strong jaw thoughtfully. "What father could be so important that Wenthaven planned to use . . . ?"

"Nonsense," Griffith said. "There must be another reason he wanted you to—"

"Swive her witless?" Taunting in his turn, Harbottle smiled directly into Griffith's face.

Taking a breath, Griffith struggled against the image Harbottle presented. "Marian has better taste."

"Better than me?" Harbottle stood, caught his foot against the rope, stumbled, and righted himself in one graceful swoop. "Look at me. I'm not some beastly Welsh barbarian who speaks an uncivilized tongue and lives in some dank, moldy castle far from the English court. I'm an English nobleman, sound of mind and limb."

"The least of the noblemen. The lowest of the high." Damn! Griffith wanted to beat that handsome, smirking face to a pulp, but he couldn't, so he taunted, "The best of the common folk stand well above you."

Rhys incited Harbottle with a soft assent. "Aye, better the head of an ass than the tail of a horse."

"Not true! I am a nobleman, and more trustworthy than any Welshman who ever trod the earth."

"Ah, he's bold for a man with his foot in a rope," Rhys said.

"Could be his neck." Griffith put his fists on his hips and grinned at the thought.

But his grin faded when Harbottle snarled, "I came to rescue Lady Marian."

Griffith was savage in his fury. "She stays with me."

"Because you force her to remain." Harbottle had found the chink in Griffith's armor, and he pounded at it. "How could she trust a foreigner, a man who serves the king she despises?"

"She does trust me, she just . . ."

Words failed Griffith, but not Harbottle. With glinting eyes and open smile, he advanced on Griffith. "At least I'd keep her under control with the back of my hand, and that whelp of hers could go to Lord Wenthaven. When I give her more brats, she'll forget her bastard. When I'm her husband, she'll advance me in court with her connections, keep her mouth shut about matters that don't concern her, and make me comfortable. That includes spreading her legs when and where I—"

Harbottle squeaked like a rat when Griffith's hands reached for his neck. Then a shrewd intelligence flashed across his face, and he slammed his fist into Griffith's stomach. Griffith doubled over in agony, scarcely hearing Harbottle crow, "I owed you that."

But he heard the shriek as Harbottle went flying under the impetus of his father's arm, and the thump as his head hit the wall. Gathering his strength, Griffith staggered back toward the door and stumbled out when Rhys opened it.

# 11

*Harbottle groaned* as the key grated in the lock.

God's teeth, how he'd enjoyed hitting Griffith. He could have hit him and kicked him until Griffith bled from every orifice. The satisfaction he'd experienced almost offset this suffering. Fingering his throbbing jaw, he stood up and peered into the full wash bowl.

He could just barely see his reflection, and he winced as he realized Rhys's fist had left a bruise. Cupping his hands, he plunged them into the icy water and dabbled the droplets on his face.

With any luck, he could contain the swelling—and the pain.

He hated pain. 'Twas the secret of his brilliant swordsmanship. He hated to be hurt.

Gingerly he touched the bump on the back of his head. Didn't those bullies know the rules governing the captivity of a noble hostage?

Of course, he wasn't a hostage, exactly. No one would pay money to have him released. But he'd been in tighter places—he'd just have to get himself out.

A slow grin spread across his face, and he studied it in the basin. What a handsome man. Good teeth, square jaw, beautiful hair, eyelashes most women would kill for. Aye, women would do a lot of things for a man of his looks. So he'd get himself released.

That was the easy part.

Deciding whom to take with him was not.

Marian? Aye, he wanted Marian, for a lot of reasons. Because she'd refused him once and taken Griffith. Because she was Wenthaven's daughter, and he spied a chance for revenge on the earl.

He wanted her badly. Was he ill? It raised his fever when he thought about her, and a shiver chilled his spine when he imagined making her repent of her boldness. He fantasized their final sword duel. She'd fight with all her skill and strength. He'd outslash her, and when at last he'd knocked her sword from her hand, he'd show her what the thrust of a real man's sword could do.

What worried him was his thought that he would marry her even if her father disinherited her. It might be worth it, to tame the vixen, but better that he should have it all: Marian, the position, and the money.

But he had to reconsider. He had to *think*.

That whiny little whelp of hers was the key. Marian had been at court when she'd conceived him, and it seemed that Griffith—and Wenthaven—considered the child important. And if Wenthaven considered him important, the whelp was worth having.

If he got himself released, and if he could lay hands on the boy, and if he could get away from the castle . . . well, then he could have Marian, and on his terms.

He smiled. A good incentive, and one well worth suffering for.

\*    \*    \*

Griffith, too, suffered as Rhys towed him into the master solar—suffered from his pain in the gut and suffered more beneath his father's disapproval.

Kicking the door shut, Rhys demanded, "Get out of those wet clothes, and while you do that, tell your loving father about this union with Lady Marian."

His father was furious, Griffith determined, and with reason. A man's wife was not his own business, but the business of his family. A man wed to increase the family's lands, wealth, and power.

Griffith had done that with his first wife, and their union had been satisfying. There had been no fights, for his wife had known her place. There had been no talk, for his wife hadn't comprehended politics or warfare. There had been hot meals on the table and a warm body in the bed—everything a man could desire.

A single moon ago he would have hooted with laughter had someone suggested he would seek his second wife without a thought beyond the swelling in his breeches.

But a moon ago he had not met Marian.

God, Marian. As inappropriate as any woman could be. Helplessly he began, "She's a fine woman. Gentle, demure—"

An abrupt gesture from Rhys cut him off, and Griffith remembered how intimidating his father could be.

"Stand before that fire and get out of your clothes."

Griffith did as he was told, as meekly as that small, disobedient boy had done so long ago. As he did, Rhys moved to the trunks lining the walls to pitch them open. With a total disregard for Angharad's organization, he flung clothing hither and yon until he'd compiled one complete, warm outfit. Holding it in his hands, out of reach, he demanded, "Now—try again, and tell the truth this time."

The truth? What truth? That Marian fought with swords and wore men's clothing? That when she recovered, she'd be as active and restless as her son? No, Griffith couldn't tell his father the truth. "Da, you'll like her when you get to know her." He rubbed the gooseflesh that rose from the chill of the air. "She's sweet and civil—" More gooseflesh rose, but this time Rhys's curled lip caused it and not any outer chill.

"Have you been in England so long you've forgotten honesty?"

Discomfit your opponent, and he will buckle. A good tactic, and one Griffith had used many times—but he had forgotten from whom he'd learned it. He couldn't help but beg, "Please, Da, my clothes."

His father snorted. "I changed your nappies and taught you to piss in the streams. You've got no secrets from me . . . do you?"

"You wish me to tell you about Lady Marian?"

"Nay." Rhys dangled a hose enticingly. "I want you to tell me the *truth* about Lady Marian."

Griffith wondered how to surrender in such a way as would placate his father. It had been so long since he'd allowed the wild part of himself—the Welsh part of himself—its freedom. Did he even remember how?

Hesitantly he found the words. "Lady Marian. When I raise my eyes to the sun, I see her. She's like a gyrfalcon, fit for a king, soaring in the windswept sky, wild and proud above even the morning lark."

Rhys threw him a linen shirt.

Griffith pulled it on and tied the drawstring at the neck. "Her feathers are summed to the peak plumage, her train and beams glow in the light of day."

Watching him closely, Rhys tossed him a tunic and murmured, "The truth at last."

Griffith paused, surprised at himself, at the lyricism he'd thought poisoned and killed by life. "'Tis not the truth, 'tis just—"

"'Tis just a Welsh soul you've buried so deep I thought you'd never find it again." Rhys threw the rest of the clothes at Griffith, then pulled a chair to the fire.

Amused at himself and at his father's complacency, yet irresistibly drawn, Griffith dressed himself and continued his thoughtful tribute to his lady falcon. "When some lesser mortal snares her and takes her to hand, with pounces and beak she tears at them until they are bloodied. But though they loose their grip, they never stop seeking the flash of wing and cry of elation that betrays her presence."

"But you may tame her?"

"No man will ever tame her." Griffith knew the harsh truth. "I can whistle until my spit runs dry, but she comes to me reluctantly. She uses not her claws and beak, but stays only when I coax her with"—he faltered—"delectations she cannot refuse. Then for a moment, while she's weary and replete, she's mine and mine alone."

Rhys quoted, "With empty hand no man shall falcons lure."

Knocked from his poetic perch and instantly defensive, Griffith said, "I give her myself."

"Not all of yourself."

"The part that matters. The part that's whole. She'll know no difference."

"Nay?" Rhys templed his fingers. "Falcons—and women, too—have a fine instinct for those whom they can trust."

Sharp and keen, the memory of the vow she had wrung from Art stabbed at Griffith's heart. He poured himself a cup of wine and drank it, trying to swallow his misgivings. "She must learn, but she will trust me."

Like the powerful report of a cannon, Rhys

knocked down Griffith's pretensions. "She'll not trust you if you never let her know you."

Griffith turned his head away, but Rhys tapped the hand hanging lax at his side and said, "What happened, happened long ago. We've all forgiven you—only you have not."

Bitterness and long-ago embarrassment had burned lines in Griffith's face. "The loss of Castle Powel was not a great thing?"

"'Twas only a temporary thing. I would not have given it up had I not known how to retrieve it. There were other ways to get you back, if not as easy."

"It should not have been necessary. I was a stupid, spoiled lad."

"Not spoiled. Headstrong. And as your mother told me at the time—if I'd handled you better, the whole incident need not have happened."

Griffith excused his father's long-ago impatience. "'Twas the strain of resisting the siege, of rationing supplies and fearing they would poison the spring that fed the well."

"Aye, and your escapade resulted from the strain of living with the siege. By the saints, man, tell the woman what oppresses your soul, and perhaps she'll willingly nest with you." When Griffith didn't answer, Rhys stretched out his legs and relaxed. "That *is* what you're planning? To build a nest with this Lady Marian Wenthaven?"

Ready to turn the subject, Griffith asked, "Do you care?"

"Our lineage is respected enough to bear the disgrace of an Englishwoman in the family, but will she bring us a dowry?"

"I don't know. I doubt it."

"Then of what use is she to the family?"

"Her connections in the court are of a weighty nature." Griffith picked his words carefully. "The queen of England is her friend."

That impressed Rhys. "I doubt your assurances of her good nature. Art seemed to be in awe of her—and Art finds little which awes him."

Griffith muttered, "I don't know why I keep that old man."

"Because you owe him your life?" Rhys suggested.

"Mayhap that's it." Griffith poured a mug of wine and handed it to his father.

Accepting it, Rhys said, "I thought you wanted another wife like Gwenllian. Many was the time I heard you say you liked a domestic woman, adept with a needle and content to stay home."

"Marian will learn," Griffith declared. "Aye, she will learn."

Griffith couldn't help but suspect his father drank to hide a smile, but when Rhys finished and wiped his mouth, nothing remained of his amusement. "I do wonder if Lady Marian's father will soon be camping on our doorstep, demanding the return of his daughter."

Griffith sank onto a bench and leaned forward to catch the warmth of the fire. "Perhaps he would if he knew where she was, but a siege is not Wenthaven's chosen method of warfare. He would rather hunt in the dun, like a ferret, and drag his prey away by the throat."

"Reassuring. Shall we keep watch lest Lady Marian disappears?"

"She's safe in Castle Powel"—Griffith hoped—"but 'tis Lionel who may be in the greatest danger."

"The father of the child seeks him?"

"I don't know the identity of Lionel's father, but he's shown no interest so far. Still, Lionel is a special child for many reasons, some of which I don't yet understand."

"So I was right. Wenthaven prizes Marian for her son."

"I suspect that's the truth, but I don't want Harbottle to realize it."

"Why should the son matter?"

Griffith wanted to explain, to ask his father's advice. But to do so without Marian's knowledge would betray Marian's trust—the trust Rhys considered unattainable. "Da, I cannot in all honor tell you, but I must warn you—keeping Marian and Lionel here could endanger Castle Powel and everyone in it. If you wish, you may refuse sanctuary and I will take them elsewhere."

"Nonsense," Rhys said with inelegant bluntness. "If I refused them sanctuary out of fear for my life, your mother would drop me off the tallest tower—and worse, refuse me her bed."

Griffith chuckled. It was no more than he expected, but he had felt he had to give fair warning. "Aye, Da, but this I can say—Marian was never Harbottle's lover."

Rhys narrowed his eyes as he examined his son from top to toe. "I wouldn't ask you to betray your honor, but don't tell your mother. She hates a secret."

Relaxing back in his chair, Griffith realized Rhys had, for the moment, withdrawn his objections to Marian. For while Griffith's duty remained with his family's advancement, still Rhys harbored a romantic Welsh heart, and that heart deplored Griffith's detachment from all who loved him. Griffith asked, "So what do we do with Harbottle? With that Gwarwyn-a-Throt?"

"A bogie, do you call him?" Rhys laughed in a burst, then sobered at once. "Don't tempt the bogies to do you a wrong by misnaming Harbottle in their image."

"Aye, even a bogie might be insulted," Griffith concurred. "Shall we keep him? He's a treacherous brute, and it might be wise to retain him within reach."

"Or should we throw him out?" Rhys mused. "The spring weather is unsettled—wet one day, cold the next. If he remained within the neighborhood, he'd soon find himself unhappy."

"He is very comfortable in his prison."

Their eyes met, and in unison they said, "We'll throw him out."


"You have to take your tonic," Angharad coaxed, holding the potion before Marian's pursed lips. "You promised Art you would."

Marian pinched her nose against the stench. "I didn't promise him I'd take it forever. I'm better now."

"So you are. This last week in bed has been good for you." Angharad wrapped Marian's hand around the mug. "So another week will be better yet."

"Another week?" Marian squeaked, and to her disgust her voice promptly failed her—a circumstance of which Angharad was quick to take advantage.

"See now, you've hurt yourself." She caressed Marian's cheek, much like a mother luring her infant. "If you'll drink it, I'll allow you some visitors."

Marian glared and wished she weren't so weak. She had thought she was going to die—now it seemed she'd come too close. The days of fever had seemed endless, a dark swirl of pain and fear, of sleeping with dread nightmares and waking only to cough until she was sick.

The malady had extinguished the spark of energy that drove her. She could lift her head off the pillow, but there seemed to be no reason to do so. She could verify, every day, that her treasure was still hidden in the bag where she'd placed it, but it seemed almost unimportant. She could sit up to have her hair brushed, and stand up to take care of her body's needs, but she didn't want to go out and face the myriad challenges her life had become. Her son was safe and being cared for, and she was weary. Bone weary.

"I'll rub your back," Angharad offered.

Marian wavered. Angharad had a way about her.

Griffith had offered his mother to her as if she were the greatest gift he could tender, and Angharad had proved to be more. She drew Marian under her wing as if Marian were a long-lost and much beloved chick. She fussed—too much, Marian thought, but with such affectionate concern Marian found herself doing everything to ease Angharad's worry. And Angharad loved. Loved Marian, loved Lionel, as tenderly as if they were her own. She baited her snare with the soft down of motherhood, and Marian willingly entered and remained.

"Tyrant," Marian muttered, and drank down the disgusting brew. It tasted like bat dung mixed with herbs, and as she knew, it could well be. It didn't bear thinking about, though, so she accepted the ale Angharad passed her to help wash the taste away and twitched her loose linen gown over as she rolled onto her stomach. "Rub, please."

Angharad sat on the mattress beside Marian, pushed the long, heavy red braid out of the way, and began to massage the neck and back muscles that protested the long hours in bed.

Marian gave a heartfelt moan of pleasure, then asked, "Is Lionel coming to see me?"

"Lionel, Rhys, and Griffith."

"Griffith?" A bit of the lassitude afflicting Marian fled, and she struggled up onto her elbows. "I don't want to see Griffith."

"You've refused him this whole week, and he's been acting like a bear waiting to face the bull. Pacing and grumping and snapping." Angharad lightly smacked Marian's rump as if it were all her fault. "'Tis time to put him—and the rest of us—out of our misery."

"I don't feel well enough to see him."

Angharad pushed her face back into the pillow. "A moment ago you were well enough to get up."

Muffled, Marian protested, "He'll make me worse."

"He'll make you better." Angharad pressed her palm into the center of Marian's back. "Just feel how your heart is pounding. 'Twill move the blood in your system, and you'll exhale the bad humors which have made you ill."

Marian buried her head in her pillow to hide her heated cheeks. If Angharad so easily recognized her confusion, fear, and embarrassment, who else would see it? Would Griffith?

Never in her life had Marian hid from trouble. Indeed, in the old days Lady Elizabeth had complained she ran to meet it. But this was different. This wasn't a fight to be fought or a challenge to be met. This was confronting the man who had taken her to the limits of her control, and beyond. He'd raided the storehouse of her body, with her own help. He'd stolen something that could never be returned—her innocence—and replaced it with a frustration that grew stronger even as she did. No, she was too tired to see Griffith—ever again.

Lifting her head, she begged, "Can't we wait until tomorrow?"

She jumped when Griffith answered her, "Not another day."

One glance sufficed her. He looked like one of the towering ancient stone slabs that jutted out from the ground. She'd discovered them in her travels around England and even more of them in Wales. Menhirs, they called them here. Battered by wind and rain, they stood, immovable, indestructible, inexplicable: monuments that defied the march of time to silently proclaim their might.

The silence in the room strained Marian's nerves— the nerves she never realized she had—and she risked another glance.

He stood closer now, no longer just a shape and a

menace, but a man. A man as hard and hot and massive as a menhir heated from within by the earth from which it sprang.

Could they communicate without words? To her discomfort, Marian found they could. As clearly as if he'd told her, she knew his fury and his desire. He desperately wanted her, yet desperately wished he didn't.

Did Griffith have a weakness? If he did, she was it, and he fought to relegate her to her proper place in his well-organized life.

Hoarse with his need, he asked, "Are you well?"

She found her voice had escaped once more and only nodded.

"We'll be married as soon as the banns can be called."

Her voice returned quickly enough. "Nay!"

He seemed to grow taller. "We must act in a responsible manner."

When facing him, she found it hard to remember more than their tumultuous, all-too-enjoyable encounter between the sheets. But she had to. She had her responsibility to Lionel. Softly, taking care not to strain her fragile throat, she answered, "I am acting in a responsible manner. I cannot marry Henry's man. Not now. Not ever."

It was odd to feel the pain that flashed over his tough countenance as if it were her own. Odd to feel ashamed of suspicions that could save her child's life.

Griffith strode to the window overlooking the bailey. He leaned his shoulder against the wall and spoke, sounding as unyielding as a menhir would sound, if it could speak. "I'll have the priest call the banns for the next three Sundays."

"A waste."

"We'll see," he answered.

"Son," Rhys said, his voice heavy with displeasure, "you can't force her to wed you."

Marian stared in surprise. Rhys stood in the middle

of the room, holding Lionel as if he'd been there the entire time.

But she'd not noticed him. She'd not noticed her baby, whom she'd been longing for. Come to think of it, she'd even failed to notice Angharad, who was still rubbing the tense place on her neck.

"We must wed," Griffith insisted. "For her safety and the safety of her child."

"We will keep them both safe," Rhys vowed. "But regardless of the danger, our priest will not call the banns until the lady has consented to the union."

Griffith hunched his shoulders and folded his arms across his chest.

Rhys watched his son and waited, but Griffith would vouchsafe no reply, so Rhys asked, "Is Lady Marian well enough to hold Lionel?"

"Aye, she can hold him," Angharad said. They were both doing their best to lighten the conflict between Griffith and Marian. "There's been no fever these last three days, and the lad is as healthy as Griffith was at his age. As feckless as Griffith, also."

Marian accepted her son from Rhys with a murmur of pleasure and hugged his wriggling body close. "Has he been a great pest?"

"Nay," Lionel took it on himself to answer.

Rhys laughed. "He's a pleasure. You've done the world a great service by raising him to be a bright and curious lad."

"Nay," Lionel said again, then plastered a kiss on Marian's lips.

She glanced at Griffith and found him watching them with a smile. The week in his own home had been good to Griffith. He had bathed and now wore new, clean clothes—colorful clothes in the fashion of the court. His hair had been trimmed and brushed until it gleamed like polished wood. In fact—as Angharad promised, the blood moved in Marian's veins—he looked like a man come a-wooing.

No sooner had she thought it than he said, "I met Marian because of Lionel. The lad has my gratitude, and I'm not likely to forget it."

Message received, she thought. If only she could say, message believed.

While Marian fussed over Lionel, giving him a pillow of his own, covering his legs with a blanket, Angharad leaped in to fill the silence. "At least you didn't meet like Rhys and I met."

"Hey!" Rhys remonstrated. "'Twasn't so bad."

"Not so bad?" Angharad turned to Marian and confided, "We met during the wedding ceremony."

"Our parents thought it best." Rhys sounded quite righteous and solemn, then he grinned. "What did they know? What did I know, for that matter? I didn't care. What did a wife matter? I was twenty-one, just knighted, a man of the world."

"I was twelve," Angharad said.

Rhys held up his hand with his little finger stuck up. "With just this many curves."

"He scared me to death."

"I thought I was supposed to."

"He entered the sleeping chamber, took one look at me, naked and shivering, and proclaimed, 'I'm not sleeping with a baby.'"

"And I left."

"You stomped out," Angharad accused.

"You're not making me feel guilty about *that,*" Rhys said.

"No." A smile played around Angharad's mouth. "I was secretly relieved. And publicly humiliated."

Rhys smiled at his wife, and Marian could almost see him wrapping Angharad in his embrace. Something existed between them: a pleasure strengthened by time and affection and old desire easily rekindled.

Griffith sighed and shook his head. "They're love-struck," he told Marian.

She did not reply. It was too easy to think she and Griffith could be a couple like this one, relating the story of their courting with practiced ease, knowing what each was going to say before it was said.

Painful to consider, too, that she and Griffith could still be star-crossed in forty years. Even to her own ears, Marian sounded husky and on the verge of tears when she asked, "What happened?"

"How did we get together, do you mean?" Angharad clasped her work-worn hands in her lap. "I grew up."

"Very nicely, too," Rhys supplemented.

Angharad scoffed, "You never even noticed. I was keeping your house and the widow in the village was keeping you satisfied, and you were oblivious of my meager charms."

"Until you flirted with my squire."

"The squire was my age"—Angharad leaned closer to Marian—"and handsome as wicked sin."

"And stupid," Rhys added.

"Saint Winifred's head! If he was obvious, it was because he thought you didn't care. And you didn't, either, until you saw someone else did." Angharad huffed with long-ago indignation. "Like a dog with a bone—unwanted until another dog desires it."

"I wasn't as oblivious as she thinks," Rhys said sotto voce to Marian.

Angharad crossed her arms across her ample chest. "Ha!"

"Oh, I'd been noticing her. Her figure had filled out very"—Rhys rolled the r—"nicely. But we'd been married four years, and it wasn't so easy to change the sleeping arrangements. I didn't want to look the fool, courting my own wife." He sighed and spoke with profound dejection. "But courting would have been easier."

Angharad subdued a faint smile, but Marian wasn't so capable. Seeing this big bear of a man cowed by his tiny wife proved too much for her gravity, and she laughed.

"See?" Rhys pointed at her and at Angharad. "See, son? Women are ever disrespectful of their sweethearts. I'm relating a tale of my own humiliation, and they're giggling."

"'Tis shocking, Da," Griffith agreed.

"Aye." Rhys cocked his eyebrow sternly at Marian. "I see nothing funny in my plight."

Marian cleared her throat and tried to look restrained. "Please go on. What did you do with the squire?"

"I sent him home in disgrace. I pulled the ungrateful whelp from a home in the village and raised him up to be my squire, and he repaid me by lusting after my wife." Rhys gestured angrily. "*My* wife!"

Marian suspected the squire's expulsion had been none too kind, and when Angharad said, "He's back, you know," Rhys almost shouted.

"Do you think I care? Stupid, young—"

Angharad interrupted. "He's not young anymore, but he's still handsome, still wrathful, and I wish you'd watch your step."

The old feud still moved powerful emotions, it seemed, for Rhys flushed scarlet, and Marian asked hastily, "What happened to you and Angharad after you were alone?"

Rhys visibly checked the irate words on his lips; he looked at his anxious wife and let the moment pass. "I stomped around all angry. I expected Angharad to grovel."

Angharad sniffed. "And I didn't."

"She was angry, too." Rhys still sounded amazed at this outbreak from his previously docile wife. "As though it were my fault."

"It *was* your fault," Angharad told him.

"So the next thing I know, my twelve-year-old

bride tells me she's sixteen and sick of being treated like a child."

"And he said if I wanted to be treated like a woman, I should act like one."

"So I took her to bed."

They'd been involved in the telling, topping each other with each addition, but Rhys's blunt statement seemed to catch them almost by surprise. They both blushed, a ruddy intrusion of color in the wrinkled, paper-thin skin of the aging. They exchanged swift, shy glances, then Rhys coughed. When he spoke again, the timbre of his voice had softened. "The thing is, bedding a virgin when you're enraged is not a good idea. Not at all. There're tears—"

"Some of them his," Angharad interjected.

"—and a man has to make amends, and it puts him in a bad position to negotiate." He wiped at the memory of ancient sweat on his brow and settled back. "Of course, that's not a difficulty you're likely to encounter, so be grateful."

"Rhys," Angharad reprimanded.

Wrapped in a cocoon of silence, the little group watched Lionel as he played peek-a-boo with the blanket. No one seemed to want to say more, and Marian dared not look at Rhys or Angharad, and most certainly not at Griffith.

Then Griffith cleared his throat. "Well, actually—"

She lifted her outraged gaze, thinking she must be mistaken, knowing he wouldn't tell them the truth.

"Marian and I—"

She could scarcely breathe, and she sat up in a flurry. "Griffith?"

"—had quite a similar experience—"

"Griffith, don't say another word!"

"—and I need your help in dealing with the consequences." Griffith relaxed against the window frame. "Don't fret, sweeting, Mama and Da always give me good advice."

Desperate to make him understand, she said, "This isn't just about you and me."

"'Tis not about you and me that I ask." Griffith bowed to her but remained out of reach of her fists. "God willing, we will work it out. 'Tis Lionel we should be concerned about."

"Griffith, I forbid—" Marian tried to raise her voice. To her dismay, she discovered it faded completely.

"The lad's not hers," Griffith said. She took several deep breaths of the chilly air, trying to revitalize her voice, but he continued steadily, "I had the proof less than a moon ago."

Angharad and Rhys exchanged dumbfounded glances, then stared at Lionel, then at Marian, then at Griffith.

Rhys recovered first. "What do you mean, Griffith?"

Pride and embarrassment warred on Griffith's face, but he drew himself up loftily. "I mean, she came to my bed a virgin."

Marian covered her face with her hands and moaned. This was it. Lionel's parentage had been betrayed.

"How did it happen she was in your bed, Griffith?" Angharad almost stuttered in her excitement.

"She . . . had a nightmare." As if he realized how absurd that sounded, Griffith rushed to add, "She truly did. She was white and shaking . . . Lionel had been kidnapped that day, and she was afraid . . . of someone taking . . ."

"Of course, of course," Rhys agreed heartily. "But you're telling us you made love with the lass. That you're no longer celibate. Isn't that what you're saying?"

"Aye, Da."

Uncomprehending, Marian lifted her head. She and Griffith's parents didn't seem to be thinking on the same level. She was worried about Lionel's pedigree and how it would influence the history of a nation. They seemed interested only in Griffith . . . and her.

Rhys rubbed his hands together with relish. *"Why* did you make love with the lass?"

Griffith hung his head. "I lost control, Da."

Angharad clapped in an excess of delight. "You lost control?"

"Aye," Griffith admitted.

"With Lady Marian?" she insisted.

"Aye," he said again.

Angharad lifted her arms to heaven. "God be praised, we have a daughter at last."

"Amen," Rhys finished reverently.

With a quick kiss to Lionel and an enthusiastic hug to the bewildered—and horrified—Marian, Angharad hopped off the mattress. "I'll prepare the wedding."

Rhys stood from the chair and joined her. "And I'll go tell the priest to call the banns."

Her head spun, but Marian swiftly objected, "But you said you wouldn't allow it until I agreed to the union."

"That was before we heard this astounding news." Angharad hugged Rhys's arm and looked from Griffith to Marian. "You've given us our son back."

It didn't make any sense to Marian, and if she'd been clothed, she'd have leaped up to confront Rhys. "But what about Lionel?"

"Lionel?" Rhys considered the boy. Lionel's head was under the blanket, his pillow on the floor, and he drummed his heels against the headboard in a steady, jarring rhythm. "Get Lionel, Angharad, and we'll leave these sweetkins alone."

"I believe Marian wants to know what you think of him, now that you know he's not of her blood," Griffith said.

"I want to know," Marian burst out, "if you'll swear to keep this secret."

Rhys and Angharad seemed at a loss to comprehend her concern. Finally Rhys spoke for them both. "If you took the lad as your own, and ruined your reputation and your chance at happiness, it seems to me there's a good reason hidden somewhere. Now, you know the reason, and no doubt Griffith knows the reason, but unless you wish to tell us, we don't have to know the reason. . . . Is that what you wanted to know?"

"Swear to keep it secret," Marian whispered, intense and afraid. "Swear."

Rhys stiffened, and Angharad gasped in audible dismay.

Griffith groaned and shook his head. "She means no disrespect, Da. If you'd met her father, you'd understand."

The haughty cast of Rhys's face tightened, then Angharad touched his chest. She looked up at him, and he nodded at her unspoken message, then came to Marian's side. He took her hand between his two callused ones. "Harbottle told me about your father, and so I do forgive you your insult. But you're in Wales now, and among your kin. And if you can't trust your kin, whom can you trust?"

# 12

*As the door shut* softly behind Rhys, Angharad, and Lionel, Marian stared after them and wondered if they were crazed. Trust them because they were kin? What madness was that?

Yet she did trust Angharad. 'Twas impossible not to. And Rhys . . . well, if Art were Lionel's companion, and Griffith were Lionel's father-figure, then Rhys was his hero. He stuck to Rhys like a burr to a sock. She blushed to remember Rhys's hurt pride when she'd demanded he swear himself to secrecy. "Why is Harbottle here?" she asked.

Griffith sighed and pushed himself away from the window. "He apparently followed your trail into Wales, and when he lost that, he asked directions to Castle Powel."

"Why?"

He stalked toward the bed, slow and silent. "Because he wants you."

"Nonsense." Her voice wavered a little, and she steadied it. "My father must have sent him."

"Your father seems to have washed his hands of

him. As have we. We turned him out four days ago
with dry clothes and barely enough food to reach
England, if he walks briskly. But he seems willing to
defy the fates to get his hands on you, for we've had
reports of a man watching the castle." He stepped
onto the dais and climbed up on the mattress. "In
fact, several reports."

She wanted to demand more in the way of explanation, but he took off his boots. And his doublet.
And when his hands went to the ties of his hose, she
whispered, "What are you doing?"

"Coming to get the answers about Lionel. Isn't this
how I got the answers about you?" He stripped off
his hose, pulled his shirt over his head, and divested
himself of his drawers in a twisting dance that kept
her dizzy with his unpredictability. "You came and
lay in bed with me, we talked, we loved, and when we
had finished, I knew your secrets."

The blood sang in her veins now, and she no
longer wondered why she should get well. It was so
she could run away. "It wasn't so . . ."

"So?"

Or perhaps, run toward. "So simple."

He chuckled, low and deep. "'Tis the simplest
thing in the world. 'Tis why the Lord God made us so
different—so we'd fit together well."

He stretched out on the bed beside her, all the long
length of him bare and brown and brawny, and held
her when she would have edged off the bed. Lying
down, she clamped her arms at her sides so the blankets were tight around her body. "Someone might
come in."

"We're in a Welsh household, and by now everyone knows the banns will be called on Saturday."
With a smile, he tucked Lionel's pillow close against
hers and lay so his head rested against her shoulder.
"Welshmen have better manners than that."

With that he seemed content. He said nothing else,

made no move, while the minutes ticked by and
Marian grew so tense that she thought the tendons in
her neck would pop. When she couldn't bear the
silence anymore, she burst out, "What do you want?"

"Several things." Lifting his hand, he traced the
outline of her breasts. "First, as I told you, I want to
hear the story of Lionel."

The covers, which she had depended on for protection, seemed suddenly thin and flimsy. "I can't tell
you that."

He sighed, and the air slithered through the loose
weave of the linen and warmed her chest. He
mourned, "'Twas what I feared, and I cannot force
the tale which should come to me freely."

His tone made her wretched, and his touch made
her remember. If she had been the experienced
woman she pretended to be, she would have different
memories to tap into. As it was, only the night in
Griffith's arms came to mind, and came so vividly
that she almost forgot the thread of the conversation.
"I can't tell anyone."

"Not even your bridegroom?"

"I can't wed you."

"Ah, that's next, then. I want your promise to wed
me."

"Nay." She didn't sound as firm as she liked, but
only because he'd pressed a kiss—one small kiss—at
the place where her jaw met her ear.

"There are advantages to our marriage."

"And disadvantages."

"Such as?"

"Lionel wouldn't be in line for . . ." She trailed off.
She'd almost given it all away, and she couldn't help
but admire his cleverness.

He smiled ruefully, a lifting of his lips that made
her long to trace them with her tongue. "First, Lionel
will be safer with me than without me." She stiffened,
and he lifted his head. "Don't you agree?"

She didn't know what to say, for her heart and her mind were at war, battling for supremacy over her body. She had scorned passion for Lionel's sake, and when Griffith proved himself passion's master, she had fled him. Perhaps Lionel would be safer with Griffith—but Marian had given Lady Elizabeth a vow, and that vow would be as dust.

"This brings us to the second argument for marriage," he said, as smoothly as a courtier, as coolly as a king. "I have spoken to our priest, for he is a wise man. The marriage vows take precedence over my vows as a knight to my lord, although both are holy and are given in the eyes of God. I would hope I wouldn't have to make a choice between my wife and my lord. I would hope I could continue in the service of my lord while servicing my wife. But in the final conflict, I would keep my wife's secrets, take care of my wife's property and children, and remain loyal to her above all others."

She plucked at the covers with nervous fingers. "I see."

"But do you believe?" His muscles rippled, from his shoulders to his toes, as he hoisted himself up on his elbow and leaned over her. "Would you like to hear the third argument for marriage?"

"I think . . ."

"'Tis only this." He covered her face in tiny kisses. Dry kisses, that acquainted her with the texture of his lips, the spicy scent of his breath, his shaven cheeks.

She closed her eyes against the pleasure and found that it only intensified.

"You frightened me, love," he murmured close against her ear. "I thought I would lose you, and I couldn't stand that."

"You shouldn't be doing this." She wished her voice were stronger. She wished her will were stronger.

"I'm only doing it to convince you to marry me."

Her eyes popped open. "So if I consented, you'd go away?"

He stared at her. She stared at him.

"Do you consent?" he asked, his face a frozen mask.

"Tell me first."

The struggle between his body and his mind raged in his silence, but at last he relaxed. His hard smile struggled with the bitter perception in his eyes. "Nay. I will not go away. No matter what you say." He stripped the ribbon off her braid and loosened her hair. "You steal my control, take my honor, yet make me twice the man I was before." Burying his face in the shiny red strands spread wide on the pillow, he whispered, "So I will do for you what you do for me."

She half laughed, half sobbed. "Make me a man?"

"Steal your control." He lifted his head, and he looked like a knight who, even before the battle, recognized victory.

She was weak, but not as weak as she had been a scant hour ago. Not so weak she couldn't fight him. As his hand hovered above the tie on her gown, she caught it in her grasp.

He smiled. "Where do you wish to place it, my lady? Your wish is my command. Would you like me to touch your shoulders, my lady? They are the most beautiful I've ever seen—strong, muscled, but with a hollow about your collarbone that denotes femininity. I've seen them from the rear, and marveled at the way they form part of your long, narrow back, the way your back narrows to your waist, the way your hips flare and tease a man with promises of heaven."

Her fingers trembled. She pressed herself back into the pillows and wondered at the hedonistic pleasure she found in his words.

"Is my hand too heavy for you, my lady?" His voice had become a drawl, sexy, slow, and low. "Place it where you wish."

Drawing on her strength, she placed it on the covers, away from her.

Still smiling, he leaned on his elbow, supported his head with his palm, and looked pointedly at the hand she had discarded. "A wise idea, my lady. Let's discuss the proper place to begin again. For my own pleasure, I like to hold your breasts. They're not too small, not too large, but so responsive. I'll never forget the sound you made when I lapped the underside of your breast with my tongue. Like a cat, remember?"

She had trouble catching her breath, and the room spun around her. Was it a return of the illness? Or a dose of the cure?

"And you wanted more, but you didn't know what. Now you know, don't you?"

Her nipples hardened, pointed at him, answered him. She slapped her hands across her chest, even though he couldn't see the evidence through the thickness of the blankets.

He chuckled. "You do remember. When I suckled them, I had to hold you down, you were so maddened with desire. You tugged at my hair, and I couldn't tell if you wanted me to stop or go on. But when I tried to stop—"

"By the saints."

"—you brought me back by your grip on my neck, and I caressed your breasts until I thought I would die of joy." He smoothed his own chest, and fascinated, she watched as the crinkly hairs sprang back as his hand passed over them. "A man might delight in such attentions, too."

Her imagination provided vivid, color pictures of Griffith's reaction to such boldness.

As he'd intended. A smile teased the corners of his mouth, and it infuriated her that he would tempt her with his words. Shaking her head wildly, back and forth on the pillow, she demanded, "Go away."

Tenderly he pushed a tendril of hair back off her forehead. "You ask too much, my love." He cupped her cheek and traced his thumb lightly across her eyelashes. "And not enough. There is much you don't know about making love. How could you? I've not had time to teach. For instance, did you know a man may kiss a woman here"—his hand rested firmly on her mons veneris— "and produce such pleasure she cries with joy?"

She pressed her knees together in instant reaction—to keep his fingers from exploring further, she told herself—but it relieved the pressure of arousal. For a moment. Then it came back, worse, almost painful, almost superb. But not enough. "Nay."

"I vow 'tis the truth. And a woman may do as much for a man."

"Would you cry?" She meant to sound sarcastic. She sounded wistful.

"Try it." He rolled over on his back and stretched his arms up, hooking his hands behind his head. His shoulders, arms, and chest were bulky with muscle, yet still his lower ribs created a ripple of his skin. His abdomen clenched as her gaze passed over it, and she thought his legs had flexed, also. She didn't know for sure. She couldn't seem to look past . . . Jerking her head up, she looked right into his eyes.

They glowed hot as molten gold. They made her squirm more than his touch, more than his words, for his touch and words conveyed his thoughts awkwardly. Now she gazed directly into the crucible of his mind and comprehended each individual temptation.

"Imagine," he whispered, "how helpless I would be as you explored me. Imagine how I would squirm when you touched my nipples, ran your hand down my stomach. Imagine how I would taste, how I would whimper when you kissed me. Lips open, wet and warm, taking me inside—"

She cut him off with her hand over his mouth.

She hadn't meant to touch him, but she couldn't listen anymore.

When had the big warrior become a Welsh poet? When had he learned to seduce with words?

He kissed her palm, and when she would withdraw, with one hand he caught her wrist. On the inside of her hand, he found the sensitive mounds with his rough thumb, seemingly fascinated by the texture, the lines. He traced the edge of each finger, circled the cuticles, until her hand flexed as protection against the sensation. Then, one by one, he took her fingers into his mouth and sucked them.

He wanted her to do that to him. She wanted to do that to him. Jerking her hand away, she sat up. The covers fell away, revealing her breasts through the thin linen, and he groaned as his gaze feasted on her. "Pretty," he said hoarsely. Then, "Mine."

"They're mine." She leaned over him, fierce with the surge of blood through her veins, well for the first time since she'd entered Castle Powel, and convinced she would live forever. "But if you put both your hands behind your head again, I'll let you taste them."

It was a calculated risk. He could have used his strength against her and taken her without a doubt. Even without a struggle, for she craved him desperately. But he wanted her to prove her desire.

Prove it she would. She commanded, "Behind your head."

His free hand hovered, close to her face, then with an expression of painful resignation he did as she instructed.

What to do first? With him stretched as a feast laid out for her delectation and the whole, uninterrupted day before them, the importance of the decision could not be overstated. Placing her hands on his shoulders, she followed the grade of each muscle of his chest, his hips, his thighs. She explored with lazy intent, still unfamiliar with most of the workings of a man's body and curious. Curious about his reactions. Curious about his exalted control.

The muscles of his face froze in anguished appeal. His toes curled, his calves flexed, and everything in between was ruddy and hard.

"You wanted this," she reminded him.

Gruffly he ordered, "So give it to me."

"All in good time." She tucked her heels beneath her, placed her hands on either side of him, and leaned over. "All in good time."

The scent of him—clean male, strong soap— greeted her. "A bath?" she asked.

"'Tis a tradition in my family to"—he inhaled harshly when she nuzzled his ear—"to bathe before a wedding. And I was determined to . . . I can't speak when you're licking at me like a cat."

"Control," she reminded him. He tasted as good as he looked, and he shuddered when she used her tongue to wet his nipple, then blew it dry.

Staring up at the ceiling, concentrating on the rafters, he said, "I was determined to treat this as a wedding day. After all, we're only doing it out of order."

"Doing what?" She rubbed her cheek against his stomach below his ribs.

"Marrying. We're only marrying out of order. We consummated first. Now we're reading the banns. Then we'll go before the priest and speak the vows."

"One consummation is all we need." She grasped his thighs and ran her tongue from his knees to his hip. "Why have another one?"

Lifting his head, he looked down at her. "Because I thought you were going to die."

Her teasing laughter died beneath the intensity of his distress.

"I thought I had found you—happy, robust, a force of nature—in your father's home, only to lose you." He unwrapped his arms and stretched them out to her. "Make love to me, woman. Make me aware of only your vitality. Chase the shadows away."

His appeal shook her to the core.

This man, this stone, needed her. Wanted her so much that his massive will bent to that longing.

Could she take such an entreaty lightly? He was requesting more than her body laid against his. He was requesting her life laid against his.

No other man had ever tempted her to give herself up to him, yet she'd gone to Griffith ap Powel without a thought or regret. She had trusted him with herself; would she come to trust him with Lionel? Did she believe he would put his vows to her above his vows to the king?

Aye, her body answered, even as doubts clung to her mind.

She kissed his outstretched fingers, and he closed his hand around the kiss as if it were a token. With trembling fingers, she folded his arms behind his head again. Her breast brushed his face and he turned his head to catch her nipple in his mouth. She froze as he sucked it, the linen of her shirt between her flesh and his lapping tongue. He didn't touch her; didn't have to. All the passion in her body clamored like a church bell in celebration, and when he stopped, she didn't move for a long, sweet moment.

Then she settled back and smiled a wicked smile. He'd challenged her, and she would respond, creating in him the life for which he entreated.

Untying the strings of her shirt in slow, sensuous sweeps, she watched his expression. Watched every nuance as she lifted the hem, revealing flesh, inch by inch. She pulled it over her head, tossed it aside.

She grasped the part of him she'd hitherto ignored and laughed aloud to see his face. "A stone indeed," she teased, although he probably couldn't even hear. And when she took him in her mouth, he groaned like a man lost to all sense.

But he could still speak. Gutturally, haltingly, but he could speak. "Now. You must come to me now."

His eyes were slits, as if he were looking into the sun, when she rose above him.

Compelled by her uncertainty, he instructed, "Ride astride."

In a flash, she understood. Arousing him, she discovered, had aroused her, and she took him into herself in slow, wet increments. He was still too large, but discomfort gave way to excitement when he trembled yet held himself still.

She was a woman, with a warrior beneath her legs and his pleasure in her care, and it gave her a power she would test to its limits.

Feigning ignorance, she asked, "What should I do?"

He glared as if he didn't believe her. "Up and down."

"Like this?"

"Aye."

"And this?"

"Aye."

"Should I go faster?"

"Aye. Nay. Oh, God. As you like."

Still moving, she leaned back and put her hands on his thighs. "Do you like this?"

He groaned pitifully. "Are you trying to kill me?"

"With pleasure." She moved her hands forward, lightly scratching his now bucking body, marking him as her own. "I'm going to kill you with pleasure."


"A criminal," Griffith murmured when he felt her movements.

"What?" Marian's voice was choked with sleep, and she sounded so confused that guilt stabbed him. She'd been too weak for such a tumultuous loving, but what could he do? If he'd waited until she was well, she'd have used her clever mind to evade him, and he needed every advantage. Now, as she became aware of their state of dishabille, as the memories of her boldness and his pleasure came flooding back, she began the slow and careful act of disengagement.

To forestall her, he repeated, "You're a violent criminal. You killed me with pleasure, and I can't remember a more enjoyable death." He used his soft, seductive Welsh accent to color his words with shades of carnality.

Movement ceased, then reversed as she tucked her head tighter into his chest. He grinned. She must think it better to be held close than to look him in the eye.

"I have been thinking"—he took strands of her hair and arranged it on his chest, intertwining the brilliant red with his crinkled black—"we can have an *eisteddfod* for our wedding."

Her shyness didn't last past his initial feint. Lifting herself onto her elbow, she pushed at his hands. "A . . . ? For our wedding?"

"An *eisteddfod*." He pronounced it carefully, as if her ignorance were the only issue to resolve. "'Tis a gathering of musicians and bards, come to sing their songs and recite their poetry."

She stared at him steadily. "I did not say I would wed with you."

He returned the look just as candidly. "Would you do this with a man whom you don't trust with your son? Do you have such a capricious instinct you dare not rely on it?"

Brushing her hair off her forehead in a gesture that betrayed uncertainty, she said, "Wiser women than I have depended on their instinct and been betrayed. And aye, you could have harmed us, but perhaps . . . you wait on another's will."

It hurt him that she even thought it, and he sat up slowly, his arms aching. "Under no man's will would I kill a child."

"Not even if you were put to the horn, branded a

traitor, your lands stripped from you? At the least, your chance for advancement ruined?"

Steady as an ox in harness, he answered, "I do not make war on children."

"Even now, you may be thinking that with the advent of other children—your children—Lionel's fate will not matter to me."

She echoed Harbottle's words with uncanny accuracy, and it irked him that she read one man's character so easily, then attributed it to him.

"If we wed, I would expect honor from you in your dealings with me, but 'tis easy, I think, for a man to dismiss a woman's expectations," she added.

"Not if she won't marry him because of them."

As if he hadn't spoken, she continued, "I learned not to trust at my father's knee, and it is a habit deeply engraved on my soul. There's more to this than you and me. At the royal court, I saw many things occur which were abhorrent to even the perpetrators. Were you acquainted with King Richard, the uncle of Lady Elizabeth?"

"Not I."

"I was." Pushing him away, she sat up and clasped the blanket before her, treating him to a vision of her spine, clothed only in the crimson-and-copper strands of her hair. "He was a kind uncle to Elizabeth and her brothers, a good brother to King Edward. Never in my wildest dreams could I have imagined the crimes of which he was capable."

Griffith brushed the length of her hair aside and laid his palm on her shoulder. "I am not flattered with any of these comparisons."

"I'm not comparing you. Nor would I compare you to my father." She sounded fierce, but she didn't turn around to look at him. Because she couldn't stand the sight of him? Because her own suspicions embarrassed her? "I'm saying that men's souls are dark and dread places, and I don't know where to shine the light of truth."

"I see." He did, and his hand fell away from the warmth of her skin, leaving him bereft. But there wasn't any use in remaining in a bed with this woman who found him so akin to the villains who littered her life.

As he slid out of bed, she caught his arm. "Do you think I should trust my instincts?"

Hope, ever valorous, sprang to life. "Aye, that I do."

"Well, my instincts tell me you're hiding something."

Then hope crashed, and unexpected rage roared through him, as sudden and violent as a squall off the sea. Unprepared, he staggered beneath its impact, struggling to channel it into coherent thought.

He'd betrayed himself. Some way, somehow, she'd heard the old gossip. Her hand tightened, and he looked down at it: long, slender fingers, a square, capable palm. It clasped his wrist firmly, as if he were one of her swords, to be utilized under her skillful direction, and he resented it. God, how he resented it.

He wanted no woman to read him with keen vision and handle him accordingly. He wanted a woman who sewed and tended her garden, gave him children and unquestioning obedience. He wanted a woman who understood it was a man's prerogative to demand answers to his questions, to shape lives according to his own wisdom. He wanted a woman who understood she had no business thinking, much less speaking, of a man's mysteries—yet he still wanted Marian.

Bold Marian. Inquisitive Marian. "Valiant Marian." He spoke aloud. "Too stupid to know she has charged the line of my authority for the last time."

She jumped half out of the covers in indignation, ready to fight. "You shouldn't be talking about marriage with me. I am not some silly girl who'll submit to a man's will without thought or reason."

He placed his palms on her shoulders, wrapped his fingers around her, one by one, and lifted her level with his face. "If you wanted a man who would let you drag him along like an out-of-control mare, then you shouldn't have bedded me. But it's too late for both of us. I've arranged our marriage, you carry my seed, and by the grace of God, we'll wed and I'll teach you your place."

His eyes blazed with solid determination, and he sounded as stuffy as he had the first time she'd met him. But the first time she'd met him, they'd both been clothed, they'd both been standing erect, and a rumpled bed hadn't stretched behind her, begging for more.

If she were wise, she would shut her mouth now and slip away from Castle Powel when she could. But she'd never been wise. "Maybe I'll teach you your place," she said. "Maybe I'll—"

His kiss smothered the rest, and he bore her back on the mattress in a passion. Of rage? Perhaps, but she could taste frustration and anxiety, and part of her understood.

He wanted a peaceful life, a traditional wife, yet he'd trapped himself with his own code of honor. He'd taken her virginity, taught her desire, and now he thought he had to marry her. Tearing her mouth free, she told him, "You don't have to."

He looked half-wild. "What?"

"Marry me. I'm not what you want—"

He growled and cut her off with another of those untamed, assertive kisses. Cupping her face in his hands, he glared at her and said, "You're mine. No matter how or why, you're mine."

"I think—"

"Don't think." He kissed her, and she struggled.

"But you—"

"No buts." He kissed her again.

"You—"

"No you. No me. Only us."

She couldn't remember what she wanted to say, anyway, and as her motions became aimless, his ardor gentled. He still crushed her, he still wanted her, and immediately, but he wanted her to want him, too. What had been a struggle became a dance, and she teetered perilously close to yielding—when a yell in the hall jerked them apart.

"Ye can't go in there!" Art's voice shouted.

Another, unknown voice replied, "This is the place, then. Good, for I'll do what must be done."

As Griffith cursed, the door slammed against the wall. Marian squeaked, and a sepulchral voice pronounced, "I bring you greetings from your lord, King Henry."

# 13

*Art squawked like a hen* when a wolf has come a-calling. "I tried to stop him, Griffith, but he wouldn't listen to me."

Griffith thrust Marian beneath the covers and rolled to his feet. Naked and furious, he stalked toward the messenger. "Oliver Churl, is it not?"

Imperturbable, the messenger corrected, "Oliver *King*. Henry Tudor's private secretary, to be precise. I bring you greetings from your liege."

Griffith glanced at the quivering lump beneath the blankets. "My liege has impeccable timing. Art, my clothes."

As Art scurried around, sorting the scattered clothing, Griffith placed his fists on his hips, drew himself up to his full height, and put himself to the task of intimidating the small, dapper man before him.

It didn't work.

"I beg pardon, Sir Griffith, for interrupting your pleasure, but our King Henry is, as you know, most impatient. He sent me to you more than a fortnight ago, and I have since traveled to Wenthaven and, it seems, over every Welsh mountain to find you."

The need for action still throbbed in Griffith. "You travel slowly."

"Not at all. I traveled quickly, since I knew not where to look. King Henry assumed you would fulfill the duties he demanded of you, rather than come to your home for relaxation. Unless"—he glanced pointedly at Art—"your servant failed to deliver the king's letter?"

Art accorded Oliver a respect he demonstrated to only a few. "I delivered it, as ye instructed, my lord."

Art's homage caught Griffith's attention, and he looked more closely at the man before him. Oliver might be too well dressed, and speak with a slight French accent, but his well-muscled body gave his clothes their shape, and his gaze held a sharp intelligence.

Of course. Henry chose his servants well. Oliver was one of the few men who had been with Henry in exile and in triumph, and he well understood his position in court.

Griffith's fury at being interrupted eased, and he pulled on his garments as Art handed them to him. "I followed those instructions," Griffith said in a reasonable tone.

"Then where is the lady Marian?" King asked.

Griffith nodded toward the bed.

Oliver's expression changed from surprise, to horror, to thoughtfulness, and then became the blank, smooth expression of a practiced courtier. "I don't remember our liege dictating these particular instructions to me, but the king's mind is ever subtle. Perhaps that is what he intended—or hoped—would happen."

Art struck his forehead. Griffith hushed King and watched as the blankets stirred. But Marian didn't pop out, and Griffith found it touching that a woman with her reputation would cower when surprised in a compromising position. Especially when she was no doubt livid about Oliver's speculation.

King seemed to find Marian's reticence interesting, also, and he kept his gaze on the bed. "The king wants you to come to him at once."

Griffith paused in the process of donning his cloak. "Why?"

"The earl of Lincoln sailed for Ireland, where he joined forces with the earls of Kildare and Desmond—and the pretender to the throne. In Christ Church Cathedral, in Dublin, they had this impostor crowned Edward, King of England."

"Mother of God," Art whispered.

Oliver nodded grimly. "Well might you say so, for they stole a jeweled wreath from the statue of the Mother of God to place on his undeserving head."

"Blasphemy!"

"Aye. When I left court, rumors were flying that they had sailed."

"How many troops?" Griffith asked.

"Their own men," Oliver replied. "Thomas Fitzgerald, lord chancellor of Ireland, leads a contingent of Irish troops. But most important, they have a company of mercenaries under the command of Martin Schwarz."

Griffith welcomed the surge of power that shifted him from thwarted lover to Henry's warrior. He welcomed the plotting, the intrigue, the language, and with a macabre relish, he said, "An impressive military array, but expensive. Who's paying?"

"Margaret, Edward the Fourth's sister."

"Ah, Margaret," Griffith said contemptuously. "That old witch will do anything to knock Henry Tudor off the throne, and she has the resources to do it."

"Let us not forget the earl of Lincoln is her great-nephew, and Richard the Third's intended heir." Oliver exhibited the cunning that made him a dependable secretary. "I listened to the travelers on the road, and they reported an army landing on the coast of Lancashire."

"Good man!" Griffith thumped Oliver on the back. "Your information is more trustworthy than the rumors at court, I trow. What else have you heard?"

"Little or nothing of use. The rumors agreed on the landing, but not what party or their destination, and once I entered Wales, the situation in England mattered not at all."

"It wouldn't, would it, Lord Secretary?" Art gave a gap-toothed grin. "The Welsh trust Henry to keep his grasp on the throne."

"So he will, while I'm living." Griffith sucked in a breath and could almost smell the lathered horses, the blood, the burning fields. He knew combat. He understood battle tactics. He knew that victory went to the man who remained standing, defeat to the man in the mud. It was clear-cut, understandable masculine labor, suitable for a knight and preferable to the quagmire of emotions that sucked him under when he dealt with Marian.

Still, guilt tugged at him as he glanced at the bed and said, "I'll come."

Art took the role of host, freeing Griffith to handle Marian. "Lord Secretary, won't ye go down to the great hall and partake of some refreshment? Ye've come a long ways, and perhaps Lord Rhys and his wife'll be in. They'll want to give ye a proper welcome."

"Ah." Oliver fussed with the fur on his cloak, fluffing it so it waved with each puff of air. "I'd be pleased to meet Lord Rhys. I'll see you soon, Sir Griffith?"

"Very soon." Griffith waited only until the door had closed before he crossed to the bed. "Love," he murmured, peeling back the blankets, "they're gone. You can come out now."

Marian's tousled hair couldn't hide the hardness of her gaze.

Disappointment pierced him. She'd listened only to further her knowledge of Henry's designs and of his own plans. "You've been spying on me," he said, repeating her accusation—the accusation that had so infuriated him at Castle Wenthaven.

She recognized his intent and answered in a remote tone, devoid of the earlier vibrant excitement. "A disgusting habit, isn't it? But one which proves profitable, as you yourself have discovered. It would seem that you leave at once."

Calculating the time it would take him to collect his men and prepare them, he decided, "Tomorrow morning. And you'll be here when I return. You'll stay and be treated with the honor my future wife commands." Her chin jutted out, and he lifted her head with his hand. He dominated her, as was his intention. "Listen to me. You're safe here. Lionel is safe. My father and my mother will see to it. If you went back out into the world, I would fear for you. So swear to me—"

Her hand flashed out and covered his mouth. "I will exchange no vows with the man who flies to Henry's side when he calls."

He groaned in disgust and pushed her hand aside. "Are we back to that again?"

"When did we leave it?"

As patiently as if he were explaining to a child, he said, "Henry is my liege. I am required by every tenet of Christian knighthood to honor my vows, and the most important vow is to come when my lord needs my services in war. If you heard Oliver King, surely you understood the threat this pretender to the throne poses to Henry."

She turned away.

Abruptly furious, he added, "And to the lady Elizabeth."

"Of course you have to go." She looked back at him and smiled tightly. "So go."

Her terse permission failed to satisfy him. "Would you trust a man who fails his vows to his lord?"

"I trust no man."

"You trust Art."

Her face softened. "I do trust Art."

"He's my own dear servant."

She nodded.

"Would Art serve me so diligently if I were not a man worthy?"

"I don't know."

He almost smiled, "Ask him."

She burst out, "Oh, sometimes I trust you. Then you go to serve Henry, and I remember my duty." She touched the side of his face with her cool fingers. "Go away, Griffith. Fight your battle, and leave me to fight mine."

"You'll be here when I return?"

She shot the words at him like a bolt from a crossbow. "Will you return?"

He almost staggered at the question—what did she mean? Was she worried he would abandon her? Was she worried he would find another?

Or was she worried he would be wounded in battle?

A slow curl of warmth started in his gut and spread to every extremity. She snatched her hand away from him as if his warmth burned her, and he found himself grinning like the king's fool.

"I will return to you, I swear it," he said, "but I would have your token to keep close to my heart."

It stabbed him when she turned her head away again. "I have no token to give to you."

"Then I will take one." He caught a wisp of her long, red hair and singled out one strand. Then with a quick jerk he yanked it ~~free~~ and dangled it before her face. "One token, to lend me the potency of Samson in the battle I face."

Guilt got Marian out of her comfortable bed before the sun rose the next day. Guilt kept her erect and gave her the power to negotiate the spiral stairway that seemed to shift beneath her faltering step. She'd overextended her feeble strength the day before, but she had to catch one glimpse of Griffith before he left.

She couldn't let him ride away without seeing him.

She might never see him again.

With a swipe of her sleeve across her wet eyes, she continued her long journey down to the bailey. The open outer door tunneled the breeze right up the tower to her, and with a shiver she wrapped the blanket closer around her shoulders. She could hear the men calling cheerful obscenities to each other as they prepared for battle.

Stupid, ignorant men. Didn't they understand they could die? Didn't Griffith understand? Didn't he realize that all his battle prowess would be for naught when a single stone from a catapult broke all his bones, or when a bolt from a crossbow pierced his armor, or when he was unhorsed and a knight rode over him? She'd just spent the night imagining all the ways a knight could die on the battlefield, yet Griffith and his men were laughing!

When she reached the bottom, she leaned against the wall, took a few deep breaths, and swallowed hard. She needed to cough but didn't dare for fear the sound would carry. This escapade embarrassed her, and if anyone—including Griffith—discovered her, she would be mortified.

Through the open door she could see the men, the boys, the horses, moving about. But she couldn't see Griffith, so she edged a little farther out. The flooring stones leaked cold through the wool of her hose. She wrapped her toes around the drop at the threshold, and then she saw him.

Laughing. Head back, arms akimbo, pleasure radiating from every pore of his massive body.

Hastily she jumped back inside, but he laughed not at her. He laughed with joy, like all those idiotic, unimaginative men who rode to war without a backward glance. Shaking, she leaned against the wall and wiped the cold sweat from her brow.

She shouldn't have been so petty yesterday. She should have freely given him her blessing as he honored his duty to his king. Instead she'd been surly, told him lies, told him she didn't want him. When actually she'd been eaten up with jealousy.

Jealousy of Henry.

Oh, if she took Griffith, she knew she need never worry about another woman. His marriage vows would be part of his rigid code of honor, and he'd not betray them. No, if she took Griffith, she'd be his only woman—and a lesser creature, knowing always she ranked below his need to fight and serve his king.

How dare he leap from her bed at Henry's call? How dare he be so sanguine at leaving the passion that chained them?

He thought she didn't know, but she did—that he hated the madness that gripped him when in her arms. Somehow he imagined it was less of a disgrace for her to betray her honor than it was for him to succumb to desire.

So the need to serve Henry was honorable, but the need to service her, disreputable.

Her jealousy horrified her. What was this emotion Griffith created in her? Was it more than lust? Was it some mewling sentiment that weakened her, turned her from the path she knew to be right and just?

She had to reject it. She would reject it—but not today. Today she faced the fact Griffith might never return.

Grimacing at the tooled red leather bag she clutched tight in her fist, she wondered how she would get it to Griffith without his knowledge. She'd packed it without a thought to the logistics, but now the facts must be faced. She must either give it to him openly—and she didn't think her pride would stand that—or she must find a way to slip it into his saddlebags.

"M'lady!"

Art's voice made her jump and whirl.

"What're ye doing down here? 'Tis cold and ye're still ill." He put his hand on her arm and urged her toward the stairs. "Ye can wave at Griffith from yer room if ye wish, but for now . . ." He stepped back and peered into her face. "Why're ye grinning at me like that?"

Wet from fording the Trent River, Griffith rode into the royal camp at Radcliffe village with Oliver King on one side, Art on the other, and a small contingent of Welsh knights trailing behind. The journey had been six days of hard riding, first toward Kenilworth, where Henry had gone when he received word of the landing and where his most trusted supporters had joined him with four thousand men. Before Griffith's party reached Kenilworth, however, they received word he had marched on to Nottingham, where his army had been bolstered with five thousand loyal English and Welsh troops. Griffith, Oliver, Art, and the knights had turned north, reaching Nottingham only to find it deserted. Lincoln and the rebel troops were moving south, and Henry evacuated Nottingham for Radcliffe to be in position to halt their progress.

"Where's King Henry's tent?" Oliver shouted to the nearest royal sentinel.

"Who wants t' know?" the sentinel demanded.

Oliver leaned down from his saddle and glared at the hapless soldier. "The king's private secretary."

"Oliver King?" At Oliver's curt nod, the sentinel pulled his forelock in exaggerated deference. "King Henry's been askin' fer ye. Ye're t' ride t' him at once. Up there, on th' rise. See his banner?"

"A comely sight," Art muttered. "And one long in coming. Do ye think we can find our way?"

The laughter he generated died under Griffith's frown, and the Welsh knights turned aside to mingle with the other Welshmen already camped. Art heaved a sigh. "Right glad to get away from ol' puckerpuss, they are," he said to the thin air.

"Well, you're not so lucky," Griffith snapped. "Stay with me and secure my baggage."

The ride to the king's tent was silent and, on Art's part, fraught with unspoken ire, much like the rest of the journey. All in all, it had been a difficult trip, for although the weather had been pleasant, Griffith's mood had not. He had been brooding, and since he had no experience in such matters, he hadn't done it gracefully.

Marian had let him go into combat without a single tear of remorse.

She hadn't sent tender messages or in any way betrayed a concern for his well-being. She hadn't even gone to her window to wave—he'd checked as he rode out of Castle Powel. Didn't she understand some of the men in this battle would be killed? Didn't she understand he himself could be hurt?

He had more than his share of confidence, so he laughed at womanly concerns. But he wanted *his* woman to fear for him, ache for him, every moment he was gone.

Before they dismounted at the king's tent, Henry himself stepped through the open door. "Griffith, where have you been? I've been making war without my most trusted adviser. Oliver, where have you been? My squire's been writing my letters, and making a botch of it."

The king's squire and his military advisers crowded around him, protesting loudly, but they were grinning. The campaign, Griffith concluded, must be going well. Handing the reins of his horse to a page, he asked, "Where's the earl of Lincoln and his troops?"

Henry slapped him on the shoulder. "A pleasant greeting."

Realizing he had been abrupt, Griffith said, "You sent for your humble servant, and I come on the wind, my king." He hitched his cloak closer around his shoulders. "Where's Lincoln?"

Henry laughed and shook his head. To the waiting assemblage, he asked, "Have you ever heard of a Welshman lacking a honeyed tongue?"

"Mayhap, my king," Oliver said, "he needs Welsh soil beneath his feet and a beautiful woman in his arms before the honey can flow."

Griffith glared at Oliver. "Mayhap the king's secretary should keep his mouth shut and his teeth intact."

Oliver sniffed delicately and demanded to see Henry's correspondence, but Griffith knew the subject was not closed. Henry's private secretary did more than write letters; he served as Henry's sieve, discarding the dross of commonplace gossip and bringing him only the jewels of information.

The scene he'd witnessed at Castle Powel was a nugget of pure gold.

Henry led the way into the tent, with Griffith and Oliver on his heels. Art followed, dragging both Griffith's saddlebags and his own.

Pointing to a bench opposite his camp chair, Henry commanded, "Sit here and take refreshment. Your squire, Art—it is Art, is it not?"

Art grinned and nodded, flattered by his sovereign's notice.

Henry continued, "Art will serve you while I reveal Lincoln's location."

With a mumbled thanks, Griffith sank onto his seat, still sour from Marian's neglect. Would the memory of the woman ever leave him?

Henry took no notice of Griffith's morose demeanor but plunged into his account. "I've received word that Lincoln wants to get to the walled safety of York."

Accepting the ale and bread from Art, Griffith

asked, "Is the man so stupid he doesn't understand that cutting across country would expose his flank to our crossfire?"

"I wish he were." Henry sighed. "He has forded the river Trent and pitched his camp along a ridge."

"That's why we're here? So we can march up the Fosseway and grind them into the mud?" When Henry nodded, Griffith grinned savagely. "When do we move?"

"Soon. This afternoon. My royal forces are better equipped and better armed than the rebels. My generals are more experienced." Henry accepted the ale and toasted Griffith with his cup. "I have more troops—my spies say the odds are two to one. Only a colossal blunder could keep the royal cause from prevailing."

Griffith flinched in disapproval. He was soldier enough to know a battle could turn on circumstance and superstitious enough to cringe at Henry's confidence. "One such blunder at Bosworth cost Richard his life, my liege."

The occupants of the tent gasped at such a blunt upbraiding, and Henry lowered his cup. "Damn, man, what vermin bites at you?"

Belatedly Griffith realized he'd been tactless, and he sought to ease the situation. "'Tis naught, my king, but my desire to protect you from the fruits of boastfulness." The occupants gasped again, and Griffith went on. "That is to say, we should entreat God to grant us victory, not challenge God with boastful predictions."

"I understand what you say—'twould be impossible not to, and be assured, I will take it to heart." Henry glanced at Oliver and raised a questioning eyebrow, and Oliver rose from his writing table and came to his side. The secretary whispered in his ear while Griffith squirmed, and when Oliver finished Henry waved him away.

"What did he report?" Griffith demanded.

"What do you think?" Henry retorted, leaning forward.

"I'm going to marry her." Griffith spoke quickly, defiantly, for his sovereign had every right to refuse the match if he desired, and Griffith knew he had but one chance to convince him of the rightness of his suit.

Clearly Henry understood. Clearly Oliver had spoken the name of the lady, for Henry didn't ask to have it defined. But Henry's chin lifted, and Griffith's heart sank. Then he pointed at Griffith. "You've been gone from court nearly a month. Why haven't you married her yet?"

Griffith exchanged glances with Oliver, who smothered a grin. The king's other aides were studiously busy, and every ear, Griffith knew, was trained on this extraordinary exchange.

"Because I've not convinced her I will marry her. She seems to fear"—Griffith looked straight at Henry—"your intervention with her son."

Henry slowly slid a hand over his chin and cheek. "I need to be shaved," he mused. "I hate to ride into battle in a disheveled manner. It might affect the morale of the troops. Art, can you shave a man without nicking him?"

Art bobbed in a bow. "I can slice a man's throat or not, as I please, and it would please me to shave ye without a nick."

"Is he boasting?" Henry asked Griffith.

"Not at all," Griffith replied.

"Then shave me you shall," Henry told Art. "Take my knife and hone it to the proper sharpness."

"If ye don't mind, my king, I would use Sir Griffith's knife. I gave it to him myself, a good many years ago, and the blade is of finest Spanish steel." Without awaiting permission, Art dumped the contents of Griffith's saddlebag on the royal carpet and scrambled among the clothing.

"Art, what are you doing?" Griffith asked in exasperation.

"Looking for yer knife."

"Have you been beaten by the stupid stick?" Griffith pulled it from his belt and dangled it in front of Art's nose. "You know I keep it always close to hand."

"I'd forgotten." After ramming Griffith's possessions back into the bags, Art took the blade and ran his callused thumb along the edge. "'Twill take but a few moments to whet it."

"Do so." To his squire, Henry said, "Bring me hot water." To the clump of milling noblemen, he announced, "I don't like an audience when I am shaved."

When Henry chose to, Griffith realized, he was capable of clearing the room in less time than it took to shear a sheep and with just as much purpose. Only Oliver remained, his pensive gaze firmly attached to the paper on which he scratched military notations.

"As to Lady Marian Wenthaven . . ." Henry's thin lips compressed into a single line as he sorted through the shiny pile of armor. "She's of interest to the Crown only insofar as she is a cherished friend of the queen's. Her son is of interest to us because the queen is his godmother."

"Is she?"

"Did you not know?"

"Nay, but it is fitting."

Henry ignored that comment with regal disdain. "So the queen is concerned with Lady Marian and her son, but as I have pointed out to her, Lady Marian has a father who is not, to our knowledge, a traitor."

He paused, and Griffith murmured, "Not quite yet, my liege."

"Not quite yet? There's the rub, is it not?" Henry flashed a glance at Griffith. "Not quite yet. I've heard tales that Lord Wenthaven is hiring Welsh mercenaries."

"I saw it with my own eyes."

"Wenthaven has ever been a thorn in my side. He's clever, with dreams that far overreach his humble beginnings. When this battle is done, I will have to do something about the earl of Wenthaven." Henry lifted a breastplate from the pile and examined it for dents. "If Lady Marian's father rebelled against me and was put to the horn, Lady Marian and her son would be a royal responsibility. As a respected king, I should teach every traitor a lesson by chopping off his head and reducing his family to penury. In this way, I would be intervening with Lady Marian's son. What's his name?"

"Lionel, my liege." Griffith was fascinated with this performance of regal distress and more fascinated that the king agreed with Marian, but in a completely different manner.

"Lionel." Again Henry ran his hand across his face, but he paused and pressed hard against his mouth, as if Lionel's name tasted unpalatable to him. The twinge faded, however, and he continued, "But, as I said, Lady Marian is a friend of the queen's, and the queen would be distressed if I so treated her former lady-in-waiting and, of course, Lady Marian's son—the queen's own godson. So if Lady Marian were the wife of a loyal subject such as yourself . . ."

He left it to dangle in the air like the bait on a fishing line, and Griffith took it without hesitation. "She would be safe, and her heritage kept intact?"

"For her *son*," Henry agreed.

"Ah, but Lady Marian has expressed concerns much like your own, and what she fears is much different from what you've foreseen."

"I would have the queen's friend be without fear."

"Nevertheless, Lady Marian has expressed a concern that if I should wed her, *I* will be put to the horn."

"In case of her father's treachery, do you mean?"

"For whatever reason," Griffith said carefully.

"You may assure Lady Marian that you are, at present, one of my trusted advisers. If she would wed you, I would treat you with all the respect your position demands, even"—Henry looked straight at

Griffith—"if you were to retire from court and concentrate on your holdings to the exclusion of all else."

By which Henry meant, Griffith concluded, he would be relegated to obscurity when he wed Marian. It was the price he would pay for his bliss.

"You would, of course, be properly compensated. . . ." Henry sounded sincere but abstracted, as if he knew compensation little interested Griffith. Coming to the heart of his concern, he asked, "Lady Marian has honor?"

"An excess of honor," Griffith confirmed.

"Aye." Henry sighed. "Of course, she must have. Elizabeth has described"—he faltered briefly, then rallied—"the queen has described Lady Marian's support through those months of terror in Richard's court. I don't know how my wife would have survived without Lady Marian's quick wit and fierce friendship. I don't know . . ." His hand shot out, and he grasped Griffith by the shoulder in a fearsome grip. "I give her to you. Take her. Take her son. Keep them from harm, from those who would use them for their own purposes. As your king, I charge you with this task. I pray you perform it well, for the consequences of failure are dire and dread."

This was no royal performance. This was the cry of a man who would safeguard his wife, his heir, his throne.

Seeing Henry now, with resolution burning in the smithy of his mind, Griffith was struck anew by the rightness of his kingship. This man would wield England into one entity, given the chance, and his vow—that nothing and no one would ever take his throne—branded fear in Griffith's soul. Fear, respect, and comprehension. A comprehension far beyond men's fumbling attempts at communication.

"I will do so, whether you wish it or no, but I must know—who is the child?"

Henry's eyes betrayed no emotion. "Why, he is Lady Marian's son."

At the appearance of Henry's cold, still face, Griffith stifled the questions that clamored for release.

"Oliver!" Henry cried.

The secretary leaped to his feet.

"Write to the lady Marian, inviting her to visit us immediately, and we will celebrate her marriage to Sir Griffith at court." Henry beamed benevolently at Griffith. "Although her father has the means, I myself will help dower the bride."

Griffith gulped in dismay. "I don't know . . ."

Reading Griffith's mind, Henry asked, "She will come. We simply must choose the messenger with care. Whom does she trust above all others?"

"Art," Griffith replied.

Art stuck his head in the tent. "Ye called?"

"Art." Henry wrapped his arm around the man's skinny shoulders. "Art, Griffith tells me the lady Marian trusts you."

Wary, Art agreed.

"Then you're the very man to fetch her to her dear one's side so we can conclude a marriage between Sir Griffith and Lady Marian. Dear me." Henry frowned. "She's the daughter of an earl, so she carries the title of 'Lady,' and Griffith is only a 'Sir.' We'll have to do something about that. Oliver, make a note. Sir Griffith needs a title."

"Aye, my liege." Oliver's face never changed expression as he selected a clean parchment and wrote the reminder in bold letters.

Griffith faltered, "Henry, there's no need."

Henry waved aside his protest. "Nonsense. You've served me faithfully, and the quest which I have asked of you is not without danger. Now, Art, how long will it take you to go to Wales and return with Lady Marian?"

"Depends on if ye stay in one place," Art answered, doubt clear in his tone.

"I intend to return to Kenilworth after this engagement"—Henry peered at Griffith—"if it is successful, God willing. Bring her there."

"Five days of hard riding to get to Castle Powel," Art said. "Returning with a lady to Kenilworth— probably ten days."

"Returning with Lady *Marian,*" Griffith said dryly, "probably seven days."

"Returning with Lionel," Art countered, "probably twelve days."

Henry squeezed Art's arm a little too tightly. "Don't bring the child. My realm is not as safe as I would like, and Castle Powel will keep him from harm."

"Don't know that she'll come without Lionel," Art said.

"It is the king's command," Henry answered.

Art cast a pleading glance at Griffith, but Griffith only shrugged. "If anyone can bring her, 'tis you, Art."

"Art will convince her." The king had grown into his royal role, for he sounded completely sure of Art's abilities. Leaning down, he picked something up. "What's this?" From his fingers dangled a tooled red leather pouch held closed by a golden thread.

"It was in Griffith's saddlebags," Art said. "It musta fallen out when I opened them."

Griffith cast him a suspicious glance but took the bag and opened it. Into his palm tumbled a gray stone, looking just like the stones that built Castle Powel. More slowly, a clinging mass slid out, and Griffith recognized the color. Lifting it by one end, he suspended a thin, bright red braid of human hair that almost brushed the ground. The sunshine became entangled in it, as did Griffith's heart.

Henry touched the glittering braid. "Your lady's token?"

"I suppose. . . ." Griffith blinked back emotion.

"Aye, 'tis my lady's token. She would have me be as strong as Samson."

"And the rock?" Henry asked.

Griffith stared at Art, who gazed innocently at the ceiling. "I suppose my squire might know."

Rocking on his heels, Art said, "I don't know nothing, but I surmise the stone is to keep you as everlasting as the good Welsh hills."

"I suppose you're right." Griffith tried to sound sarcastic. Instead he sounded as soft as new-made pudding. "Why I didn't find this before?"

Art smirked. "I don't know, of course—"

"Of course," Griffith said.

"—but Lady Marian probably didn't want ye to find it until ye came close to battle, for fear the magic would rub off."

When Griffith recovered enough to put the pouch into his shirt, Art said to Henry, "I've honed the knife, my liege. Your squire waits with hot water. Are ye ready to be shaved?"

"Shaved?" Henry frowned. "I'm going into battle, not courting a maid. Why would I want to be shaved? What I want is for you to leave on your mission."

Art staggered. "Now?"

"Of course not! Your horse needs to rest. Still, I hate to have you wait. . . ." Henry drummed his fingers on the table, then his face brightened. "I'll send you to my stable master with a royal seal set in wax, and with that he will believe you when you tell him you must have a fresh horse, the best we have, and supplies for a four-day trip."

"Five days," Griffith reminded him.

Henry didn't acknowledge Griffith by even a flick of an eyelash. "Ah, Art, what an adventure you will have. I envy you the chance to visit Wales again."

"Seems like I just left it," Art mumbled.

# 14

"*The battle proceeds* as we had hoped. My dear Lord Oxford advanced to meet Lincoln's charge down Rampire Hill. The fighting was fierce, but the superiority of my armor and weaponry soon revealed itself." Smug and smiling, Henry looked up from the field dispatch he was reading. "It would seem, Griffith, that God does indeed favor the prepared."

Frustrated, Griffith slapped his leather gloves onto the table littered with similar dispatches. He paced away, lifting each foot high, his metal sabbatons clinking each time he struck a rock. The plate armor that covered his legs made each step awkward, and the joints at elbow and knee creaked.

Griffith didn't notice. He didn't notice how the noonday sun broiled him like meat within a pot or that the heat made him sweat into the padding protecting him from the metal. He didn't even notice Oliver King's exasperated sigh or the telling glances with which Henry's personal staff communicated. Sick of inaction, he sought the words to convince Henry to send him into battle. "God has certainly favored me, my liege, with your continued patronage, but I would be grateful for the chance to smite your enemies from the face of the earth."

Untouched by Griffith's effort to be eloquent, Henry rolled the parchment. "Bedford and Oxford have it well in hand."

Griffith's breastplate glistened in the morning sun. He held his helmet tightly under his arm and clenched his teeth. He wanted to fight. He needed to fight. He'd been frustrated for days, ever since he'd ridden away from Marian, knowing she didn't care about him. Now he was frustrated as Art rode back to her, for he knew she did care. Her token even now hung beneath his breastplate, over his heart.

And Henry insisted on keeping him from battle.

But Henry wasn't as obdurate as he appeared. "You know I'm right. 'Tis foolish to engage more men than is necessary. God favors us—why fly in the face of God because of misplaced manly pride?"

Misplaced manly pride? Was it misplaced manly pride that made Griffith want to relieve his frustration with hard labor? With fighting?

"I do require your assistance with Lady Marian more than I require your assistance on the battlefield," Henry went on.

"I know."

"But if you're going to sulk"—Henry sighed—"you may go."

But for the weight of his armor, Griffith would have jumped for joy.

"Thank God," Oliver muttered. "He's been pacing for hours, and it sounds like a damned soul dragging his burdens through eternity."

Henry swung on Oliver. "Don't say that! 'Tis bad luck to speak of death before a battle."

Shriveling beneath Henry's admonition, Oliver stammered an apology.

Griffith glared. Would Oliver's words remind

Henry of the dangers of battle? Would Henry change his mind?

Henry only lifted his finger in admonition. "Stay out of the heavy fighting. Go only as a messenger. Observe the situation and bring me information about the fighting."

"As you command, my lord." As happy as a monk on Easter morn, Griffith tried to cram the helmet over his head, but the fastening chain caught on his nose. With a laugh, he unhooked the chain and dropped the helmet into place. He fumbled with the connection that would chain the helmet to his armor, but he couldn't see it and his broad fingers weren't meant to perform such delicate work.

"Let my squire do it," Henry said.

"Your squire is at the top of the ridge watching the battle with his eyes bugging out of his head," Griffith replied.

"Oliver?" Henry asked.

Oliver lifted his head from the dispatches he was writing. "With all due respect, my liege, I'm no knight."

Henry glanced around at his staff as they rushed to and fro, then sighed. "Here, I'll do it."

Remembering their positions, Griffith said, "Ah, King Henry? It isn't proper for a king to serve a knight."

"Let's not tell anyone, then." Grasping the flapping chain, Henry fastened it, then adjusted the helmet to its proper position and turned the bolts to secure it. He surveyed his handiwork with pride and said, "One never forgets the lessons one learns as a squire."

Testing the set of his armor, Griffith agreed, "It would seem not."

"I would that my most trusted adviser remains unharmed." Henry dropped Griffith's visor over his face.

Griffith waited until the ringing sound had faded from his ears before he promised, "So I will."

He hoisted himself into the saddle of his destrier and then galloped toward Rampire Hill. Once on the field, he raised his visor again. After all, how could he report on the battle's progress with restricted vision? It wasn't likely he would fight, God rot it. The battle had wound down to a few individual combats, and here and there Henry's men held hostages at sword point.

The flags of the enemy commanders were nowhere to be seen.

"Fled or dead," Griffith muttered, surveying the carnage with an instinctive eye for the logistics. Noting a small pocket of hot conflict close against the side of the hill, he decided to investigate—not to disobey Henry, of course, but simply to report the tidings as completely as possible. As he neared, he heard a confused clamor of high-pitched Gaelic and guttural German and a good Welsh voice roaring, "Bleed your green blood on the soil and nourish it!"

As Griffith spurred his horse, he loosened his weapons: his spear, his steel mace, and his two-handed sword. Two Welsh knights stood on the ground, fighting back to back as a dozen foreigners shuffled around them, attacking carefully—they wanted the armor, Griffith knew, and would take care not to damage it. It was the only thing that had saved his countrymen thus far, but their plight had attracted more than just his attention. Three English knights were galloping to the scene.

He would get there first. Through the pounding of the hooves, he heard a Welsh roar, "Die, you lickspit! Burn in—"

Griffith lowered his lance and spitted a mercenary as one of the beleaguered knights staggered. Abandoning the lance, Griffith turned and charged back to the scene. Only one knight now stood, and as one mercenary prepared to perform the death blow, the others grouped together to defend themselves from Griffith.

Raising his mace, Griffith dented a helmet and smashed the head within, but the blow from one of the war hammers knocked him off his horse. As he slowly struggled to his feet, his armor weighing him down, the English knights arrived to distract the mercenaries. Griffith drew his two-handed sword from his destrier's saddle in time to meet the charge of a maddened Irishman.

Griffith's blood sang in his veins, his teeth parted in a fierce smile, and he used his advantage of weight and height to hammer the Irishman to the ground. He lifted his sword for the death thrust, but a German war cry brought him around to face a mercenary charge.

The German was big, a match for Griffith's size, and skilled, a master of the sword. He moved well, and clearly he'd kept himself alive through a combination of strength and agility.

He was perfect.

Griffith couldn't stop grinning, his lips pulled back from his teeth, his face frozen in a grimace. After this decisive victory, there would be few serious challenges to Henry's power or to his dynasty, and even if there were, Henry had as much as told him he would no longer be in the center of any conflict that battered England. So Griffith resolved to make the most of this fight, to wring each drop of pleasure from the heat and smell, from the thrust and parry.

The German mercenary seemed to know. He laughed within his helmet and swung with ever-increasing vigor. The swords ground together, metal shrieking. Muscles strained, tendons creaked. The shouts of the other conflicts faded as Griffith concentrated on this fight, his final great contest.

For every thrust, the German had a parry. For

every sword swing, Griffith had a dodge. Time slowed to minutes, grinding on rusty gears. His arms began to tremble beneath the weight of the blade. He noted with satisfaction that his opponent's blade also quivered. His ears were clogged. His lungs burned, his reactions slowed. But the German never took advantage. Griffith still grinned, for the German *couldn't* take advantage. As Griffith wore down, so did his foe.

Finally it seemed they were fighting in slow motion. Each stroke rose and fell with exquisite care. Each blow could scarcely be felt through the double protection of armor and padding. Griffith began to wonder how it would end—with the two combatants fainting from exhaustion?

Marshaling his strength, he aimed at the German's neck and swung one last mighty blow. If it met the relatively slender protection of the gorget, the German would be at least knocked silly.

But it met with nothing. The German stumbled, deliberately falling backward, and the impetus pulled Griffith around in a great circle from which he couldn't recover. He, too, fell, a twisted pile of metal. Lifting his head, he stared at the German

The mercenary raised his visor and stared back, then started to laugh. "I surrender," he said in German.

Griffith didn't understand a word, but he recognized the gestures and knew it to be the only ending possible. The mercenary stood on English soil. He had no choice but to surrender, and he had found in Griffith an opponent worthy of receiving his sword.

Griffith signaled his willingness to accept that surrender, then struggled to stand. The rotation of his fall had pushed the metal joints at knee and elbow ajar, and he felt like a turtle knocked on its back as he maneuvered to get his feet beneath him.

He had just succeeded when an English voice

shouted, "Look out!" Griffith instinctively verified the location of his prisoner. The German posed no threat, but his horrified gaze brought Griffith's face up.

The Irish warrior stood on his feet, bleeding, dying, but holding his sword high above his head. As Griffith stared, dumbstruck, the blade descended in a shining arc right for his face. He flung his arm up, but the armor only deflected the blow, it couldn't block it. The blade slammed into his cheek. Blood spurted in a fountain before his eyes. He heard a shriek of pain and was distantly surprised he had screamed.

As his vision cleared, he saw the German, on his feet, with the Irishman spitted on his sword.

He'd done it, Griffith realized. He'd got himself killed. Something covered his eyes, but he could still see the sun. It danced in his face, heating him. Black-and-red dots began to obscure it, but the heat increased. He pushed the place over his heart where Marian's token hung, and like a vision of heaven, he saw the cool green of Wales, saw the gray stones of his home, and imagined his love, waiting patiently there for his return.

Marian watched the retreating shoreline of Wales and wondered if she'd ever see Griffith again.

Griffith. A man who forged his path of integrity through that confusing forest of right and wrong. Griffith. Strong and sure, but so far away, fighting for the king he loved. He'd triumph, she assured herself. No one could kill a warrior as massive and vital as he. No one could kill . . . She covered her eyes with her hand.

"If ye want th' lad, ye'd best be grabbin' him," the old mariner growled.

She lunged for Lionel and caught him just as he tipped over the edge of the little rowboat in his quest to touch the shiny ocean swells. He squawked and fought, but she dragged him back to the seat at the stern and wrapped her arms around him.

"Nay, Mama! Lionel go swim," he insisted.

"Lionel no swim," she told him. "Lionel go home."

He thought for a moment, then brightened. "Grandda Rhys?"

The mariner laughed, and his handsome, angry face watched them with what looked like satisfaction. He made her uncomfortable with his obvious malevolence, and Lionel made her want to cry with his obvious affections.

Rhys wasn't his grandfather. Wenthaven was his grandfather, yet it was Rhys who had treated Lionel like a child to be cherished. He had given Lionel so much unstinting love that for the first time since Lionel had been born, Marian had found herself supplanted as Lionel's favorite person. It had been odd to watch Rhys and Lionel together, to realize how much Lionel needed a masculine hand, to know that with Rhys as grandfather and Griffith as father, Lionel would grow brave and honorable.

Aye, he'd be brave and honorable, but he could be that and more, given the chance.

Why had God brought Griffith to her? Before Griffith, she'd been sure in her mind, knowing what she must do, what she'd sworn to do. She'd dared to dream of greatness, of justice, for herself and for her son.

But being with Griffith had shown her a different dream. Was Griffith a gift from God? Or a temptation from the devil?

In that first passionate night, Griffith had proved himself to be a temptation, and she had proved herself to be wise and valiant when she fled. God would reward her—so she had thought.

Instead He had taken her to Castle Powel, and that had proved an even crueler fate. She didn't believe in love. She couldn't, and it had been almost easy to dismiss Griffith's affection when no example of love disturbed her ambitions. But living with his parents made happiness seem tangible. Despite their early problems, Rhys and Angharad were happy together. They loved each other. And seeing them together almost convinced Marian to put her own happiness before the rights of her son.

That was why she'd left. Though she'd hated leaving without a word to Angharad or Rhys, they'd been calling the banns and she couldn't—

"Best keep him away from th' oars, too, m'lady, or I'll smack him wi' one an' knock him into th' drink."

Marian dragged Lionel back to her by the scruff of his neck and eyed the Welshman with unease.

Dolan had shipped all over England, he told her, stashed a lot of coin, and had come back to his home in Wales where the living was cheap and no one cared that his two gloves covered no more than five fingers altogether. So she'd hired him and his rowboat to transport her back to England. Now she wondered if she'd been impetuous.

Perhaps the mariner had shipped all over England, but not necessarily with any legitimate concern. More likely he'd been a pirate, preying on the innocent, losing his digits in pursuit of ill-gotten gains. Perhaps now that he had her in his power, he dreamed his pirate dreams once more.

But Marian had her own dreams, and one crafty old peasant wasn't getting in her way. True, she had Lionel, and he was a disadvantage in a fight, but she also had a strong arm, a sharp knife, and enough guile to lull the man into eternal repose. With a flutter of her eyelashes and a coy smile, she watched Dolan row. "You're very strong. I imagine the muscles in your arms are like tempered steel."

He stared at her suspiciously.

"Most of the men I've known have been lords, and

they're such weaklings. They only know how to lift a pen, not coil rope and lift that heavy anchor and move the oars back and forth. What do you call that?"

"Ye're woofin' me," he said. "Ye're not as stupid as all that."

He was rowing them parallel to the shore, traveling east toward the wash of the river Dee, but he kept them far enough out to sea to preclude her swimming to land, even if she hadn't had Lionel. Widening her eyes, she said, "Why do you say I'm stupid? Not everyone knows the names for all these boat things."

"I said ye're *not* stupid. Took one smart lady t' figure an escape from Castle Powel. If ye'd gone by land, they'd have caught up wi' ye."

"Aye," she said, remembering the wretched trip into Wales, and she dropped her hand on the top of Lionel's dark head.

"But a ship at sail leaves no trail, so th' sayin' goes, an' ye reasoned that out, an' reasoned out who t' ask who'd not go cryin' t' Lord Rhys." He nodded, his body bending with the rhythm of the oars. "So there's no use a-tellin' me ye're a fool."

His black eyes snapped with resentment, although she knew not why. His sensuous lips smiled, but not with kindness. He was as handsome as sin itself and, she feared, twice as evil.

"Man," Lionel said, pointing at Dolan and smiling so widely all his little white teeth showed. "Nice man."

"Hey? What's that?" Insulted, Dolan reared back and glared at Lionel. "Did he call me a nice man?"

Marian tried to hush Lionel, but Dolan insisted, "Did he?"

"He did," she answered.

Dolan transferred his glare to her. "I'm not a nice man."

"Grandda," Lionel insisted, still obviously enchanted with Dolan. "*My* grandda."

"Nay, sweeting. He's not your grandda."

Leaning down, she pulled a piece of bread from her bag and handed it to Lionel, hoping to quiet the inopportune worship. She thought she'd succeeded when Lionel took the bread and gnawed on it, dropping enough crumbs to attract the seabirds, but Lionel used the moment of silence to contemplate Dolan.

"What're ye starin' at?" Dolan snarled to the child.

"Grandda . . . Rhys?" Lionel inquired.

Dolan leaped up, making the oars clank in disarray and the boat rock dangerously. "I'm not Rhys! Ye hear me, I'm not Rhys. I'm Dolan."

Marian cowered from his fury, then surreptitiously verified the presence of her knife in her sleeve; but Lionel only watched Dolan with intense interest. With his mouth still stuffed with bread, Lionel said, "Grandda Dolan."

Sagging back onto his seat, Dolan demanded of Marian, "Can't ye make that whelp shut his mouth?"

"It would appear not," she admitted. "Why did you agree to take me?"

"I liked th' money." He picked up the oars again, keeping a wary eye on Lionel. "Can't never have too much money."

"And?"

"Am I goin' t' rape ye, do ye mean?"

"Are you going to try?"

He stopped rowing and looked her over, giving special notice to the stretch of her bodice. "Nay. My quarrel's wi' old Rhys, not wi' his son, an' if I raped his son's betrothed, I have no doubt young Griffith'd take it in his head t' slit my gullet. Nay, I'll not rape ye. Provided ye pay me twice what ye promised. I don't like skinny women." He cursed when Lionel bobbed up and scrambled toward him. "An' I don't like whelps, so keep this one out o' me way!"

Marian grabbed for Lionel, but the child was too

quick. Thrusting the damp, mashed chunk of bread in Dolan's face, he said, "Grandda Dolan eat."

Marian reached for her son, but something stopped her. The odd expression on Dolan's face, she supposed, or the way he stared at Lionel, like a tomcat about to adopt a puppy. Slowly he parted his lips, displaying a mouth full of strong teeth. Then, slowly, he took a nibble.

Only one, and not more than a crumb, but it satisfied Lionel, and Marian felt great triumph. For only twice what she'd promised, she'd gained safe passage to England for her and her son, she didn't have to fight for her virtue, and Dolan—well, even Dolan might yet prove to be one of Lionel's conquests.

Perhaps this adventure would yet prove successful.


She wasn't so complacent as she watched the old mariner pull away hours later.

"I'm glad to see you go," she said to the disappearing boat. "You're a nasty man."

Dolan didn't even wave when Lionel called, "Grandda! Grandda!"

"Nasty, nasty man," Marian insisted, half hoping Lionel would repeat it. "Nasty man."

He didn't repeat it. He only sat and cried.

She picked him up and wiped his tears. Her feet sank into the marshy ground, and her bags were piled at her feet. Her purse was noticeably thinner, thanks to Dolan, who seemed to regret his moment of softening and had proceeded to prove it with his unyielding demand for money and his absolute refusal to acknowledge Lionel.

Now she needed a horse, and it had better be a cheap one.

Worse still, she needed a destination.

She'd escaped Castle Powel knowing only that if she stayed, Lionel's destiny would remain unfulfilled.

But who in England would help her? Would her father?

Aye, Wenthaven would, for his own benefit—but who then would protect Lionel and his interests?

Only her. Only Lady Marian Wenthaven. But she could do it. She was strong.

Picking up her bags, picking up her son, she trudged toward Shropshire. Toward Castle Wenthaven and her father.

"She's gone?" Art could scarcely credit it, and his hopes sank as he stared at a grim-looking Rhys. "Ye couldn't find her?"

"Two days we've searched, and not a sign of her. How could she have gone so far with a child?" Rhys struck the stable wall with his fist.

"I don't understand it," Art mumbled. He'd scarcely stepped through the gate of Castle Powel when Rhys had found him and told him that the woman he sought—the one woman Griffith wanted—had vanished. Now Art dislodged his cap and rubbed his bald head, trying to massage some thought into his weary brain. "When I left, she had sent Griffith a token, and I thought everything was settled. Now . . ."

"There's no understanding women," Rhys said.

Art nodded. "Aye, so I've always said. Damned shame they're so fine between the covers."

"There's enough of that." Angharad stepped through the open door of the stables, bringing the sunshine of the spring day with her. "The lass was disturbed in her mind about the marriage, and we knew that, but we had the banns called anyway because we were so excited about Griffith and his madness for her. 'Tis easy to understand, but hard to fix." Slipping her arm through Art's, she said, "You know her better than any of us, Art. Give us the benefit of your thoughts."

"What's Art going to do that I haven't done?" Rhys snapped.

"Tell us where she's gone, mayhap," Angharad snapped back.

Art looked at Rhys and shook his head. Art knew the sweat and stain of the trip was ground into his clothes. He knew his face looked like scraps of leather patched together. But if anything, Rhys looked worse than Art. His eyes were bloodshot, his hands hung at his sides, and he could scarcely speak for frustration. "I've sought her everywhere she could have gone."

"Then seek where she couldn't have gone! She has to be somewhere. Don't you understand . . ." Angharad pressed her hand to her cheek. "I can't believe I'm arguing about this with you. You've been searching for three solid days, Rhys. You're tired and not rational. Get you up to bed and let Art and me find Lady Marian."

"Fine. You and Art find Lady Marian. You and Art succeed where I have failed." Rhys started out the door, then turned back. "But I can tell you where she isn't. She isn't on the road to England, and she isn't at St. Asaph's monastery, and she isn't with that mercenary troop haunting the neighborhood, because I personally spoke to the mercenary, Cledwyn, and took his camp apart."

"Cledwyn?" Art said. "Did ye say Cledwyn?"

"So I did." Rhys's bitterness seemed to ease. "Do you know the name?"

"That man worked for Wenthaven, and ye can wager he isn't here to do Lady Marian a good turn." Art scratched the prickly hairs on his chin. "She wasn't in the camp?"

"I swear it."

"They couldn't have taken her from the castle?" Art asked. "Through the secret passage?"

Rhys's weariness was almost palpable. "I plugged

the passage years ago, you know that, but I inspected it anyway. 'Tis untouched."

"Nevertheless, I'd like to pay Cledwyn a visit."

Rhys shook his head. "As soon as I spoke to them, they fled."

"Mayhap," Angharad said, "they were giving chase to Lady Marian."

"To an illusion, then." Rhys's patience vanished completely. "She left no trace, I tell you. She didn't take a horse, she's not hiding within the castle, and"—he pointed accusingly at Angharad—"she didn't go by sea."

He marched out of the stable, head held high, and Angharad turned to Art. "I suggested she might have gone by sea, and he's angry he didn't think of it. That's why he's going up to bed—so we can go speak to the fisherfolk and his pride won't be involved."

"Not until later," Art said.

"Oh, well, later he'll be rested and able to shrug it off."

They stepped into the sun, and Art saw that Angharad, too, looked tired. He comforted her with a hug. "Ye can't blame yerself for this. The lass is half-wild and a bit of a handful."

"But I can blame myself." Angharad smiled wistfully. "I know how she felt, better than most, but I wanted her for Griffith so badly. I wouldn't listen when she tried to tell me of her dreams for her boy—I thought only of my dreams for mine."

"'Tis no sin. I have those dreams, too."

"Aye, you would." Angharad touched Art's scraggly chin.

"I worked hard to bring this match to fruition, and I'll not give up now." With a hard determination, he demanded, "Tell me why ye think she went by sea."

"For all that Rhys is a hardheaded man, he's a good tracker, and his men are good trackers." Angharad strode toward the open gate with grim purpose. "'Tis impossible for Lady Marian to have gone and left no sign, unless . . ."

Art followed her pointing finger and saw, silhouetted against the ocean below, the fishing village. He understood Rhys's frustration and objected, "The fisherfolk are yer folk. They'd not take Griffith's betrothed. Not on her request, nor on anyone else's."

"Nay, the fisherfolk wouldn't." Angharad smiled with an almost wicked amusement. "But do you remember Dolan?"

"Do I remember Dolan?" Art cried aloud. "Aye, I remember Dolan. A bad seed. He was the squire who thought he could woo ye."

"That's Dolan."

"Rhys threw him out years ago."

"Aye, and he swore he'd have no more of the knight's life, and ran away to sea."

"So he did." Art looked at her closely. "Are ye saying he's back?"

"Last year, and more perverse than ever."

"I'm surprised Rhys hasn't killed him."

"Are you?"

Art shifted his feet. "Nay, I suppose not. Blood's thicker than water, and for Rhys to have the blood of his brother—"

"Half brother," she corrected.

"—half brother on his hands would be a bit of a stain."

"Dolan knows it, too." Angharad once again linked arms with Art and pulled him down the path to the village. "That's why I think we should ask him about Lady Marian."

# 15

*The crack of a twig* in the woods beside the road stopped Marian in her tracks and brought her whirling around. Vigorously she shushed Lionel, but the boy in the saddle insisted, "Why, Mama? Why?"

The reins in her hand tightened as the old gelding spied a chance at freedom and tugged, but she was wise to his tricks now, and she clutched the leather as she scanned the shadows in the trees. She saw nothing, but she had discovered she presented an easy target for looters and scoundrels and other characters even less savory.

Although she could hear nothing else suspicious, she led the horse into the bushes on the other side of the road and tethered him firmly to a branch. Each wheeze sounded like the horse's last, and Lionel still asked, "Why, Mama? Why?"

"Hush, Lionel." She pulled him from the saddle and walked deeper into the shadows. "Let Mama hold you."

He was willing. Poor lad, he was more than willing. He'd been torn from the only home he'd ever known, dragged to Wales, given into the keeping of

Rhys and Angharad while she was ill, and just as he had settled into a routine with them, she had dragged him away again. Two days of traveling had tired him, the killings of the day before disturbed him, and nothing could convince him she could keep him safe.

Now he buried his face in her neck, and her heart ached when she felt him tremble. Straining, she listened again for sound of a footfall, but all she heard was the horse's everlasting groans as it tried to free itself and gallop back toward its home.

"Mama," Lionel whispered.

She rubbed his back. "Hush, Lionel."

"Mama—Art."

"Nay, my babe, there's no Art. He's far away."

Lionel lifted his head and pointed to the trees. "Art," he insisted. "Art! Art!"

His voice got louder with each repetition, and he bounced in her arms.

"Art! Art!"

Incredulous but half-believing, she turned to face the shadows. There was nothing there. Nothing but a blasted stump with holes that looked like eyes. She patted Lionel again and moved toward it. "Nay, Lionel. See? 'Tis only—"

Like some dwarf spirit come to life, the stump rose. She stumbled backward, tripped on an exposed root, and fell with Lionel clutched in her arms. He landed on her stomach, knocking the breath out of her, and scrambled up before she could catch him.

"Art!" the boy shrieked.

"Lionel," she cried as the man-tree stooped and picked up her son.

The man-tree moved forward, and she struggled to her feet, prepared to fight this spirit for her son. But the stump spoke in familiar tones. "Greetings, m'lady." Art stepped full into the sun, and he grinned as cheerfully as if they were meeting in the great hall of Castle Powel. "What a surprise to meet ye here."

Marian placed her hand on her chest, the thump of her heart so strong that it shook her fingers.

Or were her fingers shaking on their own?

"Art, where's . . . ?" She faltered, looking to the man who stood behind him.

He wasn't Griffith. Although she couldn't see him well, she had discovered she placed every man in the world in one of two categories. They either were tall, dark, and Griffith, or they were not. She never needed a second glance. Whether she liked it or not, she recognized Griffith with more than her sight; she recognized him with her soul.

Dolan stepped out and mocked her with a bow, then said, "I'll take care o' yer noble steed, shall I?"

"Why are you here?" Marian asked him, but she saw only his back as he stomped away. Turning to Art, she demanded again, "Why are you here?"

He said the last thing she expected. "I came from Castle Wenthaven."

"From Wenthaven? What were you doing there?"

"Looking for ye."

"Mother of God." Marian grabbed his wrist. "Is Griffith hurt?"

Art's mouth curled in a crafty smile of satisfaction. "He was fine when I left him at Stoke." He scarcely waited for her heartbeat to calm before he added, "Of course, that was before the battle."

"You left him before the battle? Art, how could you?"

Art let Lionel slip to the ground and stepped forward to look straight in Marian's face. "Are ye accusing me of abandoning him in his hour of need, m'lady?"

"I . . ." Her gaze slipped away from his. "Nay, Art, of course not."

"Glad to hear it, I am. For it would be an inappropriate accusation coming from ye, would it not?"

Art's tone contained a bite she'd never heard before,

and the guilt that had dogged her every step strengthened. "Have you heard any word on the battle?"

"Word in the countryside is that Henry's forces easily defeated the pretender, and Henry's returned to Kenilworth to rest."

"But no word of Griffith?"

"What word would there be about one man?"

"Aye." On edge with frustration and uncertainty, she wandered to the rough-skinned oak and hugged it as if it were her lover. "You . . . how did you know I had left Powel?"

"Lord Rhys and Lady Angharad told me. They were much distressed at yer defection and very worried about yer safety." Art glanced at Lionel as he ran in circles, exalting in his freedom. "About Lionel's safety, too."

"You couldn't have gone from Powel to Stoke, back to Powel, and then here in only nine days. 'Tis . . ." She wanted to say impossible, but as her gaze swept him she stopped. He might claim he had blended with the scenery because he was Welsh and canny about the woodland arts, but the dirt he wore lent him a natural camouflage, and he looked worn, thin, and years older. Even those few hairs that so jauntily decorated his bald pate hung wearily. Aye, he'd traveled the distance.

"Where did ye think to go?" Art asked, as if he had the right. "Running away like a thief in the night."

His rebuke infuriated her, and she snapped, "You're just like every other man. Questioning me about my destination and intent, just as if I weren't the daughter of an earl and a friend of the queen."

"Oo, been a hard come-down fer ye, has it?" Dolan stood on the roadway, holding the reins of her piteous animal and glaring at them with evil intensity.

She drew herself up and glared at the impudent old pirate. "I've done well by myself."

"O' course ye have. That explains th' blood smeared all over yer skirt, an' th' split on yer chin that looks like a second mouth." He stepped back and studied her. "Only lower."

Art pushed up her chin with a firm grip. "How'd ye get this, lass?"

"I fell."

Dolan snorted, and Art said, "Try again, Lady Marian, with the truth."

She didn't like being treated like a child, but beneath Art's gruff exterior existed a true concern, and after a brief defiance she gave in. "There were two thieves—"

Even Dolan cried out.

"Oh, it's not as bad as it sounds. They tried to steal the horse." Funny, she trembled like a pup in the cold. She hadn't been nearly so impacted yesterday, when it had happened. "I had to . . . um . . . kill them."

Art stood, mouth hanging open, hands slack, and after a glance at him, Dolan demanded, "Ye killed two men?"

"Well, not exactly." Sweat trickled down her forehead and beaded on her upper lip, and she blotted it with her sleeve. "That horse killed one of them. Kicked him in the head. He's a vicious beast."

"The thief?" Art croaked.

"The *horse.*"

Dolan tightened the reins. "An' th' other thief?"

"Well, I had a knife, you know." She had plunged it into his chest without remorse, for the thieves had taunted her with tales of screaming women and roasted children. They had described the fate of the last woman they'd laid hands on. They had eyed Lionel and speculated on the price he would bring in a market.

She had no remorse, she really didn't, but faintly she heard Dolan say, "She's goin' down," and she found herself sitting beside the road, her head thrust forcibly between her knees.

When they let her up, she gasped for air and said,

"I'm not squeamish, but when I remember the way his muscles collapsed, that gray fog of death over his blue eyes, it just makes me—"

"Ah, well, lass, we all get that way after our first bloodin'." Dolan sounded almost kind. "An' most o' us after every other bloodin', too. But there's some that like it, an' it seems ye found a couple."

"If ye hadn't killed them, ye'd be dead, or wishing ye were dead by this morn, and this lad . . ." Art snatched Lionel off his feet and hugged him until the little boy kicked to be put down.

"I know." Marian propped her elbows on her raised knees and buried her head in her hands. As if the admission had been forced from her, she added, "Adventure isn't as much fun as I'd hoped." A silence followed, and she dared not look up. She didn't want to see their complacency or hear them tout the proper way of life for a woman and how she'd be safer within castle walls, sewing a seam. That wasn't what she meant at all, only she needed more money, more food, her suit of men's clothes, and a sword in her hand to properly protect Lionel.

And there had been a moment, yesterday, when she would have been glad of Griffith's company. But Griffith was far away, fighting for the king she despised, and Lady Marian Wenthaven had never depended on any man for anything.

'Twas a sign of weakness. 'Twas a sign of Griffith's bad influence on her and another reason to keep staunchly on her path.

As aggressively as she knew how, she demanded, "What are you doing, chasing after me?"

The odd mixture of compassion and affection on Dolan's face curdled to aversion. "That's what I'd like t' know. She's just an Englishwoman, an' a stupid one at that."

Marian's faintness vanished in a flash of fury. "I'm not stupid."

Dolan peered at her. "Where ye be goin'?"

"To Wenthaven. To my father's house. Do you have any objections to that?"

"Not at all." Dolan casually picked at his teeth with his fingernail. "But ye're on th' wrong road."

"I am not," she answered automatically, but she glanced around.

"Ye're a good thirty miles due east o' Wenthaven. Didn't ye notice when ye passed Stafford?"

"I've been avoiding the towns," she mumbled.

"We'd have found ye yesterday if ye had yer bearings." Dolan snorted. "Just like a woman."

Marian looked at Art, and he nodded. "Sad, but true. Ye missed Wenthaven." He swept Lionel up and placed him on the saddle once more. "But if ye want to go to Wenthaven, m'lady, then we'll be a-going, too." Art indicated the rutted road. "After ye."

She took a few steps. "But why are you here?"

"I can ill perform my sworn duty if I'm not with ye."

Art was playing with her, prodding her reactions, and she was dancing to his tune. First she showed concern for Griffith when she should have shown indifference. Now she struggled against her curiosity and lost. "What sworn duty?"

"To protect young Lionel, of course. Don't ye remember making me take that vow?"

She didn't believe him. He hadn't meant her to, for although his mouth smiled, his eyebrows turned down and his eyes were impatient. "You swore to protect Griffith, too," she said sullenly.

"Griffith is a man, and well able to protect himself."

"What if he's hurt?" She hesitated. "He would need you."

"If he is hurt, 'tis not my ugly face he wishes to see," Art replied.

At a loss for words, she glared until Dolan asked, "Are we going to jaw all day, or are we going?"

"Right away, my fine man," she said sarcastically.

Dolan only nodded. "Got th' right womanly attitude there, ye have."

"Who are you to tell me the right womanly attitude? You betrayed me."

"Me?" Dolan pointed at himself, then shook his head. "Did ye think yer money had bought me loyalty?"

"Nay, but I thought your spite would seal your mouth."

"Aye, an' it would, but yer friends were distressed at yer flight—distressed enough t' threaten me wi' exile if I didn't cooperate." The horse struggled to escape, and Dolan slapped him across the nose with the reins. "I've had enough o' wanderin'. I'll not be thrown out o' Powel again, certainly not over a wench like ye."

Voice shaking with rage, she said, "You are a wicked man."

He smiled, marring his dark beauty with malice. "Aye, I am. Did ye just now discover it?"

With a toss of her head, Marian flounced away from Dolan. Art followed with Lionel, and Dolan followed with the horse, handling it with ease. He asked, "Where did ye get this fine horse?"

"The horse's name is Jack."

"For Jackass?" Dolan guessed with uncanny accuracy. "Got as tough a mouth as any ass I've met. He can scarcely carry his own fleas"—he slapped Jack's rump—"but let's see how fast we can get this ass a-movin'."

Lionel's shout of encouragement drowned out Marian's cry of, "Oh, nay!"

Art put his hand on her arm. "Don't worry. Dolan'll watch over the lad."

"Dolan doesn't like children," she replied in exasperation.

Art cackled. "Perhaps."

Watching wistfully as her son and his new companions raced ahead, Marian wished she could be like them. Happy, carefree, heart whole. "What did Griffith think of his token?"

"His token?" Art acted confused, then seemed to remember. "Ah, his token! A rock and a hank of hair. Quite a token ye sent, lass."

"Did he understand . . . ?" She took a breath. "Did he like them?"

"Of course, I can't speak for the man. Not with any assurance." He waggled his heavy eyebrows. "But he'd been a surly bear until I slipped it into his bag. Aye, as surly as a bear newly awake from its winter's sleep."

"I can't believe I sent it to him. Such a stupid thing. Such a womanly thing." She ground her fist into her palm. "But he looked almost hurt when he left me, and I couldn't help but think he'd fight more efficiently if he had a bit of me close."

"When he saw that rock—representing him, I suppose—and yer hair—representing ye—he smiled so sweet, and marveled ye could send him so clear a message. He was happy to think ye'd be waiting for him when he returned."

"He didn't think that." She dragged her toes in the dirt. "Did he?"

"'Twould have been kinder if ye'd sent nothing," Art said sternly.

"Well, he had no right to think he knows my mind just because he's a wizard between the sheets."

"He ought to be. He practices when he's alone, and he's been alone a lot these last two years."

Scandalized, she protested, "Art! You shouldn't say such things to me."

"I am a tired old man, and I will say what I like." He sounded savage, at the end of his rope, and unwilling to humor her. "Ye forfeited my benevolence when ye scurried away from Griffith and the love he offered ye."

"I have my reasons"—although in the face of Art's condemnation, she had trouble remembering them—"and they are more important than Griffith and me and all the petty emotions we're feeling."

"Then ye tell Griffith straight to his face. Ye don't bolt."

"I tried to tell Griffith, but he wouldn't listen."

"Or ye didn't try very hard. 'Tis damn hard to throw love away, isn't it, m'lady? Especially when ye know ye love him back."

Stunned, she sucked in her breath. "I don't."

"Ye got all the symptoms, lass." Art counted on his fingers. "Been staying awake worrying about him, haven't ye? Been wondering if ye've done the right thing, haven't ye? Been wondering if he got ye with child, and half hoping he has, haven't ye?"

Art had been inside her head, and she didn't like it. She didn't like any of it, especially not the accusation of love. For if she loved Griffith . . . by all the saints, she did love Griffith, and the pain she had previously suffered would be nothing when compared to the pain of facing him across a battlefield.

What would he do? Would he obey King Henry and try to kill her and her child? Would he stand aside, indifferent, when they were executed? Would he try to capture them when they were put to the horn?

And if King Henry were defeated, would she have to watch him die?

Fear clawed at her, and she clutched the material over her belly. "He didn't get me with child."

"Good. I would hate to have Griffith tied to another woman who's too weak to love him as he deserves. Who weds him because of her belly and then whines forever about the grand life she missed. Who gives him a child that's half English and all irresolute."

She stopped in the middle of the road. "You dare? Say those things to me? Why, you're nothing but a—"

"Servant? Welshman?" He shook his crooked finger at her. "Aye, those things I am, but I'm worth twice of ye, my fair, frightened lady. Worth twice of any woman who turns aside from a man like Griffith."

Slapping his finger aside, she said, "A man like Griffith? Aye, an honorable man, upright, kind, noble, and as ashamed of his passion for me as any man stricken with a defect. You accuse me of weakness? I agree, I must be weak, for I could not have done as I promised if Griffith had offered me his whole self. That would have been irresistible temptation. But to perjure my soul for a man who wants to tuck me away into a corner where he can manage me and his ardor with firmness and discipline? Nay, I thank you."

Looking in equal parts amazed and relieved, Art muttered, "Ah, that's it, is it?" Staring at the sky, he scratched his scraggly chin and thought so long that she squirmed in embarrassment. He came to some conclusion at last and started down the road. "I think ye'd be better with an explanation, m'lady, about the numbskull who's wooing ye. And poorly, too, it seems. Did ye know how I lost my eye?"

She not only didn't know, she didn't care, but she guessed, "In battle?"

"Of a sort," Art acknowledged. "Step lively, m'lady, seems Dolan and the lad have gotten ahead of us. Nay, I lost my eye when Griffith did as ye have. He ran away."

Art had captured her whole attention, although she hated to have him know it. "Ran away? Why would such a strong knight run away?"

"He wasn't a knight then. Wasn't even a squire. He was just a boy, a squirming, ever-moving, loud boy who worshiped his da."

Remembering the affection between father and son, Marian said, "He still does."

"Aye, although Lord Rhys has explained, many a

time, that his mistakes are by far the greater. But Griffith won't listen. Not now, and didn't then."

"Then? When?"

"We were having a siege, ye see. Trevor, as wicked a Welsh marauder as the devil ever made, decided he liked the view from Castle Powel. Decided he liked the furnishings, too." Art peered at Marian from beneath his shaggy brows. "Liked Lady Angharad in a most unneighborly way, if ye understand me."

She nodded, not at all surprised that another man had seen Angharad's kind face and wanted her for his own.

Settling into his role as storyteller, Art said, "Griffith was bored with the siege that had gone on for months. Lord Rhys was irritable and yelled at young Griffith, and next thing I knew, young Griffith had gone through the tunnel and was outside the castle."

"A tunnel?"

"Built as a bolt hole for the family back in Edward's reign. 'Twas common enough. It had been secured against the enemy coming in, but there were no provisions for a young fool going *out*. Griffith was my responsibility, so I followed and tried tactfully to coax him back." Art shook his head. "I was younger then myself, and not smart enough to save my tact until we returned to the safety of the keep. So they captured us, and that scabrous monster put out my eye."

She gasped, and he clearly relished having her undivided attention.

"Oh, aye. He wanted Griffith to go to the castle walls and cry for his da to surrender. Young Griffith refused—trying to be a hero, ye ken—and Trevor put out my eye and would have killed me, but I saved myself with my famous fake fall into the steep ravine."

"Famous fake . . . ?" She relaxed and grinned. "You tease me."

Offended, he said, "Not at all. When ye're trapped

and ye think there's no way out, ye look about ye smartly, fer there surely is a way. Might hurt ye a bit, but there's a way fer those who seek it. And there was a way fer me, although not until they'd scooped out my eye with—"

She winced, and he cleared his throat.

"No matter. But Trevor wanted both my eyes, and he wanted Griffith to see my suffering. So he ordered me released so I could stumble about, groaning and clutching my face, and I ran quick to the ravine and flung myself down just as they shot the arrow to stop me."

"To kill you?"

"Trevor wasn't a kind man, and I doubt he'd had his entertainment from me yet. But they peered down the ravine, and I lay as still as I could, and they thought I lay dead, and didn't shoot another arrow just to be sure, praise be to God. So Griffith did as they bade and convinced his father to surrender the castle." Meditatively he said, "'Twas actually a good way to end the siege."

"Why?"

"Lord Rhys took a goodly number of soldiers and marched out of the castle without Lady Angharad, as Trevor made certain sure. But once he got inside, he couldn't find her, for she and the rest of the garrison were holed up nice and tight in the tunnel. When Trevor and his men had finished celebrating—broke up the keep bad, they did, and drank all the ale— Lady Angharad brought forth her men and trounced them." He chuckled. "She was *supposed* to open the gate to Lord Rhys, but she was never one to follow orders well."

"Rhys was angry with her?"

"Furious."

"And angry at Griffith?"

"Nay, not too. Not when he saw how angry Griffith was at himself." With a hand on her arm, Art stopped her. "Look yon."

There, in a stream that crossed the road, the big pirate and the little boy tumbled and splashed. Marian smiled to hear Lionel's laughter once more, but her heart ached for Griffith, desolate at causing the loss of his home and his mother. In fact, her heart just ached, and she dared not examine the reason. "Griffith?" she prompted.

"We thought we had got through it safe. We thought Griffith had learned a lesson, and no harm done. But as time went on, it became clear Griffith didn't ever want to feel anything ever again. He blamed his own emotions, and he wanted to become a stone man." Art nodded. "'Twas an apt token ye sent him, lass, fer more than one reason."

She wilted when she realized how cold her gift of the stone had seemed.

"He controlled himself at all times. Never laughed aloud, never cried again, never displayed anguish or pain . . . or love."

"He loves his mother and his father."

"'Tis a safe love. 'Tis not an uncontrollable desire. Aye, he kept to the milk-sop feelings, and left passion to the rest of us."

"His wife?"

Art shrugged. "A lovely girl. Quiet, biddable—we scarcely noticed when she died."

"Has he ever found anything to be passionate about?"

"Searching for a compliment, lady?"

Impatient, she said, "Besides me."

"Wales." He tilted his head and watched her as he added, "And Henry Tudor."

"Aye, I know that, too. My greatest rival is the king of England."

"Would ye want Griffith to be less than he is? Aye, he's a frightened seven-year-old when it comes to loving ye without reserve, but he's just and honorable, a fine knight, a good man, and that part of him wants justice for his homeland and peace for England. What right have ye to quarrel with that?"

What right? The right of a mother to want the best for her son, even if it meant a return to the everlasting wars of the past. "I'm taking Lionel to Wenthaven, and not as a supplicant this time. I have a gift for him." She thought of the precious parchment she kept close to her body. "A great gift. He will be in my debt."

Art thought hard, and his gaze shifted to the boy on the horse. "Ye're giving him Lionel?"

"Aye, Lionel, but not Lionel as you know him."

"Not as ye know him, either, if ye surrender the lad to yer father. I don't pretend to understand the doings of royalty, and I know ye were knee deep in some scheme with Henry's queen, but if ye continue with yer plans, who'll be hurt?" He waved at Lionel. "Look at him. He just wants security. He just needs a father. And with Lionel a-tuggin' at Griffith's heartstrings one way and ye a-tuggin' the other, surely ye'll unravel the knot Griffith's tied around himself."

She was tempted. So tempted. Art made it sound like more than an impulsive decision. He made it sound logical. Of course, she would lose, too. She'd lose her chance to live at court, but she wasn't doing this for herself. Not at all.

"Hey!" Art yelled. "Hey, hey, what are ye doing?"

Startled, she glanced at him, then followed his gaze.

At first she thought it was Dolan stooping over Lionel, and she didn't understand Art's concern. Then she realized it was a stranger.

"How dare ye—" Art started off at a run toward the place where Lionel played. "Get away from him."

Where was Dolan? Marian ran after Art. Where—"Get away from him!" she screamed as the strange man picked Lionel up. "Get away!"

Art reached them, and she saw a sword arc through the air.

"Nay!" She bowled into the man and her child, knocking them into the dirt. Lionel shrieked with pain and fear, but the sword tumbled out of the stranger's hand. She pummeled him, but her strongest blow went astray when he turned his face to her and she recognized him.

Harbottle.

In her shock, she lost the initiative. She lifted her hand again, but his fist slammed into the side of her head and she fell—not unconscious, but with a blackness before her eyes and a ringing in her ears. He grabbed for his sword as Art smashed into him, and the men went tumbling.

Marian gathered her scattered wits and crawled to Lionel, whispering, "Did he hurt you?" She brushed his hair back from his forehead, and his sobs quieted. Reassured, she staggered to her feet and took his hand. "Come on."

Too late. Harbottle snatched him from her on the run.

She spun and fell again, then rose and ran after them, stumbling into the forest, calling Lionel's name and hearing his shrieks recede into the distance. She spurted into the clearing in time to see Harbottle riding away on a good horse, a young, healthy, fast horse.

Screaming at them, she heard Harbottle's triumphant laugh as he rode away and forced herself to one last, futile burst of speed.

But she couldn't go on. Her body rebelled, and she fell to the earth, defeated by pain and exhaustion.

Slowly she dragged herself up. Slowly she traced her steps back to the road, to find the bloody body of Art stretched out, half in the stream, half out.

# 16

*The horse found Marian* as she stood over Art like a mourner and nudged her in the back so hard that she splashed into the stream. She turned with a curse, but Art's moan stopped her, and she dropped to her knees beside him. "Art." She touched his hand, and the still-warm fingers curled around hers. "Sweet Saint Mary! Art, you're alive."

He opened his eyes and stared at her as if he didn't know her face, then he struggled up on his elbows. Clutching his shoulders, she urged him back down, but he fought her and scooted backward. "Let me get out of this stream."

She assisted him all she could, and when he was free of the embrace of the water, she instructed, "Lie quiet while I determine where you are hurt."

"'Tis only a head wound, m'lady. They bleed dreadfully, but—"

She explored the slash that laid open his skull from ear to spine, and pressed her skirt to it firmly. "It's dire. Oh, Art, please don't die."

"Nay, m'lady, I—"

With her head on his shoulder, she gave over to her grief and worry, while Art lay very, very still. When she drew back, she could see he had been thinking—about his own death, probably—for he closed his eyes against her tearful gaze and moaned loudly as if he were giving up his last breath.

Realizing the need for action, she leaped back. "I need bandages and—"

The horse nudged her again, and she grabbed its reins in a flash. "You're not running away from me again," she said. "I've a use for you now." With desperate zest, she dragged the gelding to a tree and tethered it. She returned to Art with her bags and draped him with a rug, then found bandage material in one of Lionel's little shirts. Holding it aloft, she stared at it in numb despair until Art moaned again. Then with her teeth she ripped it into strips and wrapped Art's head.

"Did he take Lionel?" he whispered.

"Aye." Her voice was steady, she was proud to note.

"Where's Dolan?"

"He took the advantage and ran away, I suppose."

Art muttered a Welsh word that needed no translation.

With unthinking conviction, Marian said, "I must go to Griffith. He'll find Lionel. He'll save him."

"Griffith? Ye want Griffith to rescue yer son?" Art's sardonic gaze reminded her, suddenly, of the doubts and the fears that had plagued her and sabotaged her feelings for Griffith. But they were gone, swept away like dust before a great storm.

She trusted Griffith, trusted him as she had never trusted anyone.

Then Art dangled one of the shackles that imprisoned her in suspicion. "Ye'll have to go to Kenilworth. Ye'll have to see the king, for Griffith will be with him."

She hunched her shoulders and tried to think, but in her mind there was no room for logic or intelligence, only for emotions deep and raw. She wanted to leap up and run after Harbottle. She wanted to rescue Lionel. She wanted to kill Harbottle with her bare hands. She knew she couldn't, that she must go for help, but Kenilworth? Kenilworth was a royal stronghold.

"I've known two kings, and both were treacherous. Henry has great reasons to do harm to Lionel." Lurching to her feet, she said, "I'll go after him myself."

Flinging his arm out, Art tripped her, and when she foundered to her knees, he caught her ankle in a firm and bony grip. "Lass, ye can't do it by yerself. Ye need Griffith. If ye trust Griffith as ye say ye do, then ye must trust him to protect Lionel, even from the king." Art laid his arm across his eyes, as if he needed to shield the light as the life faded from him. "The angel of death is even now spreading her wings over my poor body. I'll be gone soon, and I don't want to die with a sin on my soul."

Quick, hot tears sprang to her eyes at the thought of Art being taken from the earth, and in the blur they created she could almost see the hovering angel. "What sin?"

"I swore to ye I would protect Lionel, and I failed miserably. Set my mind at ease before I go. Swear ye'll go to Kenilworth for Griffith."

She could do it. She had to do it.

For Lionel.

"I do believe in Griffith. I'll go to Kenilworth."

"Swear."

She dabbed at her nose with her sleeve. "I swear."

"Good lass." Briskly he instructed, "Follow this road to Lichfield, and there ye can ask fer directions to Kenilworth. Ye'll be there in less than a day."

"Shouldn't I stay until—" She choked on her tears.

He began to cough as if his lungs would burst, rolling over in agony and hiding his face in the cool grass. She rubbed his back with shaking hands, and when he could speak, he refused her. "Nay. My wicked soul won't rest until I know Lionel has been rescued. Go, m'lady. Go at once, and Godspeed."

Rising on trembling legs, she walked to Jack and untied his reins.

"Ye'll have to ride him," Art called. "Get up in the saddle quick-like, before he can react."

She nodded, put her foot into the stirrup, and leaped into the saddle.

"That's m'lady," Art said approvingly. "Just keep a tight rein and ye'll be fine."

With one last, longing glance, she memorized Art's face, then she put her heels into Jack's side and rode away.

Art watched until she was well out of sight, then sat up slowly. His head ached, and he was dizzy, but he washed his face in the cool stream, taking care not to wet the bandage. Then, inch by inch, he rose until he stood on his feet and, with a grim smile, started into the forest on the trail of Harbottle.

Art had underestimated Marian's determination and stamina, and Kenilworth Castle was secured but not yet abed when she faced the king's guard and swore at him. But the guard only looked her over in the light of the torches and shook his head. "Ye talk wi' th' accent o' a lady, but no lady would come t' th' king's palace in th' middle o' th' night, soaked t' th' skin an' lookin' like a draggle-tail, without her maid or her own man t' pertect her. Go on wi' ye now, afore I have t' fling ye out."

Shaking her finger in his face, she said, "I was set upon by a thief, you fool, and the king himself will want to hear that story."

"Th' king?" The guard laughed long and hard. "Do ye think th' king worries about every robbery that occurs on his roads? Nay, ye're goin' t' have t' do better than that."

"I was not robbed." Knowing she shouldn't discuss Lionel with this ignorant soldier, she tried to explain, "Something very dear to me was taken."

He pushed her toward the door of his tiny chamber on the outer wall of the gatehouse. "Sounds like a robbery t' me."

She put her hands on either side of the door frame and clung. "I tell you, the king will want to know about it." Had she ridden through the daylight and the starlight to reach Griffith, only to be turned away by an officious commoner? Had she urged, cajoled, and fought with that tough-mouthed horse to be stopped just short of her goal? Desperate now, she tried a falsehood. "I know the king. He'll want to see me tonight."

The guard laughed again, more coarsely.

"What's your name?" she demanded.

He looked truculent, but he answered, "Ward."

"Ward, I am a friend to Elizabeth. I was her dearest lady-in-waiting."

"How th' great have fallen," he mocked her, but he stopped pushing, too entertained to throw her out now. "An' why aren't ye her dearest lady-in-waitin' now?"

She answered carefully. "I had to retire to my country estates."

"Because ye're a slut," he said in triumph, his hand in her back.

"I am Lady Marian Wenthaven, the betrothed of Griffith ap Powel, and he will break your neck for denying me entrance."

Jerking his hand away, he stared at her with narrowed eyes. "Are ye, now? Griffith ap Powel, ye say?" His gaze swept over her. "God help ye. Come this way, an' we'll talk t' me commander."

Ever more eager, she ran ahead of him.

She had lived at Kenilworth before, when she'd been an honored part of the court. She knew the arrangement of the castle and the grounds. Once inside the gatehouse that loomed before them, she would have traversed the last insurmountable obstacle between her and Griffith.

She didn't have time to go through the many self-important authorities until she reached him—it would be hours before she reached her goal, and by then Lionel could be gone forever.

More than that, she had a need to be with Griffith, to hear his voice, to have his arms around her. She wanted comfort. She wanted Griffith. She wanted love.

Art was right, it seemed. She did love Griffith—and that love would bring her grief.

She smiled grimly when the use of his name convinced the other guards to raise the portcullis of the gatehouse and let them pass. Noting her position, she climbed the stairs to the walk on the curtain wall. To the outside, the narrow walk was bound by a stone wall of alternating high and low segments, giving the exterior of the castle its characteristic snaggle-toothed appearance.

But to the inside, all the way around the bailey, it was a sheer plunge from the wall walk to the ground. With a rough kind of courtesy, Ward kept between her and the drop. She was almost impressed until he called to his commander, "We've got a woman thinks she's a friend o' th' king an' Sir Griffith's betrothed. What think ye?" And he lifted his torch so it shone on her filthy clothes and bedraggled hair.

The commander guffawed but Marian fixed him with her haughtiest gaze until he stopped and shuffled uneasily. "My horse is outside on the drawbridge, and he's too fine an animal to leave in the rain. Bring him in at once and take him to the stable to be fed and groomed."

When Ward looked indecisive, the commander called for her to enter, and she hovered on the threshold.

Glaring at the hapless guard, she suggested, "If I were you, I'd wonder what Sir Griffith ap Powel is going to say about the way you have treated his betrothed."

The threat proved enough. With a stiff bow, Ward strode toward the stairs. Watching his back, she waited until he began his descent, then raced away into the darkness.

The commander shouted. Ward, still suspicious, shouted also. Voices in the dark joined the clamor, and she ran full into one leather-clad soldier. He grabbed for her, but she kicked him in the kneecap and knocked him in the chest, and when he staggered back, she raced on, trying to be cautious of her footing yet trying to stay ahead of the surer-footed guards.

Her goal was the corner above the castle blacksmith's. If she could just reach it, she could jump onto the thatched roof and descend on the poles. Then, with luck, she could run across the bailey to the keep known as Caesar's Tower.

She knew she could, because she'd done it with the princess Elizabeth.

Of course, she'd been a lot smaller then.

Upon reaching the corner, she hesitated, her toes cramped over the edge, her soles firmly on the walk. The night torches that lit the bailey didn't reach her; she could see nothing below. If she jumped . . . when she jumped, it would be without knowing where she landed. To put so much faith in a childhood memory, to trust that nothing had been changed in ten years— that was brave. Or foolhardy. But she had no time to debate, for the shouts were coming closer. The guards were closing on her.

She jumped.


"Does it hurt you?"

Griffith jerked his hand from the stitches in his cheek. "It aches a bit," he allowed.

"If you'd left your helmet on as I instructed, you'd bear no new scars, and you wouldn't have that tapestry on your face." King Henry watched Griffith intently. "'Tis your arm which caused us concern. You're lucky you didn't get the putrefaction, as hard as that Irish whoreson swung that sword."

"Stop stalling and play. I almost have you where I want you. Then I can go to bed." Privately Griffith damned Henry's desire to play the fashionable new game of chess so late at night, and in the royal bedchamber in the tower.

"You dream of victory," Henry accused, and moved a knight.

"You'd best be satisfied with your victory at Stoke, for you'll not have one this night." Griffith answered with a move of his bishop that captured the knight.

"You can't do that!" Henry protested.

"I beg to dissent, my liege, but I most certainly can."

"Let me see the book." Henry held out his hand, and in it Griffith placed an almost new copy of *The Game and Play of Chess*, printed by the first English printing press and presented to His Grace by the printer himself.

As Henry leafed though Caxton's gift, Griffith asked idly, "What did you do with the pretender? The young boy who claimed to be the earl of Warwick?"

Henry grunted and tossed the book aside. It skidded across the reeds, riding close to the fire that warmed them on the damp spring night.

"You can't burn it," Griffith advised. "I still remember the rules."

With a sour look at his friend, Henry ran his finger across the finely carved crown on his king. "The pretender? His name is Lambert Simnel, and he's as common as dirt. I knocked him back to his origins."

Although Griffith knew royal pretensions should be crushed, still he hated to think of a boy being put into the earth, and he stared at alternating black and white squares until the colors switched.

"Stop holding your breath," Henry said irritably. "I didn't have him killed. I made him a scullery boy."

Griffith exhaled in a gasp.

"'Twas more mercy than he deserved, but he'll prove a potent lesson to any who dares imagine he can unseat me." Henry's lips twisted; he looked less like a royal lion and more like a wolf mad with blood lust. "My son will be the next king. My dynasty will wear the crown."

Griffith leaned across the board and grasped Henry's tight-held fist. "As long as there is breath in my body, it will be so."

By slow increments, Henry's tension eased. "It comforts me to know you are sworn to me. You would be a mighty enemy."

Griffith leaned back. "And Lambert Simnel is a feeble enemy."

"If he does well, maybe I'll make him a—"

"Cook?" Griffith grinned. "I'm glad you were lenient. He was no more than a pawn."

Now Henry fondled one of his own pawns on the chessboard, sure satisfaction in his touch. "Well, he's my pawn, now. The *late* earl of Lincoln will use him no more."

"The earl of Lincoln will burn in hell forever for his treachery to you," Griffith answered, grimly certain.

Concentrating on their game, they fell silent once more, and the shouts from outside the window wafted in on the night's breeze.

Again Griffith's hand drifted to his face.

"Do they itch?" Henry demanded.

Griffith gripped his hands together. "Do what itch?"

"Your stitches, man!" Henry *tsked* in disgust. "You never used to pretend you didn't understand me. It must be the lady Marian who has so clouded your comprehension."

"She has not," Griffith said indignantly.

"Then what are you thinking?"

Feeling foolish, Griffith bent over the chessboard and muttered, "I was wondering if she'll think me hideous."

To his credit, Henry didn't laugh. He didn't even seem to find it amusing. He only sighed and pushed back his own thinning hair. "Women do make us vain, don't they? I never used to worry about my looks. But for Elizabeth, I want to be"—he chuckled—"as handsome as a youth. And for what? For a woman who cherishes me as I am. Who cherishes me, she says, for my kindness."

Griffith didn't know how to answer. He never knew how to respond when Henry spoke of his wife, for Henry and Elizabeth and Griffith and Marian were all partners in a secret. A secret that each comprehended only partially, but one which weighed on them all. Stiffly he said, "The lady Elizabeth is kind, also."

"My Elizabeth is a great woman." Henry kept his gaze on the chessboard. "As is your lady Marian. I doubt the arrangement of your face has any interest to her, and in any case—"

"I know. In any case, my face was never too handsome. Art has made me well aware of that." And Marian had made him well aware of his physique. In this time of recuperation, Griffith found himself occasionally remembering her fascination as she examined him. He occasionally remembered the touch of her hand and occasionally remembered her pleasure in his meager talents. In fact, he often had trouble sleeping, or standing, or even sitting, for his body seemed to remember Marian more than just occasionally.

He glanced at Henry and scooted his chair closer under the table, hoping to hide his condition and praying that Marian would arrive soon.

Henry's hand hovered between a rook and a bishop and finally moved the bishop. "He'll be back soon with Lady Marian."

"I pray they have no trouble on the road." Actually, he prayed Marian would come on command, but he didn't tell the king. Instead he took Henry's bishop and grinned in smug triumph.

Henry sat back and eyed his rapidly deteriorating position with disgust. "Aye, for if they have trouble, you'll be like a trapped boar, all slashing tusks and wild, glaring eyes."

"My thanks, Your Grace."

"You've placed me in check."

"Aye, Your Grace."

"Don't you know it's prudent to let your liege lord triumph?"

"I wouldn't know how, Your Grace."

"No, you wouldn't." Henry grinned at him. Renewed shouting drifted in from outdoors, and running feet began to thump along the wooden floors within the keep. "They must have found a thief. By my troth, there's a madness out there tonight."

The steps moved into the tower, then up the stairs, and someone rapped firmly at the door. The two men looked at it, then at each other, and Henry called, "Enter!"

Ward, the guard from the curtain wall, stepped in and gave an awkward bow. "Yer Grace, pardon me, but we've had a bit o' a problem. She hasn't made it here yet, has she?"

"Not that I noticed," Henry said, looking entertained. "Who is *she?*"

"A madwoman. A witch." Ward waved an arm. "A bit o' light skirt wi' a fancy accent an' a manic intention t' meet Yer Grace. If Yer Grace doesn't mind, I'll post a guard outside yer door an' keep ye safe."

"So much trouble for one woman," Henry said.

"She's mad, I tell ye, wi' th' strength o' a madwoman. She tossed young Bowey aside wi' one hand, an' he's no little man."

Suspicion swelled in Griffith. "Did she kick him in the throat?"

The guard clutched his own throat at the thought. "Nay, Sir Griffith. In th' knee."

Henry followed Griffith's thought with ease. "Does this sound like someone you know?"

"Perhaps."

Ward didn't listen or didn't understand. "Don't ye worry, we've got th' keep blocked off downstairs, an' wi' a guard here, we'll have no problem. No problem at—" Sensing someone behind him, he whipped around, but before he'd completed his move, he'd been shoved bodily into the chamber. He tumbled forward, revealing the muddy figure behind him. Then he bounded to his feet.

Griffith rose and installed himself between the enraged guard and the swaying woman. Placing one hand on Ward, he said, "She's mine."

Ward glanced wildly at the woman, then at Griffith, then at the king. "You don't say."

"I assure you, this wound has not muddled my head. This is my betrothed, Lady Marian Wenthaven, and while I understand your need to protect the king from her, I assure you I can do it as well." When Ward nodded his comprehension, Griffith removed his restraining hand and gestured to the door. "You may go."

The guard dragged his feet, giving Marian a wide berth. Moving out of his way, Marian never turned her back to him, and he watched her as closely as a man watches a wildcat. At the door, he paused and gave Griffith one last chance. "Ye're sure?"

Griffith nodded. "Shut the door behind you."

Marian waited only until the latch clicked before running to Griffith and clasping his arms in both hands. Her fingers bit into his skin. She lifted her dirty face to his, looking all the world like an orphan—an orphan whose distressed green eyes tore at his heart.

"Sweetheart, what is it? What's happened?"

"Harbottle fell on us."

Her contralto voice quavered, and Griffith clutched her, offering comfort even before he knew the outrage. "Did he hurt you?"

"Me? Nay, not me. 'Tis worse. He took Lionel. He—"

"Lionel?" Griffith's arms fell away from her. "Lionel? What was Lionel doing with you?"

"He's my son." She grasped his shoulders and shook him, desperate to make him understand. "Listen to me. Harbottle took Lionel. Griffith, we have to go get him."

At the table, Henry rose, demanding attention. Reluctantly Marian broke away from Griffith and curtsied, knowing Henry's identity without introductions. Griffith performed the courtesies in a tight voice, and the king and the mud-maid surveyed each other as keenly as if they were both stripped naked.

Then Henry gestured to the bench by the fire. "Sit down. You're tired and wet, and you have a tale I need to hear. Who is Harbottle, and why did he take the child?"

Marian did as she was told. "The child's name is Lionel. He is my son, and I could not say why anyone would wish to take him. But as to Harbottle—he is a vagabond knight who once served my father, and I fear the worst." She stood up and found Griffith at her side. "We must go at once. There is no telling what Harbottle might do with him—throw him away, or beat—"

She faltered, and four hands assisted her to sit.

Over the top of her head, Henry said, "She reminds me of Elizabeth with young Arthur. That gentle woman is a tiger at the thought of a threat to the babe."

Griffith didn't agree, but he didn't say anything. In the silence it occurred to Marian that she had come to him, hoping to find a rock to lean upon, but instead he seemed hard, cold, and indifferent.

"Where's Art?" he asked.

She died inside. "Art?"

"Aye, Art, my squire, my friend. The only one we trusted to bring you from Wales to me. Where is he?"

A fire burned at her back, but it couldn't heat her, and she shivered.

"Marian." Griffith leaned down so his face was even with hers. "Where is Art?"

She tried to say it. She really did. She opened her mouth, but the words wouldn't come. Couldn't come, not in the face of Griffith's pain.

"Is he dead?" Griffith whispered.

"Harbottle killed him."

"Was there a ravine nearby?"

She understood. "Nay. I . . . nay. I bandaged his head myself, and would have stayed until the end, but he bade me come for you." He didn't speak. "For Lionel. He was worried about Lionel. We must go tonight, for every minute Lionel slips farther away."

Griffith turned away from her and her demands, and she didn't understand why. Why wasn't he concerned about Lionel?

Henry watched Griffith, too, until his gaze fell on Marian's bewildered face. With a tact rare to kings, he stepped into the breach. "Lionel has value to you, of course. Would that be the reason Harbottle took him? For power over you?"

"Or revenge on her." Griffith found a rug and tossed it over her shivering shoulders, but when she tried to thank him, he brushed her aside and spoke only to Henry. "She hurt him badly, both in body and in vanity, and that is a possibility."

Henry asked, "Could he still be serving Wenthaven?"

Marian shook her head. "My father said Harbottle had slipped his leash. Wenthaven has no more damning complaint."

"Then might he be seeking revenge on your father?" Henry suggested. "Blackmailing your father?"

"Wenthaven wanted aught to do with Lionel. Harbottle would never be so mad as to think Wenthaven would pay to have Lionel returned." She discovered, to her horror, that she had started to cry.

Without regard to her muddy clothes, Henry sat on the bench beside her and passed her a napkin with which to wipe her face. Low and vehemently, he asked, "Does Wenthaven have any reason to think Lionel is a special child? A child of interest to more than those who love him?"

She understood him very well. What plots did he hide? What fury did he experience? What anger and humiliation did Elizabeth's spouse feel at the mere thought of the babe she had borne?

When she failed to answer, he said, "Lionel is the queen's godchild, and therefore precious above the crown jewels to her. I would never allow any harm to come to him, if it is in my power to help."

Of course, she thought, he wouldn't want Lionel in the wrong hands, to be used as a weapon against him. But her cynicism couldn't stand up in face of Henry's seeming sincerity. She'd been so sure he was like the two other kings she'd known: boastful, power mad, vengeful, and cruel. Was he saying he knew of Lionel's unsavory beginnings, but that for Elizabeth, he would forget them and protect the innocent lad? It seemed so to Marian's muddled mind, but if she were mistaken, the consequences were too horrible to contemplate.

Bewildered, she looked up at Griffith, but he watched them without expression. He had left her alone with Henry, to make her own decisions about the king's character and intentions. Picking her words with care, she said, "I have never given Wenthaven any reason to think Lionel is anything more than my precious son."

"Yet Wenthaven often knows more than one would hope."

"Lionel resembles his father," she said abruptly, then bit her lip. She hadn't meant to blurt it out like that—Henry had every reason to hate Lionel's father and every reason to know who he was. But it was a truth she could no longer hide, and one Wenthaven might have realized.

Henry leaned back with a sigh. "That is unfortunate, of course, but most children do resemble one or the other of their parents. My son, Arthur, already resembles his mother, with his fair skin and hair. To hold her own child in her arms is a comfort to her. Since she lost her brothers and so much she loved, she can scarcely bear to hear of cruel separations. Your plight would tear at her heart, for you love your son. Don't you?"

"He's my son. My"—she sketched the sun in the sky—"sun."

"That is what Elizabeth told me." Henry stroked his thinning hair in a nervous gesture. "Does this Harbottle have reason to know of Lionel's special charms?"

"Nay. Even if my father knew, he would never tell so weak a vessel as Harbottle."

Griffith interrupted. "I'm afraid Harbottle might be suspicious. While in our custody in Wales, he had access to more knowledge than was good for him." Marian gaped at Griffith in dismay, and he said, "I beg your forgiveness, Marian, but I fear 'tis true."

"Traitor!" she cried.

"Am I?" His mouth tightened, and he looked, to her tired gaze, taller and grimmer. "Then let me ask you a question. How came you so far so swiftly? We sent Art not nine days ago with strict instructions to bring you to me. King Henry instructed, also, that Lionel be left with my parents, for fear some dread deed should take him from us. How came you so swiftly, and why did you bring the lad against royal orders?"

In the flurry of her need, she'd lost sight of the explanations she would be required to make. But she faced them now, and she foundered in her duplicity.

Ironically, she looked to Henry for succor, but he frowned, puzzled. "With the crisis, I had lost sight of your disobedience. Why *did* you bring the lad? Tell us the truth."

"I don't know the truth anymore," she said in despair. "There are too many truths, and too many lies, and I can't discern the difference."

Griffith said, "The truth, my liege, is that she left Castle Powel before Art arrived, without taking an escort or even taking good sense. She was fleeing the dreadful fate of being my wife. Art found her, and died for her. Lionel is gone, but once I have recovered him for her, she will flee me again. Isn't that correct, Marian?"

He thrust his face close to hers, and his eyes glowed with the same yellow flame that had lit them the first time he had met her.

She realized that he despised her.

She hadn't thought how deceitful she had been or that she might hurt him. He'd been the man to turn to, the man she depended on. In the midst of her own grief, she hadn't thought of Griffith's agony at the death of his old friend, nor had she realized she was responsible for everything. For Art's murder. For Lionel's kidnapping.

She had tried to do what was right, and everything was horribly wrong.

Straightening her shoulders, she looked into his heated gaze. "I beg you to forgive me. I should have sought help elsewhere, but when Harbottle took my lad, I thought only of you. I knew you would save him, and I beg you to do so, regardless of his mother's transgressions."

"You knew I would save him? Or Art told you I would save him?"

"'Twas I. I'm sorry. 'Twas unforgivable to think you would care after all I have done."

"You?" His deep voice trembled, intense and hopeful. "Do not lie to me. Is it true you trust me to find your son?"

"I trust you."

"You came here, to Kenilworth, to the king's own place, without reservation?"

"Without . . ." She tried to say it but couldn't. "With almost no . . ."

With a curse, Griffith turned away. He strode to the tall, narrow window, leaned out, and roared like a wounded beast.

Beside her, Henry flinched. Outside, she knew, men cowered, and within her own breast, Griffith's roar seemed an answer to her own desolation. The tears she'd never shed in all the years of loneliness— for Elizabeth, for Lionel, for herself—now mixed and flowed with the misery she experienced at disappointing this stalwart man.

Already this wretched love brought her grief, and something brought him grief, also. Was it his love for her?

She could scarcely see, but she went to him, laid her head on his back, and hugged his waist. There was nothing to say, so she held her peace, but within her clasp she felt his trembling ease as he adjusted to the agony of loss and betrayal.

Was there hope for them? Were they bound to an ill-fated love? Or could she somehow bring Griffith to the side of right and justice? For Lionel, she had to try.

Sucking in air as if he needed the cool and damp to restore his composure, he turned in her arms and looked down at her. "You must rest."

"Nay, I must go."

"'Twill take time to prepare for this expedition, and you'll be no good to me in your present condition."

"You'll go?"

"Did you doubt it?"

"Nay. I always knew—"

He cut off her protestations. "You need a hot bath to ease your muscles, a hot meal, and sleep. Come, Marian, you know it's true."

From his place before the fire, Henry said, "Even the hardiest warrior must prepare himself before battle."

She glanced at his enigmatic face, then back at Griffith's stony one. "You'll not leave without me as I sleep?"

"I will not," Griffith answered. "Do you trust me enough to believe that?"

It wasn't sarcasm, but it sounded almost like indifference. "I do trust you. I came to you though hell had formed the barrier. I wish you could believe . . ."

And for the first time, she saw the scar.

Long and red, crisscrossed with the brown of sheep-gut stitching, it was a gruesome reminder that death could visit the man she considered as strong and immutable as the earth. It was a miracle he could speak and see. It was a miracle he hadn't died. With trembling fingers, she touched the scab that stretched along his cheekbone from nose to ear. "You've been horribly wounded."

Remote within her arms, he answered, "Aye. Through the heart."

# 17

*They woke Marian* much too early in the morning for her weary body yet not soon enough for her anxious heart. They squawked like silly geese and pushed her from one to the other as they dressed her in riding clothes that fit almost perfectly. They promised a large breakfast after the ceremony. When she demanded to know when she would ride, they giggled as if at a great wit. They placed flowers in her hair, and when she yawned widely, they tossed water in her face. Then the anonymous, fatuous clump of noblewomen and servants led her through the thin dawn light to Kenilworth Chapel, where Griffith waited with the priest on one hand and King Henry on the other.

Henry smiled too cheerfully.

Griffith frowned too darkly.

Henry said, "'Tis a fine morning for a wedding."

Griffith said nothing.

Confused, Marian wondered what a wedding had to do with seeking Lionel. If the king wished them to share a hasty mass before they left, that she could understand, but her befuddled mind failed to grasp this meaning of this riddle. "A wedding?" she asked cautiously.

Clasping his hands behind his back, Henry said, "I have decided you shall wed Sir Griffith before you go seeking your son."

Numb with shock, she repeated, "Wed Sir Griffith?"

"'Tis the right and honorable thing to do, and it is Sir Griffith's dearest wish."

*Was* his dearest wish. Marian could almost hear Griffith's correction. It had been his dearest wish, before Marian had proved herself to be all he feared—unreliable, careless, licentious, intemperate. She'd lost her son and killed Art by seeking truth and honor and Lionel's rightful heritage, and that error she needed to correct now. "Your Grace—"

Red circles bloomed on Henry's cheeks. His hands moved incessantly. She wondered at the intensity of his behest. "Sir Griffith has assured me he believes the banns have been called in Wales the requisite number of times, so holy custom has been fulfilled. As the king, I will take the place of the earl of Wenthaven. 'Twill make all equitable for you, Lady Marian, and I'm sure I can make all equitable with your father when next I see him. From my own treasure, I have selected two rings of royal value—"

In desperation, Marian interrupted Henry. "May it please Your Grace, I must protest."

He paused in midflight, quite as if this were what he dreaded. "Lady Marian?"

"You don't mean for us to wed right now?" A faint, pervasive snicker passed through the crowd, and still bewildered, she looked over at them. She recognized no one except Oliver King, standing off to the side with an official-looking document in his hand, and that only contributed to her sense of disbelief. This morning, so unlike the day before, had dawned in delicate shades of pink and gold. The king, her enemy, had offered to act as her father. The priest, the ladies, the gentlemen, were all strangers, yet not as distant from her as the man who would be her bridegroom. He frowned at her, the new slash on his face no longer accented by brown stitching. He seemed a tall and mighty monolith of disapproval, and she found it odd that she could be attracted to disapproval.

But she was. Stupidly she wished this were a true wedding, with feasting and laughter and a merry bedding after. Instead—

"What about my child?" she asked, taking care to project her voice to the king and Griffith only.

"We shall seek him as soon as we've finished here," Griffith answered, his deep tones sounding as barren as the Welsh peak of Snowdon.

Chilled by his manner, stunned by the absurdity of their plan, she sought a reason to postpone the ceremony. "We have no contract of dower and dowry agreed upon, drawn up, and ready to sign."

"I have settled the matter," Henry said. "When the ceremony is complete and the witnesses have signed the registry, then I will give, as compensation, a vacant earldom to Sir Griffith—or, shall I say, Lord Griffith—and you, to be an inheritance for you and your heirs as long as your line shall endure. Currently known as Lillestry, and located on the border of Wales not far from Wenthaven, its value is well in excess of any of the properties currently in your families."

Marian looked at the parchment that Oliver unrolled and showed to her, and she realized at once her grievance had been thwarted. The prosperous lands would indeed serve as handsome compensation for this unorthodox marriage.

She studied it until Griffith leaned over her. In a voice rich with disdain, he said, "You'll find it all in order, and you'll also find Henry does not intend to let us go after Lionel until this ceremony is complete."

Now she comprehended the wiliness of the king. With her own maternal instinct, Henry had trapped her, then done what he could to render her ineffectual in her quest to place Lionel on the throne.

She rubbed the place above her skirt that hid the leather pouch from view. Henry didn't know of the weapon she yet possessed and the power it could exert, when she chose to use it.

More, she understood Griffith's resignation to a match he obviously despised. He had vowed to care for Lionel, and he would do what he must to keep his vow. Griffith also had vowed to serve the king.

This man Henry had chosen to restrain her whispered in her ear, "Resign yourself, my lady. You're marrying the Welsh beast."

Did Griffith ever lie? She doubted it. She doubted he knew how, or if he understood why he should bother, and that convinced her to face the priest and repeat the ancient vows.

When they had finished and exchanged the kiss of peace, Marian, Griffith, the priest, and Oliver all signed the registry in neat, ink-saving print. Then Henry flexed his fingers as if in anticipation, took the quill, and added his signature with a flourish.

They were married, as married as any couple could be.

Smiling broadly, Henry took Marian's arm, then Griffith's. "And now to break our fast."

"Your Grace, we must go," Marian protested.

"You must eat first, and a hearty meal will provide for you on the trail. I've ordered other meals packed for your travels, and weapons of every sort in case, God forbid, you must fight. I do hope you're not attached to the gelding that carried you to us, for I've replaced him with a younger, swifter mount."

Henry was right, damn him. She had to eat now,

just as she'd had to sleep the night before, but she found herself subduing panic. Stupid, feminine panic, for she knew Griffith would never be affected thus. He would understand the wisdom of rest and food before a challenge. He would never allow himself to dwell on the thought of the little lad in such rough hands. He wouldn't be like her, wanting to scream at Henry to let her go.

As the great hall closed around her, cutting her off from the out-of-doors, placing another obstacle between her and her son, she calmed herself and murmured, "My thanks, Your Grace." With relief, she noted the servants standing at the ready with steaming pots of porridge and joints of meat. Gold plate on the head table was piled with bread, already sliced, and pots of honey, and Marian realized this lavish meal had been prepared to be consumed in haste.

Henry seated himself on a great chair, then indicated she should take her place on his left. Griffith sat on his right, and Marian found herself unable to refuse the insistent rumblings of her stomach. Nor did she refuse the need to hurry, and she set to with a gusto that promised an early departure.

Griffith, too, paid unceasing attention to his plate while Henry watched them both. When they seemed near to finishing, he said, "My newest lord, I insist I send men with you on this anxious search."

Wiping his eating knife on his napkin, Griffith refused with as much courtesy as Marian had ever heard him muster. "Your Grace, I beg you would not. The first duty I must perform is tracking the route of the offender, and these inept Englishmen would be nothing but a nuisance."

"But when it comes to a battle—"

"When it comes to battle, Harbottle is no match for me."

"But if Harbottle has allies?"

"If the battle appears hopeless, then will I send to you," Griffith promised.

Henry stirred a spoon in his still-full bowl of porridge and, fascinated, watched the lumps circling. "You refuse my men, yet you wish to take Lady Marian. She is but a woman, and will surely slow you."

"Not I!" Marian said, vexed at the king's censure. "I ride as well as any man, have done battle with knife and sword, and I will not be left behind when my son's life is at stake."

Henry looked at her as if she were a creature from beyond the fall of the sea, and an unattractive one at that.

"You see," Griffith said. "I cannot leave her behind, for if I did, she would follow me. Lady Marian is a strong woman, and dedicated to her son's welfare."

"Aye, she is indeed strong, and dedicated." Without a trace of a smile, Henry said, "However, I see I cannot help you with your quest, and so I send you on your way. Be off at once! The child is even now slipping beyond your grasp."

Marian stood immediately. "Let us go."

Griffith bowed with great ceremony. "Remember, my liege, my vows to you. You are my king, and none other."

Henry waved a dismissing hand to them.

He waited only until he heard the heavy door slam below before he called for Oliver King. His secretary hurried forward, and Henry said, "Gather a small force of the most trustworthy men we have about us. Order them to outfit themselves for a journey with their king."

Surprised by the command and by Henry's abrupt and hasty manner of speech, Oliver stammered, "You—you will follow them, Your Grace?"

"I will not follow them, for Lord Griffith will

honor his vows to me above all else. This I know. But he is one man, and in a matter as great as this . . . I believe we will ride toward Castle Wenthaven and see who goes to visit. It might be enlightening. Very enlightening."

Normally Griffith preferred to ride in silence. He preferred to concentrate on his tracking. He wanted no distractions.

But this silence was different. It was tense with unspoken questions, fraught with Marian's own concentration as she led him to the place where the attack had taken place and then on, following him as he took his position in the lead.

As morning wore on to afternoon, he watched her with a kind of wonder. This woman was his wife. At one time he'd thought her undisciplined, out of control, a frivolous woman of lascivious tendencies. But she'd ridden most of the day yesterday to reach him, and now she rode back, without complaint, without even an indication of the discomfort she must be experiencing.

No, she wasn't undisciplined. She was too disciplined. It was a complaint others had made of him, and he found it ironic. He found it even more ironic that, regardless of her mistaken beliefs, her lack of trust, her independence, he still wanted her.

He gave his whole attention to the task of tracking, for when they had recovered the lad and Marian's mind was at rest, he planned to created a ferment in her body. He planned wonderful things, wild things, things he'd heard whispered among the men and dismissed as impossible—but for Marian, he would try them.

"Griffith?"

Marian broke into his thoughts, and he flushed guiltily. Had she noticed his condition? Did she wonder why he shifted with discomfort?

"Why haven't we found Art? He can't have gone far in his condition."

He almost sighed with relief and debated how to answer. He hated to tell her what he suspected—not because it was the worst, but because he suspected Art had manipulated her with consummate skill. He suspected Art still lived.

Art would search for Lionel and would find him. And for all Art's age, his craftiness and fighting ability commanded respect. Griffith wanted to tell her, for he'd seen the tears that pricked her lids and the guilt that shadowed her, but he feared to raise her hopes.

"Perhaps we'll find him downstream. Or perhaps thieves were attracted to his raiment and weapons." It was evasive, but almost an answer. More important, they had broken the great silence between them. Pointing at the trampled yellow rape flowers and blue lupines around them, he said, "Harbottle met some friends on his travels. He's gone on with them."

"How many?" she asked.

"I read four, and they are cunning. They cut a straight path through the wilderness"—he waved a hand back across the undulating hills, dotted with patches of forest and strips of field—"to this place, then proceeded straight toward Wenthaven without trail or path. They must be Wenthaven's men."

"Harbottle is not Wenthaven's man," she said.

"You don't wish for your father to have such a man, but in sooth, it would appear Harbottle is Wenthaven's man."

Her face tightened, pulling the rose from her cheeks. "Do they still have Lionel?"

"Aye, they have the lad. The scat of a babe occurs along the path—have you not noticed?"

"I hoped . . . Then he's alive."

"Aye, he's still alive, but if they are making for Wenthaven, we'll not catch them before they enter the gates." He tested her with his words. "But perhaps that doesn't matter to you. Perhaps you feel safe with Lionel in your father's hands."

Grief and worry had dulled her spring green eyes to the colors of autumn, and she refused to respond to his query. She said only, "Let us go," and her palfrey leaped forward.

They followed the trampled grass straight toward Wenthaven, and Griffith almost missed the signs of a lone horseman breaking off. But he couldn't miss the sudden change when the track of the main group veered toward the river Severn. The trail led them along the bottomlands, then around toward the wilderness near the Welsh border. They made a great circle, then Griffith lost the trail.

Griffith slid from his horse and examined the confusing markings on the ground. "Welshmen. These are Welshmen we're following, for only they could disguise a trail so well that I could lose it."

Still mounted, Marian said, "I recognize this place. These are the western reaches of Wenthaven land."

Standing, Griffith looked about him. Scraps of the Welsh mountains were strewn about like stones from a giant's hand. Untouched by civilization, unclaimed by Celts, Saxons, or Normans, the primeval forest still teamed with boar and deer and wild spirits. He could hear the boar snuffling in the underbrush. He could hear the clash of the stag's antlers. He could hear the high, sweet whisper of fairies and feel the malevolent gaze of the dwarves, and he prayed to Saint Dewi for guidance.

As if to deny him his plea, the sun suddenly cloaked itself with clouds. It seemed an evil omen, as if the saint himself couldn't bear to watch their fate. But—

"Griffith, look."

He followed the direction of Marian's finger and saw, not far ahead, a glow between cracked slabs of sandstone.

"Bless you, Saint Dewi." Griffith mounted quickly and backed his steed away. "Bless you."

The sun broke out again as Marian followed him to a thick grove of ash and oak. "Is it them?" she asked as she dismounted.

"Aye, no doubt it is, and all unknowing, I almost came too close." He, too, dismounted and handed her the reins. "I want to scout ahead. Stay here. Water the horses, but don't feed them or remove their tack. We might need to leave suddenly. Are you amenable to remaining?"

To his surprise, she nodded. "If you are taken, I will still be free to do what I can—seek help, recapture Lionel, or be captured and care for my son."

Her logic was good, but he found it distasteful. He didn't want her to calmly plan her strategy should he be apprehended. He wanted her to cry and wring her hands and be frightened. He wanted her to behave like a silly woman as far as he was concerned. Hoarse with disappointment, he said, "I won't be taken."

"I know."

He started toward the sandstone slabs.

"But why don't you wait until 'tis fully dark? 'Twould be safer."

He smiled and, using his best woodland skills, faded into the twilight.

When he returned, he called her softly. A slim shadow, she moved out from between the two horses. "What news?"

"Lionel is safe," he told her first, and a soft exhale expressed her relief. "He's asleep beneath an overhang. Cledwyn leads three of Wenthaven's Welsh mercenaries. Harbottle is huddled by the fire, sword at the ready. Their horses are down by the stream, clumped together and easy to scatter. And"—he frowned—"I don't understand, but Dolan of Powel is with Lionel."

Lady Marian surged forward. "That miserable sack of dung!"

Catching her by the arm, Griffith asked, "Why is he here?"

"Because he's a pirate, a thief, and a coward. He has my baby. My baby, who cared for him." She strained against him, but he held firm and her resistance collapsed. Massaging her forehead with both hands, she said, "He was probably part of this plot from the start, and I, like a fool, asked him for help."

Her bitterness was palpable, and Griffith answered it. "You'll have your chance for revenge. They're awake now, but eating well and drinking deep. In the darkness before the dawn, when they're stupid with sleep, we'll remove Lionel from their care. In the meantime, we must rest."

"I can't rest," she protested.

"You will," he answered, beginning to feed the horses.

He could almost sense her tension as she repressed her need for activity. She was a warrior, and his heart swelled with pride as she won her battle, then joined him. Moving with a restless energy, she helped him feed and groom the horses before she asked, "If we rest, we might fall asleep. How will we be assured we will wake?"

"An easy dilemma, little warrior." He handed her a skin filled with water. "Drink all of that. You'll wake before too many hours have passed, don't fear."

Uncomprehending for a moment, she stood, then lifted the skin and swallowed until he thought she must bulge. When she had finished, he drank his fill. Together they staked the horses in the grass, then they arranged the weapons Henry had provided in a careful pattern, so they would be most useful in case of attack. After preparing a bed of boughs, they lay on it, shoulder to shoulder, staring upward without a word.

The moon had not yet risen, and in all of England there could not be a blacker night. One by one, then in clumps of thousands, the stars broke through the sky. A white glow in the east seemed first an illusion, then a promise, and the moon rose as large, full, and pure as the Virgin fat with child.

Such grandeur made their personal impasse appear insignificant, and Griffith grasped Marian's hand. It trembled in his, and she clutched his fingers with an intensity that made him almost hopeful. But when she spoke, her words shocked him so much that he almost lost his grip.

"Lionel is legitimate."

His reaction was swift and from the gut. "That's impossible."

"I assure you, it is possible. As you may have surmised, Elizabeth is Lionel's birth mother."

"Aye, and you, brave woman, took the child and the shame."

"No shame, but a great danger, for perhaps you didn't realize Lionel's father was Elizabeth's uncle."

The water he had drunk wasn't enough, he realized, for his mouth felt dry. "Richard," he whispered.

"Aye."

Griffith had speculated first that Richard was Lionel's father. Then, when he'd discovered Marian was a maiden, he'd speculated Elizabeth was Lionel's mother. He had deliberately avoided the horrifying thought of Richard and Elizabeth together, understanding well the danger of such a liaison.

Now Marian brought a greater horror to him: the image of marriage between the two most royal folk in all of England and their production of a son. A monarch son, born protected by the canopy of holy Church.

Terror coursed through Griffith's veins like molten metal through a casting. "I pray you are mistaken, for if Lionel is the legitimate son of Richard and Elizabeth, then he has a better claim to the throne than Henry Tudor."

"You know me well, Griffith. Better than any man. Do you believe I would take Lionel from the safety of your home for anything less than a meeting with destiny? Do you think I would take him to face death, except for the fear that death will seek him?"

Repulsed and dismayed, he asked, "How could he bed her? How could he wed her? He was her uncle, the brother of her father. The Church forbids such union within such close bonds of consanguinity."

"As you well know, the pope provides dispensation for royalty to wed if the need arises. Richard was confident he could receive absolution, and even sent an emissary to the pope, but he died at Bosworth Field before acquiring pardon."

Hope dangled like bait before his nose, and he snapped at it. "Then the marriage is not official."

She chuckled bitterly. "Who would give credence to such priestly quarrels?"

She was right, and a silence fell between them. In the light of the moon he watched her, touched by the struggle that turned her from a vivacious girl into a driven woman. Her dry eyes didn't blink but stretched wide and dull, telling the tale of tears shed long ago.

Griffith longed to touch her, to comfort her, but he dared not. The chasm between them stretched deep and ragged, filled with dilemmas that would grab him with clawed feet and drag him down should he try.

With memory weighing on her, she told him, "Elizabeth only did it for her brothers. Richard had put them in the tower, and no one knew what he intended. He declared himself king, and everyone feared what he intended. He invited Elizabeth to court, and we went in hopes of finding what he intended. And then"—her sigh wavered with emotion—"I wished we had never discovered."

"Did he kill his wife to wed Elizabeth?"

She sat up, but he didn't think she saw him or their surroundings. "Did Richard kill Anne? I don't know. All I know is Richard was the coldest man I'd ever met. He wanted Elizabeth, not for her youth and beauty, but for the stability a marriage with her would bring to his reign. Well"—she shrugged—"he wanted her for the same reason Henry wanted her. Union with King Edward's daughter makes the throne impregnable, doesn't it?"

Cautiously he replied, "So I believe."

"He promised her if she'd bed him, he'd release her brothers. The young king and the dear little duke of York." A bitter smile tugged at her lips. "I didn't believe him, of course, and I don't think Elizabeth did, either, but what was she to do?"

"They were dead already," Griffith said.

"We had no bodies to bury. 'Tis difficult to bid farewell until one sees . . . well." She plucked a leafing twig from the mat beneath them, then broke it and broke it again. The running sap pooled in her palm, and with a gesture of distaste, she wiped it on her skirt. Then she scrubbed at it, complaining, "It won't come off."

He took her hand and used the corner of his rough homespun to rub at the sticky juice. "Once it stains, it is difficult to remove. But see, the surcoat which you once scorned has removed it." He released her, and she stared into her palm as if she could read the message there.

"Griffith? When this is over, do you think we . . . ?"

He waited, breathless.

"But you don't know the whole story yet." She dismissed her unspoken plea with a wave of the offending hand. "He—"

"He . . . who?"

"Richard." The name sounded sour on her lips. "He got Elizabeth with child immediately, and that both pleased and dismayed him. When Anne died, he wasted no time wedding Elizabeth, but we had to do so in secret, for the rumors were circulating, and the whispers were ugly. Richard didn't seem to understand, even then, that decent folks found murder, deceit, and usurpation crimes to be punished, rather than strategies to be rewarded."

"Who knew of the ceremony?" he demanded.

"Elizabeth. Richard. The priest. The duke of Norfolk. And me."

He felt almost faint with fear. "I've heard not a whisper of it."

"The priest is dead. He died, I heard, on his way to Rome to receive the necessary papal bulls. The duke of Norfolk is dead, killed at Bosworth Field. Richard is dead, also at Bosworth Field."

"You are alive."

"Aye."

She was too calm for his liking. She didn't—couldn't—understand the danger, and he said, "And if you want to stay that way, you'll not ever tell another soul this tale which you told me this day."

"Will you kill me, then?"

He laughed in angry amusement. "Not I, my dear. Just this morning I pledged to protect you. But I also stood beside Henry at Bosworth and watched the English knights kill Richard. I heard the great vow which Henry made, swearing by the nails of the cross he would do everything he must to preserve his throne, and I warn you, if a whisper of this ever escapes, Henry will deliver you and your son from the tribulations of earthly life."

As simply as a child with its catechism, she asked, "What of my vow?"

The words, the tone, chilled him. "What vow?"

"When Richard was killed, Elizabeth knew the babe in her belly was doomed. So I attended Lionel's birth. I stood beside Elizabeth, held her hands, gave my blood when she dug her nails into me. I saw Elizabeth suffer the agony of childbirth, and saw the birth of her resolution, too. When she placed Lionel's naked, squalling body in my hands, she made me swear I would do everything to raise him to the sta-

tion to which he was born. She put her faith in me.
Would you ask me to betray it?"

He looked around at the black bowl of sky, seeking
answers, but he had only his own feelings to draw on.
"Aye, I would ask you to betray that vow. You are—"

*A woman. You are my wife. You'll do as I say.* The
sentiments came easily to him, but he knew they
would have as little weight as feathers on the wind.
He had to appeal to her logic and to her love of
Lionel. To that end he said, "Have you thought of
what this would mean? For you to succeed, you must
enlist the help of ambitious, unscrupulous men."

With half a smile, she said, "I have my father."

"Do you think he wouldn't take the throne for
Lionel, then take the throne from Lionel?" he
demanded.

"Wenthaven prefers subtle power. He would
uphold Lionel's birthright."

"And warp the lad into his own image."

She straightened. "I wouldn't allow that."

"How do you imagine you would stop him?"

"Wenthaven has no interest in raising a child. He
would gladly leave Lionel to me."

Her arrogance staggered him. "You would live at
court?"

"With Lionel. Aye, of course."

"What about me? What about our marriage?"

She blushed and then paled. "You didn't wish to
wed me anyway. We've not consummated it—"

"We haven't?"

"—since the ceremony, and I'm sure we could peti-
tion for an annulment."

"If I don't agree to such a course?"

She blushed again. "I hoped you would say that. I
knew you would see your dilemma."

His irony had a sharp, shining edge. "Which
dilemma?"

"You have sworn to uphold Henry's claim to the

throne, but you see now it is based on a mistaken premise. Examine your conscience, Griffith. Where do your loyalties lie? With Henry, or with the true king of England?"

The complex world of honor had entrapped wiser men than he, and Griffith felt the pressure of uncertainty wearing at his resolve. Defensive, he answered, "I swore my oath to Henry before he was king, and again afterward. So I swore it to the man, not the office, and you with your wily ways cannot lure me from that truth."

"But you fret about Lionel. You ask how he will grow into an honorable man under the influence of my father. If you were to take charge of Lionel, I have no doubt—"

"Is this why you chose this barren place to tell me the tale?" he burst out. "To present temptation as surely as the snake presented the apple? Am I a fool to be flattered by your confidence and seduced from my duty?"

"This sweep of events is greater than you and me, yet we can be part of it."

"We can bring England to the brink of hell. Henry is powerful, well entrenched in the running of the country, with many noble allies who command many men. They would not abandon a strong man to follow a two-year-old child, especially a child born of union witnessed by dead men and two girls. How do you imagine you, a mere woman, could break the might of Henry Tudor?"

Leaning down, she lifted her skirt, binding his eyes to the long glide of her leg clear to her thigh. The garter there was tied in a complex knot, and with care she untied it and pulled loose a leather bag. From inside it, she drew a parchment, weathered by much handling, and she shook the creases from it and handed it to him. "With this. This is the page of the registry, bearing witness to the marriage of Elizabeth, daughter of Edward, to Richard, king of England."

# 18

*Touched by moonlight,* the spidery writing blared at Griffith like the flourish of a trumpet.

Marian gloated at his wide eyes and open mouth, at the astonishment writ on every line of his body. It was working, just as she'd planned. This would convince him of the rightness of her quest and would bring him into the battle on Lionel's behalf.

Then the parchment began to shake. She watched as the shaking traveled up his arm to his whole body, and she grasped his elbow in alarm. "Griffith? Are you ill?"

The anguish and horror in his gaze slashed at her, bringing home her mistake, as did the trembling of his voice when he asked, "Why did you show this to me? Do you wish me to dispose of it for you?"

"Not dispose of it, nay!" She snatched at her precious parchment, but he held it out of her reach. "I showed it to you so you would realize all portents point to Lionel's succession."

Like the knell of a church bell at a funeral, his

solemn voice pronounced, "I am Henry's man, and this is treason I hold in my hand."

"Not treason!" she cried. "'Tis Lionel's birthright."

"'Tis Lionel's death warrant." Despite the evening chill, moisture sheened his brow. "I could take it from you."

She looked at the irreplaceable document, held above her head, and examined the width of his shoulders and the strength of his arms. She could do nothing to stop him if he chose to keep it or destroy it. Her gamble had failed, and now she could only try to repair the damage. "You could keep it," she answered steadily, "but you won't. You are too honorable."

Had she convinced him, or was she merely reading his character correctly at last? It didn't matter, for he dropped the parchment, and she lunged, catching it before it fell in the dirt.

Anchoring her wrist with the grasp of his hand, he whispered, "Bury it. Burn it. Take your knife and shred it. As long as the proof of that wedding exists, evil men would be seeking Lionel to use him against the king—as they have done now, even without that proof."

Righteousness burned in her. "What about my vow to Elizabeth?"

"Your vow to Elizabeth!" He snorted. "I read the letter Elizabeth sent to you. Didn't you?"

"Aye, I did. In it she spoke of Lionel and how tenderly she thinks of him."

"And?" he prompted.

She shrugged, impatient with this empty conversation. "She spoke of her other son, Arthur, and of her husband, Henry."

"And?" he insisted.

Bewildered, she said, "And . . . what?"

"Didn't she tell you about her love for Arthur, and how he repairs the emptiness left by the death of her brothers?"

"Well . . . aye, I suppose."

"Didn't she tell you of her husband, the king, and how he encourages her to send you money for the well-being of Lionel?" He peered at her, and her blank expression seemed to drive him into a frenzy. He caught her by the shoulders and shook her. "Don't you understand what she was saying?"

Marian shook her head. She didn't understand what Griffith wanted. She didn't see what seemed so obvious to him. She didn't understand anything at all.

Griffith pushed her away as if the touch of her disgusted him. "You close your eyes deliberately. What value is a vow extorted by a woman suffering from the exhaustion of childbirth, a woman grieved from the death of her brothers and unsure of her own fate? Don't you understand? Elizabeth has found contentment with her son and her husband, and she wants you to forget the past and move on."

Stunned by his wild imaginings, Marian stammered, "She . . . does . . . not."

"Does Elizabeth want her second son killed to make way for her first?"

Marian defended Elizabeth almost on instinct. "Elizabeth is the most loving creature in the world. She wishes death for no one, and certainly"—she gasped as the truth of it hit her, but she denied it— "her second son would not have to die."

"Don't play the fool, Marian. You lived at court. You were part of the greatest intrigue in English history. You know the truth." She covered her ears, but he took her hands away. "Arthur would have to die. Henry would have to die—and Henry is easily as devoted a father as you are a devoted mother. It would be a bloody fight."

Griffith was flinging facts at her—facts she hadn't wanted to face. Facts that scourged her as precisely as a whip in the hand of an inquisitor.

He continued relentlessly. "For Lionel to become

king, Henry must be a victim, and Arthur, and even your dear friend Elizabeth. *That's* what Elizabeth was trying to tell you. That's what you must accept."

Breathing was an effort. The bleeding of her heart seemed to have clogged her lungs. Thinking became impossible. The agony of the truth destroyed her mind.

Struggling to articulate some of her own conviction, she found herself reduced to reciting the old litany with which she'd supported her hopes. "Lionel is my son, the heir to the throne, and he deserves better than a life as a bastard."

Griffith swelled with a kind of triumph. "Aye, he does, and I've offered Lionel just that. I will make him my son, give him part of my estate, and love him as my own."

It was a great offer, a generous offer, but she rejected it unconditionally, and he knew it even before she could find a way to soften the blow. In a rage of disappointment and bitterness, Griffith said, "You would have Lionel live a life defined by threats against his person and his power, a life where life itself is a gift to be stolen by one stray arrow, by a single knife blade to the heart. That is the life of a child king. That is what you wish for him."

"Nay, not so." She shook with the same palsy that had earlier afflicted him, and his accusations drove her half-mad with grief. "I can protect him. I am not so selfish."

"Aren't you?" He picked up the hand that held the parchment and pushed it before her eyes. "Perhaps you should wonder who you're saving this for? Is it for Lionel, or is it for you?"

"Not me!" She denied it instinctively, knowing she wanted only the best for Lionel, knowing no thought of her own benefit ever stirred her soul. For that was surely the blackest sin—using the child of her heart for advancement. Only a monster, only a depraved creature, would dream so deceitful a dream. She hadn't.

"Are you seeking vindication from those who called you a whore? Are you seeking power as the king's mother? Or are you simply seeking the court life you lost and miss?"

Steel flashed in the moonlight, and she found the haft of her knife in her free hand. She pressed the tip against his chest, so hurt and enraged she would gladly cut out his heart.

"Go ahead." He loosed her and spread his arms wide. "Drive your knife deep. But do it only if I've lied."

She pressed harder.

"Do it, and know the truth has died this night."

Griffith felt each mighty thump of his heart, each pulse of blood through his veins, as he crawled along the ground, and he thanked God for ongoing service of that uninjured organ.

Griffith had always known he might end as a piece of meat on a skewer, but he'd thought it would be in battle. He'd never considered his own wife would be the butcher.

But it had been close. Too close. Marian had pressed on that knife until he'd felt the threads in his doublet give way.

Then she'd pulled back. Without a word, she'd put her knife in its sheath at her waist and had lain down. He hadn't had to wake her for their raid on the mercenaries—she'd never slept, and he wondered if it was guilt or fury that had kept her awake.

Marian. Why had God given him Marian? Was it some celestial jest on Griffith, who had sworn to have a domestic woman, content to stay home? For if he now had that woman, she would not be creeping around to the far side of the mercenary camp as he prepared an attack from the near side. She would collapse at the suggestion of fighting, and he would be alone in the dark.

With Marian, he knew he wasn't alone. He had a partner he could depend on, and depend on her he did.

Taking care to remain behind a sandstone slab, for the protection of his leather armor was not enough, he rose to his feet and surveyed the area. The mercenaries had chosen their camp well. A ring of rock towered above them in the shape of a horseshoe, with Dolan and Lionel tucked in the deepest part beneath the sandstone overhang. The fire had been built ten paces in front, and four men lay wrapped in rugs around it. It couldn't have been comfortable, for the ground sloped away beneath them, but it served as protection for the child, and that, no doubt, was their intention. One man was missing—a lookout? Or simply a visitor to the bushes?

Griffith waited for his return, measuring the distance between the overhang above Lionel and the ground. They had planned that Marian would drop between Lionel and the fire and get Lionel, regardless of the cost.

He looked again, then turned his head away. It was easier, he found, to engage in battle than to contemplate your mate in battle, and he observed her escape route with care. Ringing the front of the camp was a brook that cut deep into the sandstone, a natural defense, but also the escape route Marian would use. He would earn her the time she needed. He knew she had the courage. Now, if only her strength proved great enough and her luck proved shield enough, his lady falcon would fly away from this place.

Alert in every sense, Griffith watched the camp as he notched his arrow in the yew longbow. The missing man had not returned, but the minutes were slipping by and the moon was sinking toward its resting place in the mountains. The raid could wait no longer. He lifted the bow and pulled the bowstring taut, then took aim at one sleeping figure.

The arrow flew straight and true, burying itself deep into the body. With a shriek, the mercenary died. The other mercenaries revealed their training as they rolled away from the fire and to their feet. Griffith picked off another as he ran toward the concealing woods, but in his hurry his shot faltered, and he could hear curses as the man plucked the arrow from his leg.

He waited only long enough to see Marian jump from the overhang above Lionel, and then he raced to a new position.

The slippery sandstone gravel around the overhang served as its own protection against marauders, as Marian found when she landed and her feet slid out from under her. Knife in hand, she tumbled a few feet down the slope, panicked by her clumsiness and hoping Dolan hadn't heard.

Madness. He would have had to be deaf to miss it. Gripping her knife between her teeth, she clawed her way up the few feet to the overhang and realized Dolan was not deaf, but gone. Lionel lay tucked back into the crack of the rock, wide-eyed and unguarded, and Marian's heart sang.

Her son was alive, safe, and unharmed, and never had she thought to seize him so easily.

"Lionel," she coaxed. "Come to Mama."

He only scooted tighter into the overhang.

"Lionel, please." She glanced around, but no one appeared. "Sweeting, 'tis Mama. Come with me, and we'll go away from here."

She could hear his rapid breathing and knew that for him, abruptly wakened from sleep, her appearance was nothing more than another part of this continuous nightmare. With another glance behind her, she crawled under the overhang and reached for her son.

Before she could touch him, another hand whipped out and caught her wrist.

It came from a dark and empty place—only it wasn't empty. Dolan unfolded himself from his hiding place and pushed her farther back into the rock. "M'lady," he said. "Ye came at last. What are yer plans?"

"I'm going to take Lionel." She whipped out her knife and pointed it at him.

"Don't wave yer spur at me, or I'll show ye how t' use it," he growled. "Have ye a horse? Fer ye'll not get far without one."

Confused by what sounded like benevolence, she stammered, "I don't . . . aye, I have a horse. Two horses."

"Griffith wi' ye?"

"Aye."

"Then ye've got a chance." He picked Lionel up and wrapped him tighter in the blanket, then led her to the edge of the overhang. He peered around. "Keep low until ye reach th' steed, then spur him 'til ye're well away. Go fer Castle Wenthaven, I guess, fer these dickweeds aren't Wenthaven's men no more. They're renegades, seekin' t' make a fortune sellin' th' poor lad t' his grandfather. There now"—they heard an explosion of screams—"yer Griffith got another one. Go now!"

He handed Lionel to her, but she said, "Why should I trust you? You're one of *them.*"

"Don't be such a damned stupid twit. Who th' hell did ye think was carin' fer th' lad? I had t' join 'em, or they'da not let me take him."

Looking at his gnarled face, she believed him.

And he knew it. Pushing at her, he commanded, "Run!"

She did, and he served as a shield as she slithered into the trees. She heard Griffith shout, then Dolan urged, "Keep goin'. Don't look back!"

She skidded to a stop, and he skidded into her.

"Go on," he said again, but she couldn't.

Regardless of the precious burden in her arms, she had to know. Through a gap in the trees, she saw them, face to face in the moonlight.

Griffith and Harbottle.

Harbottle held one of the dueling swords Griffith so despised.

Griffith held a war hammer.

"Oh, God," Marian whispered. "Harbottle's going to kill him."

"Don't be so sure, m'lady." But Dolan's usual cockiness failed.

From across the clearing, Harbottle glowed with health, with beauty, with the certainty of victory. Next to him, Griffith looked large, solemn, and slow, a bear or beast too simple to embrace his fate with grace.

A yell from the woods opposite startled Marian. "Get 'im!"

But for whom was the encouragement intended?

Dolan plucked at her sleeve. "M'lady, we must go. Th' other mercenaries are loose. They can find us"—he glanced around as if puzzled—"if they choose."

The silver blade sliced the air toward Griffith's face. Griffith stepped back—far enough? Marian stifled her cry, braced herself for the shower of blood that would follow the stroke.

Nothing. Even Harbottle frowned. For a brief moment Griffith had transformed himself from a lumbering beast into a skilled warrior. But the moment passed as Griffith clumsily swung his hammer toward Harbottle's shoulder. The powerful blow whistled as it missed him in a clean sweep.

Raucous laughter sounded from the woods.

Griffith sidled closer to the ravine.

"Give me th' child," Dolan instructed. "Ye're squeezin' him."

She handed Lionel to Dolan, unwilling to turn her gaze away from the horrible scene unfolding. For she knew, as Griffith did, that if by chance or skill he won the contest, he was still the target of bolts and arrows wielded by unseen watchers.

"Come, you coward," Harbottle taunted. "Meet my steel and know I'll have my way with your woman ere the night is through." Before he had finished speaking, the sword stabbed at Griffith's stomach. It struck—and stuck.

"Ooh, leather armor," observed a mercenary.

Suddenly the situation raged out of Harbottle's control. He lunged for the sword. He retrieved it with outstretched hand, and the war hammer crashed down on the bones of his arm. The crunch of bones and his shriek of pain made Marian squeeze her eyes shut, as if that would keep out the sound.

It didn't. She heard the hammer fall, heard the burst of the skull as Harbottle lost his last battle. She would have turned away without looking, but Dolan burst out, "Th' dirty dickweed! He's goin' t' get him."

Opening her eyes, she saw Griffith dashing for the chasm that wrapped itself around the camp.

"Run, man!" Dolan urged.

Following Dolan's line of vision, she stepped from behind an oak's wide trunk to observe Cledwyn perched on one of the lofty sandstone pillars, aiming a crossbow at Griffith.

She screamed a warning even as Cledwyn let fly. On the edge of the ravine, Griffith jerked, then tumbled out of sight.

Like a ravaging wolf who has brought down his prey, Cledwyn lifted his head and howled to the moon, and from the nearby woods two howls joined the primitive chorus.

Swept from nightmare to nightmare, Marian staggered when Dolan gave her a push. "We've got t' save th' child," he growled.

As Marian fled toward the horses, a stitch started in her side and spread to her heart—or was it the other way around?

Griffith was wounded—or dead. Fallen, with no one to tend to him. Laid flat in the dirt of the ravine . . .

She mounted and received Lionel from Dolan.

Into the ravine . . .

"I'll take his horse an' ride at yer back," Dolan said.

Into the ravine . . .

Facing the east, she spurred her horse toward Wenthaven, hoping for sanctuary where before she had hoped for support.

She'd been taken in by Griffith's acting. He hadn't really been hit. He'd done as Art had done so many years before, pretended death to fool his enemies.

But why didn't her spirits lighten?

And she knew the answer.

Because Griffith had been convincing. Sweet Jesus, he had been convincing.


Teetering on the edge of the precipice, Cledwyn shrieked his victory at the still body lying below. "I got him. I got th' Welsh traitor!" He turned and beamed at the mercenaries creeping out of the trees. "'Twas a good night's work, wi' Griffith ap Powel killed an' Harbottle smashed like th' bug he is, an' Lady Marian takin' th' brat back t' Wenthaven as fast as she can go. Let's chase her a bit, lads. 'Twill be great entertainment, an' th' earl's waiting wi' a fine reward."

"I can scarce walk, much less chase th' wench," the limping mercenary said.

"Buck up, Bryce. Ye're alive, aren't ye? An' I killed th' Judas what shot ye, an' he killed Harbottle an' saved us th' trouble."

"Aye, but what about that Billy? I'd be sittin' easier if he hadn't left us t' visit th' bushes an' never returned."

Cledwyn kicked out and landed a telling blow to Bryce's wounded ankle. Collapsing with a profane curse, Bryce ducked when Cledwyn swung again. "Don't ye mention it t' anyone, especially not th' earl o' Wenthaven. If anyone asks, Billy was killed on th' trail. Hear me?" He aimed another kick at Bryce, and Bryce rolled away, crying his assent. "Hear me?" He aimed a blow at the remaining mercenary.

"Aye, we'll do it," he said.

Still raving, Cledwyn looked for another chance to vent his fury, and his gaze fell on Harbottle. With a savage grin, he rolled the body over, and the mark of the hammer showed clearly in the moonlight. "Ain't so pretty now, is he?" With his foot, Cledwyn wiggled the limp head, then rolled the body over and over until it reached the precipice. "Think we ought to say a prayer?" Cledwyn cackled and raised his arms to the heavens. "We consecrate this Englishman t' th' depths o' hell. May he roast there forever."

The mercenaries shrank back from the blasphemy, but the ravine seized Harbottle with an already whetted appetite, and the sound of his tumbling body hung in the air like a threat softly uttered.

Gloating at his mercenaries Cledwyn asked, "What say ye? Will ye follow me fer th' gold? Or will ye stay an' rot wi' Harbottle?"

"Horses," Dolan called. "Comin' fast behind."

Griffith hadn't managed to scatter all the mercenaries' steeds, Marian realized, and although she used every shortcut she remembered and a few she made up, the fighters had no child to slow their pace.

Riding east toward Wenthaven, she urged her gelding to greater speeds. The moon lit the way like an obliging torch, while the sun tinted with its first hint of gold. The wind whistled in Marian's ears and plucked at the dark veil tied tightly around her bright hair.

"Still gainin', m'lady."

Ahead she heard another sound, the faint sound of barking. Of spaniels.

"The dogs have heard us," she whispered.

The horse surged beneath her, and she realized they would make it to Wenthaven before the mercenaries. If the gate were open, they would be safe.

If.

It should have been exhilarating, but it was not. Lionel stared about him with eyes too big for his thin face. What the mercenaries had done to him, she didn't know, but he didn't speak—couldn't speak?—and she longed to hear one defiant "Nay!" She cradled him tightly, trying to cushion him with her body from the worst of the jolts .

Straining to see Wenthaven's curtain walls, she was rewarded with a glimmer of water.

The lake that protected Wenthaven lay just ahead. Breaking into the cleared land that surrounded it, she galloped fiercely for the drawbridge, crying her name to the guards. Dolan fell behind, crisscrossing behind her, trying to draw any stray bolts from the crossbow. The drawbridge slid down, slow and majestic, and it hadn't touched the ground when she jumped her horse onto it. The clatter of hooves on board sounded like liberation. The sight of her father with his yipping spaniels looked like deliverance. With Dolan at her back, she shouted, "Pull it up. Pull the bridge up, the Welsh are after us!" She skidded to a stop in front of Wenthaven. "Cledwyn's on his way with his men, and he's gone mad with money lust."

"Cledwyn? How delightful." Wenthaven looked fresh and alert, and her news seemed to pique his interest. To his men he said, "Keep the drawbridge down."

"Listen to me, Wenthaven! He kidnapped Lionel!"

"He's my man." Wenthaven snapped his fingers at the mercenaries. "Hurry, we mustn't keep Cledwyn waiting."

Exasperated and not a little frightened, Marian said, "He was going to hold Lionel for ransom."

"He took his orders from me."

He was so calm, so sure, she observed him with a keen eye. He was dressed in a clean doublet, with ruffles at the neck and stylish slashes at the sleeve. His hair was cut and combed as thoroughly as the coat of any of his spaniels. In fact, he looked as fine as any London gentleman attending a city entertainment.

It struck her then. He'd been awake at this hour of the morning. He'd been expecting her.

She'd been betrayed. Betrayed by the one man she ought to be able to trust.

Betrayed by her own father.

# 19

*Griffith panted as he pushed* Harbottle's body off of his and groaned when he stood. He'd been grateful for the swordsman's protection, unknowing though it was, for he'd feared Cledwyn or one of his mercenaries might take a final, finishing shot at him. But his imitation of a man struck by a crossbow bolt must have been masterly, convincing the mercenaries of his death.

Grimly he clawed his way out of the ravine. As he expected, his horse was gone. He had no way of getting to Wenthaven this day. The weight of hopelessness settled on him, and he staggered, going down on one knee. He dug his hand into the dirt and lifted a handful to heaven.

"Keep her alive until I can get there. Keep her alive . . ." He faltered.

If she would just *stay* alive, he would make sure she continued to live to the fullness of her years. He would make sure if he had to bind her and drag her all the way to Castle Powel. It wasn't a pretty plan— imprisoning your wife could lead to ugly whispers.

But he'd heard Cledwyn's exaltation at the success of
his mission. He realized the extent of Wenthaven's
genius. He realized, too, that should Wenthaven set
his plan in motion and lead a rebellion in Lionel's
name, Lionel was doomed.

Henry would perceive his mercy to Lambert
Simnel, the previous pretender, as weakness, and
he'd resolve not to be so weak again. He'd put Lionel
to death. He'd put Wenthaven to death. He'd put
Marian to death and probably Griffith and every
member of the Powel family.

A bleak ending to a new marriage, to a vigorous family, and to a blameless lad. Griffith alone could stop the
disaster—if he could reach Wenthaven in time.

Again he dug his fingers into the dirt, the sand
scraping as it filled beneath his fingernails, the mulch
of years past a ready reminder of the fleeing seasons.

A faint nicker floated on the air. He lifted his head,
suddenly intent and determined.

A farm, perhaps? Unlikely in the wilderness, but . . .
He rose and followed the faint scent of horse. It led
him along a winding track to a meadow, lush with
spring grass, and he almost laughed aloud at the sight
of a horse, grazing without a care in the world.

It belonged to one of the dead mercenaries, stam-
peded in the fight, and lacked saddle and bridle, but
he'd learned to ride the wild and ill-natured Welsh
ponies as a child. If Saint Dewi had sent him a horse,
then, by God, he would ride him.

And ride him he did, but only after some bone-
crunching falls. Saint Dewi's horse had spirit and his
own opinion about his destination, but the struggle
restored Griffith's battered confidence. He soon
found himself galloping along the road to Wenthaven,
wrestling the unbridled stallion. He wrestled, too,
with his dream of Marian, contemplating the ways to
make it come true.

Once he had her imprisoned, he'd teach her to

enjoy domesticity. He'd give her a kiss for every stitch she set, a caress for every healing skill she learned. She'd comprehend the pleasures of womanhood and forget excitement, swordplay, and adventure.

He must be delirious with pain.

Rising in his mind was a picture of Marian, dressed in her male garb, sewing a seam and chatting about fashion.

Aye, he was delirious.

So delirious he thought he heard Henry's voice.

"Griffith. Griffith!"

Griffith stared. It even looked like Henry, coming up behind him at the head of a large, armed troop.

"I thought it was you. God rot it, Griffith, what have you done with yourself? You look like hell's spawn."

Sweeping the king with a comprehensive gaze, Griffith noted the light armor he wore. More than that, he noted the pleasant smile, the innocent expression, relaxed manner—all belied by Henry's watchful gaze. Had Henry been following him? Didn't Henry trust him? And why not? Giving no indication of his thoughts, Griffith waited until the horsemen reached him. "You look like my king, come to . . . rescue me?"

As Henry rode to Griffith's side, he observed his bruised and dirty knight. "It appears you need rescuing."

"Not rescuing, but mayhap assistance. I ride to Castle Wenthaven."

"Ah. Our destination is Castle Wenthaven also. I've had word from one of Wenthaven's men-at-arms that Wenthaven's mercenaries are up to no good, and I fear for the boy."

"The boy?" Griffith asked.

"Lady Marian's child."

Henry still couldn't bring himself to use Lionel's name. As much as Griffith wished for the backing of the royal troop, he also wished Henry would disappear.

Marian's confessions rested heavily on his conscience,
and he feared Henry's true motives. Warily he asked,
"Who brought you this news?"

Twisting in his saddle, Henry pointed. "That man."

Griffith twisted, too, and saw him. Billy, stolid and
plain, Marian's faithful guard. How had Billy come to
this pass?

But he had no time to speak to him, for Henry
demanded, "What has happened to the lad? Why
are you here without him? And has the lady Marian
been . . . been . . ."

"Killed, Your Grace? I trust not. She rescued
Lionel from the mercenaries and is even now taking
refuge with her father."

"God rot her!" Henry's destrier leaped beneath his
hand. "We've got to stop her."

"Why?" Griffith demanded, knowing the answer yet
wanting to discover the extent of Henry's knowledge.

"Because Wenthaven intends to use her son as the
arrow to pierce the heart of my monarchy."

"Your quick mind is ever a delight to me, but
really, what did you expect? You lied to me about
your son." In the comfort of his chamber, Wenthaven
poured wine, cut bread, and acted so urbanely innocent that Marian ground her teeth.

Sinking onto the chair he indicated, she shifted
Lionel in her aching arms. "I did not lie to you."

"You did not lie, nor did you tell me all the truth."
Wenthaven looked on Lionel as a miser looks on
gold. "You left the truth for me to discover."

"With your talent for spying, that should not have
been difficult," she snapped, still hurt from the realization of betrayal, still angry at herself for seeking
sanctuary with her father.

"Ah, but first I had to realize you bore a secret.
Once the lad grew enough to resemble his father, I

began to wonder about Elizabeth's ever-open purse. Then the secret was not difficult to ferret out." He placed a platter and cup on the table at her side, then leaned close to her face and murmured, "You weren't the only one present at the birth, daughter, and although the nobility have proved close-mouthed, one servant at last proved willing to speak."

What a fool she'd been to expect anything more than this of him. This was all he could comprehend. Prestige, wealth, intrigue, and the obtaining of them were his life's blood. "You have sunk too low, Wenthaven."

"I will yet rise high." Straightening, he waved a gracious hand. "Daughter dear, I'm fulfilling your every dream. I have hired the mercenaries. I have contacted every disgruntled noble in the land."

"And told them what?" She held her breath.

"Nothing, but that I have the key to Henry's downfall."

"Think you Henry hasn't had word of this muttering?"

"Does it matter?" Honey frisked around Wenthaven's feet, adoring him with her big brown eyes and her lolling tongue, and he bent to rub her ears. "With Lionel at the head of an army, we are invincible. By the end of the year, we would be in London, placing the crown on his little head."

Remembering Griffith's deductions, she tested the truth of them. "And taking the head off of Henry."

"An unfortunate necessity."

"And Elizabeth."

Expansive and generous, Wenthaven decided, "She is your friend. We will banish her to a nunnery instead."

"And the infant prince Arthur." She waited, breathless, for the denial, wanting it so much.

Caught in a spasm of discomfort, Wenthaven examined the dog's paws and plucked from them some burrs. "Killing a child is . . . not acceptable. Richard of York proved that."

"So we would simply neglect him until he died?" Wenthaven tried to speak, but she waved him to silence, so disappointed she could scarcely contain herself. "Or drop him on his head? Or place him in a monastery until all have forgotten his existence and he's old enough to be murdered?"

"Very inventive," Wenthaven commented.

"God rot you, Wenthaven, you're as low as a snake's belly."

With a growl, Honey made clear her displeasure at Marian's tone.

"I prefer the term *ruthless*." With a frown, Wenthaven made clear his exasperation. "You've wanted to go back to court. Don't tell me you haven't. You've dreamed of being the foster mother to a king. Don't tell me you haven't. You've wanted to smear the title of 'whore' in the faces of your detractors. Don't tell me you haven't at least lusted for that."

Of course she had. Marian couldn't deny any of it. But the memory of her dreams now brought her shame. She'd wanted the monarchy for Lionel, aye. But she'd wanted it for herself, too, and that had influenced her judgment. It had taken Griffith's clear vision to see her for what she was and to hold up the mirror for her to see.

"I did want those things," she admitted. She cuddled Lionel in her lap and wished his large, watchful eyes would close in slumber at last. But despite his obvious weariness, despite her comforting presence, he still clung to wakefulness. "Look at him," she whispered. "Sleep holds no security for him now. He fears the abrupt awakenings, the monster kidnappers, the absentminded cruelties of men burdened with a child. He fears . . . everything." She rubbed his back in slow, firm circles. "If he were the vanguard of a movement to usurp Henry, he would know nothing but fear—and the nightmares of his childish mind are as dust compared to the nightmares of reality. Don't tempt me with what I want. Think of what's right for Lionel."

Wenthaven condemned her in once succinct phrase. "You're thinking like a woman."

She almost laughed out loud, but she feared she wouldn't stop. "My thanks, Father." She hadn't convinced Wenthaven. Why had she even tried? Staring at her own hands, she wondered if they would be strong enough to do all that must done—alone. For there was no one left to help her, no one. Dolan, that creeping pirate of a Welshman, had disappeared as soon as they'd ridden in. Art was dead, and Rhys and Angharad were far away.

No one. "You killed Griffith," she finally said.

He lifted one brow. "Is he dead? I had no idea."

"You know he is."

"How would I—"

"You ordered your mercenaries to kill him. You ordered that dreadful Cledwyn . . ." She faltered. Cledwyn had been grinning, openly triumphant when he swept across the drawbridge and accepted his reward. The life he'd taken meant nothing beside the money he'd won and his delight in killing.

"You're so dramatic," Wenthaven chided, pouring himself some wine. "But why should you care? Griffith was only a lesser Welsh knight. Did you have a tendre for him?"

"I was married to him."

She had surprised him at last. He stalked toward her, cup in clenched hand. "You dared wed without my permission?"

"I dared not refuse. King Henry Tudor insisted on the union, gave me away, and presented us with a large estate not far from here."

Wenthaven's eyes sparked with fury. "By God,

you're my daughter. You've got a brain in your head. Couldn't you have stalled?"

"I was anxious to find Lionel—whom you had kidnapped from me. Henry refused to let us go until the deed was done, and I had no thought beyond the safety of my son. 'Tis your fault I'm wed."

"*Was* wed," he snapped.

She thought of the ravine, of the speed of the bolt, and of the way Griffith's body convulsed as it went over the edge, and still she hoped. It was foolish to hope he lived. Yet even if he couldn't reach her, even if he couldn't help, still she hoped.

Wenthaven accused her of being his daughter, rife with deviousness and manipulation. So she struggled to formulate a plan, but she needed time. With that in mind, she stroked the black hair off Lionel's forehead and said, "Lionel and I need to rest."

But Wenthaven understood her only too well. "I don't know if I should allow you to remain with your son. You might decide to do something foolish, like escape with the lad. I can take him from you."

All thought of plan flew from her mind, and she clutched Lionel tighter. "As you already have, once, and look what your tender nursemaids did to him in only one day. He's frightened half to death. He's lost his faith in me. He's a battle-scarred child, and you want him to be king of England. Are you mad? He's just a baby!"

"He's a prince." Wenthaven's indifferent gaze rested on Lionel. "And I'll teach him to behave like one."

"How will you teach him that, Wenthaven?" she asked. "You're no prince. You're scarcely even a man."

Wenthaven's hand rose, hovered in the air, then fell. The cold and scornful Wenthaven, the man always in control, seemed braced for once, as if her contempt for him and his plan could truly harm him.

"M'lord?" Cledwyn stood in the door, molting dirt like a bird molts feathers. "Got a bit o' a crisis."

Wenthaven exploded, directing his fire at the convenient target. "I told you never to come into the keep! What are you doing in the keep?"

With a jerk of his thumb, Cledwyn indicated the bailey beyond Wenthaven's window. "Got a bit o' a crisis," he repeated, but slowly, as if Wenthaven were simple.

It was the final straw. First his daughter proved unreasonable and recalcitrant, then this ignorant, claw-toothed savage dared grin and taunt him. Wenthaven swelled again with fury, ready to rend flesh from bone, but Cledwyn hastily did what he could to divert the punishment.

"Ye want me t' talk about it in front o' yer daughter?" With unmistakable sarcasm, he added, "It might upset such a delicate lass."

Cold sense took the place of hot fury, and Wenthaven went to Cledwyn. Gripping his arm with cruel fingers, he dragged the mercenary down the hall and flung him into one of his cubbyholes. "What is it?"

Cledwyn rubbed his arm. "Got a nasty way about ye, ye do."

Wenthaven leaned closer. "You don't know how nasty."

Something about him—his voice, his expression, his stance—seemed to penetrate the mercenary's cocky assurance, and Wenthaven experienced a deep and vicious satisfaction when Cledwyn stepped back until he smacked the wall.

"I just came t' tell ye, there's a troop of soldiers outside th' walls, back at th' treeline. They've sent a messenger t' th' gate an' demanded entrance. He says"—Cledwyn took a breath—"they're from th' king."

Wenthaven's lips could scarcely move. "From the king?"

"He was bearin' th' king's standard."

"Then it's not from the king. It *is* the king."
Wenthaven thought hard. "How many in the troop?"

"Can't tell fer sure because o' th' trees, but . . . I
estimate twenty knights an' their squires."

"So small a force . . . you'd think Henry would
have more wisdom. If I could capture the king . . ."
Wenthaven's hand closed into a fist, and he smiled,
the kind of smile that made the hardened mercenary
creep toward the exit. His finger shot out toward
Cledwyn. "You!"

Cledwyn froze like a marked fox. "Aye, m'lord?"

"Talk to them. Stall them while I prepare. Do what
you must to get your men ready."

"M'lord?" Cledwyn's eyes gleamed with avarice.
"Can I wear armor fer this fight?"

Magnanimous in his anticipation, Wenthaven
replied, "Aye, Cledwyn. Tell the English men-at-arms
they are to outfit you in the finest armor in the store-
room."

"They won't like it," Cledwyn said.

"They'll do as they're told. When the conditions
are proper . . ." Wenthaven gripped Cledwyn's shoulder, and Cledwyn flinched as if he'd been branded.
"We have all of England in our grasp. Let us not fail."

Wheeling around, he left the mercenary gaping
and returned to Marian. To his daughter, keeper of
secrets. Of, perhaps, the ultimate secret? He smiled
at her kindly and scarcely noticed when she cradled
Lionel as if to protect him. In his most comforting
tone he said, "Why don't you go to your suite? Put
the child to bed. Think about everything. You're
fatigued, emotional. When you've rested, you'll thank
me for my foresight."

"Oh, Wenthaven," she began.

But he ignored her. "Cecily! Come out from
behind those drapes and make yourself useful."

Confused, Marian looked at the draped wall he
indicated.

"Come on, Cecily," he snapped. "A woman the size of a cow can scarcely hide in one of my own spy holes without notice."

The drapes rustled, then parted slowly, and Cecily stepped out.

Cecily was pregnant. Her face was puffy, her forehead splotchy. Her wrists and fingers were swollen like sausages. She moved with lumbering clumsiness.

Worse, she looked unhappy. A mouth made to pout and invite kisses now simply drooped. The languorous doe eyes showed signs of weeping. And she wadded a damp, tear-laden cloth between her fingers.

How she disgusted him.

"Cecily." Marian half rose in greeting, then faltered and dropped back onto the chair. "I . . ."

"You told me so. Isn't that what you wanted to say?" Cecily said petulantly. "I can almost hear you saying it. 'I told you so. I told you so.'"

"Nay, Cecily—"

"God's gloves, Cecily, stop yammering and tend to your duties." Wenthaven stepped across the room, as far away from the bloated handmaiden as he could be. "Take Lady Marian and my grandson to their chambers"—he bent a frown on Marian—"not in the cottage, but in the manor. Tend to them as you did before. And get that lovesick look off your face. I've got no time for more of your whimpering."

He could see the realization dawning on Marian's face, as horror and amazement took their turns. He was the father of the child. Although he tried to conceal it, he met her gaze with rueful embarrassment. "She looks like your mother," he said, sure that that excused everything. "But she proved to be like all the rest. Inferior."

The king's herald rode up to the mounted troop, and Henry and Griffith closed on him as he entered the trees and spoke. "Wenthaven's got the castle manned by Welshmen. The first one pretended to speak only Welsh and sent for a second, who spoke English—badly. After much shouting, the mercenary informed me he can't let down the gate without Wenthaven's express permission, and Wenthaven is between some woman's legs. Supposedly a man has gone to fetch him." The young knight removed his helmet and wiped his sweaty hair off his forehead. "I think they're stalling, Your Grace."

Griffith moved away from Henry's noisy wrath and scanned the high, crenellated walls. He wanted to get in, and he wanted in now. He had no time to wait for Wenthaven's pleasure, nor for Henry's displeasure. The lives of Marian and Lionel counted as nothing, except to him. Therefore he would rescue them. "Billy," he called. "Come here."

The man-at-arms moved to his side as if he'd been waiting for the summons. "M'lord."

"How do we get in?"

Henry stormed up in time to hear the question and snapped, "There's no way into Castle Wenthaven. We'll have to send for an army and besiege it."

"I'll not give up so soon." Griffith examined the walls assiduously. "We have here one of Wenthaven's own men. He will know of a secret passage?"

Billy shook his head.

"Or a postern gate?"

Billy shook his head again.

"Or someone who's in league with you who will let you in?" Griffith finished in exasperation.

Billy mulled it over and by slow degrees came to a plan. "Th' good English men-at-arms have been supplanted by th' evil Welsh mercenaries—beggin' yer pardon, m'lord—an' that's bad. 'Cept th' good Englishmen might be willin' t' knock some heads if they see me, just t' let me in."

Nodding, Griffith said, "We'll ride as far around

the castle as we can without taking a dip in the lake, and stay in plain view while we do it."

Henry eyed Griffith's horse with misfavor. "You'll be like sitting drakes. You don't even have a saddle on that beast."

"Then give me one." Griffith dismounted. "This vicious steed understands me quite well now, and he's been well trained in the ways of war."

Henry hesitated, then signaled his squire and gave the order to strip the tack from the squire's own horse. When the lad would have balked, Henry said irritably, "By my troth, we're not going anywhere. Do as I tell you, and quickly!" He watched with a brooding gaze as the transfer was made, then instructed his squire to give up his weapons as well. "Lord Griffith is determined, and will need them, I suppose, although I'd prefer a siege. 'Twould keep the miscreant caged until such time as I humbled him."

"I don't have time for that, my liege." Griffith accepted a lance and shield, a long sword and war hammer, and placed them as he had been trained. "My wife and my child are inside, and I fear for them. I imagine the queen would be most fearful for them, too."

"Of course." Henry ran his finger along the collar of his gorget. "Of course. But wait at least while my squire fetches armor. You should not be so exposed for this ride."

Irritation at Henry made Griffith adjust and readjust the strap over his shoulder. It was only too obvious that Henry struggled between his conscience and expediency. If the child were killed, convenience would be served. If Henry appeared to be the executioner, hell itself could not shelter him from Elizabeth's pain and fury. So he vacillated while Griffith took action. "I'll make do with the leather armor and the shield. It will be sufficient"—he gripped the lance—"for my heart is pure."

Henry heard both what Griffith said and what he meant. "You'll take care," he insisted, then lifted a hand before Griffith could speak. "I know you will, but your previous encounters have not been auspicious, and Griffith, I need my loyal men about me. Especially now. Especially you. Especially Lady Marian's husband and the adopted father of the lad."

Proudly Griffith realized that men had no need for the too obvious sentiment that so impressed women. He and Henry communicated very well, and he put aside the uneasiness Henry's uncertainty had created in him. "My time has not yet come, my liege, nor will I open the door to death. I will take care." With a grin that resembled a snarl, he said, "This will be as simple as kissing a maid on May-day. Just be prepared to ride when we get the gate down."


Numb with amazement, Marian hoisted Lionel onto her hip and followed Cecily down the hall. The silence stretched until Cecily demanded, "Aren't you going to say anything? Like tell me how stupid I've been?"

Words were inadequate to the occasion, but Marian tried. "How are you feeling?"

"Oh, fine. Just fine. I'm fat and ugly and sick, and he doesn't want me anymore and he won't marry me, but I'm fine."

Marian nodded cautiously. "I'm sorry."

Stopping by the rooms where Marian had wintered, Cecily opened the door, then bowed to Marian. "After you. I mean, I'm just the servant here."

"My thanks." Marian stepped over the threshold. The rooms were dim and dusty and looked like a prison. Lionel dug his head into her shoulder and whimpered, and in an instant Marian realized what she wanted. "Nay," she said decisively. "I'm staying in my mother's rooms."

"What?" Cecily cried. "You can't do that. Lord Wenthaven said—"

"He said for me to stay in my chambers in the manor. So I will." Marian nodded and took Cecily's arm. "Come. We'll be happy there."

Cecily tugged free. "You'll be happy. I'll have to climb the stairs, up and down, up and down. There's no railing, the countess's room is at the top—the very top, Lady Marian!—and I can't walk in comfort."

Ignoring her, Marian strode briskly to the tower, and Cecily trailed behind, ever the martyr.

"Don't let that worry you," she went on. "I can see that it won't. After all, you are the legitimate heir to Wenthaven. I'm just carrying his only son."

In the doorway of the tower, Marian whirled on her. "By my troth, Cecily . . ."

Pleased to have provoked a reaction, Cecily smirked. "How do I know it's a son, you ask? I consulted the witch in the village, and she told me I would prove Wenthaven's downfall. He would tumble for me, and give me a child, and after a struggle and a period of suffering, all would be well."

Marian's exasperation got the better of her. "I hope you didn't pay her."

Cecily's chin wobbled.

"Cecily, I wish you'd told me what you were doing. Did you imagine Wenthaven, with his lofty aspirations and his lust for power, would wed one of his wife's illegitimate cousins?"

Tears trickled down Cecily's cheeks, and she sobbed softly.

"I don't mean to hurt you, but *I* am Wenthaven's heir. The estate of Wenthaven came from my mother, and is entailed to her lineal descendants. It is not just my inheritance—it is already mine, although my father maintains control as my guardian. Regardless of Wenthaven's remarriage and begetting of future heirs, it will never be his." Marian put her arm around Cecily's shaking shoulders. "Wenthaven is enamored of mastery. He could have wed many times over, and increased his wealth and power through the marriage settlement. He has not—because of my mother, I suspect."

Cecily's weeping reached a crescendo.

"Let's go up to the countess's room. I'll care for Lionel. You lie down and put your feet up, and we'll think of what to do for you."

Cecily leaped back. "I won't be married off. I want Wenthaven to see this child. When he sees his son, he won't be able to resist."

"Wenthaven resists childish charms with remarkable ease." Marian got behind Cecily and urged her up the stone stairs that spiraled up into the darkness. "He resisted both mine and Lionel's very well."

"You remind him of the countess. And Lionel isn't really his grandson."

Marian stopped.

"What did you say?"

Reaching the final landing, Cecily smiled a terrible smile. "Did you think I didn't know? You've never had a child. That boy is not your son, he's Elizabeth's."

Marian bounded up the remaining steps and grabbed Cecily. "Did Wenthaven tell you that?"

Cecily wriggled like a guilty child. "I told him my suspicions, and we compared the facts. Together we—"

"Forget everything you know or think you know. Forget it! You've got a child to think of now, and if you get involved in this mess of Wenthaven's, there'll be more than you who will suffer."

"*You* don't think Wenthaven will be successful, do you?" Cecily asked.

Remembering Henry, remembering the devoted entourage around him, remembering the loyalty he inspired in Griffith, Marian shook her head.

"But I'm different. I believe in Wenthaven. I understand his ambitions." Cecily straightened her shoulders, and some of her old glow shone through. "I'd be a helpmeet for him."

"Perhaps you would." Giving up for the moment, Marian pushed open the door and stepped into the countess's room.

Home. It smelled, looked, and felt like home. Despite everything, she relaxed. She couldn't remember the last time she'd felt this way. It had to have been . . . in Wales. She jumped guiltily. In Wales, with gruff Rhys and gentle Angharad. With Art and Griffith, still alive, still well.

Tears overflowed, tears she hadn't even known she was holding back. Lionel reached up and patted her cheeks. Cecily looked at her curiously. And the comfort of the room closed over Marian like a blanket.

Lionel seemed to feel it, too, for he struggled to be put down. Marian rubbed her aching arms as she watched him explore the room, recognizing it in the touch of his little hands and the occasional smile. At last he came and stood before her. "Griffith?" he asked.

It was the first word she'd heard him speak since the rescue.

"Griffith?" he asked again.

"No Griffith," Marian answered. "Not now."

"Huh! Not ever," Cecily said.

Marian glared a warning, and Cecily shivered as she glanced around the room. "I hate this chamber. It stinks, and it feels cold."

"I'll open a window," Marian said, suiting action to word. "I don't think anyone has been up here since I left. It's dusty. The firebox is full of ash." She swept it out and laid the fire, lighting it with flint and feeding it with chips until it burned well enough to accept logs. A glint caught her eye; leaning against the stone of the fireplace was her sword, clean, erect, and waiting for her hand. She picked it up and felt the heft and balance of the blade.

It recalled earlier days, better days, the day when she'd met Griffith.

Hastily she put down the sword once more.

"Stand by the fire, Cecily, it'll warm you."

Cecily did as she instructed and watched Marian as she moved about the room, straightening it. Slyly she said, "The bed's just as you left it."

Marian stopped, remembering that night.

"I wager the sheets are the same. Don't you want to lay down and pretend you're in his arms again?"

When Marian wished, she could be as haughty as her father. "Cecily, you go too far."

Cecily burst into tears again. "I know. I know. I beg your pardon." She ran to Marian and flung her arms around her. "I'm just tired and frightened. All my dreams are dying, and I keep looking for a way to keep them alive. I think if I'm mean to other people, it'll help, but it doesn't."

Touched by the first sincere statement she'd heard from Cecily since her return, Marian patted her on the back.

"Nothing helps," Cecily muttered.

"I'm sorry, too." Marian gave Cecily a gentle push. "Now dry your tears. I'll make the bed, and you and Lionel can rest."

"What will you do?" Cecily demanded.

"I'll tend the fire." She smiled. "It will be good to put my feet up. I need to think, but I'm too tired." *And too worried and discouraged,* but she didn't say that.

To her surprise, she found she had to coax Lionel to lie with Cecily. She had thought Cecily would be welcomed as an old friend, but it seemed he trusted no one any longer. But he couldn't resist the lure of sleep for long, and soon Marian sat on a bench by the fire.

She had lied to Cecily. She no longer needed to think. She knew what had to be done and was prepared to do it.

But it hurt.

When Cecily complained that her dreams were dying, she'd struck a sympathetic chord in Marian. Marian's dreams, too, lay in ruins around her feet. The temptations that Wenthaven brandished still had the power to move her, and she still had the power to follow them.

She could go to London. She could control Lionel and, through Lionel, the kingdom. She could have wealth and power above her greatest imaginings.

If she didn't seize this chance, go with Wenthaven into battle and defeat Henry, she would never have a chance to be powerful—and she was, she had discovered, enough like her father to long for power.

Yet if Wenthaven rebelled against the king and failed, Henry would seek Lionel to the ends of the earth. She and her son would be in exile in a foreign land, seeking the kindness of a patron, begging, starving, always in fear for their lives.

But whether Griffith lived or died, she knew what he expected. She knew what was right, and she knew how to take the initiative away from Wenthaven and place it in her own hands.

So with one last glance at the bed, she lifted her skirt and untied the pouch that held the page from the marriage registry. After removing the parchment and smoothing it out, she read the words that could set the world on fire. She remembered the wedding so vividly—Richard, dark and domineering; Elizabeth, beautiful and frightened. The priest, hurrying through the rite as if it were something dirty. Lord Norfolk. And her, three years younger—only nineteen—and infinitely more naive.

The chapel had been lit by only one branch of candles. She had signed the registry with shaking fingers, and when Elizabeth whispered of her pregnancy, those same shaking fingers had stolen the page from the book.

She had never been able to view that chapel again without seeing it as if through a smoky glass. And smoke is what the proof of marriage would be. It would be best—for Lionel and for Griffith.

Leaning forward, she placed the parchment near the flame.

"Don't!"

The scream from Cecily made her jump and drop the registry page.

"Nay!" Cecily screamed again, and leaped toward the fire. With her bare hands she rescued the parchment as the edges turned brown and began to curl. "Sweet Jesú!" She dropped it on the floor and stamped out the impending flame, then blew on her fingers. "You've got it. You've got it! I always thought you did. I told Wenthaven you did. I searched the cottage, but I couldn't find it."

Astounded, Marian remembered the destruction of her home. *"You* searched the cottage?"

"Aye. I couldn't find it easily, so I tore the cottage apart. I thought it clever, but Wenthaven was angry with me. Now here it is, and you"—Cecily's eyes narrowed—"you were trying to burn it."

Marian lunged for it, but Cecily snatched it up.

"Give it to me," Marian coaxed. "You don't know what you're doing."

"Aye, I do. I'm getting Wenthaven what he seeks above all else. For this he will wed me."

"Not while I live." Marian leaped, and Cecily was no match for her. Clutching Cecily's wrist in her strong hand, she squeezed until Cecily cried aloud and the parchment fluttered toward the floor.

Before it landed, a male hand caught it.

Wenthaven's hand.

# 20

*The jeers of the mercenaries* never gave way to arrows as Griffith and Billy circled Castle Wenthaven, and their very lack of aggression made Griffith uneasy. Why the forbearance? What plan was Wenthaven putting into motion?

He prodded Billy. "Do you recognize anyone?"

Squinting at the colossal battlements, Billy said, "T' tell ye th' truth, me vision ain't what it used t' be. I can't tell th' Englishmen from th' Welshmen, an' I ain't close enough t' smell them. Damned Welsh traitors."

Griffith stiffened. "What's that, Billy?"

Resentful and angry, Billy asked, "Well, why can't they support Henry? He's Welsh—isn't that good enough fer them?"

"Wales is a poor country, with not enough land and too many hungry mouths. Those men are feeding their children the only way they can."

But Griffith's explanation didn't touch Billy. He only stared sullenly, and Griffith realized Art had been right. Until a man had his own wide-eyed, hungry children, he didn't understand the desperate measures to which a parent would resort. Griffith had a child now. He had Lionel, and he sat within range of an enemy's arrows, attempting a scheme so desperate that it was unlikely to succeed in the best of circumstances. And Billy couldn't see? "Billy, if I describe the men, would you know them?"

Billy was close enough to see Griffith's face and realized he'd better make the attempt. "Aye . . . er . . . maybe. If ye describe them well, I suppose I might."

"A black-haired man with a brown tunic on."

"Welsh," Billy said decidedly.

"A black-haired man with"—damn, the walls loomed over them, and even Griffith's eagle vision had trouble discerning details—"two or three fingers missing."

"Uh . . . lotta black-haired Englishmen, too, especially around these parts. Welsh, I suppose."

Fast and hard, Griffith said, "A black-haired man with half a nose."

"Welsh."

"A bald man with one eye."

"Welsh, I guess, although I haven't seen him around th'—"

Giving a whoop, Griffith galloped toward the wall. "Art! Arthur, for the love of God—"

Art waved, grinning, and another black-haired man appeared beside him.

Splashing into the lake, wetting himself and his horse, Griffith exulted, "And Dolan. Oh, praise be to God, 'tis Dolan, too."

He couldn't remember when he'd experienced such joy. Art! Dear old Art, alive and as conniving as ever. And Dolan, that old pirate who lived in the village and gave his father fits with his sly and surly tricks. Never had a man such competent allies. Never had Griffith found himself so blatantly optimistic.

Had he ever been a controlled and cautious man?

Banish the thought! For he now knew himself to be in a state of grace. Nothing could touch him, and he would triumph.

His two conspirators leaned out and, without a word, pointed at the gate.

Griffith indicated his approval, and the men ducked back. Laughing, he shook his fist at the gray walls that excluded him and opened his arms to heaven. "I will prevail!" he shouted. "I will conquer! I will—"

A single bolt from a crossbow smacked the water beside him.

Far above, Cledwyn stood in the crenelation and shrieked, "Griffith ap Powel, ye lickspit, I'll kill ye yet!"

As Griffith stared, Cledwyn reloaded, and Griffith tarried no longer. He might conquer, he realized, but only if he now retreated. Protecting his back with his shield, he returned to Billy, shouting, "Welsh! Saint Dewi has blessed us, those men are Welsh, and they're going to open the gate."

Scarcely waiting until Griffith drew abreast, Billy joined his headlong retreat. "But there's only two!" he shouted back.

Griffith grinned with all his teeth. "They're Welsh. Two are all it takes."

Marian stood in front of the closed door, sword pointed at her father's throat. "You cannot leave with that document. It's mine. Give it to me."

Unconcerned by her threat, by Honey's scratching demand to be let in, or by Cecily's simulated panic, Wenthaven rolled the parchment carefully. Bits of the charred edges fluttered to the floor as he said, "Don't be foolish, dear daughter. You can't kill your own father. Unlike me, you have some morals."

"My morals are at war with themselves, dear

father. Should I betray the princess who has been a true and faithful friend? Should I destroy her life, and the life of both her child and mine? Or should I kill my father, the man who bred me, then treated me with less care than a cur in his kennel?" Two pairs of green eyes locked in battle. "Do the correct thing, Wenthaven. Save me from making the choice. Drop the parchment."

His amusement was almost palpable, yet she couldn't help but wonder at him. He glittered with an almost frantic intensity. His armor, though light, was complete, and he wore the weapons of a warrior. It was as if he anticipated battle—a battle he could not lose.

"What would you do with the letter if I dropped it?" he asked.

"Burn it." At his chuckle she went on, "It's going to burn. Either I will burn it, or Henry will burn it when he burns your castle, your crops, and your vassals in their beds."

"Don't listen to her, Wenthaven!" Cecily cried. "Your own daughter doubts your power and betrays you in her faith."

With one glance Marian summed up Cecily's triumph. The stupid girl stood on a bench for a better view and baited them like a spectator at a bull and bear exhibition.

Not even Wenthaven's curt, "Shut your mouth," could dim Cecily's glow. No wonder, for Wenthaven accused Marian, "You have such faith in Henry Tudor."

"I have faith in the men who follow him."

From outside the window, a shout briefly distracted Wenthaven, but he returned his attention to Marian. "Griffith ap Powel is dead."

"There are others like him."

"You?" he sneered. Pure reflexive anger almost pushed the point into his throat, and again his teeth gleamed. "In sooth, you've become Henry's champion."

She realized it was true. If Lionel was not to be on the throne, then Henry was her choice. He was strong and stable. He had married Elizabeth, who would serve justice as best she could. He had begun a dynasty to rule a sore and aching England. Her fingers loosened on the grip, and she balanced it correctly again. "If I am Henry's champion, then I will fight to the death for him."

"A wager of battle? A trial by arms? How English. How plebeian." With the faint scrape of steel, Wenthaven pulled his sword from its scabbard. "How right."

She didn't know why, but she was surprised. Horrified, even. Aye, perhaps Wenthaven had treated her with less attention than one of his curs, but he was her father. She had thought he wouldn't pull steel on her in menace, but betrayal piled on betrayal.

"Have you changed your mind?" Wenthaven asked in a mocking tone.

But his attention was only half on her as one shout from outside the window multiplied into a dozen. Honey whined, demanding entrance.

"Nay, not so." She wet her dry lips. "A challenge, Wenthaven. We fight to the death. We fight for the proof of marriage. If you die, I will burn the parchment. If I die, you will use it. So place it on the hearth, dear father, where the winner may easily seize it."

"On the hearth?" The blades met, and his dimples flashed. "I taught you what you know, and in all our bouts you have never succeeded in disarming me. Have you learned so much? Have you such faith in your swordsmanship?"

"I do," she said, gathering her skirt over her arm. "Don't you?"

He seemed to consider, and Cecily burst out,

"Don't do it, Wenthaven. It's a trick! Don't be a fool."

Cecily was, without a doubt, the fool, and Marian blessed her for it.

"Cecily, you prove your own stupidity," Wenthaven snarled. "My daughter may wish to trick me, but I am yet the master." Sidling to the hearth, his sword still pointed at Marian, he placed the parchment on the stones. "Leave it," he commanded when Cecily made a move toward it. "Leave it. Either I will pick it up and use it, or Marian will have it and burn it—and the other will no longer care."

Marian had won the greatest of the concessions. Now she must utilize it, but she experienced no jubilation. No doubt heaven would be a better place, but until she witnessed Griffith's lifeless body, she could not easily relinquish the earth. Justice sometimes required sacrifice, though, and sacrifice required blood.

That blood thrummed in her ears as her own death toll rang in the rhythm of her heart. She leaped toward Wenthaven, her sword as liquid and shining as quicksilver. He met her thrust, but barely, and an unrestrained oath slipped from his lips. He regained his balance, and his sword shot out, an extension of his arm, slashing her skirt and . . . her arm?

She lifted it, half expecting to see a bloody stub, but as close as he'd come, he'd not nicked her. Watching her from beneath heavy lids, Wenthaven commanded, "Tear it off completely."

She stared, uncomprehending.

"Your skirt," he said. "Tear it short so you don't have to hold it. I would not have it said I won with an unfair advantage."

Only Wenthaven would worry about such a thing. Only Wenthaven had the precision to complete that blow. Frightening, to think she might have lost before she began.

"Do it," he commanded.

Nodding, she took the material and ripped along the weft until it reached just below her knees.

He had inflicted no tangible damage, but the sword thrust had been a blow to her ego—he hoped. He hoped it would be sufficient to make her discontinue this futile action. He hoped that if she were not convinced physically, she could be convinced verbally.

Not that he cared about Marian, disobedient, disrespectful offspring that she was. Nay, 'twas simply that he dreaded the prospect of taking her child—indeed, any child—under his wing. Especially a child who wailed for a dead mother.

He'd proved himself inadequate to that task once before.

The shouting in the bailey grew into a roar. Damn Cledwyn—couldn't he keep his men under control until Wenthaven had finished his business here? A pox on them all—he'd deal with them later. "Do we begin again?" he asked Marian.

"I'm ready," she answered.

Her steady, bleak stare disturbed him. It reminded him of one of his spaniels when she had been mauled by a wolf—facing death with the satisfaction of knowing she had done what was required of her. Wanting to smash that inclination, wanting to give Marian every chance, he launched a brilliant attack—brilliant even in his own eyes.

He maneuvered her across the room to the door and held her captive against the wood with a series of thrusts so quick that they created a cage around her. He would have held her there longer, but the sounds of their swordwork drove Honey to a frenzy of barking, and he feared the dog would leap off the unrailed landing in her excitement. So he allowed Marian to disable him temporarily with an unexceptional parry.

An unexceptional parry that drew blood, he noted

with disgust. "I'm slipping," he said as crimson trickled from his wrist up his arm and dripped in tiny
splashes from his elbow.

"I'm good," she answered.

"Conceit."

"Truth."

Pride was the beginning of her downfall.
Wenthaven noted it and gloated. Thrusting, thrusting, he worked her until she had to do more than
parry—she had to fight, and fight to win.

Her chest began the work of a bellows. Sweat
trickled in her eyes, and a determined smile curved
her lips. It required all of her concentration to retain
her sword and her life. He observed her as he maneuvered her over to the bed, where Lionel slept the
sleep of the innocent. The proximity to the lad distracted her, he noted with satisfaction. She watched
her footing with exceptional care and fought in
silence so as not to disturb the lad.

Wenthaven understood the feeling. Honey roused
just such an emotion in him, and he ached for the dog
now clawing at the wooden flooring, trying to dig her
way beneath the door. To his surprise, he also ached
for Marian, fighting a losing battle for her honor.

Surely if he defeated her now, he wouldn't have to
kill her. Surely the humiliation would be enough to
turn her, for now the duel pumped excitement
through her veins, and the pleasure of combat
chipped away at her stoic resignation.

He'd won the greatest part of the conflict—Marian
struggled to live again.

Now he had to persuade her to do his bidding.
Persuasion would work with her, he assured himself.
She was his daughter. She could be swayed with per-
suasion.

Employing the voice he used so successfully
when taming a skittish bitch-dog, he said, "You
don't yet understand your position. I have the proof

of marriage. With that proof in hand, I can—and will—topple Henry from his throne."

He maneuvered her to the open window, hoping to awaken her good sense. But the breeze carried the screech of metal and wood as the drawbridge was lowered. What were those mercenary morons doing? he wondered.

"Not easily," she said, panting.

"Aye, easily."

"You lie . . . to yourself. You spend too much time here." She stabbed the air beside his head as she stumbled on a silver ball. A bell tinkled as it rolled, and she righted herself. "Has it never occurred to you . . . your spies are telling you what you wish to hear?"

He didn't like that and slashed harder. "What do you mean?"

"The countryside—settled. The townfolk—satisfied. You'll not easily . . . raise an army. The great nobles grow wealthy . . . under Henry." She struggled to keep up with his intensified attack, but she used precious breath to gasp, "Go out into . . . the land, Wenthaven, and you'll see . . . I'm right."

She was tricky. Trickier than he'd realized. Would she undermine his confidence with her babblings?

She would not. But she required close observation, as did the idiots outside who were even now yelling words he couldn't quite hear. Anxious to overcome her, he said, "I'll ignore your foolishness, if you'll come with me as a convenience for the care of the child."

Her smile, so much like his own, flashed dimples at him. "If I'm . . . a convenience . . . why are we fighting?"

The forgotten Cecily demanded, "Aye, why?"

Annoyed beyond good sense, Wenthaven snapped, "Cecily! Get out of here." He saw her from the corner of his eye, standing on a bench by the door, avid elation gleaming in her eyes. "Out," he said. "Out, out, out!"

"But Wenthaven . . ."

God's teeth, how he hated whimpering women!
"Out!" he roared, his sword dipping wildly. "Get out
of here."

Cecily began to sob loudly, which sent the dog into
a frenzy. The noise outside grew in volume and in dis-
sonance, and Wenthaven cursed.

But Marian didn't take advantage of his distraction.
She seemed too enthralled with the action in the bailey. Placing her sword against the wall, she leaned out
the window. "They've lowered the drawbridge, and
there's a huge troop of knights riding into the bailey."

"Those imbeciles!"

Wenthaven leaped toward her and tried to shoulder her aside, but Marian fought for her place. "By
my troth, Wenthaven, there's one horseman who's
trouncing your mercenaries. He—"

She stepped back. Her hand flew to her heart. She
choked as if she'd swallowed wrong, and Wenthaven
gave her a hearty slap on the back before taking her
place.

He realized at once she had tricked him. No troop
of knights flooded his bailey, but the drawbridge
wavered up and down as if someone fought for mastery of the levers. Yet she hadn't lied about the lone
horseman. He wore only leather armor and carried a
shield, but he was a knight, and one of Henry's best.
He wielded a sword with one hand, disabling mercenaries with mighty swings while defending himself
with the other. Under his able guidance, the horse,
too, was a weapon, lashing out with hooves and
teeth.

"Who is that man?" he demanded of no one in particular.

"Wenthaven?" Cecily's voice wavered.

"Get out, Cecily," he commanded. Another man
joined the lone horseman from outside, but he rode
toward the manor, away from the fight, and

Wenthaven found his attention again stolen by the knight. "He looks familiar," he fretted.

"Wenthaven?" Cecily said again.

Turning with a flourish, he snapped, "I'm being invaded, you stupid—"

He froze.

His daughter, his bitch-daughter, held the proof of marriage in her hand and placed it on the hottest blue coals even as he watched.

"Nay!" he screamed, racing toward her.

Marian's eyes widened, then in defiance she pressed his most precious parchment into the fire. He again screamed, "Nay!" and grabbed her hair even as Cecily opened the door to run.

Honey, frantic for her master, sprinted for him and jumped, knocking him aside and loosening his grip.

Marian fell backward, then forward, again shoving the parchment deep among the coals. After throwing the dog against the wall, Wenthaven knocked Marian aside with one wholehearted blow of the arm and reached into the flames.

Too late.

Greedy now, the fire captured the parchment in a miniature conflagration. Briefly the words shone dark, the smoke billowed, and it was gone.

"Gone. Gone. Gone. Gone." He'd have taken England. He'd have owned England. Nobles would have bowed down to him. Peasants would have groveled. He'd have been rich and powerful. So powerful.

Again he looked at the flames, seeking what was not there. Gone without a trace.

"Gone. Gone. Gone. Gone." Beating on his leg, Wenthaven chanted as if it would ease him.

But nothing would ease him. Nothing but her destruction.

Marian's destruction. The sight of her lifeless body—smashed on the stones of the tower floor far below.

Marian could hear someone crying. Lionel crying.

She could hear him. She needed to go to him, but her vision wavered, and she couldn't rise.

The pain in her hand was too great. The pain in her head was too great. She needed to get off the floor and run. She needed to get off the floor and snatch Lionel to safety. But she couldn't seem to move her legs. She had to. She had to. Hurry, before he came after them. Before he came after her . . .

"Marian."

It was Wenthaven. It was her father. She'd thought he wanted to kill her, but he had never talked to her in that benign tone before. She'd heard him use it, but when?

"Marian?" he crooned again.

So kind, so gentle. When had she heard him sound like this?

"Come, Marian."

Groggily she lifted her head away from the stone wall and looked up into his eyes—and remembered when. When he'd taken a dog unfit for breeding to be destroyed.

"Stand, Marian."

He held his sword pointed at her breast. Poised to plunge cleanly into her heart, it created a summons she could not ignore. Using the wall for support, she crawled up until she faced him. In the doorway, Cecily watched, awed at last by that which she could not comprehend. On the floor, Honey ran in limping circles and yelped. On the bed, Lionel watched solemnly, used to seeing his mother facing a sword, unaware of any consequences.

She should reassure him, but Marian could do nothing more than stare at Wenthaven. Stare at her death.

"Wenthaven." Her gravelly voice seemed clogged with tears. "In the name of our sweet Savior, Wenthaven . . ."

"You'll face our Savior soon enough."

Knees trembling, she sidled along the wall. "You'll burn in hell if you do this."

"What news? I am in hell." He curled his fingers into a fist. "I held it in my hand, and my own vanity let it slip away. My vanity, and your treachery."

Reaching the wall's juncture, she slid into the corner and out again, heading for the door.

"What happened to your misplaced honor?" Wenthaven still spoke softly, slowly, inciting faith by his very manner. "I trusted you would leave it in place until we had finished the bout."

"My honor told me I had to burn it, even if my reward was death." She wrapped her fingers around the wooden sill, and beside her Cecily stepped out of the way. "My honor told me that was my highest mission."

His fury slipped its bounds, and he cried, "A woman's honor!"

Amazingly, she found a smile. "Aye, a woman's honor!"

"Then die for your woman's honor."

Beneath the direction of his sword, she stumbled onto the landing.

"Step back," he said.

She glanced over the edge of the wooden platform. A hole spiraled down so far, she couldn't see the bottom.

The point of the sword gently touched her throat, then retreated. "Step back," he insisted. "Step all the way back—into eternity."

Her heel met the air and her toes curled within her shoes. Keeping a desperate balance, she watched in horrified fascination as the shining tip came closer and closer.

"The stones below have welcomed other bodies." The tip began to tremble. "Your mother met her end there, and gossip claims I killed her, but nay. She died, and so dying, escaped me."

She looked at him. He looked at her. The tip straightened, and his eyes narrowed. No pity, no hope, no escape. Only a faint surprise.

Yet slowly, he withdrew the sword. "I cannot do it."

"Do it." Cecily's whisper hung in the air like the stink of rotting cabbage.

He continued as if he hadn't heard her. "It's as if I hear her still, making me vow to protect you always, to make you strong."

"Kill her." It was a goad.

He answered Cecily this time. "I can't kill her. She's her mother's daughter."

"Well, I can!"

Action suited words. Cecily ran toward her, hands outstretched.

There was nowhere to go.

Marian teetered, arms flailing. A hand grabbed her bodice and pitched her toward safety. An arm barred Cecily from completing the act.

The world spun, and Marian hit the boards atop a thrashing body.

Cecily.

A thudding sound assaulted her. A grunting.

She knew the sound. She dreaded it.

Rolling, she grasped the edge of the landing and looked. Wenthaven rolled down the spiral stairs, limp, no longer the puppeteer but the puppet. His head struck the wall repeatedly. He was unconscious.

One step cracked. He careened sideways.

She screamed.

And he dropped off the edge.

# 21

*"Lower th' portcullis!"*

The mercenaries shrieked their war cries as they tried to unhorse Griffith. The war steed squealed and reared, inflicting damage with his slashing hooves. The injured cried in agony as they rolled in the grass of Wenthaven's bailey. But Griffith heard the call anyway.

"That's it, ye dickweeds. Lower th' damned portcullis!"

With a quick glance, Griffith located the source of the command. Standing on the stairs that led to the gatehouse, Cledwyn brayed commands to his men inside.

The iron-capped, pointed teeth of the timber grill jerked and descended rapidly, putting a barrier between Griffith and Henry's charge to the rescue. No knight would risk the crushing, stabbing death of riding beneath the portcullis.

"Shut th' doors. Shut th' doors, ye dickweeds, afore th' English comes an' slices us int' meat pies." Clad in a suit of riding armor, Cledwyn yelled as a dozen mercenaries worked to close the pair of heavy wooden doors just inside the portcullis. A too large breastplate protected his chest. A too small helmet sheltered his head. Greaves covered his shins, and his sabbatons clanked when he stomped his foot. His gauntlets shone in the light as he gestured. "Hurry. Hurry!"

Soon, too soon, Griffith knew, they would have secured the iron straps that bound the doors closed, keeping him in, keeping Henry out.

He needed help, and he needed it now. Where was Billy? Where was the help promised him?

With a roar, Griffith shook off his attackers and rode to the middle of the bailey. "For England!" he shouted toward the keep. "King Henry demands entrance, and Welsh mercenaries deny it."

The mercenaries froze, looking toward the keep. Would the English men-at-arms disobey their lord's commands for the king?

"For Englishmen!"

Nothing happened, and the mercenaries began to jeer, to move around Griffith like a pack of hunting wolves. In desperation he shouted, "For your comrade Billy and your mistress, Marian!"

The lower doors of the keep opened, and English men-at-arms burst forth. Behind them ran English cooks and English maids, English laundry women and English serving boys.

In the lead, Billy yelled instructions like a true commander as the two sides joined with a mighty clash. The men-at-arms performed efficiently, as expected, but Griffith found himself impressed when serving boys used heavy silver platters as shields and maids wielded massive iron fire pokers. Laundry women beat Welsh heads with stirring paddles while cooks cleaved Welsh tenderloins with carving knives.

In the midst of the clamor, Sheldon let the dogs

out of the kennel, and with unerring instinct they attacked the mercenaries.

Cledwyn slapped his visor open and reviled his men, already hard-pressed by the English tide. But before he could join the fray, the portcullis began a slow, ponderous rise, and Griffith laughed aloud at the mercenary leader and his fury. Even above the screams, curses, and barks, Cledwyn heard, and he grinned in ugly invitation. He scurried up the stone stair to the room that housed the portcullis mechanism, knowing Griffith must follow, and Griffith galloped after him. Then, after leaping free of his horse, Griffith ran, shield and sword in hand, to the foot of the stair.

So intent was he on his prey, he almost missed when Art yelled, "Griffith. Take a look, man!"

He looked up to the landing and was blinded by the flash of sunshine on Cledwyn and his armor. Grinning and taunting, Art and Dolan dangled him over the precipice as the mercenary flailed, trying futilely to regain his footing. Griffith got only one satisfying glimpse before he swung too far and the Welshmen released him. He landed with a clang of a blacksmith's hammer against an anvil, and the bailey's dust rose to coat the gleaming armor with defeat.

Cledwyn didn't move, and Griffith looked up at his grinning comrades.

Art shrugged sheepishly. Dolan wiped his hands on his cloak and claimed, "He slipped."

Aye, Griffith reflected, two Welshmen were all he needed.

"You've killed him. You killed your own father." Cecily's wail echoed up the tall emptiness and around the crowded floor of the tower. To the crowd gathered in shock around the body, Cecily cried, "She killed her father. Do something."

Honey added to the hysteria as she made her way downstairs, step by painful step, holding up her leg and barking in pain.

"He fed you, clothed you. Do something!" Cecily's screeching exhibition of grief faded as the gentlemen and women stared wide-eyed. In desperate appeal she said, "Why don't you do something?"

"I will." One woman swept her skirts away from the shattered body of Wenthaven. "I'll pack, and I think I'll take the gold-trimmed washbasin in my room. I can sell it for a good price."

"Aye, and I want the gold plate." A gentleman tugged at his beard. "Is the table set in the dining room, do you think?"

Marian stood with Lionel clasped in her arms and watched as Wenthaven's dependents rushed to strip the keep of its valuables.

Another shriek split the air as Cecily realized no one cared about Wenthaven—or about her.

"Mama?" Lionel asked.

Marian pressed his head into her shoulder and kept her good hand over his ear. She had to protect him from this. She wished someone would protect her, yet her grief was real, a wound in her soul, as deep and painful as the burn on her palm, and she was glad. Glad.

Wenthaven, the most selfish, ruthless man to exist on this earth, had been unable to kill her. She'd destroyed his dreams, destroyed his chance at greatness, yet when he'd held the sword to her throat, he could not complete the stroke, nor could he allow Cecily to execute her.

Because she was his daughter? Perhaps. Because she was her mother's daughter? Probably.

Did love ever die?

She looked up at the great tower and knew it did not.

Her father's love for her mother. Her mother's

love for her. It was all still there, a mortar that bonded the stones of the tower. A protection. A nourishment. A necessity.

Wenthaven's rogue priest entered and with one glance summed up the situation. Kneeling beside the body, he began the prayers for the dead. Cecily's shrieking rose to a crescendo, but the priest flattened her with one quick blow. "Have respect," he commanded.

Cecily lifted her tearstained face and looked at him, then at all that remained of her lover. She sobbed again, but low and soft, holding her belly as if grief swelled it beyond bearing.

Honey reached the bottom and went to the body, sniffing it. Then she sat down and howled like a soul in agony.

"He died unshriven." The words came to Marian's lips unbidden.

The priest's cynical gaze took in her stance, then softened. "He did not. He has received extreme unction every morning since your mother died."

Shocked, Marian protested, "That's against the dictates of Mother Church."

"Wenthaven fed and clothed me when Mother Church rejected me. I obeyed him first."

With a gasp, Marian fled the dark tower.

She wanted Griffith. From the window in the tower room, she'd seen him ride in and recognized him immediately. If love didn't die, then his love for her had survived this ordeal, and she wanted to take refuge in that love. She wanted to be what he needed and atone for what she had done.

The windows she passed showed a battle almost finished. Mercenaries were running from the savage attacks of Wenthaven's men-at-arms and surrendering to a strange troop of English knights.

Had Griffith raised them to support him? No doubt. Griffith could do anything, even bring himself back from the deadly ravine that had devoured him.

Blind to the turmoil around her, Marian struggled to reach the last place she had seen Griffith. She wanted to go outside, out into the bailey, and she knew nothing else. She was oblivious of the blond cocker spaniel that scurried to catch her, then limped along behind her. She didn't notice the bloodsuckers who were stripping the keep, or the injured mercenaries running, or the men-at-arms and servants chasing them. Nor did she notice the procession coming toward her, until strong fingers gripped her arm.

She looked up into the face of her monarch.

"Where do you go?" Henry demanded.

Stupefied by his appearance, she answered, "To Griffith."

With his hand, he lifted Lionel's face and examined it. "Do you think you can take that child anywhere you please?"

"Your Grace?"

He moved to block the curious stares of his knights. "Where can we go to be alone?"

She glanced around. "We're close to . . . my father's chamber. There we can . . . speak, if you like. My father will no longer"—she gulped, and her voice grew hoarse—"need a room within this castle."

Examining her as keenly as he had examined Lionel, Henry raised his voice so all could hear. "I understand your father lost his life in the fight to remain loyal to me against his treacherous mercenaries."

Bewildered, Marian stammered, "I—I don't know what—"

"Come." Henry urged her with his hand on her back.

She resisted his direction. "But, Griffith—"

"Go and find Lord Griffith." Henry addressed the order to his knights without turning or allowing a glimpse of Lionel to slip past him. "Send him to us."

As Marian entered Wenthaven's chamber, memories struck her, sending her staggering. Only two hours ago Wenthaven had been alive, triumphant, reveling in victory as yet unachieved. Now he lay shattered, and his darkest enemy spread a cloak of protection over her and her possessions. With the falsehood Henry had purveyed, she would be more than simply tolerated. She would be elevated to the position of a hero's daughter.

She should thank him, and she tried. "Your grace . . ." But she faltered in the face of his concentration on Lionel.

Allowing only the dog to enter, Henry shut the door against the inquiring knights. "He looks like his father." His tone was unemotional, constrained, and he watched Lionel as if the child were at fault.

Lionel returned the regard, his heritage plain in the regal tilt of his chin, the straight back, the puckered lips that seemed to find fault in Henry without speaking a word.

"There's not a bit of his mother in him," Henry continued. "I had hoped I could see a bit . . . but it's no use, is it? He can't go into English society. He can't be seen lest someone recognize—"

"Your Grace, he's *my* son," she said quickly. "His father was nobody of interest to . . ." But she couldn't say it.

"You see? Not even you can lie about it. But I have a solution to this quandary." Henry advanced on her. "Give me the child."

Marian moved back a step and shifted Lionel on her hip. "Your Grace? You wish to hold Lionel?"

"I wish to keep Lionel."

He sounded smooth, kind, considerate. He sounded like her father when he performed his foulest tricks, and she looked into his eyes, seeking the truth. They glowed with a chill fire, like hot metal in the cold earth. He steamed like cold water on hot iron. The man before her couldn't be trusted, and she backed away.

He followed, his voice low and coaxing, but with a vicious intent that couldn't be disguised. "I could put the child in safe place, where he wouldn't be bothered with the demands of his heritage. He could keep company with his betters."

"Like the earl of Warwick?"

"In the Tower?" He chuckled, deep and low. "The Tower has a bad reputation, and it's really undeserved. 'Tis no disgrace to be—"

"Confined there?" After so much pain, so much effort, Marian could scarcely believe she would find herself in such a situation. She had done everything to preserve Lionel—breaking her vow to Elizabeth, burning the proof of Lionel's legitimacy, destroying Griffith's admiration for her. She had even accepted the overtures of the man before her, wanting to believe he wouldn't harm a child.

But now, stacked against the evidence of his kindness, was this proof of his perfidy.

He wanted to take Lionel away from her, take him to some fate reserved for unwanted royal children.

He moved toward her slowly, like a hunter stalking an unwary doe. "The Tower is not only a prison, but also a royal residence."

She backed from him just as slowly and thought wistfully of her knife. Yet what good would it do her? She couldn't stab the king of England. Even if she succeeded, she would have signed her death sentence, and Lionel's, too. Taking care not to irritate Henry with a sudden move, she said, "Aye. My lady Elizabeth's brothers lived there." *Before their deaths,* she meant to add, but she dared not say it.

The door opened behind them, but Marian did not take her gaze from Henry, who simply snapped, "Get out," never doubting his order would be obeyed. The latch clicked, and Henry watched Lionel. "He's very like the previous king. Is he arrogant?"

She pushed Lionel's face into her shoulder to hide his countenance and answered, "Not at all."

Lionel jerked his head away from her grasp and said, "Nay!"

Henry's smile dropped from his face, erased by Lionel's disdain for her authority. "I suppose he's aggressive, too?"

Lionel struggled to get down. She struggled to hold him and try to explain, but to her disgust it sounded like a plea. "He's a little boy. He's just a little boy."

"Not just a little boy." Henry had backed her to the wall, and he reached out for Lionel with greedy hands. "Richard's son."

Before his fingers could touch, a short, silver blade slid between them, drawing a line past which he could not reach.

"Your Grace," Griffith said, "Lionel is *my* son."

Marian couldn't move, frozen with a mixture of relief and terror and a deep-seated knowledge that Griffith would protect them despite the displeasure of the Tudor king.

Henry didn't move. He didn't turn his head to look at Griffith. His only acknowledgment was a terse, "Step aside, Lord Griffith."

By no measure did Henry indicate a concern about the sword blade or the man who held it. He knew without a doubt that Griffith was his man. He knew the vows that Griffith had made were graven in the Welsh stone of which Griffith was formed.

Griffith knew it, too. The vows of a liege to his lord were holy. He had vowed to uphold Henry in his honorable rule of England, and nothing could make him break that vow—just as nothing could make him break his vows to Marian.

"I will step aside, my liege, as soon you step back."

"This is none of your concern, Lord Griffith. Step aside."

Henry's voice was a whiplash, but Griffith didn't flinch. "You made it my concern, Your Grace, when you wed me to the lady Marian. The child is hers, and therefore mine, and I will not allow you to take Lionel from us."

Surprise made Henry react sluggishly, and he faced Griffith with a deliberateness that in itself was frightening. Jealousy, fury, and desperation combined in his eyes—a dangerous brew, especially in a king.

"Let us speak frankly, *Sir* Griffith." Henry's demotion was rapid and succinct. "The child is not Lady Marian's, nor is it yours. It is the fruit of incest and rape. It is the son of Richard, that blot on the face of mankind. It should be confined for fear of the horrors its heritage will bring."

"Lionel's heritage is the same as your queen's," Griffith answered steadily, and with more truth than Henry would admit aloud. "Richard was her uncle, yet Elizabeth is a gracious woman, kind and charitable to all, and one of the bulwarks of your kingship."

Petulantly Henry answered, "She's not my queen. I haven't had her crowned, yet."

"Is that your way of having her confined, too?" Marian cried. "Is that her reward for sacrificing herself for the good of England?"

Griffith almost groaned at her interference, although it was no more than he expected. His lady had proved her courage many times over, just as she had proved her indiscretion many times over. God grant her diplomacy now.

"I'll be king on my own merit, not on her merit or the merit of her family. Her family." Henry spat on the ground. "Look at them. Her father was a drunk and a lecher. Her mother has already betrayed me. Her uncle . . ."

"A fine marriage," Marian said. "You judge her on her patrimony."

God had ignored Griffith's plea, but Marian was

saying something Henry deserved to hear, something that might sway him from his course of vengeance. Griffith held himself still. He watched Marian, impassioned and angry, and Henry, cruel and contemptuous.

"It is a fine marriage," Henry said. "Elizabeth doesn't know—"

Marian laughed in contempt. "Doesn't she? Oh, doesn't she, Your Grace? I grew up with Elizabeth, and I assure you, although Elizabeth was never the highest scholar, she comprehends the minds and emotions of those around her more clearly than they understand themselves. She has had to. Her survival has depended upon it."

Henry drew himself up, sweeping his cape around him. "I'm the king. I've kept my feelings hidden."

"You're a man, and her husband. She knows what you think, and she understands why you've failed to have her crowned, and every day you postpone that coronation you cut her to the core. She gave you an heir, she loves him to the exclusion of . . . of all others." Marian's voice broke, and she cradled Lionel proudly. "She forgets all her former loyalty. She forgets the oath she made me swear. She forgets her own flesh and firstborn."

"Woman!" Griffith boomed. "Be silent."

She turned on him, but he wrapped his free hand around her chin and spaced the words of his command so she could read his lips, if not hear his speech. "Be . . . silent."

She quivered with indignation, defiance in every line, but his threat had penetrated the armor of her fury. Reason began to reassert itself and she subsided in tiny increments. When he released her, she bowed her head like some lesser creature and said, "I beg your pardon, my lord husband. I will do as you say, of course."

"Congratulations," Henry said spitefully. "You have succeeded in breaking the finest of Wenthaven's spaniels."

Griffith hoped that he, too, would retain control.

"Your Grace," he said, "I once found Lady Marian defending herself against a man—against Harbottle. He wanted to strip her virtue from her, and she rejected him with a kick to the throat. Yet I, rude, impetuous ass that I am, blamed Lady Marian for Harbottle's unruliness. Lady Marian said men always blame a woman when the woman is the victim."

"Did you avenge that insult?" Henry asked.

"Aye, so I did."

"But not thoroughly enough, it seems, for Harbottle reappeared to trouble us. If a weed flourishes, we should dig it out by the root. By the root, Sir Griffith."

"Henry," Griffith whispered, but the sound echoed throughout the chamber. "Don't you yet understand? Lionel is the son of royalty. The *legitimate* son of royalty. If I should kill you here—and I can kill you here, as you well know." He placed his fists on his hips and made himself a menacing presence. "If I killed you, I would be the lord protector of the king. I would be regent. I would fulfill my dream of an independent Wales without having to wait on your mercy. I would have at my side the woman Lionel considers his mother, and I would vanquish your seed from the earth. This place which you have chosen to be the resting place of Lionel could easily become the resting place of King Henry Tudor, and I would be as one with the Crown."

Henry watched him without blinking, with both terror and amazement in his gaze.

Softly Griffith said, "We have the proof of marriage."

Henry jumped. "What?"

"The proof. Lady Marian has it."

"Impossible. I searched—"

"But couldn't find it. Aye, because Lady Marian's always had it. At any time we could have turned the country upside down, had we chosen. Shall we do it now, Marian?" Griffith didn't look at her, but he sensed that she moved to his side. "You wanted to live at court. You longed for a life of wealth and influence. This is your chance. Shall we do it now?"

She pretended to consider, her head tilted to one side as she watched Henry. "Shall we let Lionel decide?"

"What?" Henry's shout rebounded across the walls, bringing a thump on the door as his men called to him. "Leave off!" he roared.

"Ask Lionel if he would be king?" Griffith nodded. "As good a method as any. Lionel, do you wish to be king?"

Still struggling to get down, Lionel said, "Nay!"

"You'll get to live in a palace," Marian coaxed, as if he could care.

"Nay!"

"And have men kneel to you and women kiss you," Griffith continued.

"Nay! Nay. Lionel down *now.*"

A sheen of sweat covered Henry's thin face. "You mock me."

"Just a little, Your Grace." Griffith took Lionel from Marian, although her embrace lingered a little too long, and swung him to his feet. "Don't climb on the chairs," he instructed the lad.

"You wouldn't really try to replace me as king." Henry wiped his forehead with his sleeve.

"Nor would you really try to have Lionel confined to the Tower." Griffith waved his naked blade in emphasis.

"Of course not."

"Of course not," Marian repeated. "Our liege lord is ever wise."

"As are Lord Griffith and Lady Marian."

"Anyone can make a mistake," Griffith said. "Only a fool insists on repeating it."

Lionel cooed with concern when he found Honey, curled up by Wenthaven's chair and licking her injured paw. With a child's sure instincts, he let the dog sniff his hand, then cautiously began to pet her head.

Did he have the scent of Wenthaven on him? Perhaps, for Honey tolerated the attention until, with a sigh, she dropped her head on Lionel's lap.

Henry watched without expression. "This proof of marriage . . ."

"Is in a safe place." Marian dared say no more.

Henry sagged with relief. "Good. I would that it remain unseen, for my queen's sake, if not my own."

"That is a vow I believe I may make, Your Grace," Marian said.

Henry backed toward the door, his gaze cold and his expression deadly. "As long as that proof is in a safe place, I believe you'll find your safety guaranteed."

Marian couldn't stand to see it end this way—Henry defeated, Griffith rejected. She was, after all, a woman. Perhaps not a conventional woman, perhaps not the woman Griffith would have chosen if fate had given him a choice, but a woman nevertheless. With the whisper of Wenthaven's countess in her ears, she cried, "Wait!"

Stopped by the plea, Henry lifted a brow. "Lady Marian? Have you more demands for me?"

"Only one, Your Grace." She went to him and dropped to her knees. "I wish to pledge my fealty to you."

She watched him as he stared down at her and realized how well Henry wore the inscrutability necessary for a monarch. In no way did he show he comprehended the depth of her submission. By not a flicker of an eyelash did he indicate any impropriety in her choice of place and time. Instead he readily took her two hands between his. "Do you wish, without reserve, to become my vassal?"

"I do so wish," she answered. "I become your vassal, to bear to you faith of life and member and earthly worship against all who live and can die. I swear this by the memory of the holy Mary, who, like me, was the mother of a son."

Henry nodded as if well satisfied, then raised her to her feet. The kiss of peace must seal their pact, but never had Marian had to kiss a man more unresponsive than Henry. He waited, silent and stony-faced, clearly expecting her to offer it freely.

To her shame she faltered. This final step proved too difficult, and she found herself unable to touch the man who had so threatened her son's life.

At last Henry said, "Think of it as my token of homage. You have no other."

She looked down at her empty hands in surprise. "So I don't." But his words broke her paralysis, and she put her arms around his shoulders and kissed him on the mouth.

He kissed her back—not a pleasant kiss, but one that reminded her of his mastery—then pushed her toward Griffith. With a grimness at odds with his attempt at humor, he said, "A saucy wench you have here, Lord Griffith. Take care, or she'll lead you a merry dance."

"I do so pray, Your Grace." Griffith received her into his arms. "I do so pray."

"You'll live on your new property on the Welsh border, of course?"

"As my liege commands, of course." Griffith gripped Marian even tighter. "But we had first hoped to go to my parents' home in Wales, where our marriage can be properly celebrated."

"That's an excellent idea. In sooth, if you stay far, far away from London, from the court, and from me, it would be even more excellent."

At the door, Henry laid his hand on the handle and paused. He seemed to be deep in thought, and

Griffith tensed. Then, without turning, Henry said, "You have my thanks, Lady Marian, for reminding me of the pleasure my queen will experience with her coronation. As soon as Westminster Abbey can be prepared and the proper celebration can be organized, the archbishop will place the crown on her noble brow, and make her queen in her own right." He stood in silence, still facing away. Slowly, as if decency were dragged from him, he added, "I will have her write you, Lady Marian, as often as she wishes. Your friendship means a great deal to her, and I look forward to hearing about your accomplishments throughout the long years ahead."

He stepped out and shut the door before Marian could reply.

For that she was grateful. Putting her face in her hands, she sobbed with relief. As soon as she could, she struggled to speak. "I was afraid . . . I'd ruined it for her. I was afraid . . . he'd blame her for my outspokenness and use it as one more excuse to plot against us. But he does love her. He truly does. And do you think"—Griffith's face shimmered before her gaze—"that he means to leave us to raise Lionel in peace?"

"Aye, that's what I think." Griffith's voice sounded deep and rough-edged, as if he, too, fought some great emotion. "Else he'd have called his guards to cut us down and we even now would be dying on the floor."

"Dying on the floor?" She blinked and focused more clearly on his face, trying to understand what caused that savage tone. The expression she saw made her leap back in horror. "Griffith?"

He followed her, towering over her like a monolith about to topple. "What I want to know is—how do you get yourself into such predicaments?"

# 22

*Stupefied, Marian could only* gape at him. "What predicaments?"

"What predicaments?" he roared. "I walk in to find you defying the king of England, and you ask 'What predicaments?'"

"I didn't—"

"Every man on the isle of Britain wants you enough to kill for you, and you ask 'What predicaments?'"

"That's not—"

"You wear a skirt torn up to your knees, a burn on your hand, and blood splattered on your skirt, and you ask—"

Losing her temper, she stepped up to him and glared. "You pompous, overgrown, arrogant man! You dare talk to me about danger, when I saw you fighting Harbottle with nothing more than a war hammer? When I watched as Cledwyn shot arrows at you? When I saw you ride into Wenthaven's stronghold alone?"

She realized someone was shouting, and she realized it was she. Glancing guiltily at Lionel, she braced herself for the fear on his little face. Instead she saw a boy petting a dog and watching the proceedings with great interest. Like a spectator at a game of ball, he glanced from Griffith to her, awaiting the next volley.

She didn't disappoint him. Pressing her finger into Griffith's leather breastplate, she declared, "I should have put my knife in your heart when I had the chance."

"You would have, but you knew I was right."

"I would have, but you don't have a heart."

"Don't I?" He tore off his armor. "Don't I?" He snatched her hand and placed it on his chest. "My heart beats for you, my lady, in triple time. If it's not beating for the horrors that truly menace you, it beats for the horrors I imagine menace you. I used to be a stable, reliable, solid man of good reputation. Now I'm always half-mad with worry, anger, and desire." His palm pressed hers deeper into the warmth of his chest. His eyes narrowed on her face, swept her figure up and down. "Mostly desire."

"Ha!" She jerked her hand away and stumbled backward. "Mostly silly—"

He didn't move but observed her with an intensity that reminded her of a stalking beast.

"Mostly silly conceit and stupid male—"

He breathed audibly through lips slightly apart. His eyelids drooped. He looked hungry and sleepy and, as he claimed, half-mad with desire.

"Mostly, um . . ." She forgot what she wanted to say. She only knew what she wanted to do.

Reach for him. Touch him. Taste him. Mate with him.

He wanted it, too. She could almost smell his arousal, feel his heat.

She held up her hand. It trembled, and she snatched it back to her side. "Now, Griffith. Now, Griffith, we haven't found a solution for—"

"For what?"

She didn't know for what.

Backing toward the door, Griffith kept his seductive gaze fixed on her. "Art!"

Art fell into the room, with Dolan atop of him.

"Listening at the keyhole?" Griffith snapped. "Learn anything interesting?"

Abashed, Art scrambled to his feet, but Dolan lolled on the floor and smirked. "Nothin' we didn't know."

"Where's Henry?" Griffith demanded.

"The king is gone. Run out of here like the devil chased him. Took his whole bodyguard." Art shook his head. "Didn't even stop to eat, and that caused some grumbling, I'll tell ye."

Griffith smiled grimly. "As I thought."

"Took ol' Cledwyn, too," Dolan said with relish. "His neck'll be stretched before this fortnight is through."

"Couldn't happen to a more deserving dickweed," Art pronounced.

Griffith marched over and encircled Marian's wrist with his fingers. Like a manacle, only stronger, warmer, and much, much more sensuous. "Take care of the child. Lady Marian and I are going for a ride."

"A ride?" Incredulous and obviously aware of their desires, Art waved an encompassing arm. "But there's plenty of bedrooms in—"

Griffith glared at him. "A ride."

Dolan elbowed Art. "He means he doesn't want Lady Marian haunted by any memories."

"That's stupid," Art said. "Where will they go?"

Laughing out loud, Dolan said, "Just about anywhere. How long's it been since ye were in a desperate hurry?"

Griffith and Marian didn't wait to hear the reply— Griffith, because he *was* in a desperate hurry; Marian because he towed her behind him like a plow behind an ox. They went out the main door, and in a blur

Marian saw mercenaries trussed together like pigs going to market, smiling servants, exhausted dogs, and a few bandaged men-at-arms.

"Griffith, shouldn't we—"

"Nay."

"But some of my folk—"

"They're fine."

"You're heartless."

Stopping so fast she bumped into him, Griffith took her in his arms and kissed her. Kissed her until she forgot her people and all her responsibility. She forgot war and grief and shame. When he peeled her off him, she dimly heard calls of encouragement, but it made no sense to her. Only his words made sense to her.

"I am not heartless," Griffith claimed. "Come with me, lady, and I'll show you."

"We can take my horse."

He smiled, the smile that had first lured her. His golden eyes glowed, approving of her, warming her, and soon she found herself before him on her own barebacked horse before she recovered half her good sense. The other half she kept at bay, asking only, "Where are we going?"

"Down by the Severn, where I heard the fairies call." His arm tightened around her waist. "I've wed you in Holy Church—now I'll call on the magic of the wee folk to bind you to me forever."

"You don't need magic."

"What will it take?"

Laying her head back on his shoulder, she said, "Only love me."

Exasperation shone from his eyes, and he sighed. "By the saints, woman, what do you think this has all been about?"

What had it all been about? she wondered with a chill. It had been about her insane ambition, and no sweet talk or mad passion could change that. She didn't want the warmth, the closeness, to slip away, but she couldn't hold on to it. Slowly she lifted herself away from him. He tried to tug her back, but she resisted. "If you knew the truth about me, you wouldn't wish to touch me."

She felt the tension in him, then he loosened his grip and said, "I doubt that."

"You were right. I did wish the throne for myself as well as Lionel."

"I know."

"I'm not his true mother, for his true mother would have never—"

He interrupted. "You're too hard on yourself."

"Not hard enough," she mumbled, and wiped her eyes.

"My mother says the only mother who always does the right thing is the woman without a child."

He wanted her to smile, and so she did, but it was a wretched thing. The corners of her mouth trembled, and she had to wet her lips before she could say, "My father almost never did the right thing."

"Maybe he did the best he could according to his knowledge," Griffith suggested. "Maybe that's all he knew how to do."

Remembering her own designs for Lionel, Marian agreed. "Maybe that's all anybody ever does."

"Those people who lived with your father . . . I was coming in as they were leaving."

Marian laughed harshly, wondering what he'd thought of the exodus of Wenthaven's furnishings.

"They said Wenthaven fell from the tower."

"Aye." She plucked at the horse's mane. "He was trying to kill me, and found he couldn't." Clutching the coarse hair in a fist, she added, "But Cecily could."

Speechless for a long moment, he stammered, "Cecily? You—you mean Cecily—"

"Is as big a fool as I am." She smoothed the horse's

mane with her fingers and remembered Cecily's honest grief over Wenthaven's body. "But she's bearing my half brother, and she's big and miserable."

"And after the child is born?"

Marian shrugged. "I suppose she'll live to plot again."

Stopping on the slope above the river, Griffith stared out at the winding ribbon of water. There he seemed to find a solution to some dilemma, for when he slid from the horse, he raised a mischievous face to her. "Would you like to give her to Dolan?'

Bracing herself on his shoulders, she stared at him. "Dolan?" she repeated slowly.

"Aye"—he grinned—"Dolan."

The vision of the wicked old mariner and dainty, pretentious Cecily rose before her eyes, and, irresistibly, she laughed. "Whom are we castigating?"

Chuckling, he drew her down into his arms. "They deserve each other."

As she watched, his smile faded. Embarrassment and distress swallowed his amusement, and he swallowed before he spoke. "You weren't the only fool."

"What do you mean?"

"You were right. Henry did wish to harm Lionel." He wanted her so badly he could taste it, but he couldn't let her blame herself when he was equally at fault. He suffered when he put her from him, suffered from the desire to take her and love her forever. Distress bred frustration, and he said, "Yet, damn it! How could Henry have duped me so thoroughly?"

"You're a man." She shrugged, quite as if that explained it. "Men like you think only of honor and justice, and never wonder about the emotions. Henry could be kind and just about Lionel—when he hadn't seen him. But then he looked on that young face and saw Richard the Third."

Griffith agreed. "It is the truth."

"Not the King Richard the Third whom Henry

defeated, who fought and died for his crown. That Richard Henry might be able to understand, and even forgive. Nay, when Henry looked on Lionel, he saw the Richard who had defiled his wife, and that Henry could not stomach."

Ugly possessiveness had warped Henry—and worse, Griffith understood Henry's emotions. He'd experienced those same emotions once—when he had thought Lionel was Marian's son and Richard had forced the child on her. Hoarse and low, he said, "Tell me now. It is safe. Where do you hide the proof of marriage?"

"I burned it."

He released her and staggered backward. "But you told the king—"

"That it was in a safe place. So it is."

"You said . . . you said you would never destroy it. You kept it for Lionel. You said it was his birthright."

Tears sprang to her eyes, and she looked at the ground.

He took her hands gently in his and turned the palms up. Blisters had swollen and burst on the mound beneath the thumb, leaving flesh marked forever with fire. Her index finger and the one beside it were shiny and purple, and redness crept across the skin like algae across a rock.

She had done this to herself to do right, because he'd showed her her ambitions and she'd been ashamed. Now he was ashamed, both about his inept judgment of Henry and about his uncharitable judgment of her. "I know my mother's burn recipe." He touched the injured hand, and she winced. "I can gather the herbs right now and . . ."

But that wasn't what he needed to say. Words were difficult, slippery beings, but he had to try to make amends. "I wanted you to give up your quest and your dream, assuming they were too immense for you to bear. I had believed my honor to be immutable, and your honor to be a lesser thing. You proved me wrong, about both your strength and your honor. I understand." He gave her back her hand. "I really do. You wanted Lionel to be king of England. You wanted to stand at his side and share his pride. Well, I . . . um . . . feel the same way about you."

"About me?"

His face flamed, and he strolled toward the river. "I've captured a gyrfalcon. Not many men can make that claim."

"A gyrfalcon?" She followed him, fascinated. "You mean me?"

"Wild and free, soaring high and taking me with you. Do you want to walk? We have the time now. We don't have to rescue anybody or fight any armies."

Her unmarked hand crept under his elbow. "I'd love to walk."

Griffith pointed toward a stand of trees. "Let's go there. That looks like a fine place to hunt fairies."

She looked at him, and he saw excitement in her eyes. "I would love to go there," Marian said, "if you'll tell me about the gyrfalcon."

What had started as an embarrassment had become a lure to his bird, and she didn't even realize it. Leading her down toward the grove, he said, "Of course, most men don't even try to capture such a bird. They fear the beak and claws, but they envy the man who possesses one."

"You think other men will envy you for having me as your wife?" She snorted. "The other men have women who sew and cook and take care of their families. Other women never fight with swords or travel alone or challenge the king. When your friends go home, they'll say, 'Poor Griffith. He'll never have a moment's peace with that outrageous Lady Marian.'"

"Aye, so they will. And at night, they'll pretend they swive the outrageous Lady Marian, and their dull wives will wonder at their burst of passion." He put his arm around her. "But only I will have the real Lady Marian—queen of my home, my hearth, my bed."

"I thought you were sorry Henry made you marry me."

"Who do you think put the idea in Henry's head?"

She pushed him so hard and so suddenly, he stumbled backward over a fallen log. "You did that?" He nodded, and she demanded, "Why did you do that?"

"Because I . . . ah . . . lost control." She stared, incredulous, and he said, "It has been ever so where you're concerned. I've been rash and foolish, sweeping you into my bed, taking you to my home against your will"—he scrambled up and glared into her eyes—"and I'm glad. By all that's holy, glad!"

"But you don't like to lose control. You resent me when I make you lose control."

This was the time he should tell her. "I wanted you to trust me without returning the gift of trust." Tell her about the previous siege of Castle Powel. "You recognized my cowardice, and gave me equal measure." Tell her how his youthful rage had cost his father the castle and Art his eye. "You gave me nothing."

He wanted to tell her, he really did. But it required more courage than capturing the castle alone, and he wondered if he could bare his naked and unadorned soul to Marian without shriveling in shame or crying out in agony. The mighty warrior inside, the one who had disciplined him for so many years, feared he might sound silly, or offend inadvertently, or—worst of all—get a tear in his eye.

In fact, he must have one, for she stepped close against him and brushed at his cheeks. "Griffith, Art told me about the loss of the castle, and how you've feared you would one day err again. But 'tis not your control I love you for—'tis the man who roars when he's angry and laughs when he's happy and loves a gyrfalcon with such passion that he tames her, all unwilling."

Gently he caught her hands and held them to his face. "You love me—for that?"

"What else?" She smiled, and her wide green eyes made him think of spring. "Do you think I love you when you're hard and cold as stone?"

"Don't you?"

"Well . . . aye. I really love you when you're pompous." She winked flirtatiously. "It makes me laugh."

Stiffly, he answered, "I'm glad I can be an object of mirth for you, my lady."

She laughed. Putting her lips against his mouth, she murmured, "Do you know when I realized you loved me?"

"When I told you?"

"I've had no reason to have faith in men's words. Nay, I knew you loved me when you drew steel on the king."

"That was stupid." He condemned himself. "Unforgivably stupid. If I had had the control on which I prided myself, I'd have thought of another way to divert Henry's wrath."

"It was, wasn't it?" She smiled, and all her dimples winked at him. "But I took care of it."

"Pardon, my lady?"

"I pledged my fealty to Henry to protect you."

His control snapped, as it always did with her. "What?" he roared.

"Someone had to do something! Henry has a part of your heart, and I couldn't have him leave in such a manner. He might have come after Lionel and me, and you'd have fought for us." She shook her head ruefully. "If there is one thing this last day has taught me, it is that I could not bear to have you die for us. For me."

"It is my right."

"Not if I don't allow it."

He was furious. She wanted to protect him. Him! The greatest warrior in Wales and England. He could see the reflection of sunshine off her copper hair as she took more steps toward the grove of trees. He could see the green eyes slanting with amusement. Starting after her, he vowed, "I'm going to chain you to my bed."

Her amusement changed to laughter. "You'll have to catch me first."

He speeded up. "Do you think I can't?"

With a shriek, she turned and ran into the trees, and her voice floated back on the wind. "Who can catch a gyrfalcon?"

"Who can catch a gyrfalcon?" He stopped running, regained control, and considered the question. "Who can catch a gyrfalcon? They are the swiftest of birds." With a grin, he walked on, slowly, to the place of solitude. Discarding his clothes in an intimate, teasing courtship dance, he whispered to the wind, "Who can catch a gyrfalcon? Only the wise hunter, using the right bait."